Penguin Books

Footsteps

Pramoedya Ananta Toer was born in Blora, a small town in central Java, Indonesia, in 1925. Some of his early works were written while in a Dutch colonial prison during 1947-49. His major work, a quartet of novels – *This Earth of Mankind, Child of All Nations, Footsteps* and *The Glass House* – emerged from a period as a political prisoner, without trial, from 1965-79 on Indonesia's Buru Island. All the books of the series have been banned by the Indonesian government since 1981, despite having become bestsellers in Indonesia. Pramoedya also completed several other works during his imprisonment. Since 1981 Pramoedya has edited and revised collections of early Malay-language writings. These have also now been banned.

Among Pramoedya's other works are *Fugitive, Story from Blora, Corruption, The Fugitive, The Sparks of the Revolution, Dawn, Not an All Night Fair, On the Banks of the Bekasi River* and *Guerilla Family,* many of which have been translated into several languages.

Max Lane, the translator of *This Earth of Mankind, Child of All Nations* and *Footsteps*, was Second Secretary in the Australian Embassy in Jakarta from April 1980 until recalled in September 1981 because of his translation of Pramoedya's works. As well as translating the other three novels of this quartet, he is also working on a book surveying contemporary society and politics in Indonesia, and is the regular political commentator for the quarterly magazine on Indonesian affairs called *Inside Indonesia*. Max Lane has also translated works by Indonesian dramatist, W.S. Rendra, including *The Struggle of the Naga Tribe*, and has published a book on contemporary Filipino politics.

Footsteps

a novel

Pramoedya Ananta Toer

Translated and introduced by Max Lane

Penguin Books

Penguin Books Australia Ltd
487 Maroondah Highway, PO Box 257
Ringwood, Victoria 3134, Australia
Penguin Books Ltd
Harmondsworth, Middlesex, England
Viking Penguin, A Division of Penguin Books USA Inc.
375 Hudson Street, New York, New York 10014, USA
Penguin Books Canada Limited
2801 John Street, Markham, Ontario, Canada L3R 1B4
Penguin Books (N.Z.) Ltd
182–190 Wairau Road, Auckland 10, New Zealand

Published in Indonesia by Hasta Mitra, Jakarta, 1985
First published by Penguin Books Australia, 1990
10 9 8 7 6 5 4 3 2 1

Typeset in 8¾/11 pt Plantin by Midland Typesetters, Maryborough, Victoria
Made and printed in Australia by Australian Print Group, Maryborough, Victoria

National Library of Australia
Cataloguing-in-Publication data:
Tur, Pramudya Ananta, 1925–
[Jejak langkah. English]. Footsteps: a novel.
ISBN 0 14 012693 7.
I. Title. II. Title: Footsteps: a novel.
899.22132

for those who have been forgotten, deliberately or otherwise

Translator's Note

This is a novel set in a time prior to the establishment of an official national language and when the choice of language was intimately tied up with social status and power. I have thus tried to preserve as much as possible of the different usages, including honorifics, of the original. These are usually Malay, Javanese and Dutch terms.

These are italicised throughout, except for very common terms, which are italicised only the first time they appear. If explanations or translations are required, they can be found in the Glossary at the back of this book. The Glossary also includes some English terms and acronyms that may not be familiar to the English-speaking reader. The explanations given have been kept to a minimum.

There are a number of people I should thank for helping in completing this book. As with the first two volumes of this tetralogy, I must thank all my many Indonesian friends for continuing to encourage me with this project. Of course, there is no need to thank them for setting such an inspiring example of commitment to the advance of Indonesian culture and society. Amongst these many people, it is natural that I should mention in particular the three men who set up the publishing company Hasta Mitra (Hands of Friendship) and started publishing Pramoedya's books. These three are: Pramoedya Ananta Toer, Yusuf Isak and Hasyim Rahman.

I should also thank Elizabeth Flann for the editorial work she did on the manuscript. And finally, I would like to thank Anna Nurfia and Melanie Purwitasari for their tolerance of my times away from home that were needed to finish this work.

Max Lane
Canberra
May 1990

Introduction

Footsteps is the third volume of a quartet of novels inspired by the life of one of the pioneers of the Indonesian national awakening and of Indonesian journalism, Tirto Adi Suryo. These novels, along with other manuscripts, were written in the last period of fourteen years of imprisonment under barbaric conditions on the prison island of Buru in Eastern Indonesia. Pramoedya, along with thousands of others, was imprisoned in Jakarta gaols and the Buru Island concentration camps for fourteen years without ever being tried and sentenced. Many, including Pramoedya, were beaten or suffered torture. Many died during their imprisonment.

Pramoedya only obtained writing materials and the opportunity to write in the last few years of his time at Buru. Prior to this he had narrated to his fellow prisoners the story of Minke, Annelies, Nyai Ontosoroh, Robert Suurhof and the characters of *Footsteps* and *The Glass House*. He had to rely on his memory of the historical research he had undertaken in the early 1960s to be able to capture the detail and colour of the Netherlands Indies of the early twentieth century.

Footsteps is essentially an adventure story, and a story of discovery. It is the story of a pioneer who discovered a new country. But for Minke, the narrator and protagonist of the story, his discovery was not of an unknown land across the seas, but the very land he lived in — then called the Netherlands Indies. In the process of discovering this country he sees for the first time the plight of its people and culture, the oppression of white colonial power and brown collaborators. In the process of the arduous struggle to understand what to do about it all, he, and many others after him, eventually created the vision of a new country, *Indonesia*. Pramoedya Ananta Toer, through his wonderfully vivid storytelling, brings us back to the very beginning, to before the birth of the nation Indonesia, or even the idea of Indonesia, to its conception.

Preceding the release of *Footsteps* Pramoedya also published a non-fiction account of the life of Tirto Adi Suryo and an anthology of his journalism and fiction. Tirto Adi Suryo was publisher and editor of the first Native-owned daily paper, instigator of the first 'legal aid service', co-founder of the first modern political organisation, co-publisher of the first magazine for women, and a pioneer of indigenous literature in the language of the nation yet to be born. All this and more is brought to life for the reader in an amazing adventure of intellectual discovery and emotion.

Neither is the personal story of Minke, the man, and all the other characters that inhabit the land he discovers forgotten. His own personal adventure continues on from *This Earth of Mankind* and *Child of All Nations*. The kaleidoscope of characters he meets, learns from and struggles against is equal to the cast of any true-life epic. And, of course, many of these are also fully or partially inspired by real historical figures.

Footsteps is a story of a beginning in two ways. It is a story not just set against the background of the creation of a nation but a story that puts you right inside that beginning.

It is also a second beginning for Minke, the boy who narrated the earlier novels *This Earth of Mankind* and *Child of All Nations*. In those novels he told of how he found out the hard way what it meant to be a Native in the apartheid of the Netherlands Indies, what 'entering into the modern world' really meant, what real and cruel injustice was and to what heights a Native could rise, if he or she refused to be cowed by the colonial world.

In *Footsteps* Minke leaves the East Javanese port town of Surabaya and arrives in Batavia, or Betawi as the indigenous people called it. Batavia was the capital of the Netherlands Indies. It was the intellectual and political centre of the colony. Today, as Jakarta, it retains that central place. He has arrived to study at the only school of higher learning in the Indies for 'Natives', the medical school for Native doctors.

He has left behind the people who played such an important role in opening his youthful eyes to the world around him. Annelies, his wife, was a victim of colonial inhumanity. Nyai Ontosoroh, the concubine of a failed Dutch entrepreneur, who had inspired Minke with her strength of character and understanding of the modern, colonial world, was engaged in her own new beginning in Surabaya. Jean Marais, the Frenchman who had fought against the Natives for the Dutch but who then became their admirer, and who taught Minke not to ignore the life of the people around him, continued to paint and bring up his daughter, Maysoroh Marais. Khouw Ah Soe, the fighter for the progress of the Chinese people, had lost his life at the hands of the secret societies. Troenodongso and his fellow farmers would still be fighting for survival in the sugar fields and rice paddies of East Java. Magda Peters, his teacher, who had crossed the boundaries of what was permissible in colonial society, was on her way back to Holland. Herbert de la Croix, the liberal Dutch administrator, had also returned home to Holland with his family, embittered by the cruelty of his own people.

Sometimes their paths might cross again but it is only the liberal Dutch journalist Ter Haar, and Mir, the now-adult daughter of Herbert de la Croix, who return to play an important role in Minke's life.

But Minke brought many new things with him to Betawi also. He had been through so much and had his eyes opened to so much in the course of just a few months in Surabaya. That he was in store for an unusual life was already signalled by the fact that he was one of only two Native boys allowed to study in the elite Dutch-language grammar school, the HBS. Here, through a school friend who later was to become his nemesis, he met the Eurasian girl, Annelies, and her mother Nyai Ontosoroh, whose own story of being sold into bondage is a gripping novelette in itself.

Annelies' mother, being a concubine of a Dutchman, has no legal rights over her daughter. It is the Dutch side of the family that has control over the still under-age Annelies. In *This Earth of Mankind* this situation, following the murder of the Dutchman in a brothel, sets in train a confrontation between Natives and Dutchmen, Islam and the 'Christian' way, the individual and the law. It is through this confrontation that Minke learns so much: about true liberal values, about what colonialism is all about, about the relationship between his Malay and non-Dutch-speaking fellow countrymen. It also teaches him what it is to wage a fight against injustice.

In *Child of All Nations* Minke's horizons are broadened even further. His adventures in *This Earth of Mankind* centred on his own entanglement in the colonial web. In *Child of All Nations,* he moves out beyond the confines of the HBS school and from the gloomy mansion of Nyai Ontosoroh. He witnesses and gets caught up in the rebellion of peasants against the sugar planter. He confronts the power of the planters and their control over the newspapers. He learns for the first time of the awakening in Asia's north— of the Philippines Republic and of the activities of the Young Generation in Japan and China. Indeed, he meets and later shelters a roving Chinese boy, a youth who had smuggled himself into the Indies to bring the message of the awakening of Asia to the Chinese community of the Indies, dominated as it was by the terroristic Thong secret societies. And he and Nyai have to face once more the cold face of colonial indifference, in the form of the greed of the family of Nyai's former master.

These struggles and adventures teach Minke about many new things. They also teach him about many old things. He is a Javanese, a descendent of the *ksatria* caste, of the noble knights of Java. His father has given up his heritage to become a salaried official of the Dutch, a noble and aristocrat in outward form only. But in his mother he finds the best of the wisdom of Java. But what does the wisdom mean for him, graduate of the HBS, speaker of Dutch, child of all nations, creature of this earth of mankind?

Minke, as narrator of *Footsteps*, tells us that *This Earth of Mankind* and

Child of All Nations were novels he wrote while waiting in Surabaya for the school year to start in Batavia. They were his story of what first made him look at the world around him. In *Footsteps,* we read of how he is still unable to turn away from reality. It presses in on him. Others drag him in front of it. Sometimes despite his own best, or is it worst efforts, he becomes addicted to it. But it is not simply a story of another series of revelations. It is truly a second beginning because Minke goes beyond simply wanting to understand the world to wanting to change it, not just for himself but for all the peoples of the Indies.

Today in Indonesia all of the writings of Pramoedya Ananta Toer are banned. This includes all his novels and short stories from the 1940s, 1950s and 1960s. His publications in the 1980s after his release from Buru Island in 1979 have also been banned. These include the novels *Bumi Manusia (This Earth of Mankind), Anak Semua Bangsa (Child of All Nations), Jejak Langkah (Footsteps), Rumah Kaca (The Glass House)* and *Gadis Pantai (Coastal Girl),* as well as the anthology of writings by Tirto Adi Suryo entitled *Sang Pemula (The Pathbreaker)* and the historical essay on and anthology of early Malay language fiction, entitled *Temp Dulu (Bygone Days).* All the books published by his publisher, Hasta Mitra Pty Ltd, have been banned.

The accusation against Pramoedya's own works are that they surreptitiously spread 'Marxist-Leninist teachings', an accusation regularly made by the Indonesian authorities against anyone standing up for the values of independence and critical-mindedness. Pramoedya's works, available freely and indeed included in educational curricula in Malaysia, have been welcomed throughout the world as a great contribution to world literature and to the world's understanding of Indonesia. In Indonesia, he is feared by the government not so much because of 'hidden Marxist-Leninist teachings', but because he represents a genuine Indonesian tradition, a tradition that follows in the footsteps of Tirto Adi Suryo, a tradition of standing up for the truth, that the current regime cannot accept. The regime also fears him because, despite what it says, his books are enormously popular amongst all those who get a chance to read them.

But the repression goes beyond the banning of books. Pramoedya cannnot leave Jakarta for any other part of Indonesia without permission from the local military command. All his enquiries about obtaining a passport have been unanswered. He has been regularly interrogated about his works. His editor, Yusuf Isak, and his publisher, Hasyim Rachman, have also been interrogated a number of times. Both have been detained in relation to the publication of his books. Yusuf, and his son Verdi, spent several weeks in a Jakarta gaol after Pramoedya spoke at a seminar at the University of Indonesia that Verdi helped organise. Like Pramoedya, both Hasyim and Rachman also spent long periods in gaol in the 1960s and 1970s.

And still it does not stop. In August 1989 two young members of a study group on the campus of the Gajah Mada State University in the university town of Jogjakarta in central Java were arrested. Central amongst the accusations against them was that they possessed, circulated and discussed the novels of Pramoedya Ananta Toer. They have already been tried and sentenced. Bambang Isti Nugroho was sentenced to eight years' gaol. Bambang Subeno received a seven-year sentence. Both received strong character references from leading intellectual and religious figures in Indonesia. During their trials Bambaug and Isti asked that these leading national personalities be allowed to speak at the trial. Their request was denied. A third student, Bonar Tigor Naipolsos, was arrested later and is still in gaol awaiting trial.

The absorbing story of struggle so engrossingly told by Pramoedya, through Minke, continues today as more and more people in Indonesia follow in the footsteps of Tirto Adi Suryo and the thousands of others who created the idea of *Indonesia Merdeka, Adil dan Makmur*— a free, just and prosperous Indonesia.

Max Lane
Canberra
May 1990

1

The earth of *Betawi* finally spread out beneath my feet. I took a great deep breath of the shoreside air. Farewell to you, ship. Farewell to you, sea. Farewell to all that is past. And the dark times, neither are you exempt – farewell.

Into the universe of Betawi I go – into the universe of the twentieth century. And, yes, to you too nineteenth century – farewell!

I am here to triumph, to do great things, to succeed. And all of you will be swept away, everything that is in my way. But not for me the banners of *veni, vidi, vici*. I'm not here to conquer, I've never longed to be a victor over others. He who wanted to unfurl those banners of Caesar's – he was never once victorious. And now he and his banners have crashed to disaster. Robert Suurhof, my nemesis, is in gaol – and all because of his greed for overnight glory. Just like Bandung Bondowoso when he built Prambanan.

No one is here to meet me. So what! People say only the modern man gets ahead in these times. In his hands lies the fate of humankind. You reject modernity? You will be the plaything of all those forces of the world operating outside and around you. I am a modern person. I have freed my body and my thoughts of all ornamentations.

And modernity brings the loneliness of orphaned humanity, cursed to free itself from unnecessary ties of custom, blood – even from the land, and if need be from others of its kind.

I don't need anyone to meet me. I need no help! Those who always need help are people who have allowed themselves to become dependent, almost like slaves. I am free! Totally free. From now on I will only be bound by those things in which I have a real stake.

With my heart, body and mind in this state of freedom I sat in the corner of the tram. There were no comfortable trams like this in Surabaya, travelling on steel rails, with a brass bell to chase away the sleepiness. Third class was crammed. First class, where I sat, was rather empty. I didn't have much with me: an old suitcase, dinted and dented in many places; a bag; and a woman's portrait in a wine-red velvet cover wrapped again in calico.

The tram moved along smoothly. The after-effect of the ship left my body

1

plunging up and down as if I was riding a thousand waves. There's talk that trams will soon be pulled along by electricity! How could electricity possibly pull a tram along?

As it left the port the tram seemed to become lost in swampland, with only clumps of forest and jungle here and there. The air was pregnant with the mustiness of rotting leaves. Monkeys hung from the vines and branches, untroubled by the clanging bell. A few of them tumbled gaily along. One even pointed at us with a branch. They were, perhaps, all conspiring to examine me especially, and now, in their own language, were crying out: That's him, Minke, the 'modern man'! Yes, that's him, sitting there in the corner by himself. That one, with the beginnings of a moustache, but his chin still bare. Yes, that's him all right, the Native who prefers European clothes, who carries on like a *sinyo*. He even travels in 'white class' – first class.

Huh!

Ah, that must be the 'Golden Star Villa', famous because of all the stories about the slaves who had toiled there in the time of the Dutch East Indies Company. Perhaps one day I'll have time to write their story.

The villa was the only thing decorating the swamps. Everything else was boring, nothing worth describing. Yet it was these swamps that had swallowed up one third of the Company's soldiers when they first arrived to occupy the area. The swamp has sided with the Natives for a long time now. On the other hand, it was this same swamp that killed sixty thousand Natives as they built Betawi. Most had been prisoners of war. And the glorious Captain Bontekoe, who began his rise to fame transporting sand and rock from Tangerang to Betawi, had also been almost killed by swamp fever.

'What is this place called?' I asked the Eurasian conductor in Malay.

His eyes blinked open, startled by this extra burden: 'Ancol.'

'Can the sailboats out there go right into Betawi?' I asked in Dutch.

'Of course, Sir, if they go up the Ciliwung.' He moved along, selling his tickets.

Then the tram entered the city. The streets were just as narrow as in Surabaya, made from the same whitish–yellow stone. Old buildings, standing from the days of the Company, lined the streets. The streets were lit by gas. Another fairy-tale, that Betawi had begun to asphalt its streets. Just more talk. And how many such fairy-tales are told in this world?

The city of Betawi! So this is the capital of the Indies, built by Governor-General Jan Pieterz Coen at the cost of sixty thousand Native lives. Who was it who worked out that figure? This is the city that was attacked and laid siege to by Sultan Agung in 1629. My Dutch schoolfriends used to taunt me during our history lessons. How many soldiers did Sultan Agung have? Two hundred thousand? How many Company soldiers defended the city? Five hundred! The Dutch had cannon. But so did Agung! How come your

Sultan's army was beaten, then? Yes, there's no doubt about it. They were defeated. That's the reality. The Dutch have controlled everything since then. Even now! Even though Coen himself died during the defence of the city and was never to see his homeland again.

Two hundred thousand soldiers, my friends had said. With cannon too. I believe Agung had cannon. But two hundred thousand men! Who can disprove it? But neither could they produce real evidence to back their claim. Ahh, that's enough of thinking like this, or I'll die of frustration!

Betawi was not as busy as Surabaya. And so clean. Big wooden rubbish bins stood in appropiate places, and the people placed their garbage there. Not like Surabaya. And there were little parks everywhere, their gaily-coloured flowers adding a touch of festivity.

In Surabaya all you ever saw were bamboo hut slums and fires, and rubbish everywhere.

1901. The paper I'd bought at the harbour announced that Priangan women were being sold to Singapore and Hong Kong and Bangkok. I was reminded of the past – of the Japanese prostitute Maiko's evidence to the court in Surabaya about how much prostitutes were bought and sold for. I put away those memories. What purpose is there in dwelling on the past? The past should not become a burden if it is not also willing to be a help.

There was one interesting editorial comment – the Malay–Chinese press was refusing to use Ch Van Ophuyzen's new Malay spelling. We don't use school Malay, high Malay, the press was saying. Our subscribers aren't graduates of the state schools. We're not going to risk bankruptcy by using such foreign spelling.

The report went on to complain about the new postal regulations obliging letter writers to use the new spelling. Trying to stop mail that used the old spelling would be like trying to hold back the sea with your bare hands, they said.

What! Why didn't I see this headline before? Staring at me in such large print? Japan was laying claim to Sabang Island with its coal station. Was this true? And the paper's comment: 'This clown's behaviour is getting more and more out of hand.' As expected, there was also a small item about an urgently called meeting of naval personnel.

The tram moved on smoothly to the clanging of the brass bell. Betawi! Ah, Betawi! Here I am now in your centre. You don't know me yet, Betawi! But I know you. You've turned Ciliwung into a canal, with boats and rafts going back and forth, laden with goods from the interior. Almost like Surabaya. Your buildings are big and grand, but my spirit is bigger and grander.

It was said that the Ciliwung was once lined by a long unbroken line of sumptuous buildings. Now they had been turned into shops and makeshift workshops, mostly Chinese-owned. And in the middle of all this, I stood out as something extraordinary. I wore shoes; most others went chicken-clawed! I wore a felt hat; most others wore bamboo *destars*. I wore European clothes; others wore shorts, went bare-chested or wore pyjamas.

The scenery was full of colour. My heart was even brighter, full of joy. Where are you all, maids of Priangan, famed for your grace, beauty and smooth, satin skin? I haven't seen even one yet! Come on, out of your houses! Here I am now. Where are all the Dasimas that Francis wrote about?

I could not find what I was looking for. The first-class compartment contained mostly Eurasians, with their dried-up skin and arrogant posing. Next to me sat an old Eurasian grandmother scratching her hair – probably forgotten to comb out the lice. Opposite sat a thin middle-aged man with a moustache as big as his arm. Next to him was a European Pure engrossed in his newspapers. One item caught my eye. A Dutch poet was soon to arrive and would read Dutch and Shakespearean poems at the Comedy Hall in Pasar Baru. The report said that he had just finished successful readings in the European capitals and also in South Africa.

No! I will not use this time to think about anything. I'll just sit here soaking up the Betawi scenery. Oh, Betawi, I've known you for a while now.

Deelemans, grootbaks, dos-a-dos's, bendys, landaus, victorias, dog-carts – all offerings from the immigrant civilisation – passed each other in every street. People in all kinds of clothes rode along on their horses. Bicycles too! And no one took any notice of them! I'll get myself a bicycle! How much would it cost? Hey, aren't they nimble, all those bike riders! They move slowly, and can see everything as they move along.

The tram left downtown Betawi and passed through the forest and swamp on the way to Gambir. It wouldn't be long before it stopped to spew out and suck up passengers. But still there was no face that lured me.

'Not yet,' said a Chinese man next to me. 'Gambir's quite a way. About a quarter of an hour more.'

In third class the bedlam never abated.

'What do you expect?' the man prattled on. 'They're gambling on the horses. This is your first time to Betawi? I thought so. People here, men and women, they've all become possessed. The races, cockfighting, dice, *capjiki*, even lizard fights. When Gambir Markets open, every gambler in the country comes. You must see Gambir Markets.'

'Are there any good shows to see in the villages?'

'There's no one crazier about watching performances than the men of Betawi. What about Solo, you ask? No. In the villages here there is *cokek, doger, lenong* and *gambang kromong*. Do you like *kroncong?* Wah-wah, *Meneer* Longsor, he's the king of *kroncong*. A great, thick, moustache, a beautiful voice. They say he's got real Portuguese blood. And he lives near the Portuguese Church too.'

4

My neighbour alighted. Prattling over, lecture over. And I myself was amazed. I'd spoken Malay quite fluently, and not only had he understood me, I had understood him too.

The Eurasian grandmother looked at me. In Malay: 'Where is *Sinyo* from?'

'Surabaya.'

'Your first time to Betawi?'

'Yes, *Oma*.'

'Nah,' she said, pointing out the window. 'That's the Harmoni Club, where all the big people enjoy themselves. An old building, *Nyo*. Not just anyone can get in there. You've got to have a wage more than 400 hundred guilders. But even if you and I had two and a half times that, we would still never see inside.'

Four hundred guilders! And my total wealth came only to one hundred and seventy guilders and so many cents, put away over years. Anyway, what would you need four hundred guilders a month for? You could buy at least three bicycles every month! And you'd still have enough left over to live well!

Straight, solid and large buildings everywhere, beautiful carriages, all crowded my view. My old *bendi* was just a heap of timber compared to these. Big broad streets like soccer fields. And the Harmoni bridge, like a wax moulding, was even adorned by statues. Cupid and Venus?

'We've arrived at Weltevreden, *Nyo*. Gambir, the Betawi call it. The last stop. Where are you going from here, *Nyo*? Ah, that's Koningsplein – the Betawi say Gambir Square – where the Gambir Market is set up. The tram will stop in front of the station. If you want to go on, you'll have to change trams. Or take a *delman*.'

I gazed out across Koningsplein field – the pride of the Indies. One kilometre square, beautifully tended lawns, no flowers, where the people of Betawi met and played, whether or not the Gambir Markets were on, whether or not they had money. This was, of course, their cure for the boredom of being stuck at home.

'Weltevreden! Last stop!' cried the conductor, first in Dutch, then in Malay.

Puh-puh-puh! Look at how big Gambir station is! A whole village under one roof. What is it that the trains offload here? No doubt the same as in Surabaya, the prosperity and happiness of the villages – for export. And imports too – things to make you forget where you are, prosperity and happiness that have been put in hock. You must always remember the nature of the modern cities. They stand upon the traffic in happiness and prosperity.

A horse-cart took me towards my destination.

Even if that were the truth about modern cities, I still considered myself a modern man, among the most advanced of the age. You don't want to be involved with progress? Then you must accept being trampled into dust.

In my shirt pocket were two neatly folded pieces of paper – my graduation

5

diploma and a summons from the Batavia medical school – *STOVIA*. Fantastic! Not just Betawi, but the medical school too must open its doors to me.

Fantastic! Incredible!

Fortress Betawi had been breached.

A school coolie took down my suitcase, bags and Annelies' portrait which was wrapped in velvet. They were all placed neatly in the office.

I handed over my papers.

'Good day! We have been waiting for you a long time, Sir. You should've been here last year, yes? Even now you're late. One week late. I hope you understand that it is only because of your high marks that we have pardoned your tardiness.'

I was offended. I was already feeling uncomfortable. That wasn't the way I should be spoken to. I wasn't even studying yet and they were already trying to box me in.

'Javanese, aren't you?'

Even more offensive. Seeing I wasn't answering and that my eyes were challenging him, he didn't ask again. He pulled out a piece of paper. He wanted me to study it.

'Can you follow that?' he asked. 'The rules apply from the moment you are accepted as a student, from the moment you enter the school grounds. They are compulsory.'

I looked him in the eyes again. It seemed that he understood my heart was rebelling against the rules. He hurriedly added: 'I am only showing you. It's up to you if you want to stay on as a student or not.'

I sat there on the couch, playing with the felt hat in my lap. There was only one place I was going. I only knew one destination – the School for the Education of Native Doctors (STOVIA). How painful all this was.

He seemed to be losing his patience and wanting to get on with his work.

'There's a room through there.' He pointed. 'Before you sign the agreement you *must* conform with the rules.'

Everywhere there are rules. Why are the ones here so offensive? As a Javanese, as a pupil, I must wear Javanese dress: a *destar*, a traditional buttoned-up top, a *batik sarong*, and chicken-clawed feet! Shoes are banned!

'Do you have Javanese clothes?' he asked.

I did, except for a *destar*. How humiliating it would be to admit I had no *destar*.

'No,' I answered.

'Do you have money?' The questions were getting even more insulting. He probably wasn't earning much more than seventy guilders a month. 'If you haven't any, we can advance you some to buy whatever you need.'

Very well. I will be a student. I took leave to go and buy what I needed.

'Your things will be safe here. We will wait for you,' he said. 'About three hundred metres from here, there are markets. Senen Markets, they're called. You'll be able to get everything there.'

I left feeling quite annoyed. It was easy to find someone selling *destars*. The stall was run by an Arab. He had deep, small eyes and wore a big, thick and grimy *fez*. He asked a terribly high price but I got it for half that. It was probably still too expensive.

To me, this was all a form of oppression. All in order to become a doctor – a cog in the machines of the sugar industry according to my new friend from the boat on which I first tried to leave Surabaya – I have to put up with all this trivial aggravation. Will I be able to put up with it all? Amazing, but here I was indeed carrying out these humiliating, degrading orders.

Back at the school, angry and offended, I went into the room and . . . farewell to you all, my European clothes! First my shoes, my trousers, my stockings. In place of my felt hat was the *destar*. I hadn't worn a *destar* for years. My honoured feet, once clothed in shoes and stockings, were now chicken claws in their nakedness. And the floor felt cold as it sucked up the warmth of my blood.

Like a bird caught in the rain, I signed my contract as a pupil at the school. I would receive an allowance of ten guilders a month and free board. In return, I would be bonded to work for the government, either on land or sea, for a period equal to the length of my training.

A Native office employee took me into the dormitory. The air smelt of alcohol and creolin. Across the way was the Ambon hospital, for the Ambonese soldiers and their families.

My bags had hardly touched the ground before we were surrounded by a milling group of students. On the bed opposite mine, I saw a suitcase with a newspaper clipping stuck on it that set my blood boiling.

Before I could collect my wits, a big youth examining my dented and bruised old brown tin suitcase, shouted in Indo Dutch: 'Look at this! Only the rottenest village boy would bring a rotten case like this!'

He seemed to be the only one wearing shoes. He was obviously not Sundanese, Javanese, Madurese or Balinese, and he wasn't Malay either. Yes, he was probably Eurasian.

Then, catching me by surprise, his big shoes flung out at my case. I felt as if he were kicking my pride and my dignity as well. The case shimmied across the floor. The office clerk tried to stop the second and third kicks. Then everyone started jockeying for a turn at giving it a kick.

Hey, you, I said to myself, are you going to take this treatment?

'Gentlemen,' I shouted in a rage, 'forget the case. Here I am. Come on, one by one, or all together, it's the same to me.'

I had never been in a fight in my life; I had never experienced such violent

7

behaviour as this. But I was ready. I snapped into position. My thighs pushed open the split in my *sarong*. My left hand undid the buttons on my shirt. And my eyes challenged them all.

They took no notice. They laughed! They were laughing at me! At me!

And then the boy in European clothes calmly tried to punch me on the nose. How dare he! My left hand shot towards his face, my right was ready to go for his chest. He stepped back. I took a step forward and my right hand advanced, and . . . I collapsed on the floor in the midst of tumultuous laughter.

I wanted to jump up, to attack again. But I couldn't. *Couldn't*! It was as if a mountain had fallen on my body. They were all holding down my legs. My *sarong* had been torn away and my underpants glared in their whiteness. I had been overcome so easily.

And it wasn't over. In just a few seconds they stripped me naked. Except for a leather belt and my *destar*. Like a work-horse without its harness.

'Ayoh! come on big man, hero, start crowing again!' the Eurasian challenged me.

They let me go even while shouting and cheering. And like Adam chased out of Eden, I ran to my bed to get something to cover my nakedness.

'Don't give him any clothes!' someone cried out in Malay to the office boy, who wanted to help me. 'Let him run round like a buffalo in the fields.'

Everyone laughed again.

'Ayoh, start braying, come on hero!'

Don't think I'd ever bray for you lot.

Everyone crowded round, pulling me into the centre of the room. And naked in front of everyone, I lost my strength. Perhaps that's how a fighting cock would feel if all his feathers had been plucked. Naked, all I could do was stand there using my two hands to cover my private parts.

'A Javanese knight with just a leather belt and *destar*!'

'A fighting cock who can't crow!'

'Let him stay here like this until tomorrow, until the Director makes his inspection. Everyone agree?'

'Agreee!!!!' they all shouted.

The lone European-dressed boy came up to me and tried to grab my hand. That was too much. Then I thought I saw the early signs of an impending attack. I dived, flinging my legs upwards. I felt my toes jab into his throat. He swayed, spitting onto the floor. Two teeth and some blood came out.

The shouting got wilder and wilder.

'Adam's run amok!'

I suddenly decided to fight rather than be ashamed. I excused my two hands and began my attack.

'Come on gentlemen, that's enough,' the office clerk cried out. 'No more, that's enough. Otherwise I'll call in the Director.'

'Report! Yes, go on and report! Our hero has gone wild.'

'Yes, report him!'

They began to surround me.

'Ayoh! try it!' I shouted.

And they didn't jump on me. It appeared they didn't mean me any real harm, they were just playing around with me. No one came forward. They just laughed. And the now-tested cock, myself, began crowing again: 'So this is how educated people behave?' And they went quiet. 'Is this what your ancestors taught you?'

'Shut up! Leave our ancestors out of it.'

'Do you all think you're better than them?'

Someone threw me my *batik sarong*. I slowly wrapped it around my waist, my eyes vigilant.

'In front of villagers you all behave like intellectuals. But villagers are more civilised than you lot!' I kept on crowing.

Remaining vigilant, especially as regards the now toothless Indo, I walked over to my bed. No one tried to stop me. The tumult had died down.

'God's own Satan isn't as big a bastard as any one of you,' I kept on crowing, egged on by their silence, 'Go on, get away, all of you.' By now I was growling.

No one said anything. They just stood there watching me, amazed at my outrageous behaviour. But they didn't go away.

I dressed again, acting as if I were some kind of aristocrat. I pushed all my things under the bed. I stood the painting in its wine-red velvet cover, and wrapped in turn in calico, on my pillow.

The office clerk had disappeared. He was probably used to these kinds of goings on. He won't report anything. Except to the people in his village, and to his wife.

I sat on my bed. I looked around at them with a challenging gaze. But they were all smiling now. One by one they told me their names. It was clear there'd be no more fighting. It seems it was all some kind of crude initiation game. And they were sorry they'd gone too far.

Don't try playing rough like that again, I challenged them in my heart. Don't try humiliating this crummy-looking old dented tin suitcase. Its contents are worth more than all of you put together, you bloody candidate doctors! You must get to know me first, like I must get to know you. Inside that suitcase are stored my best thoughts: notes, letters, including letters from friends and love letters, newspaper clippings, my two novel manuscripts about the loss of my wife, Annelies, and the experiences Nyai Ontosoroh and I had with the Dutch authorities – perhaps more than two kilograms altogether. Have any of you ever owned a treasure as weighty as that? And important letters from other people too – will you lot ever own anything like this? And then there are the letters from mother. I don't believe any of you

9

have a mother like my mother. And I don't believe any of you have had experiences such as I have experienced and have summarised in my writings. All of you, candidate gobblers-up of government wages, candidate *priyayi* . . .

No one was interested in bothering me any more, so it became my duty to start establishing better relations: 'I'm sorry I knocked out two of you lot's teeth.'

They laughed. Ignoring them all, I started moving my clothes into a wardrobe. And they watched every single piece of clothing as if I was about to start a magical performance.

'What he's got on are his only Javanese clothes,' someone noticed.

'Perhaps he's legally Dutch, a *Londo Godong*.' Someone else offered their opinion.

'He only owns European clothes!'

I pretended not to hear. Now out came my papers and books. I put the empty suitcase and bag on top of the wardrobe.

'Ahai!' came a high-pitched shout.

I wheeled around. My painting had emerged into public view. And it quickly travelled from hand to hand to the person furthest away.

'Flower of the Century's End!' somebody read from underneath the picture.

My blood boiled as I saw my painting handled by these people who had not asked my permission. I took the dagger from the wardrobe, drew it out of its sheath, and cried: 'Put it back!'

Everyone went on discussing it in the far corner of the room.

'Or shall I let this fly?'

'That's enough, everyone, put it back,' came an order.

The noise ceased. They all turned to me, and to the dagger in my hand.

'I'll count to three,' I threatened. 'If the picture isn't put back I'll let this fly, I don't care who it hits.'

One pupil, short and skinny, came across and put the picture back in its cover. He frowned: 'Yes, *Mas,* they always go too far. I myself can hardly take it here any more.'

And I knew from that moment that the two of us would be allies. I watched him as I put the dagger away. He straightened up the picture's cover, flicking off some flecks of dirt. 'Let me introduce myself, Mas, my name is Partotenojo. But they call me Partokleooo,' he said in very bad Dutch, with a heavy Javanese accent. 'Mas Partotenojo.'

'They pick on you?' I asked.

'I can't stand it, I say.'

'Where do you sleep?'

'In the corner over there.'

'Are there rules about where people must sleep?'

'No.'

'Good. You'll move over here next to me,' I suggested.

'But this bed is taken.'

'He'll have to move. Tell him.'

Partotenojo, alias Partokleooo, went and fetched the person concerned. He came across, his eyes full of suspicion. 'You're ordering me to change places with Partokleooo?'

'That's right.'

'You want to be the big-shot here?'

'If you and the others want that, yes, I can become the big-shot. Any objections? I'll help you carry across your things. You like picking on Partokleooo too? All that must stop – starting now.'

All the others gathered round again. He complained to them all. Everyone was discussing my instructions. The European–dressed Indo wasn't there. Perhaps he was taking care of his gums.

'Look, it's not because I want to be the big-shot here that I've asked you to move – except if you force me. I don't like people who play around with other people's rights.'

They talked things over among themselves. Then, all together, they helped move his and Partokleooo's things. The lunch bell rang. They all raced off. Only Partokleooo and I were left.

'It's true what you said, Mas, they're only intellectuals if compared to village folk. A bunch of barbarians!' He swore. His Dutch was really bad, with a very thick Javanese accent. His accent was both wrong and exaggerated.

'You're not a graduate?'

'I'm from a teachers' school, Mas.' He gazed at me, seemingly longing for protection. 'Come on, let's eat.' Seeing I wasn't ready yet, he asked, 'Where did you get that painting, Mas?'

'I got someone to paint it.'

'It's a beautiful painting. Did you ever meet her?'

'Yes.'

'Did you know her?'

'I knew her well.'

I didn't understand why he seemed so moved. His eyes seemed to be fixed on some spot far away. His lips trembled almost imperceptibly, then the words came out, slow and broken: 'I followed the reports about her. I didn't see all the reports, but enough. It was a terrible story.'

'Yes.'

'You haven't told me your name yet, Mas.'

'My name is Minke. Let's eat now.'

He looked at me with those questioning eyes. He followed on behind me.

'No one else need know about the painting,' I said.

'How is she now?'

'She died, Parto.'

'May her soul be received by Allah,' he pronounced, and asked no further questions.

The dining-room was full of students from all grades. They all wore Native dress. It was only the Menadonese and Indos who wore European clothes. The Javanese and Sundanese were different only in the kind of *destars* they wore. There was only one Malay; he wore a *songkok* and a short *sarong*. The *destars* were in the majority.

It looked as though news about the incident in the dormitory had spread quickly. As soon as I entered all eyes were on me. Here and there people started whispering. I took no notice and sat down with Partokleooo. Just as I sat down, a message boy came in: 'Mr Minke?'

Partokleooo waved him over. He spoke very politely to Partokleooo: 'There is someone asking whether a student arrived by ship from Surabaya today.' He held out a torn piece of paper with some writing in pencil on it.

I grabbed quickly before Parto could get a look.

'Yes, that's me,' I said. 'Who is it asking for me?'

Both the messenger and Partokleooo were observing me. And the messenger answered politely: 'A Dutchman, a Pure-Blood, he's talking with the Director at the moment.'

'Very well, I'll come when I've finished lunch.'

Partokleooo never tired of staring at me. I think he really wanted to know more about the woman in the painting. But I didn't pay him any heed.

I didn't eat much. I'd lost my appetite after the fight. I left the dining-room and went straight to the sitting-room. The visitor was none other than my journalist friend from *De Locomotief*, Mr Ter Haar, whom I'd met on the boat to Semarang a year ago.

'It's good to meet you again, Sir.' Smiling, he held out his hand. He explained that he had just arrived by train from Semarang. He'd received my letter just a little time beforehand. He'd gone out to the harbour to meet me but I'd left by tram for Weltevreden.

He talked on in his usual friendly manner until the Director came back and joined us. He introduced himself to me as if he wasn't the Director at all. He asked: 'How many pen-names have you used?'

I laughed.

'I'm proud to have a student who can write. But your task here is to study. What if you want to write again, won't that disturb your studies?'

'Writing, with so many experiences, of the world and of the soul,' my friend defended me, 'I think he'll turn out to be quite an advanced student.'

'Yes, true, but medical school is different. Mr . . . so I should use Mr . . . ?'

'Minke is fine, Sir.'

'So Mr Minke, no matter how clever a student is, no matter how rich his experiences have been, he must treat his lessons seriously. Everything must be studied in detail. You must follow things as the seconds' hand follows the seconds. A lost second can mean a lost life. You've arrived late too. You'll have to work hard to catch up.'

'Mr Director,' began my friend, 'if he was to be another couple of days late, it wouldn't matter, would it? I would like to ask your permission to take him away today. Mr Minke cannot miss such a great opportunity. What do you think, Mr Director?'

'Opportunity?'

'Yes. I myself have come up from Semarang to take advantage of the same opportunity, Mr Director, to meet the Honourable Member of the House of Representatives in the Netherlands, Mr Engineer H. van Kollewijn.'

'One of my students will meet with a member of parliament?'

'Tonight the God of the Liberals, the Radical God of the Liberals, will be holding an invitation-only meeting in the Harmoni Club,' my friend continued. 'He can't miss this opportunity.'

'Nah, just what I said. You haven't even started your studies yet and your private activities are already intruding. What will happen to your studies later?'

'A visit by the Honourable Member is a rare event. He is unlikely to be out here even once in every five years, Mr Director. Mr Minke will have many days for study.'

'All right, but just this once. Except for holidays,' he gave in. 'But have you recovered from your journey?'

'Even tiredness can be overcome with eight hours' sleep. Isn't that right?' Now my friend spoke to me.

2

There had not been time to think over and digest all my impressions and experiences of that day. I did not even have time for an afternoon nap. Everyone in the dormitory was busy trying to figure out the identity of the woman in my painting. The person who had stuck the news-clipping on my suitcase tried to question me. Perhaps Partokleooo had told him what I had said about her.

They all started to make friends, and carefully sought an opportunity to ask. The Indo, too, whose name was Wilam (his official name – his unofficial name was William Merryweather). He was the son of an English plantation owner who had been killed by the Pitung gang in an attack on his plantation. His mother, a beauty from Cicurug – perhaps a relative of Nyai Dasima, was kidnapped by the gang. She was only freed after they were finally smashed by the army. And she brought home with her a new son.

I didn't answer any of their questions, except with a smile. I began to realise that among these educated Natives there were the beginnings of an appreciation of the beauty of the European face.

After it was announced that the School Council had decided to allow me to skip the first two years of preparatory classes, the students all felt that the harsh treatment they had meted out to me had been fair.

My friend was to pick me up at a quarter to five. The other students escorted me to the front of the school, where we all waited. The unpleasant events of earlier in the day were forgotten.

For the entire length of our journey in the *delman*, Ter Haar did nothing but talk about what a great man van Kollewijn was. He was a man who had contributed so much to the Indies, he said, opening up new vistas for the Natives. Even though, yes, even though it was Sugar that enjoyed most of these benefits.

I knew very little about this god, except for the fact that he was famous. I tried to understand what my friend was saying – that one man alone could change so much! What was his secret, what were his powers? If he did not have such powers then how was it possible that he could be elevated to such god-like status, as if he were a king with the power of life and death over others? And he was just a member of the Lower House, his only task was to speak. Just to talk. Of course he no doubt had a silver tongue. I just wasn't able to picture in my mind what he would be like. I had to meet him for myself and hear from him directly what he had to say.

The Harmoni Club was impressive. Huge, magnificent and opulent. The floor was made from tiles of black stone that reflected the light from the crystal chandeliers above. The air inside was cool and fresh. The rooms were filled with enormous elaborately-carved furniture. Every suite represented the fashion of a particular period. In one room there stood three huge billiard tables surrounded by billiard cues that looked as if they were lances guarding the tables. There was a picture of Her Majesty, standing alone, wearing a full-length gown and a white sash with black streaks, in a gold-painted carved frame. It stood higher than me, and I was one metre fifty-five centimetres.

This maiden, whom I had once praised so much, was about to walk down the wedding aisle with Prince Hendrik. It would be on 1 February 1901 Netherlands time, or 6 February 1901 according to Indies time, which was a *Kliwon* Friday. There hadn't been time to decorate the ballroom for the big celebrations, as big as those at her coronation, that were planned.

'It seems that you like to look at the picture of Her Majesty, but I know you are thinking about someone else,' reprimanded my friend. 'Yes, there is a likeness. I don't think you should dwell on the past too much, Mr Minke. You have a long future in front of you.'

Suddenly he turned the conversation.

'And in this building,' he was starting up his lecture, 'the first Liberal Movement was born. Mr Dominie Baron von Hoevell called for the establishment of high schools in the Indies. Fifty years ago! Time sometimes passes so slowly! The Governor-General himself ordered von Hoevell's arrest. The club was surrounded by soldiers and the cannons were aimed at it – all because he wanted the government to build some high schools. Von Hoevell was detained, and kept in the palace that you passed on the way here, until he could be whisked on board the first ship back to the Netherlands. He was banned from ever landing in the Indies again. Have you ever heard his name?'

I wasn't sure. Perhaps I had, but had forgotten. I shook my head.

'We can say, at the very least, that it is because of his efforts, Mr Minke, that you were able to go to high school. Within ten years of his arrest, high schools were no longer unusual in the Indies. In this modern era, everything moves faster. You remember why? Because of the triumph of capital, in its search for profits. And Baron von Hoevell's activities were just the beginning of greater efforts, efforts that have made the Indies what it is today. Today the Liberals are very powerful, and even more so since the emergence of the Radical wing, under the leadership of the man we will meet tonight. His influence is felt everywhere. His voice echoes with authority everywhere – in the Netherlands, the Indies and perhaps even in Surinam.'

This friend of mine seemed to know very well just how ignorant I was. He repeated patiently all of the little I knew about *Multatuli* and *Roorda van Eysinga*. And when he got to the speeches of the lion of the Lower House, von Hoevell, and then on to the emergence of van Deventer, he brimmed over with enthusiasm as if the Liberals were the ones who were going to turn the Indies into a paradise overnight, in the way that Bandung Bondowoso built the Prambanan temples. The fight against state plantations! The abolition of forced labour! The establishment of new private plantations! Free labour! Character building through free labour! Free competition! Repay the moral debt to the Natives through Emigration! Education! and Irrigation!

'Yes, my young sir,' he said slowly and clearly, 'only free labour can elevate the dignity and value of the Native. Free labour will return to the Native the knowledge and science that he lost as a result of being forced to obey the constant orders of those who do not necessarily know any better, knowledge and science that has been so long lost, lost for centuries. Free labour will free the Native of his superstitious fears, his fears of ghosts and of the police and the government soldiers. Then there will appear the real Native man.'

And how will all this benefit the Native, I wanted to ask, but I didn't. I should be the one who could answer that question. All that I was able to utter was: 'Raden Saleh Sjarif Boestaman . . . '

'You mean the famous painter?'

'He has also proved what the Native is capable of.'

'Yes. It's just a pity that he spends his time touring Europe, visiting the salons of the French and Dutch elites, seeking fame for himself, but making no real contribution to the advancement of his people. People are saying that he returned to the Indies no longer as a Native or a teacher of his people. He returned as a non-Native and as someone who was definitely not a teacher of his people.'

It was sad, but what he said was true.

He kept on talking and talking. The more he went on, the less I seemed to understand, and the more I started to scratch my neck. There didn't seem to be any connecting thread in what he was saying. It all sounded like the chanted spells of the magician. He spoke about the debates in the Dutch parliament and the problems of the Indies.

Seeing that my nods were becoming deeper and less sure of themselves, he said: 'Ah, perhaps you're not catching all of this. I will send you a book about all the problems of the Indies. Published in the Netherlands. Written by a true Liberal. Then you'll be able to study things at your leisure.'

The clock struck once. It was five-thirty in the evening. Engineer van

Kollewijn had still not arrived. The clang of the *delman* bell and the clatter of the tram occasionally reverberated through the building.

'He'll be here soon. It looks as if he's going to be a bit late.' He returned to his lecture. 'In short, it is the Liberals who are the chosen sons of our times, the best sons of the age of capital – an age when everything has and will be brought into being by capital, when anybody – not just the kings and sultans – will be able to have anything they like, as long as they have some capital. And there is only one condition that you need fulfil to obtain capital, Mr Minke, and that is to work hard as a free worker.'

I could understand that. Even so I found myself bored by this inappropriately timed and located lecture.

We hadn't noticed several European Pures come in and sit round the big table.

Several carriages – some with one horse, some with two – stopped in front of the building. Two Europeans went out to meet them and opened the doors of the leading carriage, and then . . . wasn't that General van Heutsz descending? He was wearing a military uniform, but without any marks of rank. He wore no decorations, carried no weapons and was without any bodyguards. He didn't come straight in, but stood facing the carriage, helping out another European, a very big man, perhaps weighing more than one hundred and twenty kilograms. Was that the god of the Radicals? Was that Engineer van Kollewijn? The one who looks like Bathara Narada? So plump with prosperity?

My friend the journalist from *De Locomotief* left me and ran outside to join with the others in welcoming their guest. Ah, who cares less, I thought, none of them know me anyway. Ter Haar greeted the corpulent one and then helped steer the two guests inside, along with all the other people who had arrived with them.

My heart began pounding when General van Heutsz turned his questioning eyes upon me as he walked inside. And his gaze conveyed an order that I show him the respect that he obviously felt was his right. I showed him the due respect.

'I see there is a *sinyo* here tonight?' he asked Ter Haar, looking first at me, then at Ter Haar.

Ter Haar brought them both over to me, saying: 'Excuse me, General, Mr van Kollewijn, this is the young Native who has been writing in Dutch.'

'Ah!' cried the General. 'This is him, Henk,' he said to van Kollewijn, 'I think he's about to grow a moustache.' To me, 'I enjoy your writing very much.' He held out his hand.

The stories of the Aceh War, that I had heard so often from my painter friend in Surabaya, meant that mine trembled as it took his. His were hands that had killed thousands of Acehnese fighters in their own land, in the land of their birth. His moustache, the metal buttons he wore on his uniform . . .

17

I would remember them all as the features of this much respected and much fawned upon murderer.

His grip on my hand was tight and painful. He shook it several times. And when he let go, it fell lifeless by my side. Without realising what I was doing I was wiping my hand clean of his touch on my trousers.

Ter Haar looked the other way when he saw that. Van Kollewijn quickly held out his hand and held my hand for what seemed a long while. That left hand of his, so fat and soft, squeezed my right hand, which literally sank into his.

'And what have you been writing?' he asked with the voice of somebody who was courting me.

'Short stories!' answered van Heutsz. 'And in the European style, Henk. I never realised he was so young.'

'Short stories? You don't really mean in the European style, then, do you? You must mean in the American style?' answered van Kollewijn, trying to correct his friend. 'What do you say, young man?'

'I think probably in my own style, Sir,' I answered.

They both laughed heartily. I didn't really understand why.

'He is right,' Ter Haar joined in. 'He does have his own style.'

'That is very great praise, then,' said van Kollewijn, as he looked me over, shaking his head. As soon as his hand let go of mine, it moved up to my back, patting me: 'Come along, Sir.'

'Please call me Minke.'

'Javanese?'

'Yes, Sir.'

'The son of which *bupati*?'

'The Bupati of B – '

'Near Jepara, isn't it? That's where that famous young woman lives. Do you know her?'

'I know the name, Sir.'

Ter Haar, myself and the others accompanied the two guests to the assigned area. Those who had arrived earlier and were sitting round the table rose to greet the guests.

It was a great long oval table covered in green material, like a judge's bench or a billiard table. But it was made from velvet. Silver ashtrays shone all around the table. As soon as they all sat down, every pair of eyes rained their curiosity down upon me. I pretended not to notice.

The host introduced General van Heutsz and van Kollewijn. Then he introduced the various guests. One of the two journalists present was Marie van Zeggelen.

'I haven't seen anything by you for some time, Miss van Zeggelen. Are you planning any more articles about the heroism of the Natives?'

'Yes, I would say so, General.'

No one introduced me. The General and the Member of Parliament both stared at me. Then the General decided to speak: 'And let me introduce to you all a young writer named Minke,' he said, indicating with his hand that he meant me.

All eyes examined me with amazement.

'Or, more accurately, a short story writer,' van Kollewijn corrected him, in that personal way of his, that Dutch way.

Under such a deluge of gazes from such important personages, whether because of the colour of my skin, or my age, or because of my very appearance, I felt like a monkey that had been put in the wrong cage. Just where had I let myself be taken?

The old man across from me nodded, slowly smacked his lips and said: 'Ah, gentlemen, let us begin the evening's proceedings,' because he was the host. And he himself gave the first speech.

Engineer van Kollewijn had come to Java to witness for himself the developments that were taking place as a result of the efforts, both inside and outside parliament, of the Free Democratic Party.

There then followed a series of questions and answers whose meaning I didn't really understand. I felt even more like a monkey in the wrong cage. The questions and answers went on for quite some time. Drinks were served twice. Almost everyone had a chance to go to the toilet. Still the interview continued. The eight o'clock cannon had long been quiet, and the barracks' bugles long silent. I need not say that it was only I who did not ask questions. All I could do was look first left and then right to see who was speaking.

'You surely have plans for other activities while you are here.' The old grandfather across from me spoke.

'Of course,. It's been a long time since I've been in these beloved Indies,' said van Kollewijn. 'It would be a great waste if I concerned myself only with party affairs while I was here.'

'So what else might you be planning?'

'Well, for example, I very much hope that I can meet some of the educated Natives. It's very important to know what they are thinking now as we enter this new age. Will they be able to adjust or not? Will they welcome the new age or reject it?'

'Is there any connection between the educated Natives and your party's campaign, Mr van Kollewijn?' someone asked.

'The ties between Holland and the Indies are growing closer and closer. The demands of the modern world are bringing these two distant countries closer together. The qualifications needed to work in a modern society are higher today. This is true in the Indies as well as in Holland. This means we have a responsibility to prepare educated Natives to enter into the modern age. If we do not do this, then all the factories and machines, no matter how fantastic, will be useless because the Natives will not be able to use them.'

19

'Couldn't the factories be run just by Europeans?'

'Aha, that is the old way. But it is no longer appropriate. Gentlemen, just look at the situation today where all the railway machinists are European. There is not a single Native machinist in the Indies. Indeed even the rock-crushers used for road construction are not run by Natives, but by Indos. But the coming of trains to the Indies has not only brought new ways of doing things but also new laws. And these laws must be obeyed by both European and Native. And so why should the Natives be expected to learn the new ways and obey the new laws, when, on the other hand, they are told it is only they who must make the sacrifices?'

The longer the discussion went on, the more confused I became trying to follow it, and the more convinced I was of how little I knew and understood. And I truly tried to understand what they were talking about. Every single pronouncement of such a person as van Kollewijn, so highly esteemed, with such a fiery tongue, must be heeded closely.

He repeated what I had once read in that anonymous political pamphlet. He explained that the first decades of the Culture System, also called Forced Cultivation, had saved Holland from the bankruptcy it faced due to the huge debts that were incurred through the wars in Europe in which Holland too was involved. The profits from the Indies had also paid for Holland's own development and provided it with working capital. The Indies, he said, had not only paid in money but also in lives. Thousands of Natives died because of the Forced Cultivation system. And without those sacrifices from the Indies, Holland may have been wiped off the face of the earth.

'We owe a lot to the Indies – there is a moral debt. A debt of honour, which as Europeans, as Christians, we are obliged to repay. We must now do good for the Natives, in return for the good they have done us. And this should not just amount to a few regulations in their favour. They must be helped to become equipped to deal with the new times. And the best bridge across to the Natives that they may be so helped is the educated Natives.'

'Could Your Excellency tell us which educated Natives you will be meeting?'

'Well I have met with Mr Minke who is here with us tonight,' he nodded in my direction, 'a young man who has written short stories, not simply in the European or American fashion, but, according to Mr Ter Haar, in his own, personal style. This is indeed true praise. I'm glad you have asked me this question, gentlemen. But I wish also to ask you all a question. Is it actually possible for a Native to develop a personality, a character, of his own? Aha, I am sure this is an issue that none of you have ever really considered. The development of a personality, of individual character, is a sign that a man and his times are in harmony.'

'And do you have hopes for Mr Minke?' asked Marie van Zeggelen.

'Science and modern knowledge, gentlemen, no matter how advanced, have no character. The most fantastic of machines, built by the most fantastic of men, also have no real character. But the simplest of the most simple stories that somebody can write – they can really represent somebody's personality and character, or, indeed, could also bear inside them the personality and character of a whole people. Isn't that so, General?'

The General nodded silently.

'You yourself are a writer, are you not, Miss?' van Kollewijn asked in turn.

'Has Your Excellency ever read any of Mr Minke's writings?'

'Not yet, unfortunately. But General van Heutsz has read them, and, I expect, so have most of you here. Is that not so, Mr Ter Haar?'

'He is extremely talented. And his writings show true character. If you were not aware who the author was you would swear they were written by a European or an American with the Indies just as their setting.'

'Once again high praise indeed,' van Kollewijn continued.

'Which other educated Natives are you interested in meeting, Your Excellency?'

'Well, according to the advice of the Director of Education and Culture, Mr van Aberon, I should, of course, meet the girl from Jepara.'

'So Your Excellency will also visit Jepara, as did Mr van Aberon?'

'That would be very interesting. Then I could not only meet the person concerned but also see for myself the environment in which she lives and works.'

'Very impressive, Sir,' cried van Zeggelen, 'but could I also ask what it is about this woman that interests you?'

'She has done more than just write and more than just tell stories. She has dedicated her life to an ideal. She writes not to seek fame for herself. As a spiritual child of Multatuli, she has, in her own way, struggled in the name of humanity to lessen the suffering of humankind.'

General van Heutsz cleared his throat.

'Ignorance is always a barrier to prosperity. This is true in Europe, America, the Indies, or wherever,' van Kollewijn went on. 'Mankind needs prosperity that he may live in conditions worthy of his humanity,' he glanced across at van Heutsz. 'That is the importance of the educated Native.'

'Your Excellency, Honourable Member of Parliament, you have praised the idea of free labour. Are you therefore also in favour of the abolition of forced labour, of *rodi*?'

'*Rodi* is a traditional form of collective labour which has been used by the Indies for the benefit of the state and of society as an alternative form of state tax. It will be some time before *rodi* can be abolished because the circulation of money in the villages and hamlets is very limited. It is only in the cities that a cash economy prevails. The important thing today is to ensure that the system is not abused. We do not want to see the abuses of power that happened in Multatuli's day.'

'If we view *rodi* as a form of tax, Your Excellency,' asked Ter Haar, 'doesn't that mean that the revenue received by the Netherlands Indies is much, much greater than that which is set down in the official budget? Doesn't it mean that the official statement of annual income of the Indies is much smaller than it should be?'

Engineer van Kollewijn was silenced. There was sweat on his brow. Hurriedly, he took out a handkerchief and wiped his brow. General van Heutsz's fingers tapped upon the table. Marie van Zeggelen bit her lip. Everyone there, except the military man, waited expectantly for his answer. And van Kollewijn still didn't answer.

'Just think, Your Excellency, ten million Natives each working twenty days' *rodi* per year. At seven and a half cents per person per day of work, that's ten million times twenty times seven and a half. That's equal to fifteen million guilders a year. Fifteen million guilders that has never been accounted for or documented. Where did it all go?'

Silence.

Ter Haar went on. 'And that's not all, Your Excellency. I hear that the villagers themselves have to organise village security, something that the police should look after. And there's the emergency services too – the fifteen million should probably be doubled. See, the villages have had thirty million guilders a year sucked out of them. Once, when the Government was pressed for money, it thought of selling one of the Sunda Kelapa islands to an Arab. He was said to have offered one hundred and eighty thousand guilders. The equivalent of just a year of our debt to the villages would be enough for an Arab to buy the whole of Sunda Kelapa islands ten times over! Has your Excellency given this matter any thought, either as an individual, a member of parliament, or a member of the Free Democratic Party?'

'As free labour becomes more and more widespread, taxes in the form of *rodi* will gradually die out.'

'Yes, Your Excellency, if we calculate that *rodi* has been going ever since the Indies became the property of the Empire, anyway say from 1870, since the Forced Cultivation period, then the Government of the Netherlands Indies and the Netherlands itself owes the Natives thirty times thirty million guilders or nine hundred million guilders. And if we count too all those hidden services provided by the people to the state free of charge, the figure will probably go up to one billion guilders. The Netherlands is unable to fully repay the debt we owe the Natives as a result of the Forced Cultivation system, Your Excellency, let alone if we add all this unaccounted-for money.'

Even though I only half understood, I could still see – it was not van Kollewijn who was the god, but Ter Haar. This athletic-bodied Dutchman was tough-thinking and didn't hesitate for a moment to expose the giant fraud that had been carried out upon my people. I trembled. I am unable to explain how I felt at that moment. I was not a god. I was not yet anything.

'Yes, it's a pity that's not on my agenda during this trip. Even so, I will take note of what you've said.' His corpulent body seemed even fatter now, and white, like a big fat white ghost.

'Yes, a pity,' repeated Ter Haar. 'Does Your Excellency agree with my opinion that corruption during the East Indies Company period was just as great as that which exists today?'

'Corruption is not foreign to the Indies, especially to the Native ruling class,' van Kollewijn was forced to answer. 'Isn't that so, General?'

'It is not my responsibility to answer that question, unfortunately,' replied van Heutsz.

'A billion guilders corrupted over thirty years has nothing to do with the Natives. Don't Christians always pay back their debts? When will the Netherlands pay back its thirty-year-old debt, and the interest that's owing as well?'

General van Heutsz, head bowed, was concentrating on all that was being said, although his boredom was also obvious. I took another look around the table.

Ter Haar's question remained unanswered. Van Kollewijn tried to laugh the question off. His friend the General seemed to understand his predicament. The General interrupted the silence to ask Marie van Zeggelen: 'I think Marie van Zeggelen might be interested in other matters.'

She smiled and nodded, then: 'If the chair does not object?'

The old man looked at van Kollewijn, who nodded in agreement.

'Yes, the opportunity is now open to Miss van Zeggelen and the gentlemen to ask questions of the General, even though it is outside the agenda.'

'On the condition, gentlemen, that nothing discussed here today is to go beyond this room,' said van Kollewijn.

'With the Aceh War drawing to an end, General . . . ,' she began to ask.

'It has been announced that the war, as a military exercise, is over,' the General butted in.

'Excuse me. Now that the war, as a military exercise, is over, can you say whether there is some light at the end of the tunnel. Can the Natives look forward to peace? Or the reverse?'

'That's a matter for the Netherlands Indies Government. It's not for me to answer.'

'Thank you. But I am asking what the General's own views are?'

'An honour,' Van Heutsz nodded quickly and happily. 'However, as a soldier, it is not my job to talk about policies, let alone actually govern.'

'Exactly,' van Kollewijn backed him up.

'I mean your personal opinion,' Marie van Zeggelen pressed him.

'Personal opinion? Of course I have one, but it's not for the public.'

'Of course. But don't you think you should let your old friends, and your new ones here, know what your views are? Isn't that fair enough, General, as long as there are no military secrets involved?'

'Very well, for my old and new friends that are here with us tonight. Everyone knows from the papers that the war in Aceh was very costly. Almost the total resources of the Indies, both manpower and money, were mobilised for that conquest. Now that the war is over, the Government will, of course, be able to begin to strengthen the administration there, tighten security and restore civil order. And to unify the Indies.'

'Of course, you mean *expand*, don't you, not *unify*?'

'Unify.'

'I think the General has always preferred this new term, which in fact has the same meaning,' pressed Marie van Zeggelen.

'Nah, what did I say? A soldier shouldn't get involved in talking.'

'Very true, General. This new term of yours explains everything very clearly.'

Van Heutsz laughed boisterously. His eyes pleaded for help from van Kollewijn who was grinning, enjoying his friend's discomfort.

'Once you've begun to speak,' the Member of Parliament said, 'you must continue. What else can you do?'

All eyes were now focussed on the General, famed for his conquest of Aceh. I had been observing him closely. I wanted to get a feel for how a killer talked and behaved.

'It's not difficult to understand what the implications are. The money saved by ending the war in Aceh can now be put to other uses . . . '

His movements and the way he spoke were enough to make one feel confident in predicting that more wars would be breaking out everywhere. More Natives, armed with bows and arrows and spears, in now yet unknown places would die in their hundreds on the orders of this man. For the sake of the unity of the colony, in other words for the security of big capital in the Indies. The spilling of more blood, the loss of life, slavery, oppression, exploitation, humiliation – all this would occur at the wave of his hand. All this man sitting near me need do is point with his baton at the map, and somewhere in the Indies hell would descend to tear apart the lives of the people. Those left alive would be burdened with *rodi*, which would produce more of that unaccounted, unreported wealth for the Indies.

'No one should misunderstand,' van Heutsz went on. 'The unification of the Indies does not mean expansionism. There are pockets of power, different political enclaves, a score or so, still left in these Indies, which are destabilising surrounding regions – regions that have acknowledged the sovereignty of Her Majesty.'

'They are independent states,' said Marie van Zeggelen, 'just like Aceh before it was conquered.'

'They are not states, they are stateless regions. They have no economy or monetary system. They have no foreign relations.'

'They are independent states,' Ter Haar retorted, 'no matter how small or weak.'

'They use old Chinese coins, not their own coinage. In the Batak area, for example, they use the Spanish dollar,' answered van Heutsz.

'That's no criterion. Some of them do have foreign relations. They all have systems of government. They have their own defences. Isn't that so, Your Excellency?'

Engineer van Kollewijn just smiled silently.

'And they are a source of strife,' van Heutsz stated firmly.

'Perhaps they think we are the source of strife, General.'

Van Heutsz laughed and nodded vigorously. He seemed to be enjoying the debate. Then: 'That's why we make, buy and use guns.'

And whoever does not make them, buy them and use them . . . now I understood – they become targets and victims.

'And what about East Papua? And South-east Papua? Are they on the list of regions to be 'unified'?'

'Ha-ha-ha,' the General laughed again. 'I haven't got any list. There is no list. No one has ever made a list.'

'And anyway,' Ter Haar added. 'East Papua has become Germany's burden. The South-east is Australia's.'

The discussion turned more and more into a debate. Van Kollewijn cleverly avoided becoming involved. His obese body didn't seem to move at all, except for his head. And that only with difficulty.

'And West Papua is a heavy burden for the Indies. But we all know that west, east or south-east, it's all a matter of the prestige of the Empire. It's got nothing to do with strategy, or colonial welfare, or even geo-politics.' Ter Haar kept pressing van Heutsz. 'Are these pockets of power you talk about important only because of the prestige that would flow from their conquest or do you say it's a matter of territorial integrity, General?'

'Prestige, territorial integrity and power.'

'The party of the Honourable Member of Parliament, His Excellency van Kollewijn, is campaigning to repay the debt of honour we owe to the Indies – I hope this will not turn out to be just a promise used for political purposes.'

Van Heutsz seemed offended. He stopped laughing. His cheerfulness disappeared. His moustache trembled. 'If I was in power, the Free Democratic Party would be allowed to implement its program, on the condition that there were no more colonial wars in progress, that is to say the wars would have to be finished first.'

Obviously such wars were going to continue. These murderers were still thirsty for blood, the blood of Natives, of my fellow countrymen.

'Excuse me, gentlemen,' interrupted our elderly host, 'I think we should return to our official program. It will not be so easy for General van Heutsz to leave the Indies. Even though it might be somewhat difficult, it is possible for us to meet him. On the other hand, this is a rare opportunity for us to speak with His Excellency, the Honourable Member of Parliament Mr van Kollewijn, who may get out here only a couple of times every ten years.'

The questioning turned again to van Kollewijn and proceeded rapidly. Everyone deliberately ignored van Heutsz, who was on the verge of losing his temper. Everyone had asked some kind of important question. I was the only one who had not said anything. No doubt everyone was assuming that I felt inferior among these high-level European Pures. Then, all of a sudden, van Heutsz turned to me and said: 'Mr Minke . . . you have a very easy name to remember. You too must have some important questions.' He smiled, perhaps to help subdue his anger.

I showed no nervousness. Thanks be to God! I was the only Native, and the only juvenile, present. Acknowledgement by the conquering General of Aceh, it would be said, was still a real acknowledgement. I felt Ter Haar nudge my leg with his feet.

'Thank you, Your Excellency. Concerning this question of free labour, Your Excellency, does it include the freedom to evict farmers who do not wish to rent their land to the sugar mills?'

'Your question's not quite clear,' said van Kollewijn, while looking one by one at each of those present. He was obviously preparing an answer. Or he considered my question to be totally stupid.

I repeated my question. He still didn't answer. My nerves were on edge. I was afraid that my question was about to be disregarded as ridiculous. Was my question wrong or stupid? Everything was quiet, and the quiet tortured me. It was just a few seconds, but it felt like eternity. I caught Marie Van Zeggelen rocking her bag. Ter Haar shuffled on his chair. Why wasn't my question answered?

'Is that sort of thing still happening?' asked van Kollewijn. His eyes spoke to van Heutsz.

'I haven't heard of anything like that, Your Excellency,' a journalist answered.

'We haven't received any reports of that sort of thing,' someone else commented.

I've had it, I thought to myself. I must be ready.

'You're related to a *bupati*, aren't you, Mr Minke?' asked van Kollewijn.

'You're not mistaken, Your Excellency.'

'I'm quite amazed to hear you ask such a question, Meneer Minke. Have you perhaps been in contact with the peasants?'

'No, Your Excellency, but I did by coincidence witness such an incident.'

'Where did it happen, Mr Minke?' asked van Kollewijn very politely.

'Sidoarjo, Your Excellency.'

'Sidoarjo!' one journalist cried out.

'You mean, Mr Minke, that you witnessed what happened amongst the Sidoarjo peasants last year?' van Heutsz suddenly asked with rather excessive respect.

Something had given me the courage to bring forward this otherwise unknown incident. Meanwhile Ter Haar was nudging my foot under the table. He was obviously warning me. But it wasn't his warnings that were foremost in my mind at that moment, rather the fate of those peasants and their families, and their friends. I had made a promise to them. So I told the whole story, from the beginning until the peasants' uprising and the deaths of all the peasants.

As soon as I had finished Ter Haar hurriedly spoke out: 'Excuse me,' he said, 'Mr Minke is a medical student.'

'You mean he hasn't studied the law?'

'That is right, Your Excellency.'

I remembered all the problems I had experienced with the law in the past. And I became somewhat afraid. No doubt this god before me would seek to entangle me again with the law, and would accuse me of not reporting what I had witnessed.

The atmosphere became tense again. And I too was tense.

'Yes, it does seem that Mr Minke here does not understand the law. You could be in trouble because of this, Mr Minke. You should have reported what you knew before the uprising occurred, then the authorities could have acted to prevent it.'

'I am not speaking just about the uprising itself,' I spoke out, overcoming my fear. 'The question is, does "free labour" mean the freedom to evict farmers from their own land?'

Among all those present, only Ter Haar and Marie van Zeggelen did not seem to be offended by my question.

'Your question, and indeed your whole story, is not so important,' answered van Kollewijn, 'but even so it could bring you into contact with the police. They could charge you with covering up evidence.'

'Excuse me, Your Excellency, but I do not have any business with the police.'

'But Mr Minke, it's very difficult for anyone to say they do not have business with the police. The security of the state is protected by the police. Therefore everyone, from the smallest baby to the oldest grandfather, has business with the police. Also, you knew of the situation before the uprising took place. And you didn't report it.'

'Yes, it's true, I didn't report it to the police. But I did write a report for everyone to read, before the uprising,' I answered, and my fear disappeared with my next sentence, 'But the newspaper refused to publish it; the editor was even angry with me.'

Van Kollewijn nodded, like some kind of all-knowing god.

'Furthermore,' I went on, 'as far as I know – and I hope I'm wrong – the police have never taken action to investigate the eviction of those farmers by the sugar mill.'

'Do you think I could read that article of yours?' van Heutsz asked.

'Because I was so disappointed after it was rejected,' I replied, 'I tore it up on the way home from the newspaper office.'

And it couldn't have been otherwise: all eyes were now focussed on the wayward child present, that is to say, me. Van Kollewijn did not answer my question. Neither did van Heutsz. And the, according to himself, all-wise host looked at me with accusing eyes: you, uninvited, a rotten Native, you have ruined this meeting, which should have been a beautiful evening.

He spoke: 'The discussion has been very useful tonight. Our thanks to His Excellency the Honourable Engineer van Kollewijn and also to His Excellency General van Heutsz and to all our invited guests. Good evening.'

Everyone stood to honour the VIPs as they left. But instead they did not leave straight away. Both van Heutsz and van Kollewijn held out their hands to me.

'I was very happy to hear what you had to say,' said van Kollewijn.

'You speak clearly and with courage and honesty,' said van Heutsz.

'Who brought you here?' asked the official host.

'Perhaps we can have a more private talk?' said van Kollewijn.

'Unfortunately I am bound by my promise to the school Director to catch up with my studies, Your Excellency.'

'I judge from your attitude, Mr Minke, that you have experienced some tragedy and disappointment in your life. Would it be all right with you if I invited you for a discussion one day?'

'If the school Director permits it, Your Excellency Mr General.'

'Good. If I get the opportunity, I'll try to arrange it.'

They left the club. As soon as the group broke up, the host from the club attacked Ter Haar.

'And I, representing both the management of the club and all its members, condemn you for bringing a Native here. You know the rules.'

'Be as angry as you like, Sir. In any case, both van Kollewijn and the General appreciated the chance to meet Mr Minke. They have even asked for another meeting.'

'But not in this club.'

'That's up to them.'

'Get out!'

'Yes, Minke, we don't need to stay here any longer. What for, anyway? We don't want to hang around haunting the place. Come on, let's go. And thank you to our host, who has been so kind. This is the first time a Native has set foot – other than as a waiter or coolie – inside this building which was built on the land of his own ancestors. Good evening.'

So we left the old man there, muttering.

In the *delman*, Ter Haar began again. 'Next time you must be more careful when you start talking about things that touch upon power, that is to say, Sugar. You must be fully equipped before you go into the field of battle. We were lucky the old man knew when to end the session.'

'So you're not angry with him?'

'No need to be angry. He knew he was breaking the club rules. It was against the rules for you to come into the club. Perhaps because of his age, or because he was hoping for some kind of praise from his guests, he didn't comment on your presence even after he saw you there. Or perhaps we just outmanoeuvred him!'

'So you had some scheme in mind when you took me to the Harmoni.'

'Forget it.'

'And what I said really did put me in danger?'

'It did worry me. You enjoined battle without knowing the lie of the land. Don't worry. Yes, they're free to interpret your story any way they like. Perhaps you were in league with those peasants. You might even have been the brains behind the uprising. But don't worry, if anything happens, I'll be by your side.'

I listened carefully to what he said, making sure that I remembered it all. Just as I had made promises to people in the past, now Ter Haar was making such a promise to me. He was a friend. And people must have friends, said my mother. It was true, friendship was more powerful than enmity. Ter Haar had proved himself a Liberal who did not bow down to Sugar, but only to the principles of humanity. How beautiful was his spirit, like an orchard in the middle of this desert.

'Mr Minke, mixing with the powerful is like going among wild animals. They fight each other, their hunger for victims is insatiable. Their hearts are like the Sahara desert, dry and harsh. Even the ocean would disappear in that desert. I hope you're not offended by my giving you this advice. It is very stupid to enter a den of wild animals unarmed.'

There was no traffic. It was after eleven o'clock in the evening. Only the gas lamps along the streets were there to look up at the moon.

You, oh Remus, oh Romula, drink up all you can from this wolf. So you may grow into a builder of Rome. People say all the Europeans in the Indies are wolves. What is Ter Haar doing here in the Indies except that he too is after prey. Be careful, Minke! Watch out for van Heutsz too! And van Kollewijn. And beware too of that sympathiser of the Native cause, Marie van Zeggelen. Look, if the Natives today had the courage to rebel against the Dutch, like Sultan Agung, then I might be facing Ter Haar not as a friend but as an enemy – and a relentless one at that.

My first day in Betawi had been packed with so many different experiences. I would never forget it for as long as I lived.

I arrived at the dormitory. All the lights were out. There was nothing for me to eat.

3

Partokleooo threw himself energetically and selflessly into the task of helping me catch up with my studies. As a trained teacher, he was able to explain very well all the lessons I had missed. He also went through with me the speech that the Director delivered at the beginning of the year: 'The Native people of the Indies have an average life expectancy of twenty-five years.'

You could not imagine how much this shocked me, as Partokleooo repeated it all to me, sitting there on the bed, propped up against the wall.

'Are you sure your notes are correct?' I asked.

'Yes. Do you want me to go on or not? Very well, I will continue. The majority of the Javanese die from parasitic diseases when they are still children. Short indeed are the lives of the Javanese. They lost all their ancestors' knowledge of medicine during the chaotic times of long ago . . . '

'What did he mean by "chaotic times"?'

'A time of great natural calamities, he said, and a time of great decadence and destruction among the Native communities wherever the Dutch were not in control . . . And so the Natives lost all their healers and there was nobody to take their place . . . and so the people of Java fell victim to the thousands of parasites that inhabit the equatorial region. So now the Government, as an act of good will, is providing you all the opportunity to work for humanity, to fight these diseases, to lighten the suffering of the sick . . . '

'Humph! How beautiful!'

'Every student who fails in his studies,' he continued, repeating the Director's speech, 'is guilty of allowing his own people to die of these diseases, is guilty of inhumanity, and should be punished accordingly. Doctors make a great contribution to society. Everyone supports their work . . . '

And so on and so forth. I gradually caught up with my lessons. I was also helped by Cupid's Bow. From his name you might think he was European or Indo but no, he was Javanese and as Javanese as you could be. He was the son of a veterinary assistant from Ponorogo. No one ever used his real name any more, except for the teachers. None of us ever called him either just Cupid or Bow. He didn't like it at first and often lost his temper with us. But nobody took any notice. In the end, he had to learn to live with it.

'Why are people so strange,' sighed Partotenojo. 'Look at me, nothing wrong with me at all, but just because I'm a bit shorter than other people, I get called Partokleooo as if I'm *loyo*, pathetic and hopeless. But other than being short, I'm really quite handsome and attractive, aren't I? Then look at Cupid's Bow, he sticks out too much, even more than a European or a Jew.'

'What do you mean "sticks out"? Flat as anything is more like it.'

'Flat? Yes, if we're talking about his nose.'

'Hush!' I reprimanded him, offended. He wasn't talking about his friend's nose protruding, but his upper lip.

I was also almost given a nickname of my own. After I had left with Ter Haar that night, the students had all got together to decide to call me Gemblung – stupid one. When I woke up the next day, I found the room empty. The shoes I had been wearing when I had collapsed into bed the night before had disappeared. The mirror revealed to me that my face had been painted in coconut oil with black and white stripes. There was a huge moustache curling right up to my eyebrows. And around my neck there hung a necklace and a piece of cardboard on which was written my new nickname.

But this new nickname was cancelled the moment they found out who I had been out to meet that night – VIPs as tall as pine trees. They then had to look at me differently, even though the reality was that I was nothing more than onion fertiliser.

And that wasn't all that had happened. They had also taken the portrait out of its cover. It had been decorated with all kinds of comments written on bits of paper and placed around the bottom of the portrait. I don't know how many had given their comments, but there were quite a few. But they had to take it all back too after I threatened to make an issue out of what they had done. No educated person, no matter where they are, would violate the rights of others, I said. Only barbarians engaged in that kind of behaviour, and they were barbarians whether or not they had sat on school benches and could read and write. I am ready to defend my rights, I said again, if it is the case that you people do not understand about rights.

But it isn't my intention to bore you all with stories of the misbehaviour of children. Nor is it my intention to note down for you every boring, and sometimes disgusting incident that occurred in the dormitory. In the midst of all this unpleasantness, the only bright spots were my friendships: with Cupid's Bow, with Partokleooo and even with Wilam.

It turned out that Wilam was not the type to hold a grudge. He was considerate and helpful. The stories that proceeded forth from his gullet, now missing two teeth, were always interesting, especially the jokes he told about the English plantation owners.

It was he who told this story for the first time: 'Do you all know why it is forbidden to have a *guling* in the dormitory?' He laughed happily at his question.

'Nah, listen well and I will tell you about it. You will not find a *guling*, that pillow that you all like to have with you in bed, anywhere else in the world. Anyway, that's what my mama told me. Maybe things will be different in ten years' time, who knows? The Natives of the Indies have only been using them for a little while. They started copying the Dutch. Everything pleasant brought in by the Dutch is immediately copied, especially by those cotton-brained *priyayi*. The English laughed at the Dutch for using the *guling*.'

'Only a few of the Dutch brought women with them,' he continued. 'It was the same with other Europeans. Once they arrived here they were forced to take concubines. But the Dutch were also known to be really stingy. They wanted to return to Holland as wealthy people. So many of them didn't want to take concubines. As a replacement for a mistress, they made the *guling* – a mistress that can't fart. Hey, you, Kleooo – have you ever come across a mention of the *guling* in any of the Javanese literature you have read? No, you haven't. And you, Sutan, what about in Malay literature? A big zero. It just didn't exist. It was a pure Dutch invention – the mistress that doesn't fart – 'A Dutch Wife' . . . '

Whenever he was about to end a story, he always raised his nose and poked out his upper lip as if he were a he-goat.

'And do you know who was the first to give them that name? Raffles, the Lieutenant Governor-General of the Indies.'

'And the English in the Indies,' added Kleooo, 'what was the first thing they did when they arrived in the Indies? They asked for a Dutch Wife, a non-farting mistress. The Dutch, who considered the English the most miserly and greediest people on earth, named the *guling* "the British Doll". . .'

'You're making it up, Kleooo!' everyone chided him.

'No I'm not. My father worked for twenty years for the Dutch masters,' Partokleooo boasted proudly.

My friend had become much more confident since we had become friends and he was protected from being bullied. He was only ever bullied before because he didn't know how to defend himself.

And I myself? It was only my friendships that provided relief from all this boredom.

It took me only four months to catch up in my studies. It was true that there weren't really any subjects that were difficult for me. Even so I soon began to feel that medicine wasn't for me. From the very beginning, our studies took the form of learning rules and categories. We were forced to bow down to things, dead and living, so that you disappeared among all that you learnt. The learning you received made you feel worthless, drowning your personality. Perhaps it was true what some people had said – I was not meant to be a doctor.

Most of the students had to study Dutch, except for me and two others. On the other hand, we were obliged to learn one of the regional languages. I chose Malay. I was also freed from studying English, German and French.

I had no chance to do any writing. Every hour was taken up by study. There was no time left for enjoying life. Buy a bicycle? No time, let alone for learning to ride one! It would have been wonderful to be able to go to a shop and learn to ride. My savings remained frozen in their hiding-place.

In the sixth month of study, all first-year students began to get Saturday afternoon off. Students in the two preparatory years did not receive that privilege. Anyway, as soon as Saturday afternoons became free, everyone went off to have a good time. Except Sikun. After going with the other students a few times I became bored. I started to spend the afternoon in the library and was still there when my friends arrived back at the dormitory.

So, as time passed I understood better and better that I was becoming a person alone among all my studies, among the jokes and laughter, the temptations and games, boasting, cynicism and insults.

The medical school was not for me.

Among the Javanese students there were only two who held the title *Raden Mas*. There were four *Raden*. Most were just *Mas*. There was only one person with no title at all – Sikun.

Sikun had been a clerk in the Tegal District Administration Office with a wage of 175 cents a month. He had worked for five years without any rise in his pay. A butcher took him as his son-in-law and he soon had two children. The butcher was very proud to have a son-in-law who was an office worker. He showered everything upon his son-in-law. He paid for private tutoring that Sikun received from a bankrupt Dutchman. Sikun studied Dutch and the other subjects in the *HBS* so that he could sit for the HBS graduation examination. He went to Semarang to sit for the examination and passed with the lowest marks in the exam. And now he found himself at the medical school with a salary of ten guilders a month. He had brought his wife and children to Betawi. He used every opportunity available to visit his family in Tanah Abang where he could escape from the insulting barbs of his titled fellow-students.

The children of the upper echelons of the Native Civil Service did not generally wish to become doctors, to engage in work that involved working for one's fellow human beings. They preferred to govern, to wield power, to toady, and, most importantly, to be toadied to. My brother once came to me in Betawi. He said straight out that he was sorry for me because I had not applied to join the Native Civil Service. His attitude made me study even harder. After he had been appointed a Police Supervisor, he became even worse. Oh well, goodbye. People, even brothers, go their own way down the road of life.

Most of my friends also felt sorry for me: I had thrown away the chance to be a *bupati* – the highest position that any Native can achieve! And what would be my salary after I graduated from medical school? I would start with a mere eighteen guilders a month. I would have to work more than eleven hours a day. The highest my salary would ever reach, after thirty years of service, would be eighty-four guilders. And that was only if it was thought I had given good service.

But at the moment, yes now, with pocket money of ten guilders a month, food and board provided by the school, a young man could do whatever he liked to his full satisfaction. He could pay off the most expensive bicycle, or send home five guilders a month to his family, or send his younger brother to school, or marry and set up household in Betawi. And even without the money he could already begin to attract prospective wives – he was a medical school student! A position was already impatiently awaiting him. A house with all its furniture, and transportation and servants. There would be no need to hunt out work. No need to end up in an office. He was one of the cleverest of people. He had spent six years just studying! Just studying, mind you! Eight years, if you counted the two years of preparatory classes. Only the chosen few could survive such a long time. Eight whole years!

But neither was it unusual that many of the students had spent all their money before the month was up. And so we would all go off (sometimes I too would go) to Waterloo Park to listen to the military band and to look over, with wild and lecherous eyes, the *nyai* who were taking their children out for walks.

All the students at the medical school had a basic knowledge of the character of the concubines. They could be coaxed and cajoled easily. They opened their hearts easily. Indeed they made it easy to be coaxed and cajoled and they gladly would invite you home if their master was away. They were lonely people in the middle of a civilisation that was not their own. They needed the attentions of the young Native men, like they needed chilli and salad.

And everyone boasted about their experiences with this or that *nyai* and whatever it was that they had got.

These were all stories that worried me inside. This was all the opposite of what mother had taught me – never trust a woman, who is not your wife, who is willing to accept that which you can give her. And now, all around me, dashing young men, with the trappings of education, free individuals, with ten guilders in their pockets, are all chasing after what it is that the *nyai* can give them! Would mother think that they too, these men, could not be trusted? Mother said such women were basically prostitutes. And perhaps also men such as that were also prostitutes.

My respect for mother grew even greater. I did not know whether mother had ever faced temptation and yet had still remained true to her words. And my respect for Nyai Ontosoroh in Surabaya also grew greater – she who had stood straight and firm in the face of the great tests that stormed down upon her.

But was I better than my friends? Were my moral principles better or stronger? When I recalled again my own experiences in love and passion, they were so crystal clear in my mind, unsullied by any material desires. Now those memories were a source of strength for me. But once you used your lover's money, that time you were in B – ! Fifteen guilders! Huh! That was to pay for a telegram I sent to her, and even that I later paid back to her.

And my friends were buying and selling love with the concubines! Perhaps it was just that they were playing around and were able to get both pleasure and money at the same time. But that which they did was such a serious thing, even if it was not accompanied with feelings of the heart. Not with their hearts? Huh! Could you in fact put your heart away in a cupboard?

I never felt superior to them, and I should not feel like that either. I was not something so special. Everyone is born equal, isn't that what Rousseau had said – the father of the French Revolution? The real problem was how to lead and be led, how to carry yourself and be carried.

Aha, you say that everyone is equal. Then why do you still use your title, *Raden Mas*? Huh! that's a legal matter. Should I leave myself open to be thrown like a beggar before the Native courts?

Yes, all these things made me feel even more lonely, as if there was no way for me to make any real or intimate contact with the world around me.

Every Saturday afternoon as we left the school grounds, you could see the parents of prospective brides making sure they would remember our faces. These were residents of the hamlets of Ketapang, Kwitang and also Abang Puasa, whose residents killed *Nyai Dasima*. They were hunting after a medical student son-in-law! Even Kwitang had become a hunting ground for students. This was not only because of the number of parents there who were hunting after sons-in-law, nor because this hamlet's young women were particularly attractive to students, and not because, in any case, we students were respected by everyone everywhere. There was a more fundamental reason – every student needed a family. There he could get out of his traditional clothes, change into European clothes and become a *sinyo* once again. In European clothes, we could wander wherever we wanted, neutral in identity, especially when chasing after the *nyai*.

36

Then the students would return to their adopted family, dress again in their traditional clothes, and go back to the school dormitory.

All the inhabitants of Kwitang knew about this custom, and the hamlet's families ruthlessly competed among themselves to win the chance to look after one of us. And always there was a young daughter of marriageable age. The tradition of keeping such daughters out of sight until she had a partner had been destroyed by the medical school.

A student need only nod, need only say 'yes'. The next day or the day after, he would have a wife. It could be his first, or just a new one.

Eheh, you candidate doctors!

I was no different. I also had a family. It was headed by *Ibu* Baldrun, an old woman, a widow who lived off her husband's pension. She had two adopted sons. My friends were amazed that I had picked a family like that.

Whenever I wanted to disappear into the city, I would go to Ibu Baldrun's first and change into European clothes. To wander off in Javanese clothes, especially when the sun was at its hottest, would turn your head into a mountain with a thousand streams of tears, with your hair feeling as if it was going to fall out at any moment. And how much worse it is when your dandruff is acting up. Even the scratching of the sharpest of finger-nails can provide no relief. And then to walk chicken-clawed, barefoot over the stone streets, with the droppings of all the city's beasts of burden everywhere . . . uh!

'*Denmas*, Ibu doesn't understand why Denmas chose to live here. There's no pretty young suitable girl here. Do you want Ibu to find you somebody?'

And she went on to say that it was time I took a wife. And I said, well if it's a question of destiny who I marry, then it doesn't matter where I go, does it? She laughed and didn't raise the issue again.

I kept my European clothes there and also the bicycle I had eventually bought at the Van Hien bicycle shop in Noordwijk. There was a huge crowd of children who turned out to watch me learning to ride. And yes, after three days I had mastered this supernatural beast. My friends soon after also started to buy bicycles.

Ibu Baldrun's house turned out to be a good place to get some privacy. I used it as my postal address. And so it was to that house that my mother came to visit. This happened seven months into my studies. Taram, Ibu Baldrun's eldest son, came to the school at the end of the afternoon classes and told me that I had a guest from far away who was waiting for me at his house. And so it was that I met again that most honoured of women. She looked at me in amazement. I knelt down before her. Her look of amazement still did not go away. Her eyes caressingly inspected me, from my feet to the top of my *destar*, and then she breathed a sigh of relief. Then: 'I would never have thought, Child.'

'What would you never have thought, Mother?'

'That you would, of your own free will, become Javanese again like this.'

'Forgive me, Mother. But I am not dressed like this of my own accord, but because of the school rules. Your son must go chicken-clawed like this, Mother.'

'From the tone in your voice, I can tell that you more and more dislike being Javanese, Child.'

'Is it so important to be Javanese, Mother?'

Before I could say anything more, I flung myself to the floor when I saw tears come to her eyes as she turned away to look at the sky outside the window. I kissed her feet and once again, for the umpteenth time, asked her forgiveness.

Fortunately Ibu Baldrun didn't understand Javanese.

'Now I understand why you have been so unhappy in your life, Child. It's your own fault, the result of your own actions, and because the Dutch have taught you to forget who you are. You are not happy wearing Javanese clothes, and you do not like your mother because she is not Dutch.'

'Forgive me, Mother,' I tried to stop her going on.

'You do not like the rice you eat and the water you drink.'

'Forgive me, Mother, forgive me, forgive me.'

'Perhaps you are not even happy that you were born?'

I could not stop her from continuing to talk. Her words seized hold of me, setting my nerves on end all over.

'As long as you know that this is the cause of all your suffering. Oh, my child, haven't I told you again and again – learn to be grateful, learn to give thanks, my child. You, you must start practising now. Nah, be thankful, be grateful for everything that you have and everything you can give to others. People are never satisifed by dreams. Learn to be grateful and to give thanks while the day of judgement is still far off.'

Her gentle voice thundered down upon me, more powerful than the thunder of the gods, than the magic spells of all the *dukun* of Java. It was the voice of a loving mother.

'If you have heard all that I have said, then stand up. If not, then remain kneeling down before me so that I may repeat it all.'

'Your son heard it all, Mother, every word, and I will never forget any of what you have said.'

'Then stand up.'

I stood, and she was still gazing at me in amazement, with half-open mouth.

'You are growing a moustache . . .' she said suddenly.

'Have you forgiven me, my mother?'

'A mother always forgives her child, even a child like you, whose only achievement is to bring suffering upon himself. I have come because of your suffering, Child. You have not answered any of my letters. No one will tell me what is in the papers any more. They are all learning to forget you, Child.

They say that your blood has been judged and found wanting. But that blood is of my own blood. Your father forbade me to go to Surabaya. But I went anyway, I took no heed of his fury. It was I who gave birth to you, Child, no one else. There was no one at your most recent addresses. And the people at the old ones could not help me.'

'Forgive me, Mother.'

'I always forgive you, Child, even when you don't ask. You always need forgiveness.'

'Mother, oh, my mother . . . '

'Close to me here, you call out for your mother. But when far away, you never once heard my cries.'

'Forgiveness, Mother.'

'That fine and luxurious house at Wonokromo had new owners, people said. With the help of a new acquaintance, I obtained an address in Wonocolo. I went there. She was living in a bamboo house. I stayed there. I didn't meet my daughter-in-law. I heard that she had gone away. Ah, Child, do you not feel humiliated to be left by your wife just like that? I, as old as I am, cried in front of her. Was my son worth so little as a son-in-law? You are growing a moustache now. Why are your eyes so moist? When you were a little child you were not as sentimental as now.'

I realised I was sobbing and that there were tears in my eyes. I wiped my eyes with a handkerchief.

'You, you, you never told me all that really happened . . . '

It was better that I kept quiet and absorbed all these heart-rending emotions. How great were my sins against this noble woman!

She stopped talking when Ibu Baldrun brought in some drinks. The atmosphere relaxed somewhat. I found myself acting as interpreter of a strictly female conversation that meant little to me.

And things got even better when it got close to four o'clock. It was time to return to class. I promised I would ask permission to sleep out that night.

It wasn't so easy to get permission. The European in the office refused and wouldn't change his mind. He said impertinently that he didn't care who had arrived – my father, my mother, my fiancée, or even a corpse!

'Well if that's the case, I don't need any permission,' I said.

And at ten minutes past seven I arrived at Ibu Baldrun's. She was very happy to see me. She hadn't been able to communicate with her guest. Now the interpreter had returned.

Mother was being massaged in her room. I followed Ibu Baldrun into the kitchen. Her two sons were eating there, after which they helped wash the plates and bowls.

'Heh, you shouldn't be in here, Denmas,' she reprimanded me.

'Why not anyway, *Bu*?'

'Don't make it a habit, Denmas, pity on your wife later.'

'Oh, why is that?'

'She'll be worried skinny, if you're always interfering in the kitchen.'

Early next morning I headed off to school. I was immediately summoned by the Director.

I was reprimanded: 'What were the reasons the Civil Service Academy rejected your application to enrol?'

'I did not meet its moral standards, Sir.'

'And you acknowledge that you signed the agreement to abide by the school's rules.'

'Yes, Director. But even so, Sir, the obligation to honour one's mother is not nullified just because of the existence of the medical school.'

'You've become very big-headed since you met those VIPs,' he said, annoyed. 'Don't forget, your behaviour here will determine what kind of work you'll get later.'

'I was forced to choose between the school regulations and the obligation to honour one's mother. I chose the second. If you consider that to be big-headed or undisciplined then thank you very much but I don't think this school can teach me anything worthwhile.'

The Director was silent. He sat there thinking, with angry staring eyes.

'It is all in your hands,' I said then.

'It's a pity you've got such a good brain, otherwise . . . '

'And while my mother is in Betawi, I will not sleep in the dormitory.'

'You are a real rebel, aren't you? Yes, perhaps you'll be an important person one day, or a madman unable to adapt to your situation and environment.'

Finished with me, he sent me out. And without asking permission, I slept outside from then on.

Mother told me a lot of things that I already knew and so I was mainly just nodding and agreeing. She also spoke a lot about the new agricultural business being built by Nyai Ontosoroh in Wonocolo, about the new big corrals and barns, and about how it was all under the management of the Native woman. She was looking after everything herself, running off here, there and everywhere, sometimes to look at a new barn under construction, then to inspect some cattle. Two male supervisors were in charge of clearing the forest, carpentry and other trade work.

'What a remarkable woman!' Mother praised Nyai Ontosoroh, 'I myself saw her actually have an argument, in Dutch, with a European Pure . I don't know what it was about. And she also built a stone building across the way from the old house.' Mother smacked her lips, relishing her memories.

'I was there a week. She was always stopping me from going back to B – . Really, Child, I enjoyed staying there. No Javanese man could do what she was doing – so much, so quickly, and all at the same time. And she was a Native woman! And in the afternoon, inside that bamboo house, she still had time to do all her calculations. Sometimes she would receive people from the town who came to her for instructions. Incredible! Incredible! And even though she was so busy, she always made sure her guest was looked after.'

Mother said nothing about my father or my brothers. It seemed my elder brother had never told her about his visit to see me here.

Another time she said: 'You don't seem as vibrant as you were before, Child. You're daydreaming a lot, not listening to what I say. Find a wife, a true Javanese girl, so there is someone to lighten your suffering. Don't think about things past. What can you do anyway? Do you remember what I told you when you were getting married before?'

'I remember, Mother, I remember it well.'

'Come home when you have holidays, choose a girl you like.' She stopped talking to suck some more juice out of the betel nut in her mouth. 'Are only Dutch women or women with Dutch blood good enough to become your wife?'

'No, Mother.'

'So you'll come home in the holidays? Do you want me to come and get you?'

'No need for you to come to Betawi, Mother. I will arrange things myself.'

'Don't you ever marry without telling me. Don't humiliate your mother. Has your mother ever forbidden you to do anything?'

'Never, Mother.'

'Why didn't you even tell me you were coming to Betawi? And don't say "forgive me" again, I always forgive you. I know you are not happy. You think of yourself too much, just like the Dutch, your teachers.'

And then came a question more difficult than any school exam I had ever had to undergo: 'Don't you love your mother?'

'There is no one I love more than you, Mother.'

'Are you speaking with your lips or your heart?'

'With both, Mother.'

'Why do you try so hard to become other than your mother's son?'

Her gentle voice and her deep love were threatening my European-ness. And I felt like an orphan of the modern age, without even traditional ties to kith and kin. I had left East Java to become a person. And now the love and compassion of my mother stood before me as a judge who would allow no appeal.

'Why don't you say anything, Child? You can't speak with your heart any more. You've become a black Dutchman in Javanese clothes. If that's what you want, then so be it. But tell your mother what she should do in order to love you.'

'Ah, Mother, love has no conditions. Mother will always love me, as you have done in the past, do now and will do in the future. So bless me in my struggle to achieve my ideals.'

'Keep talking. You have begun to talk. You used to have so much to talk about, you knew so many stories that you became a man of letters. Now you look so tired. Speak, Child. Tell me all, so that once again I can feel I am a mother worthy of her child. Don't think about whether I will like what you say or not. I know your world is far away from your mother's. But perhaps I might understand a little of what you say.'

'I once told Mother about the French Revolution.'

'I remember. If everyone had equal rights like that then what rights would a mother have over her children?'

'She would have the right to love them, Mother, to raise them and educate them.'

'Is that all?'

Her love was now playing the part of prosecutor and judge! How must I answer?

'I'm so sorry for you, Child, you're so tortured by my question. Listen, I demand nothing of you. As long as I can see you I am happy, and if I can touch you then I am even happier. But to see you knotted up inside like this makes me suffer too. Become whatever you like. Become a Dutchman, I will not object.'

'Forgiveness, Mother, please do not say that again,' I screeched my request in a pathetically pleading voice. 'You sent me to school so that, as a Javanese, I would have the wisdom and knowledge of Europe. Both of those things change people, Mother.'

'I understand, Child, but should they not change people for the better, and not for the worse.'

'Your blessing, Mother, your blessing.'

'But you must not suffer so much.'

'I do not suffer.'

'Don't you think I know my own child? I have known you since you were in my womb. I have known your voice since your first cry. Even without your letters, without seeing your face, from far away, a mother's heart can always tell, Child. How much you have suffered so that you can become what you want. You do not even want to share any of it with your mother. Yes, I know that Europeans want to bear all their burdens themselves. But is that necessary when you have a mother?'

'Tell me, Mother,' I begged.

'You have caught the Europeans' disease, Child. You want everything for yourself just as you tell about them in your stories.'

'Mother!'

'That is Europe's disease. Shouldn't you learn to think of others too? Haven't I told you, learn to be thankful? Don't say anything, wait. You once told me yourself that, for Europeans, when they say "thank you" it was just a pretence. They do not say it with their hearts. You have become like that, Child. I haven't forgotten your stories. The clever try to become cleverer, the rich richer. No one has any gratitude in their hearts. Everyone is hurrying around trying to be better. Isn't that what you yourself have told me? They all suffer. Their desires and ideals become monsters that rule over them. Do you remember?'

'I remember, Mother.'

'So what is the use of the French revolution then?' and her voice was so gentle, as it had always been ever since the first time I had heard it. 'You said it was to free men from the burdens made by other men. Wasn't that it? That is not Javanese. A Javanese does something with no other motive than to do it. Orders come from Allah, from the gods, from the Raja. After a Javanese has carried out the order, he will feel satisfied because he has become himself. And then he waits for the next order. So the Javanese are grateful, they give thanks. They are not preyed upon by monsters within themselves.'

'Mother, I have learnt much in my studies. I know now that life is not so simple.'

'What teacher has told you that, my child? In bygone days, your ancestors always taught that there was nothing so simple as life. You are born, you eat and drink, you grow, bring children into the world and do good.'

'But there is a power that just swallows up good deeds without trace.'

'The teachers of our ancestors also knew that, Child. They called such forces ogres – they came in all shapes and sizes. And they never defeated our ancestor knights in battle.'

'But today they win all the time.'

'That is because things are in the hands of the wrong *dalang*.'

'Mother, I will become a true *dalang*.'

'My child is already a man of letters. Now he wants to be a *dalang* too. What else do you want to be? You'll no doubt become a doctor. You want to achieve so much! How much suffering you call down upon yourself, suffering that will knot you up inside even more, taking away your happiness. What will there be left for you to give to others, to Allah, to the gods? Your ancestors taught and received simple teachings. Your teachers teach about the unlimited potential of men. Your ancestors knew how to be grateful, even though they didn't pronounce it with their mouths. You are taught to say thank you all the time, but your heart is mute and dumb.'

'Doesn't Mother want me to be a *dalang*?'

'Even though mother does not like it, your teachers are taking you to some secret destination, across some infinite distance. When you were little you liked – you were even crazy about – *wayang* stories. Now you have forgotten them all. It's up to you as to what you want to do. But don't suffer so much, because suffering is a punishment.'

And how great was the chasm now that stood between mother and child. This was not just a historical chasm. What should it be called?

'There is punishment, my child, for all those who cannot place themselves in the order of things. If it were a star, it would be a shooting star. If it were a forest, it would be a forbidden forest. If a stone it would be a kidney stone, and if a tooth, an uneven one. Ah, you are bored listening to these words of your mother. Rest now, my child, rest, and enjoy your rest.'

Yes, I was exhausted from listening to the wave after wave of wisdom and of trying to pass this massive test.

'You know, Child,' she went on to add, 'don't believe too much in this French Revolution. What did you say was its slogan: Equality, Fraternity, Liberty? If that were all true, Child, then what would be the position of the Dutch here in Java?'

I lay on my bed. Ibu Baldrun's sons were asleep on a mat on the floor in a cloud of mosquito repellent smoke. I gave thanks that I had a mother who was so strong and firm in her beliefs and her thoughts. She was a Javanese woman and she had her own wisdom. And I would never be able to marry a woman like her. Forgive me, Mother. I am travelling another path and will make a different choice. I will write a long letter, in Javanese, to you, my mother. I couldn't do it face to face. You are right, Mother, you are dealing with a son whom you no longer know, except for his name . . .

But it is not a punishment, Mother, it isn't, Mother, truly it isn't.

4

And it did indeed turn out that Engineer H. van Kollewijn decided to leave Semarang and travel by train to Mayong. In Mayong, he was met by the Jepara Regency Carriage, which took him to town.

As the carriage slowly entered the town, children lining the streets shouted 'Long life! Long life!' and waved the Tricolours. The rotund Member of Parliament and the fat Assistant Resident of Jepara-Rembang occasionally acknowledged the children with a nod and gave them a little wave. The carriage entered the Regency of Jepara. And the *penembrama* – the traditional welcome for VIPs, with music and singing – was cancelled.

A newspaper article explained:

For the first time in history a Javanese woman has brought about a major public event. She is receiving an honoured and grand guest. The daughters of the Regent, seated in rocking chairs under the pendopo, *awaited the arrival of Engineer H. van Kollewijn. As soon as the carriage entered the Regency courtyard, they all lined up behind their father ready to welcome the honoured guest.*

Those who have studied Javanese custom and tradition will note this was a unique occurrence – Native women welcoming a man, a foreigner to boot, whom they did not yet know! And for those whose interest is politics, they will note that this was the first time a member of the Dutch Parliament felt the necessity to call upon a Native girl, with whom he was not yet acquainted. He isn't there to propose, but to discuss . . . no one knows what they discussed. No journalists were allowed to witness their conversation.

A sensation for the turn of the century! I think the Javanese will remember that event for a long time to come. And it would be the source of untold stories and rumours and guesses. But we know for sure what happened. The Member of Parliament offered her the opportunity to continue her studies in the Netherlands. And this offer occupied the thoughts of all those Javanese who knew about it. But that was all that they could do – think about it.

I wasn't so impressed by his offer. What impressed me more was this girl's initiative. Perhaps it was her way of denying the reality of her situation. Just like me. And what kind of initiative!

This girl, hemmed in by the Residency walls, imprisoned by the walls of custom, locked away in nubile seclusion, had given to the local Dutch

Assistant Resident a wedding present for Queen Wilhelmina. And the present then began its journey. First of all, from Jepara to Betawi. From the Assistant Resident to Governor-General Rosenboom. It was a teak box carved by Jepara's greatest craftsman, Pak Singo.

From the Governor-General's hands, the box crossed the ocean to the Minister of Colonies. And in the hands of the Honourable Minister, the box was presented to Her Majesty at her wedding reception. It was Engineer van Kollewijn's people who made so much of this. And people were made to understand that Dutch and European carving was no match for the teak carving of Jepara's Pak Singo. Then people started to talk about how wonderful it would be if the Queen's throne and all the Palace's furniture were carved in the Jepara style. Javanese pride swelled with pleasure, caressed and massaged by this talk.

It wasn't long before orders came flowing in to the Jepara maiden. And it wasn't long either before the craftsmen of Jepara went from being poverty-stricken, miserable and powerless to being honoured, respected, wealthy and sought after. The girl had brought energy and life where before there was dejection. She had brought change. She had wiped away a spot of poverty, of powerlessness.

But it's not my intention to note down all this kind of thing. There's something else – about Engineer van Kollewijn again. This god, who wants to pay back the Indies the debt it is owed, moved everyone with his compassionate and just heart. His fiery tongue had lashed out against the Government for wrongly hanging somebody – a Chinese from Cibinong. The victim had already lain for ages as a pile of bones in his grave. The Honourable Member made an announcement: This man is innocent!

His Excellency's name had not been raised to these new heights of honour for long before there was another report in the papers. He and van Heutsz had decided to make a brief visit to Padang to watch a public multiple hanging. So it turned out that he had an interest in hanging people after all. But then it was only criminals that were hanged. People said: Criminals – so what? Aren't they just pimples on the arsehole of the *raja*?

Who was the first to say this? How would I know? But the fiery tongue, and divinity, of Engineer van Kollewijn – in my eyes nothing was left of them but a bundle of bones, just like the Chinese man from Cibinong . . .

I had been a student for nine months. The boredom was hardly bearable any more.

Then one afternoon I was sitting in the library filling in time and I started flicking through the *Government Gazette*. Who would read the *Government Gazette* except someone who was bored? Its cover was in good condition. You could still smell the glue. And I read: '. . . the registration of the establishment in 1900 of an organisation of Chinese subjects of the Indies to be called Tiong Hoa Hwee Koan . . . ' Huh! what's the use of publishing useless information like that in the *Government Gazette*? As I reflected on this, I remembered something else – my Chinese friend. Yes, he was dead now. But, I asked myself, did he have any connection with this Tiong Hoa Hwee Koan organisation? Then there was something else, the task he'd given me – a letter for . . . ah, what was the name?

Conscious once again of the promise I had made back in Surabaya, I left the library and bought all the Malay–Chinese papers that I could find. I soon found more reports about the organisation. This wasn't surprising because it was considered to be the first modern social or political organisation registered by the Government in the Indies. It had established its own primary school with its own curriculum. The children would be educated to be modern Chinese able to continue their studies back in China or anywhere else in the world. They did not teach Dutch, only Mandarin and English. They also listed the names of the teachers. And the English teacher's name was Ang San Mei.

It seemed that the God of Luck was smiling upon me. Ang San Mei was the name of the person I had to seek out.

The following Sunday, I set off to find this person. I rode off on my bicycle early in the morning. In my pocket was my friend's letter. This person would no doubt be an interesting acquaintance. Perhaps this person would also be a *singkeh* unable to speak either Malay or Dutch, let alone Javanese.

I had an address for a house located in one of the small alleys of Betawi. I was just entering the filthy and dirty alley when a Chinese girl emerged out of the alleyway's mouth. She was slim, almost skinny, pretty, slit-eyed and pale. She walked quickly without looking round. She looked straight ahead as she went along. My own neck also suddenly became stiff.

My eyes reached out to grasp her beauty. I climbed down off my bike. I stopped. She passed me and my head swivelled around to watch her. The hinge hadn't rusted. God and all creation seemed to whisper to me – admire her beauty, her eyes, the way she walks. And once again I became a philogynist, enthralled by the allure of a woman! Why were her lips so pale? And how silken and clear was her skin, as if you could see right through it!

I wanted to chase after her and introduce myself. No! I knew that her people generally looked down upon Natives as inferior. We just passed in the lane, that's all.

I walked my bicycle through the lane. I felt like a horse suddenly burdened with a fully-loaded cart. That woman was so pretty, so interesting. Her strange narrow eyes just made her more exciting.

I found the address. It was a tiny bamboo place, stuck tightly in between two others. Did she come from this place? Her beauty was such a frail beauty.

Could such a disgusting environment as this produce someone so lovely? Ah, why won't that image of the white-gowned Chinese girl disappear from my mind?

A Chinese woman, wearing black pants, a black blouse and tiny black shoes, shuffled out to greet me. Her Malay was strange and barely understandable. Her voice was loud and jarring.

'Mr Ang San Mei?' she repeated my question. 'There is no Mr Ang San Mei here.'

'Do you know where I can find him?'

'Don't know. There is Ang San Mei here, but not Mister. She Mistress Ang.' She looked at me with suspicious eyes, obviously wishing that I had never arrived. And obviously hoping that the conversation would end there.

So Ang San Mei was a woman. Mistress Ang.

The old woman didn't invite me inside, let alone offer a chair. And she didn't ask any questions either. I tried to find a way to continue the conversation. She didn't understand. And when she spoke, I didn't understand. Because I never thought I would become a mute, I hadn't studied sign language. Neither had she. So all we could do is stand there and stare at each other. Good God! She's been here who knows how many years and still couldn't speak Malay!

I took out the envelope, which had a message written in Chinese on the outside. For Ang San Mei. She couldn't read. Illiterate to the marrow of her bones. She took the letter from my hand and went inside and didn't come out again. Oh, no! And what about me? Was I supposed just to turn round and leave without a goodbye or anything?

I was still stunned as I stood there holding my beautiful bike. The foul stench from the drains was already starting to make its presence felt. I picked up my bike and started to manoeuvre it round in the narrow alley. It scraped a fence. When I'd turned around, heh, the pretty narrow-eyed girl was there in front of me. Now it wasn't my neck but hers that seemed fixed in its place by a rusted hinge. I nodded as I left the front yard. I glanced back and saw her go inside. So she was Ang San Mei. I had no reason to go back. I kept walking my bike. I slowed down. Surely something would happen.

Yes, from behind me came shouts.

'Mista, Mista, kum beck, pliiiiiiiiis!'

I stopped. I wasn't wrong. English! I turned round and she waved to me to come. As if hypnotised, I picked up my bike and walked towards her, step by step. Her slender arm was held out to greet me. Her voice sounded so beautiful as she spoke in English: 'I'm Ang San Mei. I've been waiting for you for so long.'

'You've been waiting long, Miss?' I asked.

'You're Mr Minke, aren't you?'

Her hand was still in mine, and she wasn't objecting.

'Yes, that's right. It's been very difficult for me to get a chance to look for Miss Ang.'

She politely withdrew her hand and invited me inside.

The veranda was very narrow, about one and a half metres. There was nothing but an old bamboo bench. After she dusted it, we both sat down.

'I felt it when we passed earlier that you were the one I'd been waiting for. So I came straight back. Why has it taken you so long to come, especially as I do not have your address?' Her English was fluent and very correct.

I started to tell her all about how busy I had been. She believed me.

'Thank you for the protection you and your family gave to my late friend, though I am sure he also expressed his gratitude to you.'

I observed her pale thin lips and her brilliant white teeth. I looked at her feet – they hadn't been bound.

'Why are you looking at my feet?'

'Oh, nothing, it doesn't matter.'

'It's only by accident that my feet have escaped their humiliation.'

'Yes, I'm sorry, Miss, forgive me. A Chinese woman with feet like you, Miss, it means that you haven't been brought up in the traditional way.'

'I was brought up and educated in a convent, Mr Minke, in a Catholic Convent in Shanghai.'

This girl's frankness was amazing.

'Have you told others this?'

She smiled, and looked at me with those shining eyes. 'What is there that I shouldn't tell a good friend of my friend?'

'Thank you, Miss.'

She didn't say anything about her friend who had died – who had written that letter to her.

'Why am I called "Miss" by a good friend of my friend? Call me Mei. No one calls me that now. My friend didn't put his trust in people easily. He had sharp instincts about people. Whoever he trusted, so too must I trust them.'

'Thank you, Mei. You're extraordinary,' I said, admiring her frankness.

'Thank you.'

'The letter won't need a reply,' I said.

'Yes,' she was silent for a moment, 'you're right, it won't need a reply. I haven't even read it all.'

'You know what happened?'

'I know,' she shook her head weakly. Then her hands moved nervously as if she wanted to grab hold of something from another dimension. 'I read about it in the newspaper.'

'How did you know he left a letter?'

'Everyone, including myself, believed in the power of his sixth sense. An extraordinary person.' Her voice was full of praise, but also sadness.

'I have never met anyone like him.'

'He said he chose Surabaya because it was the most difficult area.'

'So he trusted you.'

I nodded.

'He didn't give his trust easily. I will go to the most difficult area, he told me before he left. You will receive news from me in one way or another. If you don't receive any news from me for a long time, then sooner or later someone will seek you out, I don't know who. Perhaps that will be my last letter ever.'

She kept on talking. Her voice exhibited more and more adoration, but it also became sadder and sadder. Glassy-eyed, she looked down at her shoes, turned away her face, then stood and turned round as if to walk away. It seemed she didn't want to show her feelings.

I turned round so as not to see her face. And I realised how deep the relationship between the two of them must have been. A relationship between two close comrades, between a young woman and a young man – it was not just a relationship between comrades-in-arms. They were bound by intimate and close emotional ties. I also felt her loss.

'You have my deepest, my truly sincere condolences, Mei,' I said.

'Thank you. You are the first to share my loss all this time. No one else knew about the relationship between the two of us.'

Soon I felt that I had known this girl for a long time, as if we had been at school together, as if we'd been educated together for years and years. She was quickly able to get hold of her emotions again. She took out the clips from her hair and held them in her lap, sometimes fiddling with them. She was seated calmly now in her chair.

'Can you tell me what he said to you?' she asked.

I told her everything, just as I had noted it down in my diary. She listened to every word. She made no attempt to correct my English. That we were out of town, when he left our house. That he left this letter. Then he was caught by the Surabaya Thong Secret Society and how he died.

She bowed her head again. Her voice was like a sigh: 'I never guessed things were that difficult. He never told me.'

And I told her of my admiration for him.

'Did he ever talk to you about the Surabaya Thong?'

'No.'

'About the Yi Me Tuan?'

'No.'

She held out her hand again to thank me for the protection we had given her friend. And this time it was as if she was the one who didn't want to let go. Her hand was cold.

'Are you ill, Mei?'

'Perhaps I am, I don't know.'

'Do you want me to take you to the doctor?'

She laughed and let go of my hand. Her teeth shone and she shook her head slowly.

'No need to go to that trouble. You're studying to be a doctor yourself, aren't you?'

'I'm still in my first year, I don't know anything yet,' I said. 'Where did you go to school?'

'A Catholic high school.'

'Where?'

'I told you, in Shanghai.'

'And why were you brought up in a convent?'

'As far as I know, I was always there.'

'And how did you come to meet your friend?'

'Could we not talk about him any more?' her voice was sad again, then suddenly, energetically, she asked: 'May I wish you well in your studies?'

'Of course. But school is so boring.'

'Why do you stay?'

'I don't know what else to do. It's the highest education that you can get in the Indies.'

'Don't know what else to do?' she asked, amazed, in such an intimate voice that it set my heart pounding, 'as if there isn't much work to do in the Indies.'

I gazed into her eyes and for some reason they were shining brightly. I felt that the cultural and racial barriers between us, me as a Javanese and she as a Chinese, for some reason that I didn't understand but could only sense, had been magically made to vanish. It was as if the two of us had come out of the same factory, called the modern age.

'I read your name in the papers.'

'The person who wrote that never met me. I think all she knew were the names of the teachers. No one knows me, because no one needs to know me. I prefer it that way.'

'But I know you now.'

'You are the trusted bearer of a special message.'

'I understand, Mei.' It had suddenly come to me that she too was probably in the Indies illegally. Just like her friend had been. 'But you seem to have had more success.'

'What do you mean?'

'The setting up of the Tiong Hoa Hwee Koan.'

'Ah, that? Well, it's all very fragile. Tomorrow or the next day, there may be no place for me there any more. The old thinking is still trying to dominate there. They only want Chinese to be taught.' Then she seemed to be jolted by something. 'I'm sorry. I keep thinking you're him. Your voices are so alike, except perhaps your English is better. Perhaps I'm not thinking too clearly at the moment.'

'You're too tired, Mei. It shows in your face.'

'And if you don't really want to be a doctor, then what do you want to be?' she asked, changing the subject.

'A free individual.'

She laughed gaily. And I didn't understand what she was laughing at.

'Is that funny, Mei?'

'Funny? How do you imagine this free individual to be? With no responsibilities? You can't mean that. You're just playing around. A friend of my friend wouldn't be like that. Perhaps you're just using the wrong words.'

Her remarks made me uncomfortable. She smiled at my discomfort and those narrow eyes almost disappeared from her face, changing into little ridges. All the signs that she was ill also disappeared. Her pale lips turned red.

She started to lecture me. 'Don't misunderstand what is meant by "Liberty" in the slogan of the French Revolution.' I couldn't see why she'd suddenly started talking about the French Revolution.

She went on. 'Even some of the French have interpreted this to mean they are free to steal and free of responsibilities towards anyone. They start to act completely arbitrarily. They are only after greatness for themselves in their own country! All of the educated Natives of Asia have a responsibility to help awaken their peoples. If we don't, Europe will run riot throughout Asia. Do you agree?'

I recognised her friend's voice in what she was saying. Who have these young people studied with? Were their teachers better than mine?

'If we make the wrong decisions about how to face up to the modern age, then we might end up allowing Europe to become the despot of the whole world.'

'We've moved onto this kind of subject very quickly,' I said.

'Yes, we trust each other, don't we? I have had no one with whom I can discuss things like this for a long time now.' She paused. 'Could you excuse me for just a minute?' She stood, nodded, smiled and then, with that beautiful way of walking that she has, went inside.

This sickly beautiful girl was just like her late friend. Pretty, looks fragile, yet like him has the courage to leave her country for faraway places because of her ideals. And she not only dares to strike out on such an adventure, but is also daring in her thinking, and in her friendships.

I guessed that she had gone inside to read the rest of the letter.

Then, from inside, came that exquisite voice: 'Come and sit inside, my friend.'

The room I entered was suffocatingly small. It went across the width of the shack, about three metres, and was two metres deep. I could see an even smaller room off to the side. The walls were made of plastered woven bamboo, but the plaster was peeling off everywhere. The furniture consisted of a table and a bench made of timber from a durian tree. On top of the table were two Chinese books, and the table itself was covered with scratched calculations. There was not a single picture hanging from any of the walls. I could hear voices coming from the neighbours all around, but there was nothing to be heard from inside.

She came out from the other room wearing blue silk pants. Her sleeveless blouse was from the same material, and it was decorated with a picture of a dragon on the front. In these silken blue clothes, she looked even paler. Her eyes were red. She'd been crying. She carried a school-bag. She took out another Chinese language book and from inside the book, a sheet of paper.

'I've received two letters now from a Native woman,' she said. 'But they're written in a language I don't understand. Perhaps you know her. Could you translate this for me?'

The letter was from the girl from Jepara. She wrote that she had read in the papers about two modern Chinese girls. She wanted to meet them and had tried to find their addresses. She had found Ang San Mei's address through the help of her friends in Betawi, and had sent her letter as soon as she had received the address. She wanted to correspond and to exchange ideas. She was interested to find out about emancipated Chinese women, both back in China and in the Indies. And, was the fate of women in China as terrible as it was for Javanese women? Was there polygamy everywhere? Where Chinese men only interested in their own pleasures and did they treat their mothers' kind without care or responsibility?

I also found out from this letter that the girl sitting next to me was a graduate of the Shanghai Teachers' College and was fluent in both English and French. The girl from Jepara expressed her regret that she only knew Dutch. She started to learn English but had to give it up because there were no teachers or reading material available to her.

In my opinion, read the letter, *no people anywhere can be respected if their women are oppressed by their men as is the case with my people, and if love and compassion is reserved for babies only. Everyone listens full of awe to the cry of a baby as it takes its first breath. After that the father pays no more heed, while the mother, as soon as the baby can crawl, once again becomes her husband's slave. Sometimes I just can't understand what respect and honour mean to men, and what it means to them that they are willing to let the whole nation lose its honour and dignity.*

'An interesting woman,' Mei commented, 'are Native men really like that?'

'I think she's right.'

'Yes, they're mostly like that in China too.'

'But that wasn't your experience, Mei.'

'Only because I was raised in a convent, away from society.'

'You're Catholic?'

'Yes. Someone exiled by her own people.'

'But you've dedicated your life to your people. A people who have rejected you? You've forgiven them?'

'Our Young Generation works for China and our loyalty is to China. The Young Generation fights against the rule of the Empress Ye Si who is propped up by the Western powers. This girl from Jepara wants to start with the customs of her own people. A pity.'

'Both are important,' I said, 'they can be struggled for together.'

'That'd be too difficult. What else does she say?'

I looked at her. Her eyes were no longer red. I read her the second letter. It went on to talk about the emancipation of women in Europe. The girl from Jepara wrote that she thought women in Europe were demanding too much. Women and men should have the same rights. But no more than that, she said. Special rights for some means oppression for others.

She also asked whether she was doing the right thing in writing because she had received no replies. She had found someone to translate the replies if they were written in English. She told how she had an older brother who understood English and who would, perhaps, be continuing his studies in Europe next year because there was nowhere higher for him to study in the Indies. He wasn't her real brother. Her real brother had left the year before and would already be beginning classes at university.

'A progressive family,' commented Mei.

The letter went on to say that she herself had only graduated from primary school. She was now in seclusion, which was the custom in Java for women of marriageable age. Her only friends were her books and letters. The only people who could actually talk with her were her sisters. Her life was a silent one. The author had the greatest respect for Miss Ang, who had left her country without the protection of her family – such a big step!

The letter went on to ask Mei's opinion about marriage, which the letter's author argued should be the foundation of a long-lasting and intimate relationship between man and woman. What did Miss Ang think of a relationship which was so formal and so temporary and so easily severed that those concerned could then go spreading stories of each other's weaknesses and sins. Would not such a marriage only make a man and a woman less honoured and less worthy? Was this how it was in China too?

'Worse,' answered Ang San Mei. 'Whenever one of my sisters married, everyone wished the married couple a hundred children and a thousand grandchildren. I don't know how many women have been married to the accompaniment of that prayer. Except if she's being taken as a concubine – then there's no prayer – but just as many children.'

'What about your appointment?' I asked suddenly. 'Aren't you going now?'

'Today is for my guest,' she said. 'This woman is a good person, she doesn't think about herself at all.'

'Do you like her?'

'I will answer her letters. Would you translate for me?'

'Of course. You tell me what to say, I'll write it out.'

'Now?'

'Yes. I might not have the chance another time.'

She seemed nervous. I guessed she probably didn't have any paper.

'You work it out first in English while I go and get some paper,' and without waiting for a reply, I got up and left.

It turned out not to be so easy to find a stall that sold paper. When I got back half-an-hour later, she'd written out her reply on a piece of dirty wrapping paper, which I pretended not to notice. I immediately translated it into Dutch. She went into the cooking area and brought out two glasses of creamed avocado. As if she knew it was my favourite. The two glasses stood there next to each other like two lonely lovers.

'It's too hard for you to write with these glasses in the way. Ayoh, let's drink first,' she said.

I hesitated to take my glass. She had spent her no doubt limited and much-valued money to buy this expensive drink. The avocado was only used by Europeans. Natives weren't familiar with it yet. In Betawi there was only one avocado plantation and it had been opened by a European. Natives weren't planting them yet. We clinked our glasses in a toast. She laughed and her teeth gleamed. And her eyes, now only slits, were black, covered by her long eyelashes. The way she held her glass for me to clink with it, the way she raised her chin, all set my heart pounding.

Here was another kind of beauty in yet another place, with different origins as well. And what kind of beauty was it? Why was this girl, whom I had just met, so impressive? Why did she impress me as being beautiful? It was a beauty that wasn't empty, that was backed up by character and knowledge. Was that it?

And how surprised I was when I realised that she wasn't putting her glass to her own lips but to mine. As if commanded my glass too went to her lips. We were just about to drink, and the two of us burst out laughing.

'What?'

'This was his custom too.'

No doubt she was referring to her late friend. But I didn't respond to what she had said. And she suddenly seemed to be lost in thought. I put my glass to her lips and, silently, she began to drink. And I from her glass. She laughed again, but I couldn't see if her eyes were laughing too.

She put the glass down on the bench beside me. I followed suit, then continued writing.

55

'It looks as if many of the Malay papers have published stories about you,' I said, on another subject.

'Perhaps. I've no idea really.'

I continued writing.

'Why don't you correspond with her too?' Mei asked.

'You can introduce me in this letter,' I said.

'Yes, put that in.'

Mei's letter told of the fate of women in China. In the villages they had to work as hard as the men – in fact, harder, because they had to look after the household, manage the children, and give birth, as well as cope with menstruation. They did everything that men also did, except read and write. Many also fought in the wars, some even becoming war heroes. Generally, with perhaps the exception of those from the upper class, Chinese women were trained to work and they coped with all the difficulties they faced by working and striving. Because of this, they could survive anywhere in the world.

And, my friend, I do not think you could find anywhere in the world one of my fellow countrywomen who has killed herself or died of hunger, even though she has found herself in a foreign country, went the letter towards its end. *You need not be so surprised that I am here in a foreign land either. You too would do the same if you were a Chinese woman. I think, my friend, that it is the middle-class and upper-class women who are the dependent ones. In Java, too, I think the peasant women have more rights because of their responsibilities – in looking after the land, and the animals, and the household too. The less a person's responsibilities, the less their rights. But I don't really know what the situation is in your country. I have not yet had the opportunity to visit the interior of this beautiful green land of yours.*

And that was how I ended her letter.

'I'll post it,' I said.

'Thank you.' She smiled at me.

'How could anyone do anything else but help you, Mei? It could only be because they didn't know you.' I changed the subject. 'Mei, it looks as though the papers have been reporting on you a lot.'

'I don't know. I only remember once, when our school was being opened, there was a European woman there. She tried to start up a conversation in English with me. I don't remember her name. It was just small talk. I wouldn't talk about myself, about what I was doing or where I had come . . . '

I studied her closely and she knew I was studying her. The longer I looked at her, the more beautiful she seemed, despite her thinness and paleness. Or was I just a womaniser, as my friends used to accuse me. No, it wasn't just a matter of being a philogynist. Was it wrong for me to be attracted by her beauty? Was it wrong that I had a sense of beauty and had glands in my body?

'Why are you looking at me like that?'

'It's not my fault,' I said.

'It's my fault?'

'Yes. It's your fault. You're too attractive.'

'How many women have heard you say that?'

'And how many men have you questioned like this? With words so cutting?' I asked.

She laughed, and her eyes disappeared. She dropped this subject and started to talk about other things. The conversation became more and more relaxed. Then she invited me to take lunch with her. We went into the back room, which wasn't at all as I expected. It was just a kitchen with a sleeping bench. There were no other rooms.

We sat on the bench to eat. Its bamboo mat was rolled up and I could see a bag inside it. There was nothing else in the room except some kitchen utensils. I could see out the back through the kitchen door. The backyard was about two by three metres. There was a big, high wall of a building at the rear of the yard.

There were only the two of us. And that was the first time I ate noodles fried with mushrooms and a little meat. Incredibly delicious. Out of kilter altogether with the overall condition of this bamboo hut. In the middle of such poverty as this, where did such delicious food come from?

I watched her cross herself. Then she began eating, using chopsticks. I used a spoon and fork. Her lips shone with the moisture from the food, making her even more attractive. She obviously hadn't eaten since morning.

The small-footed woman wasn't to be seen anywhere. Who knows where she had gone. All the while we were eating I tried to fathom this mystery of a girl. Educated, but living in the midst of poverty, so free in receiving a man she didn't know. Without even a piece of paper to write on. I'd finished my noodles. So had she. And I could have eaten two more plates. But I knew that she would be going without in order to feed me now.

And this somehow reminded me of the raft-maker's widow who supported Troenodongso by selling sweet potatoes.

Mei took the plates out into the kitchen and washed them.

Yes, there was nothing here. Just an old bag hanging from the bamboo divan. Probably everything she owned was in that bag.

She came in again and suggested we go out and sit on the veranda. So she hadn't tired of me yet. And she was just like Khouw Ah Soe. She always got excited when the topic changed to the Japanese Young Generation, and her own Young Generation.

'Mei,' I called to her, 'did you know Khouw Ah Soe for long?'

Her face became gloomy. And I didn't press her. I heard her draw in a long breath.

'A diamond of a youth, brilliant,' she praised him again, 'I prayed always for his safety.' Her voice became reflective again. 'In the end, he died without ever seeing his closest friends again.'

'Nor his family?'

'He was an orphan like me. But he was brought up a Protestant.'

It seemed certain to me that Khouw Ah Soe and Mei had been engaged. It was probably true that they slipped secretly into the country together. She was probably forced to take this job as a teacher, after her fiancé was killed by the Thong secret society in Surabaya.

I regretted that I had brought her thoughts back to her friend just so that I could find out what their relationship had been. Quickly I steered the conversation onto all sorts of other things. By this time even my young eyes could hardly see – the sun had almost set.

'I'm very happy that you have spent so much time here with me today. I'm so happy to be able to meet a friend of my friend. Please come here often. It will help me so much if you can translate any letters I receive that I can't understand or answer.'

It was time for me to go, though reluctantly.

On the way home, I had a lot to think about. Perhaps tonight, she would not eat. And she surely wouldn't be having any breakfast tomorrow. So thin and pale. Was she really happy that I had come? Or was it just because I was somebody her late fiancé had put his trust in? She had been left by her loved one, and now she had to struggle hard to make a living. But she felt no humiliation because of her poverty. Neither was she ashamed in front of me.

I went back the following Sunday. This time I brought things for cooking – rice, meat, vegetables and spices.

When I arrived, I found her daydreaming on the veranda divan. She jumped up happily as soon as she saw me.

'We'll feast today, Mei,' I said fixing our program. I showed her the things I'd brought. 'Come on, let's eat.'

'Since when have you been able to cook?'

'Beginning today, here with you. You're not doing anything today, are you?'

'I thought you'd come. I've been waiting here.'

'No other guests today?'

'You're the only one I'm expecting.'

'What about that small-footed woman?'

'A neighbour.'

'So you really live by yourself?'

'I thought it would be best.'

'What about your meals?'

'I get meals from next door.'

We started cooking. Happiness and poverty looked on together.

'Being close to an educated young man,' she went on, 'I feel secure. Nearly all the uneducated men of my race look upon women as nothing more than something to vent their lusts upon. And occasionally those who are educated are even worse. So our educated women feel disgusted whenever some man looks at us, even from afar, let alone if they approach us.'

That was a warning bell. How strange was the way she guarded herself, and how gently it was that she shielded herself.

'Not every educated man is like that,' I said.

'All the educated ones are the same,' she said coolly. 'They use their education to oil their tongues in persuasion. If uneducated, then their lusts just speak directly.'

She had begun to punish me even before I had committed any crime. You, Mei, you force me to stay in line. Her delicate voice and gentle tones reminded me of my mother.

'I think I'm not one of those educated men that you're talking about, Mei.'

'Well, why are we cooking together like this?' she asked, laughing. 'You're not cooking anyway, you're just chatting.'

All I could do is answer with a nervous laugh.

'Why haven't you learnt Malay?'

'I've started.'

'What if we go out for a walk?'

'What about the cooking?'

'Later on, I mean,' I said in Malay.

She smiled and mumbled some strange-sounding answer that I couldn't understand at all.

'Later,' she repeated in English, 'when we can.'

'Why don't you find somewhere better to live, Mei?'

'This is good enough. I'll only be in the Indies for five years. I don't need anything more.'

'You're not happy here in the Indies?' She didn't answer. 'What if we take a trip to the countryside one day? Breathe the fresh country air?'

'That would be very nice. When we have some holidays.'

I went the following Sunday as well. And brought more things to cook. Mei wasn't home. There was a letter stuck to the door. She was sorry but she had work to do somewhere else. I left the things I had brought on the veranda divan and set off home full of disappointment. How I missed her. If I couldn't meet her every week, it would be more than just a trip in vain, more than being bankrupt, but a loneliness that would be more painful than I could bear.

I deliberately did not go on the fourth Sunday. Nor on the fifth. A letter arrived.

You have learnt to forget me, she wrote, *even though you know I have no other friends at all. The third Sunday you came, I was worried about seeing you. Some of the Chinese community here had threatened me with trouble if I kept daring to receive a Native man in the house. So I tried to find somewhere else to live. I found somewhere but I've had problems again. It seems a girl like me, without protector, without family, can be treated like anybody's property. So I moved again, to board with a quiet Chinese family. But the master of the house, seeing that I was by myself, began to treat me as if I wanted to be taken as a concubine.*

It would be different if my late friend was still here near me.

I must be strong as I have always been. But lately I've been more anxious, worried and hesitant. Sometimes I feel I've lost all faith in myself. Could we meet this Sunday morning? At Kotta station at nine o'clock? I look forward so much to seeing you again.

She wasn't there when I arrived at Kotta. I walked up and down so that she would see me easily. I was really very anxious. Perhaps she was just playing a trick on me. No, I said to myself, she had no reason to do that.

Ten minutes later, a young Chinese boy came up to me. He asked nervously in Malay: '*Tuan* is waiting for *Encik* Teacher Ang?' He had round eyes set in narrow pock-marks of eye sockets, and he fondled a filthy tennis ball.

I hesitated. He might be someone sent by those who had threatened Mei. So what? They can bash me up then. Perhaps Mei does truly need me at this time.

'Yes.'

'Encik Teacher Ang is sick.' He held out a letter.

'How did you know I was waiting for her?'

'Wearing European clothes, she said, perhaps with a bike. A Native boy, brown hat, called Minke.'

'Clever boy,' I said, and pinched his cheek.

I read her letter. It was true, she was ill. I went with the boy to where she was staying. When we got close, the boy asked to be let off the bike. He pointed out to me where to go.

The people at the house didn't like a Native coming inside. They were suspicious. Did I care? I wasn't there to see them.

'Yes, Ang San Mei does live here. But she's ill.'

'I need to see her.'

They seemed to object to an alien entering their house. But when they saw I wasn't going to leave, a woman carrying a baby was forced, frowning, to take me to Mei. I heard her growl. Who cares? They weren't going to lose anything by having me here.

Mei was stretched out on the bed. She was asleep. And the woman began to hesitate again.

'She was my friend at school in Shanghai,' I said.

The woman began to relax a little. Perhaps she had never been home to the country of her ancestors and felt inferior before one who had. She took me inside Mei's room.

On the table beside her bed was a vase of drooping flowers and a glass of water. I noticed the absence of the little Chinese messenger boy with his tennis ball. I think he didn't want anyone to know what he had done for Mei. He wasn't about, though it was obvious he was the son of the woman at this house.

I went straight to Mei. She had a temperature. My heart went out to her. There were no signs in the room that she had any medicine. Why was she so alone among her own people like this? Did she carry some contagious disease, or did they regard her as a trouble-maker?

I sat on the bed, and took her hand. Her temperature was quite high. Her lips were more than just pale. They were bloodless, and open a little, and her beautiful pearl-like teeth shone through.

She opened her eyes, and stared at me. Then without speaking and without smiling she put her hand on mine.

'Sorry I'm sick. I hoped you'd come., though it's more than I have the right to hope. It's a pity you're not a doctor yet.'

'What did the doctor say about your illness?'

'There's no doctor and no medicines.'

'You've got such a fever. Is there a bitter taste in your mouth?'

She nodded.

'I'll be back soon. I'll buy some medicines.'

When I arrived back from the shops with medicine and food I found that woman in Mei's room. Her eyes were full of suspicion again. I tried to be respectful, but she didn't seem to realise it. Well all right. I didn't have any business with her anyway . . .

Mei was sitting up in bed massaging her head. I gave her two red quinine capsules with a glass of water.

'All right. Enough. Take this woman away from here,' the woman said in Malay.

'But she's still ill. Let her stay another week,' I said. 'I'll fetch her in another week. Isn't that so, Mei?'

She nodded. It seemed she was beginning to understand some Malay. Then I suddenly thought: How will I pay to look after her? Where will I take her? And I didn't understand either why she nodded in agreement. Why, all of a sudden did I have the courage to come forward as her protector? She wasn't allowed to stay in any other but those *kampung* set aside for Chinese by the Government.

'I'll stay with her today,' I said to the woman. 'Don't be angry. Why do you want to get rid of her so quickly?'

She frowned and went away.

Mei happened to be in a room outside the main house, in the kitchen building, because she was working there as a cook. And it happened too that I had the rest of my money from Surabaya with me. It wasn't that I wanted to appear generous or anything. When I read her letter I imagined that she might be in some desperate trouble like her friend had been in Surabaya, surrounded by a hostile community. And indeed there were no signs of food in her room anywhere.

'You're so good,' she whispered weakly.

'Go back to sleep, Mei,' I said and laid her back down on the bed. 'Where's your blanket?'

She pretended not to hear and closed her eyes.

'Where are your clothes?' and before she answered I had picked up the leather bag on her pillow.

When she heard her bag being taken, her hand moved out weakly to stop me. I took no notice. Inside were some underclothes and the white dress she had worn the first time we met. I took them all out and spread them over her.

'You don't have a blanket, Mei?' She didn't answer. 'You'll be warmer like this. You must have a terrible headache. But you must eat, Mei.'

'I don't want to eat.'

'Malaria always takes away the appetite, but you still must have something to eat,' I encouraged her. 'I brought you something, a snack. You mustn't let yourself waste away like this.'

'Were you this good to him, too?' she asked, her eyes shut.

I put the food in her mouth, as if I were feeding a baby.

'If you can't chew just swallow.'

She shook her head, refusing to take the food. But I made her eat until the food was all finished.

'Just rest for a while. I'm going out but I'll be back soon.'

I rode off on my bike like a knight on his horse off to rescue a maiden in distress, ready to fight any doer of evil. And I felt proud, that today I might be bankrupted helping somebody in need, unable to help herself. It would be a poverty that brought satisfaction. I strode into a shop and bought some plain biscuits, syrup, dried foods, canned meat and fish and a can opener, a towel and a blanket. I calculated that there was enough dried food for a week. I added a can of milk as well. And some fresh food for today. And some medicines to help get her strength back.

Yet I was still far from bankrupt.

She wasn't asleep when I arrived back. I put her clothes back in the bag and covered her with the thick blanket.

'Why are you crying, Mei?'

'Were you this good to him as well?' she repeated.

'What, Mei?' I asked, pretending I didn't hear.

She covered her face, and I heard her sobbing. She was remembering her loved one who had now passed away. And I had to respect her feelings.

'Enough, Mei, no need to keep thinking about the past,' I whispered in her ear. 'He did what he had to do. He never betrayed his promise or his work. He indeed was a diamond of a youth. He faced everything with courage.'

She was quiet.

'You must get well. You must get strong.'

The woman with the baby came back. She must have seen me carrying all the things for Mei: 'If Tuan is going to take her away in a week's time, you must pay the rent for the room in the meantime.'

'Of course. How much per day?' I asked.

'Twenty-five cents.'

'Fantastic. Like at an inn. And that would be for full board.'

'Well, only if that's what Tuan wants. I'd rather have the room empty.'

'All right. Here's seven times twenty-five cents.'

'Plus three times more, because she's been sick three days already.'

I took back the coins and gave her a shiny silver *ringgit*.

'I'll get the change,' she said.

'No need, take it all.'

'But you have to get a *setali* back, Tuan,' she went away but soon returned with twenty-five cents change. Then she left the room without another word.

Mei lay there silent for a long time. I kept quiet so she could get some sleep. I took out pencil and paper and began to write. I had been meaning to write to mother for quite a long time. In a few more days, the holidays would arrive. And with Mei sick, I didn't want to travel home.

Forgive me, Mother. I am truly not able to come home these holidays, because I have a friend who is ill and whom I must look after. Mother will not be angry with me, I'm sure. But if my friend recovers, then I will come home straight away.

'Minke', Mei called me.

I went over to her.

'You must sleep, Mei.'

'Have you sent that letter to the girl in Jepara?'

'Yes.'

'How did she reply?'

'There hasn't been any reply. It looks as if there won't be any reply.'

'How old do you think she is?'

'A year older than me.'

'Is she married yet?'

'I don't know. Maybe yes. Maybe no.' And I couldn't help smiling to myself. Ang San Mei will be better soon. Perhaps she is even jealous.

She had no more questions so I went on with my letter. I could hear the woman cooking next door in the kitchen and the smell of frying pork wafted into the room. I had never eaten pork. The smell was so strong it gave me a headache. My thoughts wandered to my mother, to what she had told me the first time I went to Surabaya. 'You are going to a big city, where you will mix with all races. You have your own people. Show them that you are a good and well-behaved Javanese. Your ancestors were Islam, so too your mother and father. Never ever must you eat pork. It is one of the least burdensome prohibitions, Child. You mustn't break this rule. It's not hard to do.' And I have never gone against that prohibition.

Ang San Mei had fallen asleep. The shudders from her fever had disappeared. Sweat started to form on her forehead.

I finally finished my long letter to mother. I wrote about my situation, my studies, my friends at school, my teachers. There was not one sentence that touched on the differences between mother and child. I presented myself as a good and obedient son, just as she had always been a good mother to me. The differences between us were differences of education, methods and goals. It was a matter of the end of an era, of changes in the times. There was nothing left that my mother could defend. Java was being continously defeated by Europe, by its people, its earth, its ideas. Java's only triumph was in its ignorance about the world. And Java truly did shut itself off from the world.

Mei awoke again in the afternoon. I went across to her.

'I feel a bit better now,' she said calmly in English. 'You should be a doctor, Minke, you'll be a good one.'

'Of course.'

'You shouldn't have any doubts about being a doctor,' she said again. 'You mustn't be lazy in your studies. There must be so many of your people who are sick like I am now.'

'I will cure you and all of them too, Mei.'

She smiled such a sweet smile, and I smiled too, perhaps even more sweetly.

'And if they're all looked after like this, they will all be cured too.'

'Naturally. And you know what I would have done if you hadn't eaten when I asked you to a while ago. I would have chewed the food for you and dropped it straight into your mouth from mine, like a mother bird.'

'That's going too far,' she said, eyes shining. 'How will you find a place for me? I can't go out looking while I'm sick like this.'

'Don't worry about it,' and in my mind's eye I saw Ibu Baldrun. 'Nah, it's almost four o'clock, Mei. I'll go home now, yes? Make sure you eat well, and don't forget to take your medicine. If you don't want to eat for yourself, eat for me, as much as you can manage. Will you do what I have asked, Mei?'

'Happily, Minke. You've been so good to me.'

Before I left, I kissed her on the cheek. And no protest came from her lips. At the door I turned round. I saw her cover her face with her two hands and her shoulders seemed to be convulsing.

I kept going.

I cycled straight back to Ibu Baldrun's in Kwitang.

'She'll want to eat different food than us,' Ibu Baldrun objected.

'Just the same as us, Ibu,' I answered.

'They have different customs than us.'

'She is very polite and helpful,' I said.

'She'll do that revolting spitting.'

'No. She is the same as me, no spitting.'

'The neighbours won't like it.'

'I'll talk to the neighbours.'

'A *sinkeh*,' Ibu Baldrun still objected. 'She'll speak in some strange language.'

'She is an educated person, Ibu, she is trying very hard to learn Malay. It's true she can't speak it yet, but she is working very hard at it.'

'She'll turn out to be a bad girl, Child?'

'Don't worry, Bu, I'll be her guarantor. I will kick her out myself if she turns out to be no good.'

'But she's not yet your wife, Denmas.'

'It's not a matter of being my wife, Bu, she's my friend.'

'Why doesn't she live with her own people? It must be because of something she's done that they don't like her.'

'She is an orphan, Bu. That's the only reason, Bu.'

'Will Denmas take her as your wife?'

'Who knows, Bu? God's will cannot be foretold.'

'She will be on display here every day?'

'That'll all stop after a week, Bu.'

'What if the hamlet chief finds out. She should be in a Chinese hamlet.'

I pretended not to hear.

For the next six days I didn't leave the school complex once. During rest times, I hid away in the library. I didn't care what I read. I only went to the dormitory to sleep or after bathing to change clothes. I knew that, because of my strong feelings for her, I had taken on a big responsibility, namely, to help a lonely girl in distress. I had made a promise to her, and I would keep it.

By Saturday night another question was haunting me. Why hadn't Mei received any help from her school, from the Council of Teachers, from the Tiong Hoa Hwee Koan? She had signed a five-year contract, hadn't she?

She was definitely my late friend's fiancée. He had used a false name. There were those who said that the name he used was a southern Chinese name. But he himself was from the north. It was pretty definite that Ang San Mei was a false name too. What was her real name? Was it too a southern name? Ah, why bother so much about a name? I've been called by my nickname now for years and years. No one has ever objected. I know her as Ang San Mei. Why worry about what her real name is?

The next Sunday it was four in the morning before I fell asleep. Then I awoke again fifteen minutes later. I was restless. Rather than be at the beck and call of all these vexing thoughts, I decided to write. And so I began to write about this girl from across the seas.

Her work as a teacher was perhaps just an attempt to obtain some kind of legal existence, I wrote. (I didn't give her name.) Her fiancé had died in Surabaya. So in one blow she lost both lover and leader. She was left alone in Betawi. She tried with all her might to fit in with her people. The Chinese living in Java, she said, did not like the new immigrants very much. People said that they were seen as being as alien as the Natives or Europeans. So Mei was forced to stay away from them too. How alone she was. As time went on she lost more and more weight, she didn't know what to do . . .

By the time the bell rang for everyone to get up, I had finished the story of our first meeting. My pen flowed magically. I felt that this story was as good as any I had ever written. It was my first piece since arriving in Betawi. By nine o'clock it would be on its way in the post to one of the leading magazines in the Indies. Then I would have to wait. The next thing I planned was a story about my late friend, but I would write that in English.

By seven o'clock in the morning I was off to see Mei. She looked much better, but still pale and even thinner. There was no one at home except Mei and the boy who had met me at the station last week.

The boy wasn't afraid at all. He came straight up to me and told me that everyone had gone to Tangerang.

'Today Encik Teacher Mei will go. All this time I have been the only one who has helped her,' he reported to me. 'When Encik Teacher Mei goes I will have no one to help any more.'

'You can help others,' I said, 'who are sick or who need help. What's your name?'

'Pengki.'

'A helpful child, and polite,' said Mei, pinching his cheek. 'I will never forget you, Pengki,' she said in Malay. Then in English: 'He was my student before.'

Outside as we were about to leave, his face began to tremble as if about to cry.

'You have brothers and sisters. You can look after them' I said, and I caressed his head, 'Do you want to see Encik Teacher again?'

He nodded.

'Can you read Latin letters?'

He nodded.

I wrote down the address on a piece of paper and gave it to him.

'It's a long way from here. You'll have to take a tram. Do you have any money for a ticket?'

He shook his head and I gave him twenty-five cents. But he refused to take it.

'You can come and visit, but be careful and ask permission from your parents first.'

'Won't Encik Teacher be teaching any more?'

I translated the question for Mei. And the girl crouched down and held the boy by the waist and spoke to him in Mandarin. She kissed him on the cheek, then she led him back inside. We thanked him for his help. Then we left, and we knew he cried.

'He'll forget all about it soon,' I said.

'He'll remember this all his life,' said Mei.

We rode along together on my bike to Kwitang. Mei had very few things, which she carried on her lap. And she herself didn't weigh much either.

She had been dismissed at the school. Her contract had been unilaterally cancelled. She had been declared unfit to teach because she was seeing a Native man.

I knew that I had to accept responsibility for looking after things now. And I did it happily.

'Don't be afraid,' I said, more to bolster my own courage, 'you are not alone.'

'But you must become a doctor.'

'That's not so important.'

'Don't say that. What about your family, your parents, and you yourself and your people? They need you.'

My people needed me, she said. We sat on the bench at Ibu Baldrun's and in the dark I gazed at her face. It was still pale. Did my people need me?

We were sitting outside in front of the house. Mei held my hand as if I might run away.

'Don't worry. I will keep up my studies. You musn't get upset about such things. You have to get better.'

'Give me a month. When I'm strong again, I'll begin my endeavours once more.'

'Don't think about that now,' I said. 'Your health is the most important thing at the moment. That is your job now. Forget everything else.'

I had calculated that I had enough money to look after her. The board at Ibu Baldrun's was three and a half guilders a month, plus another one and half for medicines. I still had five guilders a month left over from my allowance. Then there were my savings from Surabaya.

'You'll get into difficulties because of me.'

'Don't you think I'm your friend, Mei? Don't you believe in me?'

I couldn't see her face in the dark. I stood up to go but her hand still held mine.

'I must go back to the dormitory. I will come again tomorrow evening.'

'Your studies won't be disturbed?'

'Don't worry about such things.'

She kissed my hand, let it go and stood up.

'Come inside, Mei, you're still not strong.'

I took her inside and handed her back to Ibu Baldrun. Then I went back to the school. I felt relieved. Ibu Baldrun had shown a liking for Mei as soon as they met. There was still food set aside for me when I got back to the dormitory but I wasn't hungry. My mind was busy working out what was the next thing I had to do. And I decided. I would try to earn some more money as I had done in Surabaya. School was now second priority. I would start writing again.

I went back into the library, grabbed a pen and wrote about the tragic story of Khouw Ah Soe. A short, concise story. I did not give his real name. Then I read the papers, after which I went to bed.

The next day, before going to see Mei, I went to Kramat. I visited one of the auction papers there and introduced myself. Mr Kaarsen received me with some suspicion. I gave him my piece and he read it. Yes, he read it – in just a few minutes. Nodded. He offered me cash straight away – seventy-five cents. The best a sugar cane worker could get for a day's work.

'I'm sorry, Sir, but I've never been offered as little as that.'

'Don't be upset. Our paper is given out free. If you want more you have to go to a daily. We can easily fill up any empty space ourselves. But if you would like to write advertisements for us, we'll pay one *talen* for an ad in Malay, three *talen* for one in Dutch and a *rupiah* per ad for English. Except we rarely publish anything in English.'

I took my piece back but accepted the offer to write advertisements. I agreed to spend one hour a day writing up the advertisements for customers as they came in – just as I had done in Surabaya. And I needed those *talen*.

It turned out that Ang San Mei had never had any practical education, in the sense of being trained how to turn her abilities into money. From a very early age she had prepared herself to be a teacher. Having left her country to travel to the Indies with her fiancé, she had turned to becoming a propagandist, a grass-roots organiser. And perhaps she had failed. She was stranded in a foreign country, separated from her friends who had died or who were far away. Deserted and helpless like a bird with a broken wing.

'No matter, Mei, at least I've got back the energy and enthusiasm I used to have,' I often humoured her. 'As long as you get better, all will be well. I'm really happy to see you studying Malay so hard.'

Two of my stories were published. I was paid more than ever before. And what was more important – people were beginning to take notice of me in Betawi. Anyway, that's what I thought. And once my stories began to be published, there was pressure to write more and more, each time dipping into my store of energy, of which there wasn't too much left. I knew I was losing weight, and Mei wasn't putting on any either. My eyes became sunken. Mei's lips were still pale.

Then the long holidays arrived. I graduated up a grade. It was Mei who was ecstatically happy. The dormitory was silent. There was no one left. But before they all dispersed, they couldn't restrain themselves from making comments about my relationship with a Chinese girl and how they knew I wouldn't be going on holidays.

Until then I had always assumed that among educated people the personal affairs of others were their own business. I was wrong. Their education was just a thin cover over their continuing support for the old, evil ways. There had even been those who had contacted Mei herself, thinking that she was some kind of street woman. And, of course, there were the anonymous letters. Someone even threatened to bring in the authorities, saying that we were conspiring to get around the residential rules for Chinese.

The Director himself had also summoned me. He closed the conversation with the following words: 'It would be best if you severed the relationship. Nothing should disturb your studies. The Government has been generous enough to give you the opportunity to study here. You should be thankful.'

'Meneer Director,' I answered, 'it is true that I have a relationship with a female friend, just as everyone else has here at the school. Even you, Sir. Nothing is disturbing my studies here. None of my marks are below average.'

'Your marks could drop.'

'Anyone's marks could drop, not just mine, And, on the other hand, they could get better.'

'You've lost weight. Your health is being affected.'

'Yes, people can lose weight, Director, and they can also die.'

My relationship with Mei went on undisturbed, thanks to the support of the hamlet chief. One by one all problems were taken care of. And more than that. More and more of my writings were published. And it was none other than the Director himself who was among the proudest of my admirers. He had a famous student.

I took Mei on holidays to B – .

She enjoyed her trip into the country. 'The land here looks so closely-packed, just like at home,' she commented. 'Except here there are no flowers anywhere. No parks.'

I booked her into a Chinese-owned *losmen* and then went off to see my parents.

69

Father was away seeing the Resident in Surabaya. I was only able to meet my mother and my younger brothers and sisters. And this time mother did not greet me with the same pressing questions. I couldn't reject anything she said nor could I answer back. There was nothing for me to reject. My duty was to listen.

'So you decided to come home, after all, Child?' she greeted me. 'Why are you so thin? Even worse than before.'

I was afraid the questions would come thundering in again – questions that would infiltrate right into my soul, would shake my emotions to their core, and make me love her even more deeply, despite her obsession with the old Javanese ways. But she didn't ask those questions, rather she begged and pleaded: 'Come on now, *Gus*, ah, you're already an adult and I still must call you Gus. Come on, tell me what is the matter.'

So I told her all I knew about Mei. I didn't have the courage to look her in the face. The seconds passed after I had finished my story. She said nothing.

'Mother, is this relationship a sin?'

'Will you take her as your wife, Child?' she asked, and I could feel that she was suffering.

'Is there anything else I can do, Mother?'

'There are many *bupatis*' daughters awaiting a proposal from you but you wouldn't like any of them. You always want something different.'

'Mother mustn't be sad because of this.'

'No, my son. I am happy, and even happier if you are happy. The kings of your ancestors always dreamt of taking as a wife a Chinese princess, or one from Campa. But they never made such a one their princess.'

'Mother, all I need is such a princess.'

'But her religion is different.'

'And were not the kings of my ancestors also of a different religion?'

'Perhaps. And perhaps there is nothing to worry about if it is indeed what you want. When do you want to marry?'

'That is up to you, Mother.'

'You can marry whenever you like and wherever you like.'

'A thousand *sembah* for Mother's blessing. May she come and meet you, Mother?'

'You have brought her here, my son?'

'She is staying at a *losmen*.'

'I will go with you and fetch this daughter of China.'

And so we departed to fetch her.

Mei was sitting in the foyer of the *losmen*. Alone, in her best clothes, she looked fresh, and like an alabaster statue. She was wearing a long white dress and a red scarf.

'Mei, Mei, this is my mother, here to fetch you.'

She smiled, and went up to mother, and made obeisance to her by clasping her two hands together before her chest and bowing her head.

'Is this my daughter?' my mother asked in Javanese.

Mei glanced at me seeking a translation, and I translated for her.

'Here is your daughter. Ang San Mei is her name, Mother,' said Mei.

'Why are you here at this *losmen*? Why didn't you come straight home? As if you didn't have a mother here in B – !'

'Who knows, Mother? I am just a foreigner here.'

'Who has made you feel like a foreigner? Come on, let's go home, Child,' and she took Mei by the shoulder and guided her outside the *losmen*, straight into the carriage. I arranged for her things to be put aboard and instructed that the bill be sent to the Bupati's house.

Mother treated her as a child who had come from her own womb. Indeed she showered Mei with even more care than that, to make up for missing out on looking after her first daughter-in-law. She herself prepared Mei's room. She called my younger sisters to look after and befriend her, and to teach her how to wear Javanese clothes. And she summoned all the *gamelan* players to play that night, even though it wasn't Monday.

Mei seemed happy to be among my family. I prayed that my father would not return home while she was here. The atmosphere would change completely if he arrived. Even my decision to go to medical school had made him furious. Imagine how he would react to my marrying a foreign girl like this!

We holidayed like a prince and princess for three days in the region. This time there were no invitations for me to visit son-in-law-seeking local officials. Doctoring was servile work – a goat-class occupation – not like governing.

On the evening before we left, my mother gave Mei a pearl necklace and ring.

At first Ang San Mei refused to take them. I advised her that it was not good to refuse. She took my advice and accepted the gifts. Mother also gave Mei *batik* that she had made herself, and some special herbal medicines for women. And then she asked: 'When will you become man and wife?'

Mei and I looked at each other. We had not yet talked about marriage. I had not even proposed. We had never discussed it.

I told Mei she should answer. 'What does Mother think is best?'

But Mei answered: 'Am I worthy to be your daughter, Mother?'

'Worthy of becoming the wife of a good husband,' answered mother. 'So when will you marry?'

'I don't know, Mother,' Mei answered.

'Perhaps in a little while, Mother,' I translated.

Mei glanced at me and said: 'I don't trust your translation. You grinned while you spoke.'

'I said we would marry soon.' I spoke in English. 'This is also a proposal. I know you won't refuse.'

'Why are you proposing only now? Too scared except in front of your mother?'

'You're grinning too,' I said. 'I don't believe you haven't been waiting for me to propose.'

'What are you two arguing about?' asked mother.

'She wants to have nine children, Mother,' I translated Mei's answer and then told her what I had said in English.

She blushed. She bowed her head and whispered: 'You're too bold in front of your mother.'

'Ah, I forgot,' and she called one of my sisters to come, 'a girl so beautiful shouldn't be without earrings.' She spoke to my sister: 'Let me take your earrings to be a souvenir for your new sister. I'll give you some new ones later.' Then mother tried to put them on Mei. But she couldn't. She wasn't sure what was the matter.

'Allah on high!!' she cried. 'Your ears haven't been pierced?'

I had never paid any attention. But she was right.

'How will you wear these earrings?'

'There's no need, Mother,' I said.

'No need? A girl undecorated by earrings? Where do such teachings come from? Except if you can't afford it?' she was angry at me. Then she took hold of Mei's hand and clasped it in hers: 'Why are you so thin? Both of you?'

'There's a time for people being thin, Mother,' I answered.

'Yes, there is such a time. There are also reasons for it,' mother replied. 'I have never heard of any teaching that says you must starve yourself!'

'What did she say?' asked Mei.

'She said that you would be prettier still if you put on a little weight.'

'When things settle down a bit and things are calmer, I will put on more weight, Mother,' said Mei.

'To be thin like this, Mother,' I translated for her, 'means you can move more quickly and get around better. Rather than having to carry around all that unnecessary meat.'

'Ah, you'll say anything. You must be thankful and patient so that fate smiles upon you. Yes, let's hope all will turn out well for you, Child. Let's pray that everything you both desire is granted to you.'

And so we accomplished the difficulties of facing my mother without hurting her feelings.

We then travelled on to Jepara.

Jepara, a town so much mentioned in our history, was a silent place as if it had never played any role in the past at all. The town centre was like a deserted tiger's den. There was nothing of any interest at all. Yet we knew that inside the silent houses people were working with wood, turtle shell and ivory making objects of great beauty and expense. But all that was left of the past were some old ruins that people called 'the Portuguese Fort'.

'Yes,' sighed the girl we had come to visit, 'the golden age of Jepara is over. Now it is just a silent and forgotten place.'

She received us accompanied by one of her younger sisters, who mainly sat and listened.

We spoke in Dutch and once more I became an interpreter.

'Your Dutch is very good,' she praised me. She didn't wait for my response but continued: 'I value greatly and give thanks to all Native men who know how to respect women. No doubt so do you, Sir. I'm sorry I haven't been able to reply to your letter yet.'

She spoke and acted confidently and quickly. Then she turned to Mei: 'You must be happy, Miss, to be young and free.'

'This freedom, my friend, is the result of my own efforts, and of a struggle of the spirit that was also quite difficult.'

The girl from Jepara said that she understood that such freedom was open for all to obtain. But she said that such freedom should not be bought with the love of one's parents. What was the meaning of freedom if it caused suffering for those who loved you and had looked after you? Wasn't that just the transfer of one person's suffering onto others?

I got the impression that she was talking about her own situation. She was struggling to make her thoughts submit to what was proper. And she was alone, without the company of any modern individual, alone by herself, trapped, and only she could resolve her situation. All anyone else could do would be to offer suggestions.

After she found out that Mei was an orphan, that she had never known her parents, she bit her lips and turned away, and her lips went white as she bit them. Everyone knew that she loved her father, and that her father loved her more than any other of her sisters or brothers. She was a pearl to her father, and it was she who had brought fame and honour to her parents, her family and her name. And it was she who had brought life to the woodcarvers of Jepara.

But she was also a person of the modern age, a Native, one among only a handful, who had to think for themselves, who had to free themselves from all the old ways, whose ideas might not be understood by those around them, whose ideas might indeed even provoke hostility. She was a free thinker whose body was hostage to her environment, and whose freedom was caged in by her love for her father. And she herself did not have the strength to free herself from her captivity. She represented the tragedy of the change of times. She suffered no less than any other woman who lived under the yoke of a man's rule.

'If you obtained such freedom,' Mei began again, 'what would you do?'

The girl said that beside her and around her the suffering resulted from ignorance, while above her there was knowledge, science and excessive power, which were all used to maintain the suffering below.

'You sound like a follower of the Buddha.'

She laughed and said that she was not proposing the acceptance of suffering; she was just explaining how it was the result of certain situations. There should be enjoyment too. But in Java suffering was endemic. It was part of the marrow of life. Many people did not feel the suffering because they were not aware of it. And so it was that the Dutch often said: 'Happy are the ignorant, because they do not suffer so much. And happy are the children who do not yet need the knowledge to be able to understand.'

'It's not so with all children,' said Mei, and she began to tell the story of her own childhood. It was a hard time, she said. She did not know who her parents were, she had so many responsibilities, as well as her studies, and the discipline and all the rules as well. 'I think the best time in a person's life is when you are able to use the freedom you have won for yourself.'

This much-honoured girl inspected Mei and seemed suspicious of her physical weakness. She herself was plump, perhaps four centimetres shorter than Mei. Her face was roundish, while Mei's was oval. She replied that perhaps what Mei had said was true. With such freedom people could also freely show their pain at their failures. Without such freedom, even your pain had to be kept from those you loved, for the sake of that love.

Her voice pierced our hearts. I could understand her sufferings. She was a person of the modern age, someone who had studied in order to be able to understand, and who had come to understand and then to realise her own sufferings, and that of others like her and of her people. But she was still imprisoned by custom, by her parents' love, and by her situation as an unmarried elder daughter.

'But weren't you offered the chance to study in Holland?' I asked.

Yes, it was no secret, she said. But what could be achieved in Holland? Wouldn't she end up even further away from reality and more isolated from her world?

Turning back to Mei she said that she and Mei had different starting points. She started with a happy childhood, while Mei did not. She wanted every young girl to have the same happy childhood. She wanted to teach them, to educate them – her voice shook reflecting her inner troubles and restlessness. She wanted to give such girls a new foundation in life where they were taught that men must respect them, based on their real achievements and qualities.

She had begun to prepare her plans. But nothing could be achieved without freedom. And then she said that in Priangan there was a young woman who had actually started the kind of school she herself had always dreamed about. Her name was Dewi Sartika. She would try to write to her. And what about that kind of endeavour in China? Had such schools been started there?

'I don't think so,' answered Mei, 'But there are already many women teachers in China.'

'Why aren't there any schools like that?'

'My educated countrymen have set themselves a task they think is more important – the liberation of Chinese society as a whole.'

The girl from Jepara was completely taken aback. And I could understand why. We knew very little in the Indies about China or the Chinese. All we were taught was some geography, the names of provinces and towns and rivers and so on. The only other thing we knew was that China was an independent country but with several areas where foreign powers had special privileges. I only began to understand more about China after I'd been with Mei for quite a while. The education of children of the kind that our friend wanted was seen as less important than the overall task. At least that was the case as far as Mei knew.

'No. Children's happiness, and also the happiness of adults, in the midst of a sea of unhappiness is a strange thing. Those who are happy just pretend to be, or are indeed happy but because nobody else is. Isn't this immoral?'

'I don't know what to say,' said Mei.

Our friend seemed lost in thought, her head bowed and still. She truly was somebody who liked to think and liked to discuss things with other people. She had a democratic spirit, she wasn't offended by others because they had opinions of their own. But everything she said seemed to be motivated by an anxiety, a general insecurity.

She said further that everything had a beginning. And the beginning was nothing other than the proper education and training of the children. She looked at each of us in turn hoping for either support or rejection, or both at once.

'That's not the only way, my friend,' said Mei, 'It's only one way among many. The old and the parents must be educated too. And you must gather capital as well. Without money, the most you can teach is six or seven people. Even after a thousand years, you still won't have finished.' Her face lit up and lost all its paleness.'We have our own way.'

'What is that way?'

I translated the girl's question to Mei, and she answered straight away: 'Organise, my friend, form associations, with many people, tens, hundreds, yes even tens of thousands, all becoming one powerful giant, with a strength greater than the sum of all the members put together . . .'

I translated and translated.

'. . . with giant hands, giant legs, and with tremendous vision and abilities and resilience . . . '

The two of them talked and talked. I translated and translated.

But how else could you begin, this girl asked, except through education and schooling? Being a student and teacher together. Being a teacher and student together. Loving and being loved. Being loved and loving. Everything is a result of struggle. And not always a short struggle either. And old fashioned love that is not oriented to the future with its complexities and richness was also wrong and had to be corrected. To correct his, you also need struggle, vigour and the appropriate actions. There is love everywhere, even among animals. Without love, can people suffer life?

Once again I got the impression that she was wrestling with her own feelings and thoughts – the tragedy of a modern person who cannot find a way out of the limitations of her own thinking. A thousand gods would not be able to free her from them. Only people themselves can solve this kind of problem, said one article I'd read. The gods are not as compassionate now as they were in our ancestors' days. The modern age has forced people to take responsibility for themselves. To grab it out of the hands of the gods. There was no longer *deus ex machina* as in the legends of earlier times, said the article. People today were under the whip of their own consciousness, and they could not get away from this any more, now that responsibility for themselves had been stolen from the hands of the gods.

'In the end,' Mei was saying, 'even love is a thing, even though sacred and mysterious, and abstract, and every "thing" is subordinated to humankind. It's up to us how we use it.'

'None of my European friends have ever spoken like this,' said the girl from Jepara. 'Your thinking is very severe.'

'Not severe, my friend,' said Mei, 'but obedient to necessity. Everything must bow to our will, whether concrete or abstract.'

'As we are conquering the laws of nature.'

'That is only a part of it.'

The discussion became more and more serious, and I translated and translated. Whatever else I thought, I had to respect this primary school educated girl who was shackled by her own exalted thoughts without any proper response from those around her, shackled by the love for her parents, and with all her ideas coming from her love for her fellow beings. She thought she could not escape and made no effort to escape. Truly a tragedy. What a torturing burden for this young soul were her own thoughts!

I think that if a man proposed to her, she would be able to decide quickly on whether to say yes or no. She refused to let herself leave an environment of love for one without love. She refused to accept her fate as a Javanese woman where a wife is but the property of her husband. She rebelled against such a way of life. She wanted something new. She knew what she had to do in order to reach that new something but she lacked the courage to do what was necessary.

It was better that I didn't intervene in the discussion. It wasn't that the issues weren't interesting. On the contrary, they were all part of the problem of coming to grips with the modern era.

Suddenly she asked Mei what Mei had been doing while she had been in the Indies. Mei, in a rather strange way, turned the question back on her. Mei answered that she was doing whatever she could, given her situation, and this was mainly writing for the public and privately to various people. Then our friend invited us to stay longer in Jepara.

'I'd like to very much,' said Mei, 'but I don't think I can this time.'

She asked me where I worked. I told her I was still at the medical school. She was very pleased to hear that. She told me about her brother in Europe and suggested I write to him.

'I have read your articles in *Bintang Hindia* and *De Hollandshe Lelie*,' I said to her. 'Very interesting.' She was so pleased.

Mei said that I also wrote.

'Oh yes, where?'

She held out her hand to me for the second time. She didn't say anything about the letter she had written to one of her friends about my earlier experience. And I didn't say anything either.

'Won't we be late?' Mei asked suddenly.

The girl from Jepara was at her most enthusiastic now that we were talking about what we each had written. But time did not permit. The two girls shook hands emotionally, and the girl said, 'Happy are you, my friend, to be able to do what you yourself want, to do what you think is right for yourself and your people.'

'Yes, and it is all through struggle,' replied Mei.

'Yes.'

She also shook hands with me. And I couldn't but notice her eyes. This person, who was the prisoner of love, shouted out with her eyes for a love that she had never yet known.

Our carriage left Jepara and headed towards Mayong. As soon as we were seated in the train for Semarang, a word escaped from my lips: 'Tragic.'

'She could achieve more, much more, than she thinks '

'Such a pity,' I whispered.

So we continued our vacation in Bandung.

Mei enjoyed our travels very much. But she was still thin and pale. It was anaemia, low blood pressure, she was always pale and on the verge of illness. But throughout the journey to Bandung she chattered happily about the scenery. She was still shy about speaking in Malay, even though I had tried several times to get her to try, so she kept up her commentary in English, often oohing and aahing at what she saw.

A girl from a far away country who had followed her fiancé in his struggle. Alone and without family, brought up in an orphanage. And I was in love with her. Perhaps she still loved her fiancé and his spirit. Perhaps she was waiting for my proposal just so she could reject it. And I, a man, a connoisseur of beauty, who has never loved with that kind of love that so many people have spoken or written about, could not but be crazy about this beautiful girl who was in a class all of her own.

Sometimes I tried to work out what I meant to her, but I could never be sure. I was someone whose ideal was to be a free human being. From the very beginning, she had corrected me on that. On the other hand, I saw her as a simple girl with her head filled with idealism. And how did she see herself? No doubt she thought herself pretty. Perhaps she thought of me as simply a slave to her beauty!

She turned away from the window.

'You keep on staring at me,' she said, embarrassed. 'What are you thinking?'

'I was just imagining that you were already my wife.'

'But you haven't even proposed yet,' she said. 'At your mother's . . . '

'You won't laugh at my proposal? On the train like this, Mei?'

She bowed her head, and played with her fingers on her lap. Even with my eyes closed I knew she was hiding her feelings. I had already observed that talk of this kind always took her back to old memories, to my dead friend.

'You like living in the Indies now, don't you?'

'To me everywhere is the same. Where my friends are, there is my country. Without friends, all this would be unbearable. And it would be the same in one's own country, if you had no friends . . . '

'Mei, will you become my wife?'

'I'm so weak and my health is not good. Everyone says I am thin.'

'I will be a good doctor for you.'

'In six or seven years' time?' she looked at me, then she moved across to sit next to me and whispered to me through the bang and clatter of the train: 'You will regret marrying me, Minke. It will bring you many difficulties. In any case, if my health comes back to me, I will and must help you. But, do you think I can regain my health once more?'

'You are already better than you were six months ago.'

'I would like very much to accept your proposal, Minke, I would be very happy. But is it possible?'

'You yourself know that you and I don't like to delay things.'

'But you must take a broader view, think about the consequences. You should think about this deeply. What do I mean to you? Your people need you much more than I do. Look at the forests out there.'

'At this moment there is not one tree upon the earth that has any business with us.'

I held her thin hand and it trembled. She had accepted my proposal in her heart. But perhaps not yet in her mind.

Seeing me become silent she started to talk to me like a mother to her child, full of love and worry.

'In six or seven years you will become a doctor. Those of your people who are ill will come to you. They are all poor and will not be able to pay you, but you are not seeking riches, are you? So you will share in the poverty of your people. Is it right that I burden you even more? I think not. But you will find out that your people are not only sick in body because of poverty, but also sick in spirit because of another kind of poverty, a poverty of modern knowledge and understanding. And you will have to heal their spirit too so your people will become a mighty and strong people. What is it that I can do to help you in this? I think you know what are the possibilities,' she breathed in as deeply as she could, one of her short gasping breaths. Then she continued: 'Now perhaps you will ask yourself. What else is there that binds us two together except the future?'

'So you agree that we should marry?'

'Your mother is very good, Minke,' she answered.

And so we were married in a mosque outside Bandung at nine o'clock in the morning.

Our wedding present was far too magnificent – the Boers of South Africa were defeated by the English army, an army undefeated for ten years. The Dutch farmers, the Boers, who had founded two small republics, the Republic of Transvaal and the Republic of Oranje Vrijstaat, had surrendered, and England had increased its power and expanded its conquests.

The Dutch farmers had gone to South Africa to seek a better life. Then the English arrived. The Boers fled, crossing the river Vaal, and set up the two new republics. Then gold was found in the Transvaal area. The English returned across the river and war could not be avoided.

Gold! Hope for the future! Defeat for the small and weak. Victory for the big and powerful.

'The English have brought so much trouble to the world,' said Mei. 'Empress Ye Si could not hold them back. In fact, she's ended up working with them. But we can now count the days that Europe will reign over the coloured peoples.'

That was the first time in my life that I had ever heard such an idea.

'There have been so many Europeans who have caused so much suffering in the world.' She told me about Sir John Hawkins, the Englishman who pioneered the slave trade between Africa and America, so that forty million Africans ended up dead or condemned to a life of slavery.

And I had never come across this story before. I had never heard it from anyone or read it anywhere, in school or outside.

5

Once back in Betawi, Mei started to regain her health, and to get her colour back. As the wife of a Native, she no longer had to worry about the residency laws.

Ibu Baldrun grew fonder and fonder of her, even though there remained a huge gap in culture and beliefs, tradition and language. And Mei worked as hard as she could to fit in with her new situation.

Ibu Baldrun forbade her to enter the kitchen. Mei was kept busy with the lighter household chores. Ibu wanted my wife to be healthy, plump and glowing. And Mei became like her own child.

Mei herself didn't pay much attention to her health. She threw herself perhaps too intensely into her study of Malay, even to the extent of learning the Betawi pronunciations. Her Malay quickly improved. Then an old sickness returned – restlessness at being dependent, even upon her own husband. She started giving Mandarin and English lessons to the children of rich Chinese who lived near Kramat. But when I came home from the auction paper office, I always found her waiting on the veranda reading books that I was never able to read. So we would sit and talk about the day's events or about something she had just finished reading. It was during these evening discussions that I began to learn much about China.

I also learnt the background to Mei's departure from China for the Indies, although she herself didn't link her departure to the situation she explained. She and her fiancé – at least that's how I thought of him – had fled from China after the failure of the Yi He Tuan rebellion. Empress Ye Si, with the backing of the Western colonialists in China, carried out a vicious crackdown. Even though the rebellion failed, its organisations continued the struggle against the Ching Dynasty. Mei was a member of one of these organisations, I don't know which one. She mentioned some of their names, but they were too hard for me to remember. So as not to get her suspicious, I never asked her to spell out their names. If I did try to write them down, they'd probably be something like this: Pai Lian Chiao or the White Lilies; Siao Tao Hui or the Little Knife Union; Ke Lao Hui or the Union of the Old Brothers; and many others that I can't remember. It seemed her connection had been with the White Lilies or the Little Knife Union.

I was also able to form the impression that she thought the Thong Society was the strongest Chinese organisation in Java. This movement had been founded by Chinese who fled their country after the failure of the Tai Ping rebellion in the middle of the last century. The Thong didn't like the new wave of exiles, especially not those from the White Lilies movement. This was because the White Lilies not only wanted the overthrow of the Ching dynasty but also wanted a total reformation of China and the founding of a republic.

From many of her other accounts of different things about China, I concluded somewhat hesitantly that China was experiencing a period of instability and turmoil. It was different from Japan, which was growing stronger and more assertive. And when I turned to my own country, I also found stability – the stability of Dutch power.

Her stories always contained so much, were about such important and substantial things. I was always embarrassed when she asked me what I had been reading or what new things I had learnt at school. But I couldn't let her stories pass without countering with one of my own. I once decided to tell her one of my best stories from the medical school – about Diwan, a permanent patient at our hospital. He lived in a cage. He was considered a threat to the community. He was suffering from satyriasis, gonorrhoea and syphilis. He had carried out one hundred and nineteen rapes, fifty-one against humans and the rest on animals.

She seemed to sicken after hearing this. I waited for her to ask what satyriasis was. She didn't ask.

'What was his occupation?'

'He peddled stuff he had scavenged.'

'What schooling did he have?'

'He's illiterate.'

'If he had an education he would be even more dangerous. Do you remember how our friend in Jepara talked about how life could be its own cage? That would make a more interesting story than satyriasis and venereal diseases.'

'But it's a medical student's story. Diwan's got haemorrhoids now.'

'So?'

'It's important, Mei. Because he can cause us to pass or fail our exams, to go up a class or down.'

'Ah, you.'

'So you need to listen to this story. Something different from what we heard about in Jepara. Diwan is always used in the symptomology exams. Any student who doesn't try to get him on side by sending food and so on is bound to fail. He will pretend to have this or that symptom, and you will make the wrong diagnosis.'

'And you know all his diseases?'

'He's got another cartload of diseases.'

'I like stories about people who are sane and think clearly. Even if they've got sick bodies like me.'

'But there are many who are ill in this world for whom medical knowledge might turn out to be important, Mei. You mustn't forget that.'

'Yes, the sick must be attended to. But that which destroys life and society does not need to be cured so that it can resume its destruction. It's more important to cure or replace a sick environment than a sick individual.'

'Then what would happen to all the patients? Who would look after them?' She laughed.

'Why are you laughing, Mei?'

'That's for other doctors to worry about. My husband will be doing more than just curing sick bodies. He is also going to cure a way of life that is rotten. You'll always remember what our friend in Jepara said, won't you?'

And suddenly I realised the purpose of all her stories about the Tai Ping, Yi He Tuan, the White Lilies Association, the Small Knives Association and the Union of Older Brothers. She was leading me to think about what I wanted to do with my life . . .

Every evening at nine I would set off for the dormitory. Mei always walked with me to the gate. She would stand there until Ibu Baldrun called: 'Don't stay outside too long,' and Mei would go inside.

And when I looked back and she was gone, I would hasten my step.

*

1904 was a very important year in our lives.

How could I not say it was important? Like thunder out of a clear sky came a letter addressed to me at the school. Everyone there, staff and students, was excited. I had received an invitation from the Secretariat of the Governor-General to attend the reception to celebrate the appointment of Governor-General van Heutsz, who had just replaced Governor-General Rosenboom.

And just because of a letter everyone now looked upon me with respect, admiration and amazement. The Director and all the other staff reminded me to arrive on time and behave properly so that the school's name and reputation would rise in the eyes of society.

So on the appointed evening my wife and I attended at the Rijswijk Palace. Ibu Baldrun had dressed Mei in Javanese clothes. And I too wore Javanese clothes in accord with the invitation, which indicated that people should dress according to their race.

Before we left home, Ibu Baldrun still had time to ooh and aah as she admired my wife in her Javanese clothes, although she oohed and aahed more about the fact that Mei's ears weren't pierced.

All the invited guests were standing in line before the palace steps: the influential officials, residents and assistant residents, sultans, *bupatis*, directors of government departments, leading plantation administrators, the big importer-exporters, consuls . . . And among these leading figures were my wife and myself! Who wouldn't have been amazed. Me – a leading figure in society!

People were summoned by name to enter the palace. Their names were then called out again by the Governor-General's adjutant. Only the foreign consuls and residents were not summoned. They were the first group to enter. The *bupatis* were called next. Then finally came the one I had been waiting for – my father. He left the *bupatis'* group, and walked confidently and lightly as if walking on a cloud. There was a slit at the back of his shirt so that his bejewelled *keris* could be displayed. His left hand held the tip of the beautiful *batik* that he wore as a *sarong*. At his waist his diamond-studded *keris* challenged the other *bupatis*. And his belt shone with the brilliance of nine kinds of precious stones. He strode along, his last step falling exactly at the end of the path. Then he ascended the stairs into the palace with eyes fixed on the reception area inside.

'My father,' I whispered to Mei.

'What should I do if we meet?'

'Let's hope we don't meet.'

'That's not the right attitude.'

'I don't like patriarchs, no matter who they are.'

'But he's your father.'

'You have never had a father, Mei.'

Then came the summons for myself and my wife, and I too ascended the stairs, the youngest of those invited, with a narrow-eyed wife with alabaster skin dressed in formal black, who quickly became the centre of attention, and who would have guessed that she had entered the Indies illegally!

There were important men and women all about us, all dressed in black. The women carried fans made from sandalwood and peacock feathers, or Japanese paper with drawings in silver or gold ink, or silver jewellery, or silk. Everything was gleaming, including my wife. And even the room itself was brilliant, more brilliant than daylight. It was lit with electric chandeliers. Even the shadows could not find a place. And the air was thick with scents from around the world, especially Paris. The women were wearing all their best jewellery, made all the more gleaming for being on black backgrounds.

In the midst of this hubbub of the Indies elite, there was one person whose glances shot about restlessly – father. He wouldn't dare leave his group – the *bupatis*. But this night the name of his son had been called out among the guests. He wanted to check for himself, he wanted to make sure there was nothing wrong with his hearing. The son in whom he was so disappointed had been honoured with an invitation just like himself and was now here amongst the rulers.

He would never understand. Neither did I.

Before we left home, I had said to my wife: 'We will be entering the den of wild animals.'

When I told her that we had received this invitation from the heavens, she laughed: 'To attend a reception for a person who has instituted permanent humiliation upon your people,' she said. 'There's no harm in it. Let's have a look.'

And now we were in the wild beasts' cave. All these here in their formal dress were members of the wild animals' pack. We were just observers, witnesses.

'Have you ever been to a reception like this?'

She shook her head. She looked so beautiful, like a flower in bloom. I was proud to see so many eyes turn in her direction. And it seemed that she was used to being stared at by men. She didn't feel awkward; neither did she flaunt herself.

There's no need to retell the details of all the formalities. It was just the usual speeches, shaking of hands, toasts, taking of official photographs, drinking of liquor, laughter and competitive display of riches.

But one thing did happen that was out of the ordinary. When I shook hands with the Governor-General, he remembered me.

'Ah, Mr Minke,' he said, as if he wasn't the highest official in the land, as if he wasn't the representative of Her Majesty. 'You look very handsome with your moustache, Sir. It's a pity we haven't had a chance to meet again. You have no objections, do you, to us getting together to have a bit of a chat now and again?'

'Of course not, Your Excellency,' I answered. 'And this is my wife.'

He had already put out his hand.

'You have shown great ability in choosing a wife, Sir. Congratulations.'

'Congratulations on your appointment, Your Excellency,' Mei said in English.

'Thank you. Thank you.'

Such a long conversation had held up the queue behind us. And I could also see my father standing a little away across in front of us, examining us closely. Perhaps he will be angry with Mei and me for not bowing down before this Governor-General, general and victor in the Aceh War. Why, we even dared smile as if he were an old friend.

After the formalities were over, the guests moved about as they wished. Father would now have his chance to look for us.

We sat near a big pillar that had the Tricolour wrapped round it. Mei was watching what was happening around her. We had no acquaintances among all these big-shots. We hadn't yet joined this pack of wild beasts. And then what I had been fearing happened – my father found us.

I greeted him with a deep bow. He seemed to like that.

'And this is my wife, Father's daughter-in-law,' I introduced Mei.

My wife also bowed reverently before him.

'And why haven't you visited Mother in B – ?' he asked Mei.

'I just follow what my husband says,' I translated.

'What language is that, Son?'

'English, Father.'

'God Almighty! A daughter-in-law who speaks English!' and to me: 'You've got a strange way of choosing a woman.'

After the reception was over, we went by carriage to his hotel, Hotel Des Indes. He was very friendly and asked many questions of my wife. He ordered someone to take us home and asked that we come back the next morning. He promised to send a carriage. He didn't try to lord it over me. It was as if he had never behaved in the past the way he had, as if the past had not left its wounds within me.

And I knew it was all because I had received an invitation from the Governor-General's office.

Only Mei went back the next day. That afternoon, when I was working at the auction paper office, I tried to imagine the two of them sitting across from one another, unable to speak one with the other. They probably spent their time just oohing and aahing, shaking their heads and grinning. Or would father think to hire a hotel translator? He probably would never think of doing anything like that.

But when I got back to Ibu Baldrun's, it was something different that I found. Father, dressed in an ordinary suit, was waiting. Ibu Baldrun was busy preparing a meal for a *bupati* – she was cutting up three chickens! Mei was entertaining father. She was wearing far too much jewellery. No doubt father had bought it for her at the hotel. And it wasn't just any jewellery! Ai! how the Javanese aristocrat likes to show off when he gives gifts. Never caring if it will take him years to pay it all off later, or that it will only be repaid with great difficulty. The main thing is to defend one's prestige.

Father greeted me as if I were also a *bupati*. He didn't demand I crawl along the floor. We all sat on the same divan. He was extraordinarily friendly. Perhaps he was proud that he had a son and daughter-in-law who had received an invitation from the Governor-General. He'll be telling that story everywhere. My son's not even a *bupati* and he has already been honoured with such an invitation! He and van Heutsz chatted and laughed together! None of his children-in-law nor any of his other children had ever received such an honour.

Now he didn't feel humiliated to be sitting at the same level as his son and daughter-in-law. And it was Mei who was the first to be honoured in that way. It was the first time father did not feel cheated not to receive obeisance. Perhaps he already understood – in his grandchildren's time, in the future, making obeisance would disappear from the face of the earth.

Only those with a slave mentality would still be doing it.

He asked about Mei's antecedents.

'She is a person who was born into this world without ever knowing her father or mother.' He listened as if he was capturing some kind of secret knowledge, 'she was brought up in an orphanage in Shanghai, and graduated from teachers' college. Then she came to the Indies to find me.'

'So you have been in contact with each other through correspondence.'

'That is the case, Father.'

'It seems that the search for a mate no longer bothers about crossing land and sea. It's only crossing different ages that is not possible,' he said. And to my wife: 'When will you come to B – ? I and your mother will put on the biggest wedding party ever for you both.'

'I don't think that's necessary, Father.'

'You don't regret not having a celebration?'

'It's not a matter of having regrets, Father. It's just that our situation doesn't permit us to go to B – I'm too busy with my studies and my work, and so too is my wife. She doesn't want to leave her pupils.'

'You both work! Why should a woman work when she already has a husband? Is the husband worth so little that the wife must also go out and struggle?'

Now the trouble would start. We didn't answer.

'Only among peasants and in the villages, that's the only place where you find both working. Or among the peddlers and small traders. And peasants and peddlers do not receive invitations from His Excellency the Governor-General. You two do not properly appreciate the honour.'

Seeing a somewhat unfavourable situation emerging, Mei retired to the kitchen. And so this patriarch now had his chance to once more become my king.

'My wife has been offended by Father's words,' I threatened.

And I could see that he was trying to keep himself under control. He was reflecting. He adjusted his *destar* and whispered: 'That's the trouble with taking a wife who is not Javanese.'

'I have also been offended.'

'You!'

His eyes moved around everywhere. But there was nothing and nobody to help him. He was a foreigner in this place.

'Perhaps that's why you two didn't tell anybody about your marriage?'

'We married for our own sake,' I said curtly. 'As for whether good or bad comes from it, we also assume responsibility for that. We do not interfere in others' affairs, nor do we want anyone to interfere in ours.'

He had to work harder and harder to control his fury. He no longer radiated the same friendliness as he had earlier. And when he saw that I wasn't going to speak any more, he began, with great deliberateness: 'If that's what you

86

want, very well, it is what you want. Your parents can only pray for your well-being, your happiness, your safety. We can do no more than that.'

Dinner passed in silence. There was no more conversation. Father returned to his hotel, his feelings kept to himself. And that was the first time I refused to acknowledge his authority.

But this wasn't the only important thing to happen in 1904.

The appointment of van Heutsz as Governor-General gave rise to many fears among those pockets of the Indies archipelago that had so far been able to retain their independence. War would find its way into all those areas – that was not difficult to predict. Even early on after van Heutsz's appointment, many of the inhabitants of these areas fled into the areas under the control of the Netherlands Indies. None of them wanted to have to defend their homelands, still free and independent, in the face of rifle and cannon.

Van Heutsz and the whole Indies ruling class understood how these free states feared the rifle and cannon of the Netherlands Indies. The General deliberately postponed taking any military action against them. And this was not because the cannon belonging to the free states numbered more than seventy. On the contrary, his strategy was to exhibit mercy and compassion. He banned the practice of the burning of widows at their husband's funerals that was then prevalent in Bali. No longer would women be fated to become ashes as they joined their husband's soul. And he was praised to the heavens, especially by his fellow Europeans. The Government also went out of its way to be seen to be abolishing slavery in the areas it controlled.

The whisperings and rumours and other unclearly sourced talk all said these actions were meant to be a cover for bloody military actions that were being planned. People waited, certain there would be war. It wasn't for nothing, people said, that a general was made Governor-General, the highest official in the Netherlands Indies, the representative of the Royal Netherlands Crown. Look, they said, even the flea-sized republics of the Transvaal and Oranje Vrijstaat in South Africa were gobbled up by the British. Do you think the Dutch won't do the same here?

But none of this happened. The threat from Japan and Russia was a greater worry for the Netherlands Indies. The Germans, French, English, Russians and Japanese were all eyeing the coal station on the Indies island of Sabang. And some people started saying that van Heutsz would not start anything in the Indies while the cannons of Europe's navies could set the Indies on fire at any time. People called this Sabang politics. This was why a general was made Governor-General. The coal station at Sabang was a big source of foreign exchange for the Indies, but it must not become the reason for the destruction of the whole Indies.

There was no military action from van Heutsz. But there was something else: the implementation of one of the policies from the platform the Liberal Movement had been campaigning for – the Ethical Policy, *EMIGRATION*.

I got all these ideas from the auction paper. One afternoon at the paper, a white-bearded priest came in, together with a flaming-red-faced man. The crucifix hanging around the priest's neck seemed to want to comb his disintegrating chest-long whiskers. Both were Pure-Blood Europeans. They sat down on the guests' divan, and, ignoring anyone else present, continued their argument – in German.

'Impossible, my friend,' said the priest. 'Van Heutsz is a soldier. There are only guns in his skull, and the little brains he needs to be able to use them for killing.'

The other man, in his short-sleeved white shirt, undone buttons and white pants, rubbed out his cigar in the ash-tray: 'But those with small brains are usually scared of bigger killers. How many warships does the Indies have? And anyway they're already falling apart. How many warships could the Netherlands send? Even with another hundred ships, we could not secure the Indies' ten thousand miles!'

'But the Netherlands is an ally of the British! And the English rule the waves!'

'Once van Heutsz fires on one of the free states, Father, one of his colonial rivals will come to their aid. He won't move before the crisis between Russia and Japan comes to a head. Killers are always afraid of their more expert rivals.'

My boss winked at me. I went across to the two men. And in my broken German, asked what I could do for them. They went quiet, and left without excusing themselves.

After he heard from me what they'd been talking about, my boss repeated one of his most common instructions: 'Make all our customers understand: there will be no war! I don't care if it's a German, Swiss, Belgian or English, who is thinking of selling his mine or plantation. There will be no war! Even with the support he's got from the Liberals and the campaigners for the Ethical Policy, van Heutsz will not risk the Indies.'

This was the message that we repeated to all our clients: There will be no war. War will not come. What we did announce every week was – emigration and . . . emigration. Emigration for the Javanese pea- sant – a caste that have become the grass eaters and are no longer of use to the meat-eating caste. Grass-eating animals can still be a meal for meat eaters. And in the human world? Mankind has civilisation, he doesn't pounce and kill in one go, people still have a chance to redeem themselves, even in instalments.

And so it was with van Heutsz's promise. For the emigrants, everything was guaranteed – transport, tools, kitchen utensils, food for six months. You could repay in instalments – in accord with the spirit of human civilisation.

Thus propagandised the busy village officials! But there were only a few Javanese farmers who pulled up roots and moved. Because, said an anonymous leaflet, the land was filled with a mystical power that bound the Javanese peasant to his land. Even when the land was no longer his. Those who did pull up roots were those without grass among the grass eaters, those for whom the earth provided no livelihood at all.

Sugar! hissed Ter Haar in a letter to me. *Sugar needs land. It's all tied in with sugar. People are sent to Lampung to protect the Sunda Straits. The straits are undefended while the coast is unpopulated and unoccupied. Don't think that van Heutsz has thought of all this himself. It's all tied in with our stategy of defending ourselves from the threat from the north. Because all those stronger than us are to the north.*

And Mr Kaarsen for the umpteenth time soldered onto me his ideas: 'No other general could have conquered Aceh except van Heutsz. That iron-hearted man will do whatever he thinks he has to do. Even the tiger's whiskers would droop before him. And look at the emigration policy. Does he force anybody to go? See how he can show great compassion to people as well. He is moved too by the plight of the peasants who have no land, who have no secure livelihood. So what does he do for them? They can open up as much jungle as they are able, and that land will become theirs, and they're even given a money stake as well.'

'Very generous. And whose forest is he giving away, Sir?'

'Government forest. Yes, Mr Minke, it's no longer guns that determine how things go. It's no longer Pasopati or Rujakpolo who rule with their magical weapons, but the genius who can use his weapons in a game of out-manoeuvring his enemy. You too, Sir, if you had weapons and could use them properly, you too could decide what happens in the world. Even a cat could.'

'A cat?'

'Or a *biawak*, and you don't even have to own them. You can get guns on credit.'

It was also in 1904 that Mr Kaarsen reported that it would be van Heutsz who started to implement the second plank of the Liberal's plat-form – education, the establishment of primary schools for village people. According to Kaarsen, van Heutsz was trying his hardest to get the support of the Free Democratic Party.

The Russian-Japanese crisis exploded. And the Tsushima Straits wit-nessed the destruction of the Russian armada. Japan ruled the waves; and Asia rode the wind. The war did not spread. And the Sabang coal station returned to raking in profits without having to worry about any threats from anywhere.

Before I could digest all this, let alone come to some kind of appropriate conclusion, something extraordinary occurred at school. There was a 'public lecture'. It was announced that any member of the public could attend – even from outside the school. And everyone would have the right to put forward their opinions, ideas and criticisms.

'A demonstration of democracy,' I said to Mei when I suggested she come along, and after I had learnt a little more about the meaning of democracy. 'It should be very interesting. Just think. Everyone will have equal rights to put forward their views and criticisms. It's like a fairy-tale. Would you like to go, Mei?'

The 'lecture' was given by a graduate of several decades before – a retired Java Doctor from the palace in Jogjakarta.

The doctor was a small, thin, bent man. He wore a *surjan* and a Jogjakarta *destar*. His long moustache drooped at the side of his mouth. His eyes were sunken, yet they shone in his old age. He bowed to different people around the hall as he entered. Several teachers, all Europeans, followed behind him. He looked like a genuine *priyayi* of the old school. His movements were smooth and refined, as were his words and his voice.

He sat in the front row with the teachers. When he was introduced to the gathering by one of the teachers, he stood up and, stooping, walked over to the podium, nodded to the teachers, and the students, fixed his *destar*, brushed the sleeves of his *surjan* with his hands, placed his hands on the podium, cleared his throat, gave a fatherly smile, and began.

'May God give his blessing to you teachers, students and other people present here tonight.' He spoke in thickly-accented Dutch, with a true Javanese accent. 'I give thanks for this opportunity to meet you all, who have been willing to waste your time to listen to my simple words. However my voice may sound, I very much hope that what I say tonight will be heard not only by your ears, but also by your hearts.'

I gave my wife a bit of a translation.

'He speaks so slowly,' she whispered.

'You must be patient when dealing with a true Javanese aristocrat, who has been educated in the old Javanese ways of writing and speaking,' I answered in a whisper.

'What can he say with such a weak presence?'

'How do I know? Let's listen and observe this demonstration of democracy.'

The retired Java Doctor continued with his speech.

'Today's medical school is more advanced than it was thirty years ago. The science of medicine has also added much to its store of knowledge. More and more germs and bacteria and their characteristics are being identified as a result of the new methods of making cultures. And more than that, the new generation of medical students looks more dashing, more enthusiastic, more handsome and more interesting.'

A happy murmur rose up from the students.

'He's clever with the polite chatter,' whispered Mei.

Of course, he went on, the teachers are also cleverer, more knowledgeable, have greater understanding, and are wiser. So therefore the number of students has also grown.

His thickly-accented Dutch almost brought the non-Javanese students to laughter, which they had to strain to keep under control. I myself began to doubt whether this bent, old and weak retired doctor with his thick accent could possibly have anything to offer. His opening wandered, was full of trivial chit-chat, boring and uninteresting. And it was made even more tedious for me by the fact that I had to translate it all. I began to regret inviting Mei.

He'd been practising as a Java Doctor now for thirty years. None of the students had yet reached forty years, which was the best age of all. At that age people start to look back and ask themselves: What have you contributed to this life, hey, you, educated man? Medicine only for the sick patient, or for a sick way of life too? Already you students can probably imagine asking yourself that question one day. The reason is simple. Students are among the educated class, a class who have had the opportunity to obtain greater knowledge and understanding than their fellow-countrymen. Intelligent people, clever people – not those with only scientific knowledge – will always be interested in the problems of life, and especially the vital aspects of life. They will be interested in thinking about them, solving the problems, and making some contribution. The vital aspects of life were, he went on, happiness, suffering, love and compassion, service, truth, justice, power . . . In a few years' time, the students here will be out practising as doctors, excelling in one of the vital areas of life – suffering. The most intense of sufferings, a suffering intertwined with poverty, with powerlessness.

His words came out faster, took on more substance, and became more interesting.

All the time he had been a doctor, he said, he had been saving money in the bank. Who knew if one day it would be of use? He lived from his pension, had never touched his savings. Now in his old age, with only a little strength remaining (he lifted up his little finger, pointing to his fingernail), he found himself having to face more and more of the big issues of life. Sometimes they came in a group, sometimes unexpectedly. Sometimes people weren't aware of what was needed because they just didn't have the capacity to understand. He didn't know if among the students there were any who knew, knew what was really needed . . . yes, what was it they should know? He seemed to be plucking at the air for an answer – an old man who'd forgotten what he had to say.

People laughed, and he seemed to be encouraged by the laughter.

Yes, what . . . He grasped about again . . . something, something that is absolutely not a laughing matter.

There was more laughter, even from Mei.

'Because,' he said, at last, 'What I am talking about is the awakening of a people's consciousness. Not the decline of a people.'

The laughter ceased.

He pointed northwards. Up there was to be found an Asian people who stood tall and firm and were respected. They were recognised by all the civilised peoples of the world as their equals. What other people had achieved that recognition except the Japanese? We are far, far away from Japan but we still feel the waves that it has made – we, the educated. And this is even more the case for the intelligent. What is it that we should understand from this? It is that the emergence of Japan has begun to change the face of the world. Only those who understand this will grasp what is happening. It would be a great pity if there were among the students any who did not understand what had made these developments possible. Come on then, who here among the students, or anywhere in these Indies, understands what was behind this development?

He looked down on the first row – the teachers – then shifted his gaze to the rest of the audience. No one attempted an answer to his question.

He seemed disappointed that there were no answers. He went on: 'No, none of you understand. It is only the Eurasians and the Chinese Mixed-Bloods who understand what has to be done. Indeed, it was actually the Chinese who first showed that they understood the lessons of Japan. They responded to Japan's awakening. They organised themselves. They organised themselves here in the Indies so that they could begin the process of awakening their own people – through education. Their first organisation was the Tiong Hoa Hwee Koan. And it was the first organisation of its type in the Indies – the first modern organisation.'

Then he asked another question: What then is a modern organisation? Again there were no replies.

Such an organisation, he explained, was not only organised democratically but was also recognised by the authorities – in this case, by the Netherlands Indies Government. And furthermore, he added, such an organisation stands before the law with the same rights as a Pure-Blood European! Such an organisation is recognised under the law as a body corporate.

This organisation, he said, was founded in 1900 when we Natives were still asleep, asleep in our cradle of ignorance. It was a beautiful and peaceful sleep. And it seems that nothing has changed today. He asked that he be forgiven if this was not truly the case. So we Natives have been left behind not only by the Chinese but also by the Arabs who live here in the Indies. Three years after the Chinese, realising their deficiencies compared to Japan, began their struggle, the Arabs did likewise. They established a similar organisation called the Sumatra Batavia Alkhariah. While all this was happening the Natives continued to sleep peacefully.

Quiet and an atmosphere of concentration descended upon the auditorium. No one noticed his accented Dutch and his strange style of speech any more.

The Arabs established their first organisation in 1902. Now a more advanced one was being established, the Jamiatul Khair. It had a similar program to that of the Tiong Hoa Hwee Koan – it emphasised education. It had also registered as a legal body, so it too now had the same status under the law as a Pure-Blood European. Both the Chinese and Arab organisations were working to bring their people into the modern era. The Chinese brought in teachers from China and Japan, while the Arabs' teachers came from Algeria and Tunisia. If we Natives began organising now we would be starting from behind. The score at the moment is Chinese 4 – Natives 0; Chinese 4 – Arabs 2, and Arabs 2 – Natives 0. That's how many years we are behind.

He reminded us that we students of the medical school were the most highly educated Natives in the Indies. Then he asked us another question. But first he took out a white handkerchief and wiped his mouth. There was no glass of water for him and the thirstier he became the more he wiped his mouth. Then came his next question: Were we Natives willing to lag so far behind the Chinese and Arabs? Even if we started now, he said, we would still be at least four years behind the Chinese. Such an organisation would have to get legal recognition this year, if we were not to fall yet another year behind. And if this was not done, it would mean that the Native people of the Indies would never have anyone who could represent them before the law, who could defend them before the law. He said he could not imagine anything sadder than there being no one here today, the cream of the educated Natives, who thought that their countrymen needed and deserved to be defended.

To be a doctor, a public servant, a servant of humankind – this was not enough! He called on us to start organising, to educate the children, to prepare them for the modern era, their own era.

He explained how he had come to this realisation only in his old age after he had seen the rapid progress made by the Chinese community. Then they were followed by the Arabs who awoke and started to try to catch up. And what about us, the Natives. All of you? Will you awake too, or will you stay asleep? What will happen to you all, if you never begin?

He was out taking a stroll one day, thinking about all these things, he went on to tell us, when something happened. A man had been injured in an accident with a horse-cart. If he wasn't helped quickly he would die of loss of blood. The old doctor bandaged him up as best he could and then took the man off to the hospital.

It was then that he realised that it was only because of his patient's helplessness that he had ended up in hospital. Over tens of years he had tended to at least one person a day. This meant he had looked after about thirty thousand patients altogether. And of those less than one per cent had come to him voluntarily. No one ever came to him if they were only a little sick, or had only a small injury. They were nearly all illiterate. They only ever visited a doctor if they had been involved in an accident or if some official had ordered them to do so.

Some had died in his arms because they had come too late, when too much damage had already been done. Most returned to society rehabilitated to their former state. The thief returned as a thief. The clerk returned to his desk. The blackbirder for European companies went on kidnapping Javanese.

As he walked home from the hospital that day, the old doctor had reached the following conclusion – even with decades of service as a doctor, he had made no meaningful contribution to the advancement of his people. It was true that medicine was a humanitarian profession. But what a waste it would be if all it amounted to was patching things up so that things could go on without ever changing. He wanted to help further the advancement of his people. A doctor must not only cure the disease of the body, he must also awaken the spirit of his people, anaesthetised by their own ignorance.

So he didn't go straight home. He turned right and set off for the bank. He withdrew all his thirty years of savings. Mind you, he was a Java Doctor, not a European doctor, so his savings weren't that of a European. Java Doctors were not allowed to accept fees for their services. All he had was his salary. Nothing else.

And he had used that money to travel throughout Java. Everywhere he urged the Native leaders to set up organisations that could help advance the people.

'Now I stand before you, students of the Batavia Medical School, where I too once studied to be a doctor, and where I now call out to you all, as an old man with little remaining strength, as a retired Java Doctor. You must realise that you are being left behind! Wake up! Get out of bed! Rub your eyes so that you can see better and more clearly what is happening! Begin, Sirs, begin! Start now! Organise! The further you are left behind, the harder it will be to catch up. You will lag further and further behind the Japanese. We will be a people who remain the servants of our own guests.'

He stopped, exhausted.

'That's how the young doctors in our movement also talk,' said Mei. 'I think it's no accident that it's always the doctors who are the first to think this way.'

And the retired Java Doctor went on: If a doctor cures a murderer so that he returns to society to do more murders, then the doctor too is an accomplice . . .

The noisy students and trouble-makers forgot they had to yack and make trouble. Every accented, slow and drawn-out Dutch word that came from him was like another heavy millstone resting on the backs of us in the audience.

But the doctor has no right or power to stop a murderer returning to his evil ways just because he has cured him. And if the doctor had killed his murderous patient, then all that would have happened is that a murderer would have been murdered. Yet, if the doctor let his murderous patient live, then others might die as the victims of his former patient. You students are not being taught to be doctors like Tanca, are you? Who knows about the physician, Tanca?

No one knew.

It's worth knowing about Tanca. He was typical of the kind of doctor-murderer that practised during the period of the Majapahit Empire. Emperor Kala Gemet Jayanegara fell ill. Some said it was a skin disease, others said it was a stomach ailment. Tanca operated on him. You didn't know that they did surgery in those days, heh! Ever since there have been more than a thousand people on this earth, people have been operating on each other. The emperor underwent the operation. With or without orders from somebody else, Tanca murdered his patient to bring an end to the troubles that were inflicting the empire. There have always been the Dr Tancas. He was not the only one. Now we are in the modern era. Nowadays a person is not held responsible for everything that happens in the world. Our responsibility is only for that little portion of the world's activities that is our own work . . .

'He's stretching the point here,' I whispered to Mei.

During all his years as a doctor, he went on, whenever he cured a patient who was a good man, of noble heart, he too felt a right to be happy, knowing that such a person would go out to light up the world around him once more.

In the modern world, everything is specialisation. People will become alienated from each other. People will only have cause to meet because of business or they will meet by accident only. You will no longer be able to tell if the person you are treating is a good man or not. But we can make a guess that our patients will not be honourable, or at least, not so honourable. Such an honourable character is the result of a good basic education. It is such an education that gives rise to good deeds and actions. The peoples of the Indies do not yet educate their sons and daughters. Our people still live as barbarians, and they, as a people, are indeed barbarians, unable to achieve any honour for themselves, let alone for their people as a whole.

'Stop!' suddenly his voice became harsh, jolting everybody.

He did not mean to pass over the honourable achievements of the peoples of the Indies. But going into this modern age also meant that old values had to make way for the new. The old ways of honour will experience a change of form. And if the form changes, so too will the content. There is no form without content, no content without form.

It was the task of the Native doctors not only to treat wounds and cure disease, but also to treat and cure the soul, and also the people's future. Who would do this if not those of us who are educated? And indeed is it not also true that the mark of a modern man is his ability to overcome his environment based on his own abilities and efforts? Those individuals who are strong of character need to join together, to raise up their weaker countrymen, to bring light into the darkness, to give eyes to the blind.

The most advanced of individuals, the most capable, can stop developing, can be drowned in the ocean of backwardness and bad traditions because of two reasons – lack of opportunity and lack of finances. The peoples of the Indies are too poor. It is the duty of those who are not too poor to pay for the education of Native children. They must pay the way for those Natives who are clever, have talent, but are poor. This will help prepare them so all can live in accordance with the modern age instead of being its victims.

In order to do all this, there must be organisation. A big association of people who can manage things and look after the finances. It will not matter who is in need of help – the child of a *priyayi*, a carpenter or a farmer.

Then he went on to tell us how he had made this call in many of the big towns of Java. He had met many well-educated and important Javanese. But there had been no response. He felt like a wanderer shouting in the desert. And now he summoned the students of the medical school: Build an organisation – now! Unite! If we do not begin today, the peoples of the Indies will be condemned to live as barbarians for eternity.

He descended from the podium. He looked exhausted. Only when he had sat down again with the teachers was he given a glass of water which he drank to its last drop.

Then there was a question and answer period. But this was a new idea. We Natives had never experienced this situation where you were allowed to ask questions of someone like this in public. None of the students spoke up.

Perhaps the retired doctor was very disappointed to see this 'demonstration of democracy' receive so little approbation. Once more the request was made for questions. But modern organisation was as alien as the leprosy bacteria.

Suddenly Mei whispered many ideas to me, and I decided to ask them: 'First of all I apologise, Doctor, for my own ignorance. What do you mean by an "organisation"? In Japan, advanced and patriotic individuals are financially looked after by the Emperor. In China this is done by organisations of students who collect money wherever they can, including overseas. What's the right kind of organisation for the Indies?'

And even without looking I knew that everyone in the hall was turning to look in my direction – not to look at me, but at my wife. Indeed no one knew that we had been married for these last few years. I felt uneasy being the object of their stares. Especially as my questions actually came from Mei.

I could imagine Mei's eyes shining brightly in anticipation of learning something new about the Indies. She had been urging me for some time now to set up an organisation but I did not know how to begin. She said I should talk it over with my closest friends, but I had no close friends. I was still kept busy by my own affairs and the affairs of both of us together.

The retired doctor returned to the podium. He explained incident by incident all that the Japanese Emperor had done to modernise his country and people, beginning from the arrival of Admiral Perry at Yokohama.

I already knew about all these incidents, but I hadn't realised how they all linked together to become a huge, impressive mountain of actions.

He acknowledged that he did not know much about the Chinese organisations, but he was still able to tell of some that I had never heard of either. I translated it all for Mei. And that wasn't all. He also told of how these organisations sent people all over the world, wherever there was a Chinese community.

Mei squeezed my arm.

He told of how a few years ago there was a young Chinese man killed in Surabaya, that he was sent from China, and that people thought he had been killed by the Old Generation who opposed all forms of modernisation and renewal. And it wasn't only men that were sent overseas, but women also. And the foundation of the Tiong Hoa Hwee Koan in the Indies was certainly a victory for them, whatever obstacles had been put in their way by those with outdated views.

Mei prodded me with her elbow and whispered something else to me. She mentioned the name of Dewi Sartika. And I passed it on: 'What are your views, Sir, on the efforts of Nyi Dewi Sartika in Cicalengka?'

He nodded several times, praising this woman from Priangan. He hoped that many would copy her actions, men as well. He said that he was disappointed he had not yet been able to visit her to express his admiration for her. But, he said, the efforts of one person, backed at the most by one's family, or perhaps only her husband, cannot produce all that much. An organisation, only a big organisation can do that.

'And what are your views on the girl from Jepara?'

He said she was a person who could have won the heavens as well as grasp the earth. It's a pity she did not understand her own strength. He bowed his head, speaking under his breath. And then we learned that that extraordinary girl had only recently passed away.

Mei let out a cry. She quickly covered her mouth with a handkerchief. 'So young?'

Ah, what is not possible in this world? The old man said that he had visited Rembang to meet her, to listen to her call to the Javanese. But the Rembang *pendopo* was full of people paying their last respects. He recognised Dr Ravenstein, who had treated the girl. Seeing him sitting on the floor, the

European doctor nodded and then left. He would never get to meet this woman from Jepara. That brilliant and noble-hearted woman had died surrounded by the sad wailing of the people of the area. *Inna lillahi* . . . that brilliant soul had gone to meet the Lord. Such an outstanding woman. And still there was no man to equal her . . .

With news of her death, the cry of the doctor for us to start an organisation became an anti-climax. The questions and answers came to an end. No one else wanted to speak. Once more he tried to convince us: Start organising now. Study about organising in the modern way.

The old man, the shouter in the desert, agreed to receive us where he was staying, at six o'clock in the evening. Perhaps he was pleased to receive such a request.

We walked home to Ibu Baldrun's.

'Perhaps he also knows your names, Mei.'

'He might know our names, but he doesn't know us.'

I knew she was never afraid of being caught by the police.

'Don't be angry. See, even I have never asked your real name.'

'Thank you. I think we've been happy enough, haven't we?'

Between us it was as if we had signed an agreement not to talk about names, and that we would not have children for an as yet unspecified period of time. She seemed certain that no one could know who she really was.

I still remember the letter I translated for her some time ago. It was a reply to a letter from Jepara just before the woman from Jepara had married a *bupati*. At the time, there were many rumours that the Governor-General was pressuring her father not to put off her marriage to a suitable husband much longer. Perhaps, at that time, only she herself was unaware of those rumours. All the students at the medical school knew. I also told Mei about the reports. And Mei had commented: 'Believe me, forcing someone to marry like that could easily happen here, as it could in any other backward country.'

It was reported that the Resident for Central Java had made a list of suitable candidates. Apparently it was a very long list, including people from outside Java. This modern girl, alone in her traditional, pre-marriage solitude, must be married, silenced in the marriage bed.

At the peak of the rumours, Mei received a letter from Jepara. It said that the girl had decided not to dishonour or disappoint her parents. She would take the middle path, she would marry, and await the freedom of being a widow. It was the only way that she could carry out her ideas, the only way.

Now she was as free as she ever would be.

The evening meeting with the old doctor began with an avalanche of questions from Mei. What was his source of information about the men and women sent out from China? From where came the report of the murder of the Chinese man in Surabaya? What were the relationships between the different organisations?

The old Java Doctor did not give a clear answer about his sources. He gave the names of some of the young supporters of the Old Generation group. Now, he said, there had been a wave of revenge against the Old Generation members accused of being involved in the young Chinese man's murder. There was chaos in Surabaya. Blood had flowed. This had all taken place within the Chinese community itself. The police had not been able to intervene. The leaders of both the Young Generation and Old Generation organisations had entered the Indies illegally.

And the troubles had only been about how they fix their hair – pro and anti pigtail. A group of young men surrounded others just to cut off their pigtails. Sometimes those who were surrounded did not lose one strand of hair. It was the attackers who were left bruised and swollen. *Silat* had spoken.

Did he know if any of the Young Generation had been arrested? No, he didn't know.

6

Dr van Staveren explained that the syphilis bacteria had finally been definitively identified by the German zoologist, Fritz Schauddin. He had also been assisted by another German syphilologist from Bonn, Dr Eric Hoffman. This meant that *Treponema pallidum* and syphilis could now be distinguished from gonococcus gonorrhoea. Most syphilis patients also suffered from gonorrhoea and for a long time it had been impossible to distinguish between the two diseases.

This evil bacteria has had quite a long history. It spread as an epidemic all over Europe around about the time Columbus returned from his newly-discovered continent. The epidemic started in Spain and Italy. People began to speculate that it had been brought to Europe from America by Columbus's men. It then spread to France and Germany. A few years later an epidemic broke out in the Netherlands and Greece and then later in England and Scotland, followed by Russia and Poland.

The result? Poor old Diwan was taken out of his cell and he became the subject for our study of *Treponema pallidum* and gonococcus.

One afternoon, while sitting outside the house, I told Mei about Fritz Schaudin and Eric Hoffman, and also about Diwan.

She didn't get angry like the last time. She just sat there staring at me as if waiting for me to tell some more interesting story. But I had nothing more interesting to tell.

'So you haven't heard?'

'Heard what?'

'I read about it in a Chinese paper at the home of one of my students . . .'

War had broken out in the north. Russia had sent trainload after trainload of soldiers across the icy wastelands of Siberia to Manchuria. The non-European world, even to the smallest island in the ocean, had been swept up into European empires. And Russia felt left out.

Japan would quickly be defeated by the Russian armoury, the newspaper report had said. Trainloads of medals were already on their way to decorate the soon-to-be-victorious Russian soldiers. What threat were the yellow-skinned soldiers of Asia? One sweep at them and they'd all be scampering away. A huge armada had left the northern harbours to make a journey half-way round the world, staggering all the way from a boycott by coal suppliers. Through the straits of Malacca up to Vladivostok they headed, ready to cut off Japan's supplies from the crest of the ocean's waves.

Japan had not been prepared to sit idly by without conquests of its own – it wanted Manchuria for itself. It had become a matter of honour for a country to be able to enslave another people, to rob and exploit another people.

And in Betawi, the Japanese shops, barbers, drink-sellers, prostitutes, peddlers, all flew the flag of the Rising Sun. Japan was on everybody's lips.

'I haven't read any reports like that,' I said.

'It's impossible that the report I read was a lie.'

At the medical school, none of the Dutch papers in the library mentioned any news of the war. I still didn't really believe that the report was true.

Then about a week later the Dutch press carried a report containing just a snippet of what Mei had told me. The Malay language papers followed. The news flowed everywhere like water finding the lowest spot to rest. Everyone wanted to know who was winning in this war between the baby and the giant. Those educated in *wayang* tended to barrack for the Japanese; no new knights were born, grew and became mighty without being tested, they said.

I too became excited. At the school no one could stop talking about what was happening, discussing what was going on. The eternally snow-capped Mt Fuji took a hold on our minds.

Then one afternoon, when I thought I'd mastered the issues, I explained to Mei the course of the big naval battle that had taken place in the Tsushima Straits, a story of old sailors and old admirals, all of whom had sworn to deliver a victory for the Czar or die . . .

She was fascinated by my story. Her narrow-slit eyes gazed out without blinking. This always aroused my passions, as she knew, but this time she just ignored the signs.

'What is there to admire?' she said coldly. 'Whether Russia or Japan wins it will be no victory for humanity. And if Russia is defeated, it will not be a defeat that benefits humanity. They are two wolves fighting over their victim.'

She went on to tell me about the rise of British imperialism, beginning with the invention of the steam engine by James Watt, opening a new chapter in the history of industry, giving rise to the accumulation of capital and the separation of labour from capital, which brought the enslavement of the coloured peoples by English capital.

'Minke, I don't think it was an accident that you told me the other day about *Treponema pallidum* – that's how you say it, isn't it – and gonococcus. That's what Japanese and English imperialism are like. Two bacteria, each wanting to ruin the world the way Diwan's body has been destroyed. What? Why are you making such a face?'

'Yes, Mei, perhaps I know what you're getting at. But there is still something that you don't seem to want to recognise. How can you not admire an Asian people, from such a small country, so courageously taking on a European people from such a huge country as Russia?'

'Japan is not so different in size from England. Ordinary human beings eat things that are smaller than their mouths. Those bacteria, as well as England and Japan, do the opposite.' She spoke slowly and her voice was hard, inflamed with hatred, burning, tense with conviction. 'Surely you remember what happened to our friend in Jepara? These bacteria eat up both the flesh and the world they live in. You of all people should understand this!' she said bitterly. 'And isn't it true that all the nations that the Europeans have conquered these last three hundred years have been much, much bigger than their conquerors? And that the small are not always defeated, and that indeed it is the big ones that are usually defeated by them? The tiny bacteria can also bring down an elephant.'

I regretted having told her the news with such enthusiasm. She had a different starting-point and perspective.

'I'm sorry we differ on this matter. Look, these two kinds of bacteria that you have reported about have no nationality. Both of them are only after victims. Without victims they themselves would die. There's no need to barrack for Japan. You know that we fight against the Ching dynasty, even though it is also Chinese, because they not only collaborate with those bacteria, they themselves are another kind of evil bacteria. Forgive me. Can you understand?'

Japan's victory greatly worried Ang San Mei. The rising power of Japan had also worried my late friend in Surabaya. They may be right, I thought. Though Japan may defeat Russia and swallow up Manchuria, China would be its first real victim.

'It may not only be China that is grabbed by Japan but all the weaker countries of Asia that have not yet been conquered by Europe. And perhaps even those that have been gobbled up by Europe could also be taken over.'

Before we had properly finished our converstaion, a friend from school turned up and hurried me out onto the main street. A luxurious coach was waiting there and a European dressed in civvies handed me a letter, once again from the Governor-General's office. I read it quickly as he ushered me into the coach.

It wasn't long afterwards, just before sunset, that I found myself sitting on a garden chair facing Governor-General van Heutsz.

'Nah, Sir,' he began, 'I'm glad to be able to see you again. How are your studies going? How do you spend your time? Does your wife get any of that little time of yours? You've been writing so much these last few weeks. Ah, so you see, I am one of your readers, and, yes, perhaps you could also say, one of your admirers.'

'Your Excellency . . . '

During this unofficial meeting with the Governor-General, a meeting that was completely unexpected, there were two main questions he put to me: as an educated Native what would be my reaction to a Japanese victory – if indeed they won – and, secondly, what was being done by the educated Natives from and for this modern era?

These questions made me feel like a primary school student who had forgotten to learn off his homework and now was called to recite in front of class.

Van Heutsz understood my awkwardness, saying: 'No need to answer now. If you prefer you can present your answers in one of your excellent articles. Whatever newspaper you write in, it will reach me. You must do this. This month. I know it may disturb your studies a little, but you are quite good at scheduling your time, are you not? And also, you know, writers can often see aspects of things which others cannot.'

The meeting lasted only a quarter of an hour. When it was over, he presented me with some of Multatuli's books. He had them ready on the seat beside him.

I did not go home to the dormitory but went straight to Kwitang. But Mei was not home – something that greatly surprised me. Ibu Baldrun repeated to me over and over again that this was the first time that my wife had gone out alone at night. She had asked Ibu Baldrun's permission to go, saying she would be back around midnight or even later. She had taken the front door key with her.

'At first, I wouldn't let her go,' Ibu said in a pleading tone, 'but she said you would understand and would have permitted it, so I gave her permission. Forgive me if I have done wrong, Denmas.'

Ibu Baldrun did not know where Mei had gone. And I had no idea either.

I went to bed but tossed and turned unable to sleep. I was restless. Jealousy ran amok within me. Our quiet and secure life was threatened, for now and forever.

Once you are afflicted with jealousy there are no words of wisdom that can cure you.

'Such a good child as she will not do anything wrong.'

Ibu Baldrun was also beginning to get restless.

A jealous heart is like a claw whose clutch becomes deeper and deeper. That night I needed her to discuss the questions I had been asked by van Heutsz. Very well, my plans would have to be cancelled. But I would not go back to the dormitory. The Governor-General's questions had been wiped from my mind by evil imaginings about what my wife was up to.

I turned off the light and pulled down the mosquito net. As I tossed and turned I tried to humour myself. Mei would never do anything that she shouldn't. She was a careful, calm person. But jealousy knows only its own

103

laws. It's like a fire that plays at burning the rice husks. Whether or not there is anything there to burn, all you know is that you can feel the burning heat. Even so, I eventually fell asleep. I woke up at three in the morning. I heard her mumble, I don't know in what language. Perhaps she was asking who had pulled down the mosquito net. In the darkness, she started climbing into bed. She was startled to find someone else in there with her.

'Mei!' I reprimanded her, 'where have you been?'

She didn't get in after all.

'I knew you would be angry. I'm sorry,' she lit a lamp.

'Where have you been?' I got out of bed.

'I'm sorry. But there's no need to make a noise.'

I grabbed both her shoulders and shook her. 'Answer. Where have you been?'

She looked at me calmly as if nothing had happened.

'I know that you do not want to know where I have been – and will not want to know where I will be going in the future. But you do want to know what I am doing and what my work here is.'

Then I realised that I was standing before the fiancé of my late friend – a woman who did not belong to herself, a young woman who had surrendered her youth to the ideals of her organisation. Her soft and gentle face was now like stone, polished by her concern at the world's sympathy with Japan in its war against Russia, a war going on at some faraway point on the north of the globe. She was worried about something that was abstract, but that had been made concrete by her own ideals – the fate of her country and her people.

Silently I climbed once more into bed. She put out the light and climbed in also. She probably hadn't eaten since afternoon.

Suddenly she embraced me: 'I'm sorry, my husband. I must do this. If not those with Chinese blood, who then will work for our country? You would do the same for your country and people, yes?'

Ah, such words, such a tone of voice! The dancing flames of jealousy inside me melted into softness. For just a while? Forever?

'You haven't eaten yet, Mei?'

'I'm tired, sleepy.' She fell asleep, with me in her embrace until morning.

But I could not sleep. My thoughts wandered everywhere. Ah, how I admired this woman who was now my wife. She had become a part of my own self. Her hurt was also my hurt. And today, I knew, she would be more faithful to that other something far away to the north. To her hopes for her country and people. And I could not possibly go with her. How complicated and disorderly are the hearts of humankind. She still embraced me. I could not bring myself to move out of her arms. She was tired. And that small and slender body of hers, and her heart, all of it, or perhaps half, would no longer be mine. Mei, oh, my Mei!

From that morning we knew that our marriage had entered the beginning of its final stage. She would become further and further apart from me until finally we no longer were together. Forever. She would be lost in the cauldron of enthusiasm for a victory for the Young Generation of her people.

Before I got up, I kissed her. She was still asleep. And that was the first time I had done that. It felt like a parting kiss. Slowly, she opened her eyes.

'My husband,' she called out, still half asleep. It had only been in these last few hours that she called me 'my husband'. Her voice was calm, she spoke without emotion, still lying in bed. 'For almost five years now our life together has been blessed with health and happiness. What woman would not be happy to be your wife? My husband, you are a man with an understanding heart. You have never done anything to hurt me. Next year you will be a doctor. I am worried that I will not always be able to be with you. I must work, I must work harder.'

She was saying goodbye.

'I understand, Mei,' I changed the subject. 'You must bathe.'

'You bathe first. You must study.'

So I bathed first. When I came out I was served with breakfast of fried bananas and coffee, then Mei went off to bathe.

And when she came back and sat down beside me, I began: 'I want to talk with you tonight about the possibility of a Japanese victory.'

'Forgive me, but I don't think that is necessary. We must work. We face the Japanese bacteria. If I am not here this evening, don't be angry. I will always be faithful to my husband. There must never be any evil suspicions that spoil the thoughts between us, as husband and wife.'

I listened to her words and it felt as if we would never be together, not that evening or ever again. I had been overwhelmed by this feeling so many times in the last few hours. Had I become so emotional and sentimental? And I sensed what was going to happen.

I watched her secretly as she dressed. She stood before me like a creature from another universe whom I had just met. The paleness had returned to haunt her lips once again. The exhaustion from last night was already threatening her health. And she did not and would not understand that it was happening.

Listlessly I walked the several hundred metres to school.

The news that I had received a letter from the Governor-General's office caused great commotion at the school. The Director summoned me.

'So, Sir, you have had an audience with the Governor-General, representative of Her Majesty the Queen in the Netherlands Indies. May perhaps we know what he wanted you for? It may have certain consequences for our school?'

My answer greatly enthused the Director, who volunteered to help me perfect the answers, using all the material that could be obtained. He suggested that the students hold a meeting to gather together everybody's opinion on the matter. I readily agreed with the idea but was reluctant to let him find out about my writing activities. So the Director volunteered to prepare a list of questions to be answered in writing by the students. Once again I agreed while, at the same time, asking permission to sleep outside the dormitory for the coming week. He quickly agreed.

The questionnaire was soon reproduced, to be given out to the students the next morning.

After I had finished writing copy for ten advertisements at the auction paper office, I went straight to Kwitang. Mei was busy writing in Chinese. There were five pages of writing on the table. Silently I came up behind her and started to stroke her hair.

'Is that you?' she asked, without raising her head. 'I'll be finished in a minute.'

My hands moved down to her chest, and she kept on writing as if nothing was disturbing her.

'It looks as if you can write too,' I said.

'These are just notes needed for the moment, not like the stories you write,' she answered.

She finished her work, went over the the corner of the room, and started to duplicate her notes, fifty copies of each page in all. She paid no attention to me.

'Hurry up, I want to talk.'

'I answered you yesterday. Work! I've been urging you for a long time now to carry out what that old doctor suggested. And still none of you will organise. What now? Is there nothing you can do? Look at these – fifty copies to be distributed to fifty addresses. Tomorrow they will spread to fifty more and then more again. And others will start talking about what they say and so the ideas will spread further and wider. Of course, that's the theory. It could reach either more or less than that. Public opinion is changed this way. These too are bacteria but not evil ones. These indeed fight gonococcus and *Treponema pallidum*.'

'People have known how to do that for a long time now.'

'Yes,' she answered, 'it is indeed elementary. Even a small child could learn how to do it. But without an organisation not one copy will reach an address, let alone multiply like bacteria.'

'It's easier if you do it through a newspaper, without having to do so much work, Mei.'

'Not everyone owns newspapers. And those owned by the Old Generation will certainly oppose what I'm saying. Now, I'm sorry, I must go.'

She put the papers in her bag, which so far had only carried her clothes, stood before the mirror, put on some make-up and combed her hair.

106

'I want to be with you tonight, Mei,' I said.

'I'll try to get back.' And she left.

'She spent the whole morning and afternoon just reading and writing,' said Ibu Baldrun disapprovingly. She sympathised with me.

'There's something she has to do. In fact, I've asked her to do it.'

And I too began to write, to prepare the answers to van Heutsz's questions. The answers from the other students would just be used, at most, as complementary material. Anyway, they wouldn't be ready until tomorrow. And what can be hoped from those whose only dream is to become a government employee, no matter in what capacity, whose life is made up only of waiting for their salary? I found it more difficult to write than if I was writing of my own will. Every sentence got stuck, entangled in issues that I didn't fully understand. Instead all my friends, people that I loved, appeared before my mind's eye. And they all confronted me, unsullied by prejudice, competing for my allegiance, embracing each other, standing shoulder to shoulder in a single line.

I did not finish writing.

While I sat dazed in the middle of a sentence, Mei's two hands slipped across my chest. When I grabbed her hands they were cold.

'Mei, you came?' I stood up, embraced and kissed her.

The pocket watch lying on the table showed twelve midnight.

'You've been out in the cold air too long. Remember your health, Mei.'

'I've brought home some Chinese food for you.'

'So I'll eat pork?'

'No. Who said anything about pork? You've been so suspicious and angry these last few days. It's midnight and you're still up. Come on.'

We ate silently. Now and then we would steal glances at each other. She was trying to size up how I was feeling. And I was doing the same.

'You're not jealous, are you?' she said, diving straight into my personal problem. 'Jealous. I never dreamt that any husband of mine could be jealous because of me.'

We finished the food, and Mei went on: 'Since a child I have been told to be *correct*, to behave *correctly*. It was implanted into me that a correct attitude was a basic requirement for all people who wanted to have relationships with other people.'

I didn't like the way she was talking that night. She was just looking for a way to justify what she was doing.

The next day, with a pile of answers from the other students, I worked at the auction paper office. There were twenty texts that I had to work on – advertisements, that is. My boss had expanded his business to take in orders for advertising copy that would be used in the dailies as well. With these twenty texts done I would have earned enough for us to live for the next month. It wasn't until two in the morning that I finished and headed straight for Kwitang.

It was a dark night. People said that there had been a break in the gas pipes. All the street lights had been turned off. Just up ahead of me were two people wearing black pyjama pants. Perhaps they were criminals. I slowed down. Then one of them headed off into the lane where we lived. The other turned into a different lane. The first stopped outside Ibu Baldrun's fence. From the way she walked and the shape of her body, it was obviously Mei.

'You're out walking very late.' She got her reprimand in first.

'You're only home now, Mei?'

'I waited a long time for you outside your office.'

We went inside. I was not able to study the other students' questions. I had run out of strength. Mei had brought home some food once again so we sat down to eat. Silently.

'I hope you're not jealous again.'

Once again I didn't like the way she spoke, even though I understood that she was deliberately trying to goad me into facing my jealousy.

It was the next evening before I had a chance to study the other students' answers. Mei was not there. I was alone in the room. Page by page I examined what they had written. I was right. There was nothing interesting, let alone anything actually worth studying. Page after page, I continued. Ah, here was something interesting by Wardi. There was nothing from Wilam. He had left the school after a year to go to live in India. Partokleooo's answer was completely useless – he had no concepts of present and future. Wardi's and Tjipto's answers were quite interesting but too personal to be used.

The next evening as I was leaving my office, I saw Mei. I decided not to go back to Kwitang but to follow her. She stopped suddenly as if deliberately allowing me to watch her. She was wearing men's clothes, black pyjama pants and a black shirt, just like a *silat* fighter. And my grandfather had once told me that you should beware of skinny *silat* fighters, the skinnnier they are the better they are! I don't know whether grandfather was serious, but I didn't feel I had to be afraid of my own wife! Mei was met by another person. He was big and tall. They went into a restaurant together.

I also entered and ordered something to eat.

Mei, my wife, sat in the corner with this man who I had never met before in my life. The two of them talked and laughed, chuckled and guffawed. I didn't know what they were talking about. I could not overcome my jealousy. I hid myself in the shadows of some colonnades. A hand, with all of its five fingers, seemed to force its way down my throat to squeeze my heart in its grip.

From afar Mei looked even more beautiful, more waxen, like a dried flower ready to crumble at the touch of some rough hand. Beside her was a strong, handsome man, perhaps the player of some heavy sport.

108

I didn't touch my food, I knew it was all pork. I suppressed my feelings. Mei and her friend had finished eating. The young man paid the restaurant owner. But Mei seemed to want to pay for her own food. They argued loudly in a language that was as alien to me as that which decides man's fate. My jealousy subsided a little. She was still my faithful wife, I thought as well as prayed. Only – until when?

They left. I quickly paid my bill.

'Didn't you like your food, Sir?' asked the proprietor.

'There was not a thing wrong with it.'

'You didn't even touch it.'

I ran after them. They were walking beside each other, but not close. Suddenly I saw him take Mei's hand. She pulled it away. How long can you keep it up, Mei, and how long will you want to? Yes, I was jealous. But did I really love Mei? Or was I just offended because my rights were being violated?

They disappeared into a *delman*, which took them off in the direction of Kotta. I was left on the side of the street. There was no way I could follow them now. There were no other empty *delmans* about. I ambled home to Kwitang, and finished my answers for van Heutsz, reading them over and over again. Then I put them in an envelope to be posted the next morning.

Next morning, when I awoke, Mei was not there. For the first time in our marriage, she had not come home.

Her face announcing her condolences, Ibu Baldrun asked me where my wife was. I answered that I had told her to take a holiday in the country. She didn't believe me. She said that she didn't want her family's name to be hurt because of the behaviour of her lodgers. I convinced her that Mei was not doing anything wrong.

'Yes, before she was always a good girl. Always stayed at home at the proper times. Always helpful and obedient. But now she is hardly ever here and seems to prefer wandering about in the streets.'

She did not relent even when she saw my expression change as she said those things about Mei. Instead she warned me: 'Even her own husband doesn't know where she's gone. Fix things up, Denmas, fix things up well. Don't let things get out of hand.'

Yes, the joy, the happiness, the peace, that our marriage had brought us, was gone. And my heart reminded me that I must appreciate what I had lost. This girl, who once had been so helpless, had once again found her arena of struggle, after years of just giving private lessons. I didn't know if she had been in contact with many people all this time. And I didn't know any of them, not even their names! Perhaps all this time she hadn't been giving private lessons at all. Don't dream about the happiness of marriage. You are being burned up by jealousy, Minke. You have lost something. The hope in you still pleads for something. What else are you waiting for, Minke?

I went back to the dormitory and did not visit Kwitang again.

Whenever Mei wanted to meet me, she came to the office at the paper in Jalan Kramat. Her face was drawn and becoming paler. Her eyes looked yellow. It was very likely she was not getting enough sleep.

Whenever she came I gave her all that day's earnings. She always counted it, and noted it down in a book. She always gave me back a quarter for my own shopping.

Month after month, for almost a year.

Then one day she asked: 'Why do you never come home?'

'Who will I find there? Look at yourself, you're just skin and bones. Your eyes are more and more yellow. I'm worried . . . Stop for a while, Mei. Don't go out so much. Stay at home . . . But it's up to you.'

'Forgive me. Let me have another three months. After that I will be able to be a proper wife again. I've been very unfair to you these past months, not like a good Chinese should be to her husband. But I'm sure you know that I'm truly thankful that you have allowed me to make some contribution to my country and my people.'

She went again, I don't know where, and I went back to the dormitory.

We both lost weight and I became a daydreamer. Every time I met Mei her eyes were more yellow. She was showing more and more symptoms of hepatitis. I truly respected her dedication to her people. How many men have touched her without my permission or knowledge? It was impossible that this had not happened. I had thought about stopping her money. But that would not be the act of an educated person! I must be better than my parents and my ancestors. I must carry out my duties as a husband.

'Mei, go to the doctor.'

'Do I look sick?'

'Yes. Don't put it off. Just this once do as I say.'

Then she did not appear for a week. She must be exhausted from illness, I thought. She will need me now.

I walked slowly to Kwitang. She was lying sprawled out on the bed. Almost all of her skin had turned yellow.

'Mei!' I shouted and embraced her. 'You're ill, Mei.'

She cried. She knew I understood she was very ill. Her liver was inflamed and there was already signs of swelling. This illness would take her to the grave – as certain as the ticking of a clock's hands. The science of medicine and my world would not be able to save her from her disease.

'I thought you would not want to see me again, my husband. A wife who has divided her loyalties.' She sobbed.

'Shush, Mei. I have always admired you so much. You have been able to do what I have not.'

110

'I know you did not come to condemn me.'

'No. Why didn't you send news?'

'Soon you will be a doctor. You don't have long to go, do you? You've come to treat me?'

'Of course, Mei. Have you been to a doctor?'

I examined her – her eyes, heart, pulse, and the swelling in her stomach.

'No, I am not going to a doctor. I know you will cure me. You, my husband.'

'Of course, Mei, I will cure you. Where are your friends? Why is no one bothering about you?'

'They do not know where I live. They do not need to know.'

She needed to be looked after in a hospital. Mei, ah, Mei, my narrow-eyed girl of satin skin. Look how you are now.

'I'll be the one to shed the tears, my husband,' she said hoarsely. 'You mustn't shed a single tear for me. You will be a doctor. You must not fail because of any tears.'

Ibu Baldrun no longer seemed to have any concern for Mei. Even though she knew I had arrived she did not come in to see me. When I came out of the room, she greeted me with a scowl. I knew I was in the wrong.

'Forgive me, Ibu, causing you so much trouble all this time.'

'Yes, what have I done, Denmas, that things should come to this?'

'A thousand apologies, Ibu, it is all my fault.'

'So what is going to happen now?'

'I know you no longer like my wife, Ibu. But believe me, she has done nothing wrong.'

'You have not been home yourself either, Denmas.'

'Work and study have kept me busy.'

'That's not why you haven't been home, Denmas.'

'Tomorrow I will take my wife to the hospital,' I said humbly.

Mei called me from our room.

I went back in. She signalled me with her hand to come nearer: 'I don't want you to take me to a hospital. I want to be near you. Only you can treat me.'

She had more faith in me than anyone else.

'Treat me yourself, no one else.'

Mei was asking something of me that was impossible.

'I know you are not yet a doctor. I want to see you become a doctor. Are you listening?

'I'll make out a prescription, Mei. Quiet down, now. I'll be your doctor.'

She wanted to see me as a real doctor. It might be her last wish.

I wrote out a prescription and asked Ibu Baldrun's son to take it to the apothecary.

I stayed with her. In this helpless state, she looked even more beautiful.

'I'll stay with you in the hospital tomorrow, Mei. I'll stay with you all the time.'

'As long as I am with you,' she answered. She nodded. 'You must become a doctor, my husband. A very good doctor.'

Two hours passed. The child still hadn't come back with the medicine. If the prescription did not get through, then I would be in big trouble. I was not yet permitted to write prescriptions. And when the boy did return, he was escorted by the police.

'You wrote this prescription?' asked the policeman.

'Yes, Sir.'

'Who is sick?'

'My wife.'

'You are a doctor?'

'A medical student.'

'So you're not yet a doctor?'

'Next year. I'm a student,' I said, beginning to lose my temper.

'Very well, come with me,' he ordered.

'My wife is very ill,' I whispered.

'There is some explaining you have to do first.'

'Fine. Go with him,' said Mei. 'Don't worry about me.'

I was not ashamed to be arrested in front of Mei, even though I knew her faith in me would disappear or at least be lessened by this. Indeed I did not yet have the right to write prescriptions. And I had not written it because of ignorance. But because I wanted by wife to have faith. Let what must happen, happen. She knows I tried everything. Let the prescription be something that changes this gloomy atmosphere.

I was thrown into a cell. There was also an interrogation that evening, although only brief. When they realised that I was indeed a medical student, they gave me a better cell and treated me much more politely.

The next day the Director fetched me from the police station and took me back to his office. He asked me to tell him everything. I also told him how I had to look after my wife myself.

'Don't you realise that you have already broken more rules than anyone else?'

'I more than realise, Sir.'

'And who will pay for your wife's medical expenses?'

'You must also know that there is very little hope for my wife, except if God wishes otherwise. And you must also know that I must do my duty as a husband.'

'Where will you get the money?'

'I will get it.'

'You have put your studies at risk as well as written a false prescription.'

'No, the prescription I wrote was correct. I know I did not have the right

112

to do so, I have broken the rules, but I have not written any bogus prescription. I knew what medicine she needed.'

'Very well, take care of your wife as best you can. You can miss classes whenever you need.'

For two months Mei lay in bed in hospital. The operation to draw out the infection from her stomach resulted in another infection. She got worse. Every morning when I came to see her, it was more and more obvious how weak she was becoming.

Then on top of all this she contracted another intestinal illness.

'Promise me truthfully, my husband, that you will become a doctor.' Those were the words she uttered every time we met. 'Forgive me for all the trouble I have caused you. Promise me, my husband, you will become a doctor to your people who suffer poverty and humiliation. Cure their bodies, make healthy their souls, show them a way to live, rouse them to arise.'

She could no longer take proteins, only glucose.

'Shush, Mei. You'll be better soon.'

Meanwhile I had fallen behind in my studies, with no way to catch up, especially with my practical studies. Now I stayed with her every night, all night.

At three in the morning, when I was sitting in a chair next to her, she moved her lips. Her voice was so weak. I held her hand, now only skin and bones.

She died without leaving behind a word.

I returned to my lessons. I knew I had no chance of passing the examinations. Inside me, I was all churned up and in turmoil. I did what I had to do like a machine. I think it is what they call patience, having faith, and a cartload of other names. All was done because of duty, as a man and a husband, as a candidate doctor, as an educated person. I don't think any sane person could censure me for what I had done. Getting married before graduating? Who is it that is still so eager to judge relationships between people? That Mei met me, and I met her, each from a country so distant and so alien from the other's, was not something I'd wished for. Nor was it something Mei had wished for.

The other students often asked how my wife was feeling. From my sunken eyes and cheeks, they understood without needing an answer. And their sadness at my loss was also sincere and genuine. Each came up to me to offer his hand and to express condolences. One by one I shook their hands. And those hands were cold like my heart.

Through my downcast eyes everything seemed downcast – the windows

113

and doors, the bed and the old clothes hanging on the clothes hanger.

The air I breathed still seemed to smell of the coconut oil mixed with jasmine and *kenanga* that I had rubbed into Mei's hair while she had been ill. She was constantly in my mind's eye, sprawled out helpless on the hospital bed. And her faint voice still echoed within me, reminding me to make sure that I became a doctor.

Ah, Mei, I never even knew your real name. You have gone with the knowledge that I have never hurt your feelings, nor your body. For you, Mei, I have worked, studied, written a prescription before I was permitted to. And you've gone on before me. I never did wrong towards you, Mei. That my studies were in disarray was not your fault, neither was it mine. It was just misfortune.

And once again what happened was different from what I had prepared myself for.

The Director sat at his desk. Before him were several sheets of paper weighted down with a bottle of ink and a ruler.

'Mr Minke,' he began, 'please accept my condolences on the passing away of your wife. And those too of all the staff, the teachers and the students.'

'Thank you, Sir.'

'Even so, it seems there are still more troubles that we just cannot avoid. I know your results and your behaviour here. You have shown a special, individual development. I have tried to explain to the Council of Teachers that you have even attracted the attention of the Governor-General.'

An opening speech which heralded disaster.

'It is the opinion of the Council of Teachers that the two major breaches of the rules by you indicate that you cannot be relied upon to be a satisfactory government doctor. You are expelled from the school. At the start of these coming holidays, you must leave the school and the dormitory.'

I will never be a doctor, Mei, I screamed within me, forgive me, Mei. I will never be able to keep my promise to you.

'Why don't you say something? Don't you regret what has happened?'

'Before she died, my wife reminded me over and over again to make sure I worked hard to become a good doctor.'

'It's a pity that possibility has now been closed off to you.'

'What can one do?'

'And that's not all, Mr Minke. This is your letter of expulsion.'

I took it and put it in my pocket without reading it.

'And this is another letter that you must sign.'

I read the letter. I had to repay the costs of my time at the school and at the dormitory. Four years times eleven months times forty guilders. Two thousand nine hundred and seventy guilders – enough to buy two big brick buildings complete with luxurious fittings. At the bottom of the letter was a sentence: I agree to fully repay the above amount at the rate of—per month.

114

'If you go and see the Governor-General, you'll surely be able to find a way out of this. Try it.'

'I will repay all my debts, Sir.'

'You'll go to your father?'

'No.'

'To the former Assistant Resident?'

'No.'

'To the Governor-General?'

'No.'

'You'll pay it yourself? Impossible. Even as a doctor you would be earning less than twenty guilders a month. If you pay it off monthly, it will take you at least ten years.'

I signed the letter promising to repay the debt within three months.

The Director's eyes popped out in disbelief and he cried out: 'A thousand a month! How is it possible! Even your teachers could not pay that much off so quickly. Don't get yourself in more trouble. Be careful. Remember, there will be legal consequences.'

'So be it, Sir. May I go now?'

I stood to leave and walked towards the door. He raced after me, held me by the shoulders and gazed at me with his brown eyes. He bowed his head without saying anything.

I went back to the dormitory and packed quickly. The dormitory was empty, everyone was at classes. An employee helped me carry my things to a *dokar*.

'You are not the only one, Master, to experience this,' he said, trying to humour me.

The *dokar* took me to Kwitang. I went into Mei's room. It was just as it was before. I felt weighted down with sadness. I still saw Mei everywhere – her smile, her teeth, her voice. Mei! Mei! And I remembered the first time we met in the old bamboo shanty in Kotta – a girl alien in the midst of her own people. And she was sick and I took her away from that place to this room . . .

Then suddenly something pressed in on my chest and I burst out sobbing. How lonely will life be without you, Mei.

'Enough, Denmas,' Ibu Baldrun comforted me. 'Don't think about her too much.'

These words of comfort choked and squeezed my heart even more. Who else would think about her, if not me? She, who never knew father, mother, brothers or sisters?

'Don't dwell on her so much, Denmas. Don't hurt yourself too much,' she said again. 'Surrender everything to He Who Gives Life. Humankind just carries out His plans.'

Those words, so often spoken when people die, now seemed full of real

115

meaning for me, moving my emotions even more. Mei, what were you able to achieve in your short life? You were determined to work for your country and your people, so far away and abstract. A country and people who did not even know you! In illness you first met me. And in illness you are taken away from me forever. Almost five years we were married. Long enough to know that you were truly worthy of being loved. A diamond that brought brilliance into my life, that made me go crazy with jealousy. And all that is passed now that Death, the great teacher, has come, leaving behind this chaos inside me.

After the second week of mourning, my mother unexpectedly visited me. She came straight into the room and embraced me: 'What terrible fate you have, Child. What is it that you have done? Twice married, twice abandoned by your wife!'

I bowed down before her, and kissed her feet.

'What's the matter with you, Child, that it is always like this? And no children either. She was ill and you did not tell us. When you were married, the same. And now when she dies, also silence. How far apart are we now, Child. And when your Father came to Betawi, you did not honour him either.'

She pulled at me telling me to stand and then told me to sit on the edge of the bed.

'And you have never wanted to come home.'

'No need to talk about this any more, Mother.'

She looked at me from behind her tears.

'What has been wanting in my prayers for your safety? Your happiness? Your triumph? So that this has happened?'

"Mother, let's not discuss it any further. Your son can deal with all this.'

She sat there silent, watching me for a long time.

'You are paler than you were before,' she began again. 'I can't bear to see you suffer like this, Child. You yourself know I suffer the most when I see you suffering. More than when I gave birth to you.'

So that things would not go on and become even more involved, I took her out of the room. She had to restrain herself more in front of Ibu Baldrun. And we sat at the bare dining table without a table-cloth.

She began to ask Ibu Baldrun about Mei's and my life together. And the two women, neither of whom could understand each other, began talking noisily. Each going off in their own direction, one north, one south. I could tell from my mother's eyes that she was truly saddened by my fate. Seeing that I was not translating for them, the two of them went silent.

I went back into the room. Mother followed me inside.

'Mother should not be sad because of your son,' I said finally. 'I had great happiness living with Mother's daughter-in-law. Truly, Mother. She came into my life in a proper way and she left it unsullied also. I never hurt her feelings nor her body. I stayed with her and looked after her to the last moment.'

'And you're so thin, Child.'

'Enough, Mother, no need to keep harping on how thin I am. I am just coming out of mourning. I am leaving behind the past.'

I left the house very early the next morning. I had decided to set out to find the money to pay off my debt of almost three thousand guilders. I needed some money for capital. My boss at the auction paper, who was now running an office preparing advertising copy, had offered me a permanent job when he heard I had been dismissed from school. I had to refuse. In the meantime, he offered me an advance of twenty *rupiah* on my casual work and I took that. Everyone at the office was very good to me, they offered to do this and that for me, and expressed their condolences. Everyone has been so good to me, Mei. Because of you. And I made a promise to myself, a vow, that I too would do good to all good people.

I went to the post office and sent a telegram to Wonocolo, Surabaya, reporting my failure at medical school, my dismissal and my financial difficulties. I did not report about my marriage and the death of Mei.

At home mother still kept on urging me to come home. I used every way that I knew to explain that I couldn't go home to B – . I would not leave Betawi. I would rebuild everything that had collapsed now about me. I wouldn't even promise that I would go home later. I did not listen to mother's urgings that I marry again. I knew that she was made to suffer even more because of my attitude. To end all her urgings and pressuring, I was forced to say: 'Give me another five years, Mother.'

'Five more years! And what things might happen during the next five years, Child. Your mother may be called home by the Almighty.'

'I pray day and night for a long life for you, Mother.'

On the eighth day of mother's stay, a bank cheque arrived from Surabaya to the value of three thousand five hundred guilders. After I cashed it at the bank, I went to the government cashier's office and paid my debt. I then went to see the Director to show him the receipt.

He gaped at it in amazement. And he seemed to regret the decision that had been made. He said: 'That was a far too heavy fine to impose on you. And you never made any protest. Would you like me to try to get the amount reduced?'

I made no answer.

'So what will you do now after your failure here?'

'All I want to be is a free individual, Director. I will regard this dismissal as a blessing.' He returned the letter I had signed promising to repay my debt. I tore it up and threw it in the waste-paper basket.

My former school friends had assembled in the courtyard. I deliberately put on a tearless, happy front. They were all disappointed at my dismissal,

117

with only one more year to go.

'I much prefer to be a free individual, my friends, than a government doctor. We will meet again one day out there in the real world.'

Mother returned home to B – disappointed, not knowing what my plans were. She knew that I could not do what she asked. Having failed to become a doctor, there were now a thousand opportunities open to me. Overcompensation was pushing me to be even more ambitious in my plans. Go out now and fight for whatever it is you want!

I deliberately rented a house just near my school, in Kampung Ketapang, where many Native students boarded. I also bought some fine furniture at an auction for inside the house. I made sure everyone would know that not only did I not regret having to leave medical school, but that I was glad I was not going to be a government doctor.

I took out the portrait I owned from its wine-red velvet cover and hung it in the sitting-room. It dominated the room like a queen ruling over her empire, grander even than Queen Wilhelmina. In my bedroom I hung a portrait of Ang San Mei. It wasn't a very good portrait. Perhaps you could even say it was a bad painting. It was painted by one of the village artists in Kwitang, a neighbour who had seen Ang San Mei several times. It took him a week to paint it. I stayed with him several hours a day while he was painting. The combination of colours wasn't right. But that was what he was able to do. And he had got her profile right.

For the next few weeks I thought I would enjoy this beautiful freedom – no responsibilities, no ties, no need to sell my services. Kaarsen had come three times to offer me work. Three times I told him I was looking forward to a long rest. And every time he came he had to stop to admire the portrait hanging in the sitting-room: *Flower of the Century's End*.

On the fourth visit, he asked: 'Could I borrow that portrait, Sir? Just for a week?'

'I'm sorry, but no.'

'Perhaps I could rent it?'

'Also no, I'm sorry.'

'What if I hired an artist to come here and copy it?'

'It's a pity, but I'm afraid I still must say no.'

'How much do you want for it to be copied?'

'This painting is for me alone to possess. Forgive me.'

'What a pity. It's exactly right for the advertisement we're doing for the show on at the Komedi Building. What are your objections? It's just a painting, isn't it?'

'You cannot buy its history with money, Sir.'

'Very well. How is your work going?'

He reminded me of the cash advance I had received from him.

'I will return the advance to you.'

'That's not what I'm after. Your departure has put my business in a lot of trouble; we're making a loss. You rejected my offer of permanent employment. But the business has achieved such a good reputation. Now an English circus has arrived in town and has given us even more work. Well, I've thought a lot about what to do and here is my offer. I'd like you to become the deputy manager of my company, though holding no equity. I'm sure you'll agree.'

Without giving it much thought, I agreed. An agreement was drawn up on the spot and we each signed it. I was to receive seventy-five guilders a month, with no payment for individual advertising copy.

When he left I sat back feeling that I had already achieved much more than even a government doctor of ten years' standing. I looked up at the painting for a moment and then went and lay down in bed.

The picture of Ang San Mei always drew my attention. And every time I looked at it I was taken back to the times just passed. And I could still hear her reminding me: become a doctor! I shook my head. I've failed, Mei. Your hopes were in vain.

Doctors were considered to be the most educated of the educated Natives. Without a sharp mind and a resolute will, you could not possibly graduate. Only a chosen few could graduate as doctors. But, Mei, a doctor is not the only good and honourable profession there is. Even writing copy for advertisements should not be considered dishonourable work, though it may perhaps not classify as an honoured profession either. Then it seemed Mei refuted what I had just thought. All right, it's not so worthy a position but at least it pays more than a government doctor who has ten years' experience. It's easy work. Clean. I'm not dependent on the Government. I'm free, Mei. That's more important.

The narrow-slit eyes of my wife stared out at me, never to blink again. But, even so, in my heart they still shone strongly, like the first time she urged me to start organising: Are you going to let your people stay bent under the burden of their ignorance? Who will begin if you don't?

I reflected once more on everything she had said, all that she had worked for, the sacrifices she had made. She had never talked about what she had achieved. She had only talked about the Young Generation and its great energy, its goals and its analysis of what was happening around it. And she had spoken about them all – the bacteria that was British imperialism, its twin, Japanese imperialism, the Emperor Ye Si, who was yet another kind of bacteria, the rousing summons of the old doctor, the outlook on life of the girl from Jepara . . . Don't leave that old man to cry out to the desert-like hearts of the educated Natives. He had spent his whole thirty years' savings. I hope your heart, Minke, is not a desert, like the Sahara, the Gobi or Karakum deserts.

Was it right that I was enjoying myself like this and accepting the position

119

as number two man in the business? Ssst! Even working in an auction paper you soon learn new things, like the collusion between capitalists and Government officials. All at the expense, of course, of the weak and power-less. I had never imagined that auctions could be a disguised form of bribery!

It had become the custom that any Government official who was being transferred to another town would auction off all his furniture before he moved. The Dutch and Chinese businessmen from his area would then calculate how important this official was to their businesses and plantations and bid for the goods accordingly. The more important he was to them, the higher they would bid. The Resident of East Sumatra was able to pocket 43 thousand guilders in one such auction! An ink bottle sold for 500 guilders, a globe of the world of the kind found in a study sold for 650 guilders, a desk ruler went for 120 guilders. The buyers? Those businessmen who had dealings with the official. And the prices could go even higher if the businessmen knew that the official concerned was in a position to act even more tyrannically towards the Natives so as to be able to further help their businesses. But those who lost their land, or who lost their freedom when forced into becoming contract coolies, could do nothing, except run amok blindly or pray for the next seven generations.

All my past experiences were paraded before me. What was there that I had not yet experienced? All those I had met along the way, simple people, educated people, whether conscious or not, had brought me to where I found myself today. I felt ashamed when I remembered all the lectures, expla-nations, teachings and hopes that Ter Haar had showered upon me. How people had cursed the war in Aceh, how Marie van Zeggelen had acclaimed the struggle for freedom waged by the native Acehnese and Buginese. I remembered the anonymous pamphlets telling the story of the forced labour system and of how many people had died because of it. Of how the Acehnese had fought the Dutch for a quarter of a century – women and children too! Of Multatuli, Roorda van Eysinga, Van Hoevell. Of the greed of sugar and the barbarism of the plantation administrators. Of the rebellions of the Javanese peasants which were always broken by the power of sugar. Of the Batak peasants who had also been conquered – but by tobacco and rubber! Of what I learned in *Millions from Deli*, a story written by the Dutch lawyer J. van der Brand who had worked in East Sumatra.

Brand had exposed the exploitative practices of the tobacco plantations in Sumatra. I don't know whether he was just a good European and Christian or whether he was influenced by the thinking of the Ethical Policy being propagated by the Radicals. The Dutch Government felt obliged to send an investigator, Judge J.L.T. Rhemrev, to check on the veracity of Brand's allegations. The results of Rhemrev's report – the tobacco plantation workers' plight was even worse than Brand had reported. Perhaps that was why the results of his investigation were never published. The Minister for

Colonies, J.T. Cremer, a former manager of the Deli Corporation, could only say that when he was in Sumatra there were no such practices. He said he thought that the hot tropical sun seemed to affect the morals of some Europeans who lived there.

How easy it was for Cremer to look for excuses – as if the weather had changed since he'd been there. The Native rulers of Sumatra had sold off their people's land to the tobacco plantations. They had overturned and subverted their traditional law to give up the people's rights over their ancestral lands. Over the last thirty years thousands of hectares had been sold off by greedy sultans to the tobacco capitalists, and also to the sugar plantations.

I recalled the reports in the *Sumatra Post* of the cruelty of the European plantation owners, who never ceased in their search for fertile land . . .

And the way Native officials oppressed their own people . . .

I jumped out of my bed and went over to the portrait of Ang San Mei – a portrait that was like an idol I worshipped.

And the last letter I had received from Ter Haar:

Yes, we must keep watch on van Heutsz. He is a major colonial figure. And don't forget, he is a general who has not won any international wars. He has achieved victories only over the Native peoples of the Indies. And even Aceh was never completely subdued by him. The Acehnese are now fighting back even harder, their determination aroused by the Japanese victory over Russia.

'Yes, Mei, I will study all this over again!'

7

I studied once more all the notes I had made in my diaries. I took out all my correspondence. I put aside everthing I had never really understood. I started to properly digest and assimilate those sections of the newspapers that I had marked with red pencil and that now lay heaped in the corner of my study. Gradually I began to build up a clearer picture of what had been happening during those years.

The most interesting materials were Ter Haar's letters. Beginning from the very first one. If I order them in my own way, they read like this:

Dear Mr Minke,

I am now in Semarang. Engineer van Kollewijn would not allow me to accompany him to Jepara. We don't know what he and the girl discussed. When he arrived back in Semarang, he would not say a thing about what had happened.

It would be a mistake to think the meeting he held in Jepara was not important. Everything that a Member of Parliament does has a political purpose, even if it is only talking with a housemaid.

It seems that the girl is being fought over by the different political groupings. Van Kollewijn's visit was just one of many. You may remember how she handled the first attempt to force her to marry? Or perhaps you've never heard the story. Among us journalists it is a public secret. When the crisis came and the emotional stress became very great, she fell seriously ill. People were predicting that she would break with her family and convert to Protestant Christianity. Dr N. Adriani and Dr Bervoets, the founders of the first mission hospital in Mojowarno, also visited her on behalf of certain political groups.

It's a pity we don't know what really happened. So this information is just for your information, not for publication.

And what about yourself? I'm sure you've been able to make contact with the Liberal group in Betawi. I'm sure the discussions have been very interesting. It's a shame there is no Liberal newspaper in the Indies. De Locomotief has to self-censor itself all the time just to avoid incurring the wrath of the Sugar Syndicate and the Agricultural Traders' Association. We must learn to avoid all the obstacles that are put in our way by the Government and big business and we must learn to navigate the corals that lie under the sea that are there because of our own desires.

Even so, our paper is still considered the best in the Indies, with the biggest circulation and with the best reputation as a source of reliable information.

You're not interested in seeing Semarang? I'll take you to see the Soerja Soemirat Association, an organisation founded by local Eurasians. It is the biggest and most successful social organisation in the Indies. You would learn a lot from the experiences of the Soerja Soemirat. It runs a mechanical repair shop, a technical school , an orphanage and a few small businesses. I think you would admire how these, mostly poor, Eurasians have been able to band together and, through some manufacturing and trading, look after themselves. They are not dependent on any Governement authority or any of the big companies. They are taught, and teach each other, how to stand on their own two feet . . .

The next few letters I can combine together like this:

Do you remember our conversation on the way home in the delman after the meeting at the Harmoni club? It looked then as if van Heutsz was going to get the support of the Liberals. Perhaps he and van Kollewijn had made a deal of some kind. Van Heutsz may soon be installed as Governor-General. If this happens, then there will be an evil alliance here in the Indies between the Free Democractic Party and the military.

Then Ter Haar went off to the Netherlands. His letters from Holland were mainly personal. At the beginning of 1904, he returned to the Indies and visited me at the dormitory. He said it was now certain that van Heutsz would be made Governor-General. He had emerged the lone victor after an almighty fight among all the generals. He was the one who suggested the new position of armed forces chief, which the rest were now fighting over. In the meantime, he will take the position of Governor-General. Yes, a clever move. He would now have the highest position in the land. And tribute for life from every Resident he appointed!

A few months later van Heutsz was appointed Governor-General of the Netherlands Indies and Ter Haar wrote me:

We can only pray that the idea of the territorial integrity of the Indies is not going to mean war. Now that the Aceh War is over, the army has all its forces at its disposal. It can do whatever it wants. If war does come, let's hope it does not mean that more of the independent parts of the Indies will have to suffer the hell that Aceh did. I am worried about the talk in military circles here, that after Aceh, it will be Bali's turn.

The military's calculations are that the Balinese will be just as fanatical as the Acehnese, even though their religion is different. The Natives there were always fighting each other though, they are saying. And the colonial authorities were also involved. And they would be victorious over the Balinese as well as the Acehnese. They are also saying that the divide and conquer policy was not working. The Dutch had been in alliance with the king of Buleleng for twelve years and still they had not conquered Bali . . .

I wrote to him that his letter reminded me of two reports I had read about

123

Bali. One was to do with prohibition against the ritual cremation of widows at their husband's funeral and the other was about the ransacking of a merchant ship, the *Sri Kumala*, that was wrecked on Gumicik beach, near Sanur.

He answered:

The Netherlands Indies excercises no authority in Bali. The ban on the cremations was just propaganda, to boost Europe's image as humanitarian and as having law. Holland had no effective authority in Bali, not even in the friendly kingdom of Buleleng. The Balinese, who are a proud people, did not hear and did not listen to the Dutch prohibition.

The newspaper reports are true. The ship Sri Kumala, *which was wrecked off Sanur, was sacked by the local people, who also killed the crew. Emissaries from the Netherlands Indies Government travelled from Batavia and Surabaya to Denpasar to demand compensation of one thousand ringgit.*

My friend Minke, I think it is all part of a scheme, worked out by van Heutsz's military, to start a war with Bali. They have to find an excuse. There must be a reason, some proper grounds, to attack another party because that's the European way of thinking. Not like the Asian kings – they attacked other kingdoms giving no other reason than that they wanted to be stronger than the others. Europe must have a reason, even if it is just made up and isn't really true, but there must be some excuse for the action. To satisfy their intellect, my friend Minke, not their morality, neither of which Natives have anyway. The odds are one in ten, my friend, that van Heutsz will almost definitely implement his plan to 'unify' the Netherlands Indies.

Do you remember how van Zeggelen attacked van Heutsz that time? She wasn't wrong about him. I'm sure if war breaks out between the Netherlands Indies and Bali, she will go to Bali and show her support for the Balinese heroes, just as she did for the Buginese and the Acehnese in their defeat.

Or do you think the Balinese might win?

Perhaps the Balinese could have won if they hadn't been so lax during the last several years. Did you know that twenty years ago the black market for weapons in Singapore was dominated by the competition between Aceh and Bali? The Acehnese used the dollars from their pepper, the Balinese used slaves. The Chinese traders of Singapore had enough slaves, especially women for mistresses, so Bali lost out. The weapons flowed to Aceh. Then the Dutch attacked Aceh and the war started. Bali felt safe again. Bali no longer tried to arm itself. Now it's too late. Bali will be defeated. There are no grounds at all for thinking that Bali might win. Even so we can still pray that there will be no war.

Then a letter from my old correspondent Miriam de la Croix arrived from Holland. She had married a lawyer, a thirty-eight-year-old widower.

If you write to me, don't use my family name, wrote Mir Frischboten. *My husband was born in Bandung. He is fluent in Sundanese and Malay. Unfortunately he can't speak Javanese. He wants to go back to Java and open a practice in Bandung.*

I have told him a lot about you and he very much wants to meet you.

There are rumours going about that there is trouble in Bali. Is it true? There are no reports in the papers here, just gossip, especially around the stock market. If it is true, what is your opinion about what is happening?

Oh yes, I forgot to tell you that the authoress Marie van Zeggelen has arrived in Holland. She has been giving many lectures about the Acehnese war. I went to listen one time. She was glorifying the Acehnese women who went forth into battle with the men, to die or be wounded. And that has never happened in Europe, although here the movement for women's rights is now at its peak.

She told of the loyalty of the Acehnese fighters to their country, people and religion. She told of their defeat, which they suffered stoically – in a war which was completely different than the Boer War in South Africa or the wars that had taken place between European countries. A special Acehnese kind of war: one that did not know night or day. The only war during three centuries of Dutch presence in the Indies that had independence as its goal.

Everyone is saying, including Father, that the Balinese have learnt a lot from the fall of the Javanese. It won't be so easy to conquer them. Is it true what they're saying, that the Indies will invade Bali? Tell me something about Bali. They say the men are all handsome and brave and the women accomplished in many things.

I answered Mir Frischboten's letter by passing on what Ter Haar had told me. I had no choice as there was no other material to use. There was still almost no news at all in the papers about Bali.

This is what Ter Haar had written me:
I will tell you what little I know about Bali.

It's true not much has been written about Bali. One day if I get a chance to go there, perhaps I will have more to say.

The emissary from the Netherlands Indies who went to Denpasar met the Raja of Klungkung's First Minister, I Goesti Agoeng Djelantik. What van Heutsz had been hoping for happened. As had been predicted, Djelantik rejected the claim for compensation. People said that the First Minister was indeed speaking officially on behalf of the Raja of Klungkung who was in the Asmarapura Palace in Klungkung itself.

'We will pay compensation in the form of the tip of our spears.'

And so van Heutsz now had his excuse for invading Bali.

One company of troops landed at Sanur and another two landed at Kuta. They were both under orders to march on Denpasar.

If you read the next issue of the army magazine, you'll get a more detailed idea of what happened – though you must remember not to accept everything it says as the whole truth.

It's indeed pitiful to see a country that has not yet been touched by the spirit of the modern era. They can never win, no matter how brave and strong are their warriors. Look at Bali. The Klungkung Kingdom engages in hardly any trade. So it cannot afford a decent-sized standing army. It's immoral in these

125

times to rely simply on the loyalty of the people, especially when you've been using the people as a source of luxury and comfort for the king and his family. Yes, even though the writers and the priests have tried to teach loyalty through religion and even by deifying the king, such a country will be defeated.

Perhaps you disagree. Please let us know your views on this matter.

I answered his letter by saying that I was too busy with work and study to give it any thought. And, in any case, I didn't have any information upon which to base my comments.

In his next letter, he rebuked me with the following words:

How can you be so apathetic about the disaster that has befallen your fellow countrymen? Don't you feel their suffering as your own? Yes, they are Balinese but they are of the Indies and therefore also your countrymen. Their skin is the same as your skin. The water they drink and the rice they eat is the same. You cannot use your studies as an excuse, no matter how much work you have to do. Being apathetic about what is happening is the same as helping the army vanquish the Balinese people. Why can't you put aside just a few minutes to think about them, to discuss with your friends what is happening?

He was right. The Balinese were my fellow countrymen. But it was also true that I had no chance to discuss what was happening to the Balinese with the other students. They were all busy with their own affairs. Most of them didn't even read the newspapers. Newspapers cost more than cigarettes. Most gave priority to the latter. And they were already satisfied with the prospect of being appointed a government doctor when they graduated. So, in the end, I never discussed it with anyone, not even with my wife.

Mir Frischboten raised another issue:

My husband heard news that the Netherlands Indies Government had taken a decision to exile a sultan from the Moluccas. He and his family had been exiled to Java. He said they had been confined to somewhere around Sukabumi. Is it true? If so, could you let us know what has happened?

Her letter reminded me of what happened to the girl from Jepara. Was it Mir's questions that were supplying information, consciously or otherwise, to van Kollewijn? Governor-General Rosenboom felt it was necessary to silence our friend in Jepara by condemning her to the matrimonial bedroom. What about Mir? And wasn't it possible that I was also being used by people in Holland as a source of information? At the very least were they getting what I had received from Ter Haar?

So what was Mir Frischboten really up to? Who else received letters like this?

And as for me, why was I never able to answer any questions based on my own knowledge? How was it that they knew far more about what was happening in the Indies than I, and I lived here?

But as usual all these questions went by the board because of my studies and work. I never answered Mir Frischboten's letter. And I didn't enquire of Ter Haar about the sultan from the Molucccas. So I didn't hear from Mir for quite a while. But Ter Haar kept on writing.

His next letter was no longer so accusing:

Yes, you're not to blame. It shouldn't surprise anyone that you don't know much about the Indies. It's the journalist's profession to seek out news and analyse events. It's the task of a student to seek information and explanations from his teachers and his books.

One week ago two army platoons were despatched from Surabaya to Bali. I don't know how many have been sent from other areas. It seems that the army is finding it difficult to cope with the resistance. It's amazing when you think that it's only six kilometres from Sanur to Denpasar and only eleven kilometres from Kuta. They've been fighting for twenty days and Denpasar still hasn't fallen. Do you understand what that means? Spears and arrows have fought off rifles for twenty days! You should feel proud. Twenty days!

One week after I received his letter, the papers announced that Denpasar had fallen. Denpasar fell thirty days after the army attacked.

In another letter Ter Haar reported the news behind the news:

It was a courageous fight, rarely equalled anywhere in human history, perhaps one of its kind. The King of Klungkung, I Dewa Agoeng Djambe, ordered all the kings's family, and the families of the other nobles, men and women, to fight a Perang Puputan, a fight to the last person.

Your fellow countrymen, men and women, these courageous Balinese, went forward into battle. The women, with their babies on their backs, carrying spear or keris, charged like flying ants diving into fire. They would never return to their homes. They would remain on the battlefield bathed in their blood or the blood of their babies.

When I heard this news, my friend, I stood and bowed my head in memory of these heroes, not one of whose names I knew. A great love for these courageous people rose up within me. It is a pity you cannot leave your studies for a while. I want to go to Bali. I would very much like to have you go with me. You would be able to write a story about this never-to-be-equalled heroism. It is a pity that I am not a writer.

But even with the fall of Denpasar, Bali had not surrendered. The centre of government in Klungkung would not surrender. It could not yet be subdued. They had not yet got their hands on it. The war would continue . . .

If Marie van Zeggelen had written to me, perhaps she would have said the Balinese war was not fought because of the desire for independence and freedom as was the case with Aceh. This was one of the old-style wars of resistance against the Dutch that had occurred all over the Indies.

I read Ter Haar's letter over and over again. Day after day I waited for Ter Haar's next report. Each time I read his letter I was more impressed with the courage of the Balinese. They were not yet acquainted with modern

European science and knowledge but they were prepared to sacrifice their most valuable property, their lives, so as to not have to bow down before the Dutch. And at the school that I had now left, they were happy just to know that in the future they would be employed by the Government as a doctor, the same Government that was raping Bali. In the name of the territorial integrity of the Indies!

I would never serve the Government, that conspiracy of murderers. I left my desk, went into my room, and stood before the portrait of Mei. 'I'm sorry I never told you about this. You have gone without ever knowing that there was a people that fought the Europeans to their last man, woman and child . . .'

The portrait remained silent, refusing to speak.

What must I do now? Struggle in the modern era? Suddenly I remembered Ter Haar's words that day – a long time ago – aboard the ship from Surabaya: Political struggle today must use modern methods – organisation. Become a giant, said the old doctor. And Mei too. And each part of the body would be stronger than the sum of the individuals who were in it. Begin to organise! Your heart is not a desert, is it?

If your people had the courage to fight like the Balinese, to the last man, woman and child as in the Puputan War, but using modern methods! But how? Organise! Organise now! cried Mei, the old doctor, Ter Haar. But how? How? HOW?

Begin, and you will find the answers, resounded Mei's voice from several years before.

I bowed my head, went back to my desk. I took out my diary and wrote these words: 'Today I begin.'

That evening some of the students from the medical school came to my house. We all sat and chatted beneath the picture of *Flower of the Century's End*. The room was filled with smoke. My housemaid was busy going back and forth looking after my guests. There were also some who had been my juniors. There were sixteen in all.

They were all talking about girls, a subject that never ran dry. There was a new student there who sat silently through the whole conversation, just staring at the picture.

'You seem to be really taken by that picture,' someone chided him.

He turned away without answering, and then seemed to fall into a silent reverie.

'You're usually quite cheerful,' someone else commented.

'Can we discuss something more serious,' I suggested. Before anyone had a chance to protest, I continued: 'Have any of you heard what has happened in Bali?'

128

Not one knew what had happened. Not one.

The rowdiness disappeared. Everything was quiet. I told them about Bali, about the attack on Denpasar and how the war escalated, and about the Puputan battle.

'There has never been such a heroic war in Java, or in Europe.'

'But they were defeated,' interrupted Partokleooo.

'They lost only because they weren't properly prepared. As human beings and heroes, they are worthy of much more admiration than the army.'

'Perhaps. But they lost,' insisted Partokleooo, who had never read a newspaper in his life. 'Not being prepared is just an excuse. If you decide to fight the army, it means you've calculated that you are prepared and that you do have the ability to win.'

'I know what you're getting at,' interrupted Tjipto. 'You want to talk about what preparations are needed, what are the conditions that have to be fulfilled.'

The one who had been admiring *Flower of the Century's End*, with the round face, smiled, and looked at me with gleaming eyes, but he still didn't say anything.

'Begin', Tjipto encouraged me.

And I began to explain my views about what the backward countries, very backward countries, such as ours, needed to survive in the modern era.

'It is precisely fulfilling the appropriate conditions that makes you modern. First you must have modern science and knowledge, then modern organisation and modern technology.'

'We're starting to get more modern science and knowledge,' someone said.

'But we don't have any modern organisation yet,' I quickly added.

'So you make technology the bottom priority?' someone asked disapprovingly.

'Exactly. What we need now is organisation.'

'The old doctor failed in his efforts,' interrupted Partokleooo.

'He didn't fail completely. His voice lives on in the hearts of some people. It's just that no one has started yet,' Wardi supported me.

'At the very least, my heart is not a desert in which he cries out hopelessly,' I said, 'and I think that goes for many of us.'

'It's easy for you to talk like that,' contradicted Partokleooo, no longer timid like a rabbit. 'You're not studying any more. You're not being hounded all the time by the teachers. Why didn't you talk like this before?'

'Up to now all anyone has done is talk about organising.' The round-faced youth made his voice heard, 'no one has ever dared try to do it.'

The maid come in and told me that the locksmith had arrived.

I excused myself for a few minutes and went out back.

The locksmith was a young, full-blood Chinese. I took him into my room to open my wardrobe so he could make a key mould.

'There's the wardrobe,' I said.

But he didn't move straight away. He stood instead in front of the painting of Mei, glancing back and forth between me and the portrait. Only after a while did he come away from the painting. He took out a big bunch of keys from under his pyjamas and tried several of them. None of them worked. Only then did he try the master key, with its many teeth, and after a bit the door opened. He studied the master key for a moment and then made a mould in some soft wax. Using the mould he made a dummy key from tin and tried it.

'It works, Tuan,' he said. 'Tomorrow you will have a new key.'

He didn't leave straight away, stopping again in front of Mei's picture. He glanced across at me, and, putting on an innocent air, asked: 'There is a picture of a Chinese woman here, Tuan?'

'Engkoh knows her?'

He looked at me again, his accusing eyes also full of suspicion. He neither nodded nor shook his head. Perhaps this locksmith was a memeber of the Young Generation and a friend of Mei. Or he could also be a member of the Old Generation. If he was the latter then he was a potential murderer or kidnapper of my wife. It was clear from his behaviour that there was no other possibility. Whether he was from the Old or Young Generation, he was looking for Mei.

'She died, Koh,' I said.

He seemed stunned and bit his lip.

'Her name was Ang San Mei. You're looking for her, aren't you? She was my wife.'

He seemed nervous. I guessed he was indeed a friend of Mei.

'While she was sick none of her friends came to see her.' He bowed his head deeply. 'You didn't come either. She died peacefully in my arms in hospital.'

He didn't say anything, pretending not to understand what I was talking about. He asked permission to leave, his head still bowed down. I escorted him outside, down the steps and across the yard to the street.

I went back to my friends. From my chair I could see the locksmith. He couldn't make up his mind what to do. He walked back and forth, stopping occasionally to look in the direction of my house. Perhaps he had smuggled himself into the Indies like Mei and her fiancé. Perhaps he was someone new, who had just arrived. Perhaps he too was a university student, and now wandered about Betawi in pyjamas as a locksmith. Whether or not he was a locksmith, maybe he was also working away for his country and people, even though they might not know it. His English might also be as fluent as my late comrade's or Mei's. And such lack of pretensions!

My country has not been conquered by a foreign people as yours has, chided Mei's voice. Your work will be more difficult than mine. Your method

130

of work will also be different. And you still haven't started.

The locksmith disappeared from view.

'Gentlemen,' I continued, 'two years ago the old doctor, who had spent all his savings to travel around on his mission, said that we were already four years behind the Chinese who had founded the Tiong Hoa Hwee Koan. And we were already two years behind the Arabs. Now we must add a further two years. So what will we do about it, my friends?'

They had not been able to come to any agreement while I was out attending to the locksmith. They suggested that I begin, but that they couldn't afford to disrupt their studies. They would not be able to pay the school if they were expelled.

'I do not mean to disrupt your studies, gentlemen. Even so I ask you to at least think a little about what we've discussed. The others have brought in teachers from China and Japan, and the Arabs from Egypt and Algeria. They insist on not teaching Dutch, but English instead. Their graduates continue their studies in schools in Singapore or other British countries. They will return to the Indies as first-class graduates. We will be left even further behind. And still we are not making any efforts. None.'

The discussion had spoilt their evening. The gaiety had disappeared. The round-faced student returned to silently gazing at the picture.

'It's only a picture,' someone teased him.

It wasn't even nine o'clock before they had drifted back to the dormitory. When the curfew horn blew there was not a single one left. It was my fault, they did not need an organisation yet.

The next afternoon the locksmith returned as promised with the new key. After he had handed it over, he forced himself to ask: 'Don't be angry, Tuan, but may I ask where your wife is buried?'

If he knew his friends might come and ask for her to be moved from the Moslem cemetery where she was buried. No. She will be buried in the earth that I had bought for her, and for myself in the future. I would not tell him where.

And he didn't insist.

'She didn't leave behind any writings?'

'Yes.'

'May I see them, Tuan.'

I knew that her friends had a greater right to them than I. I went inside and tried out the new key. It worked. I took out a bundle of Mei's writings and gave them to him.

While standing in the door, the young Chinese man silently read through them. I didn't know what was in them. And while he was reading I was able to study the young man's face. A free man, selling his services cheaply, yet with an interest in papers, dedicating himself to his country and people. No one can possibly love their country, echoed Mei, if they aren't familiar with the materials that tell about it. If they are not familiar with its history. And especially if they have never done any service for it.

He sat down at the kitchen table and was served coffee and fried bananas. I stood next to him as he read. His bag, which was canvas and had once been white, rested across his legs. After he finished reading, he become lost in thought and then he glanced up at me.

'What do they say? I asked in English.

'They are not for Tuan,' he answered in Malay.

So he did understand English.

'Yes,' I said in Malay, 'but what do they say?'

'They are not for Tuan,' he insisted.

'Very well. Then take them all.'

He bowed politely and left, taking with him the letters and his old canvas bag. His pyjamas were old, and washed thoroughly as if they had never ever been dirty. So unpretentious. He knew one of the modern languages. He was educated. What force was it that gave him the strength to work so hard for a country so far away, with an income of just a few cents here and there?

I was engrossed in trying to estimate my own strength. I must also be able to do it! I shouted.

I will begin. I had obviously failed with the students from the medical school. There was no other choice than to use the tried and tested method of calling out to people, explaining and giving information. But call out to whom? In public meetings? On a one-to-one basis? And if individually, who?

I chose the latter.

While thinking about just who I should approach, I left the house and went for a walk through Kwitang Kampung. Remembering what my friend Jean Marais, the painter in Surabaya, had once said, I started to observe more closely all the people about me. It was clear that I could not ask these people to discuss the issue of a modern organisation. They know nothing of their own country. Most probably they rarely ever leave their *kampung*. They have never read a book. Illiterate. Their ancestors only ever knew the epic tales of heroes greater than the gods, yet who were always defeated by the colonial army.

The little children were playing in the streets as usual, with only bibs covering their chests. A tuft of hair on the top of their forehead. Snot dribbling down about their mouth. In a few years they will have grown up to become the illiterate youth of the *kampung*. Only one or two of them would get to learn to read and write and would end up as a foreman over the others. Most would die due to one or another parasitical disease. Could they reach forty? And if they did survive until forty, if they overcame the diseases that inflicted them, would their life be any better than it was when they were children? They would continue to live within their narrow destiny. Never having any comparison. Happy are they who know nothing. Once you can compare your situation with others, once you have that knowledge, only restlessness and dissatisfaction ensue.

Along the side of a lane was the leather workshop owned by the man Da'im. His workers slaved from nine in the morning until nine at night, working half-naked to make harnesses and horseshoes. I often passed this workshop. None of them knew me, although they all knew who I was. I thought to myself, if the breadwinner was tied to his workplace like this, how much more so his children and his wife.

The local *dokar* owner, wrapped in a *sarong* and wearing a Chinese shirt, nodded and gave me a friendly smile. Perhaps he was on his way to an opium den. His lips were blue and he had sunken eyes. And standing over by the foodstall was Mat Colek. Everyone was afraid of him. People said he was a thief and a paid killer. Perhaps, like Abang Puasa in Francis's story of *Nyai Dasima*, Mat Colek seemed to think humankind was his personal herd of cattle, the same attitude displayed by British, Japanese and European imperialism. He also nodded a greeting. Perhaps he remembered the time his jaw was dislocated and couldn't be closed any more and I helped him. Maybe if I hadn't fixed his jaw that time, he wouldn't be able to ride herd over his cattle. Aha, over there is Mak Romlah, walking along, chewing *sirih* and expelling red spit onto the ground as she goes. She is a madam kept busy looking after many prostitutes.

Young men dressed in pyjamas were off to earn some money and young Moslem women, their heads covered, were heading off to unknown destinations. What lived within these young people's minds? Marriage, bearing children, multiplying snotty-nosed, naked, bib-wearing babies, getting divorced, marrying again?

And out there to the north, Japan had defeated the Russian army and navy.

And still I could not think of who I should approach.

I looked back over my past. Not everything had gone smoothly, like a train shooting along its rails. All these people around me had never known any of what I had known. They probably had never even sat in a classroom. They knew nothing else except making a living and multiplying themselves. Beings kept like a herd of cattle! They don't even understand how badly off they are. And neither do they know of the giant forces building up to the north, eating everything in their path, never satisfied. And if they did know, they would not care.

Among all these people I felt like an all-knowing god, who also knew how pathetic would be their fate if the bacteria of the north kept spreading. They would become cattle ridden over by criminals and imperialists together. Something had to be done. Something! Was organising the only way? I could not answer. I didn't know. And if we had an organisation, then what?

Was their situation any better before the people and land of the Indies had fallen into the grip of the Dutch? My teachers at school had taught that things had been worse. The *rajas* had never cared about the health and welfare of their subjects – only about how to rob them and use them for royal pleasure. And, damn it, I had to agree with my teachers.

Ibu Baldrun kept pushing me to marry again. She rattled off a list of candidates: 'It's better Denmas take one, two or even three wives rather than take a mistress,' she said.

I left her house. I continued my stroll. Now I began to think about mistresses. As everywhere else people here looked at mistresses somewhat askance. They were considered to be only slightly higher than prostitutes. Except of course if you were taken as a mistress by a foreigner. Nyai Ontosoroh in Surabaya had been able to prove herself to have a high social status, higher than a woman who was legally married. My mother was not ashamed to be with her, even to have her as the mother-in-law of her son. And the children of mistresses taken by foreigners all seemed to be more advanced than the children of genuine Natives. They received a European education and they absorbed either the best or worst from both their parents. And once they were adults, society eventually acknowledged them.

And so what about taking mistresses and what about prostitution? Well it began with them using their only capital – their bodies. The Resident of East Sumatra also prostituted himself, didn't he? With his power? And what about all the Native kings who had prostituted themselves, selling their authority to the Dutch? To the plantations? Even to the extent of hiring out the villages and their people? The aim – money, money, to get money without working. There was risk! What isn't without risk? Life itself is a risk. Every tooth lodged there in your gums is at risk.

Ah why was my head full of mistresses and their children, and prostitutes? It's another issue! My late comrade, the late Ang San Mei, the locksmith and his friends, had they ever come face to face with the problems of prostitution and the keeping of mistresses? Had the organisation they praised so much answered them then? How is it to be done? How? How? HOW? Everything that we are fighting, Mei once said, has the one source – our own backwardness, and our stupid, groundless and excessive national pride. And our backwardness made us choose the Empress as our symbol, the Empress and all her power and all her instruments of power. The empire had to be overthrown and replaced with a republic.

Would that guarantee change?

A start must be made by beginning, she repeated over and over again.

At the corner of a lane across the way, a man and wife were arguing. The children were looking on. The wife was roaring her protests against her husband: You're hardly earning anything, every year there are more kids, and now you go and take another wife!

Wasn't life so often hell for the women who gave birth to it? Surely there was more to life than this? What was the meaning of life if this was all there was?

When I got back I ordered that all the front doors and windows be shut. I was receiving no guests, no matter who. I had to think everything over. And my pen flowed across paper. The voices of the old Java Doctor, of Mei, of Ter Haar, echoed within my mind, of the rise of Japan until its victory, of the time we first met until the time we separated forever. In the end, I concluded, a progressive people can look after their own welfare, no matter how few they are or how small their country. The Netherlands Indies Government has an interest in limiting Native people's access to modern knowledge and science. The Natives must look after themselves.

I jumped up from my chair, marvelling at whether the logic here was right. I thought it over again and again.

Suddenly I was interrupted. A postman arrived and asked me to sign for a registered letter. From the Director of my former school. A summons to come back to school? What did school mean to me now?

But it was something else. He wrote to say he was sorry and that they had overcharged me regarding the money I repaid the school. There was another letter giving me authority to obtain a refund from the State Treasury Office – eight hundred and sixty-five guilders.

I would return it to Mama in Surabaya.

A good omen. A good omen.

None of the newspapers would publish my article. They turned it down coldly. All the editors I had got to know returned it without comment. Finally I took it to a small paper that carried no advertising. Its pages were small too. After reading it the editor asked me: 'So what do you want the Natives to become, Meneer? You want them to become white people?'

'I want them to stand equal with and not under your people,' I answered.

'Here is not the place for this,' he said. 'I don't think the paper that would publish this has been born yet.'

What Kommer had always said turned out to be right. They allowed no road that leads to a better life for Natives. The Natives would have to struggle for themselves. This is a basic truth that must be faced.

The scribe I had hired for a week had finished his work. He had made twenty-three copies of my translation of the Constitution of the Tiong Hoa Hwee Koan. I had changed it here and there according to my own thoughts. There was also a covering letter and another calling on people to help establish the organisation. I also had these copied.

I checked over the copies and addressed them. The clerk put them in envelopes and put stamps on them.

'Post them now and then come back here,' I said.

Ten minutes later he was back. And so his work was done. He would collect his pay and go.

'Tuan,' said Sandiman, 'if you're satisfied with my work . . . ' He didn't go on.

'What is it, Sandiman?'

'Were you disappointed with my work?'

'There was not one word that was wrongly written.'

'Allow me to work for you.'

'I can't afford to pay a monthly wage.'

'I have no wife or child, Tuan. Any wage will be all right.'

'Ten guilders?'

'That would be fine, Tuan.'

'And what happens when I don't have any money?'

'Whatever you decide, Tuan.'

'And if I have no work for you?'

'There will always be work, Tuan. I can also sweep.'

'And if one day I can't afford to supply you with rice any more, then what?'

'I don't think things will ever reach that stage, Tuan.'

And so it was that I obtained a helper.

He was born and raised in Solo. His older brother was a soldier in the Mangkunegaran Legion. His brother had suggested several times that he also join, but he did not like the soldier's life. He left his brother and came to Betawi seeking new experiences.

'Why didn't you look for a job in a sugar plantation?'

'No, Tuan.' He always spoke in Malay.

'What are your hopes for the future, working for me like this?'

'It is not my future that concerns me now.'

'Very well, that's your business.'

It turned out he did not have a place to stay so he moved into my house. He stayed in the room at the back. And his only clothes were the ones he was wearing. That was all he owned in the world that could be touched and seen. He did not bow and bend all the time like most Javanese. And he did not raise his thumb every time he told me something was ready. He spoke school Malay not bazaar Malay.

Sandiman soon proved himself to be a very good assistant. Every morning when I awoke there was a newspaper beside my coffee. Breakfast was waiting in the front room. He noted down both my ingoing and outgoing correspondence, washed the floor, swept the yard, fixed up the garden, scrubbed the window frames and tidied up the tables and chairs, as if I were some rich man whose money he could hope for.

One afternoon when I arrived home he handed me a bundle of letters. There was a letter from Ter Haar and some replies to the materials I had sent out. Not everyone replied and only four supported the idea. One of these was the Bupati of Serang.

The Bupati of Serang was well known in educated circles as a student of Dr Snouck Hurgronje. He was the student Mir had told me about long ago, the boy Snouck Hurgronje had used as a guinea pig. Guinea pig or not, he was well respected by both educated Natives and Europeans. People said that he not only always scored nine out of ten for his French, but he was a diligent reader and was never afraid to speak out his mind, no matter to whom.

If someone as widely respected as the Bupati of Serang publicly supported the formation of a new organisation, then no one would have any excuse to be suspicious or apathetic. People would flock to join. I would try him first.

The next day I handed the house over to Sandiman. To Serang!

The train journey was slow. The rain meant that every time the furnace was stoked thick, black smoke spewed out. It was evening by the time I arrived. I had to book into a very simple inn.

I believed this Western-educated *bupati* would be a modern man. He would certainly be different from Bupati Lebak Kartawidjaja of the time of Controller Eduard Douwes Dekker, as told in *Max Havelaar*. He was the first Javanese to use a surname. He would be somebody with whom you could have an open and frank discussion.

A messenger took me to the *pendopo*. And, ya Allah, I would have to once again crawl across the floor to seek audience with him. No doubt to be followed by innumerable genuflections of obeisance. How could it be like this between two modern people? This kind of barbaric custom could not be accepted.

The messenger bowed before me and then backed far away.

Should I cancel this initiative? It would be very easy. But I needed this person. The organisation will need public acceptance. And his blessing will help. It would even be good if he were to join. This kind of tactic must not be given up. The organisation must be founded and must succeed.

I took off my shoes, I adjusted my *destar*, and I crawled across to the appointed place. I crawled, though not as slowly and slimily as a snail. Crawling!

The *pendopo* was no different from any other in Java, even its decorations were standard issue. And I stopped, sitting squatted in front of his chair. What kind of show was this?

I must not be offended, for the sake of the success of our enterprise. My hands moved naturally together to make obeisance to him when he came in and sat down. As soon as my hands came down, I heard his voice, speaking in rapid Dutch: 'Is it Raden Mas I find before me here?'

'You are not mistaken, Gusti Kanjeng.'

'Greetings, Raden Mas.'

'A thousand thanks, Gusti Kanjeng,' I answered and once again raised my clasped hands in obeisance. 'May Gusti Kanjeng always be blessed with happiness.'

'I have received your letter and I understand your intentions, Raden Mas.'

'I thank you a thousand times for giving my letter your attention, Gusti Kanjeng. I have come in the hope that Gusti Kanjeng may be willing to spend some time further discussing the idea.'

'It was very interesting. When will such an organisation be founded and what will be its name?'

'That will depend on its founding meeting. If Gusti Kanjeng could find time, perhaps, to attend . . . '

My words disappeared in the wave of uproarious laughter that burst forth. I could see that his *kain* was shaking because of his laughter.

'The Bupati of Serong attend such a meeting. Heh, Raden Mas, who do you think the Bupati of Serong is? Your equal?'

Was this the person that everyone talked about as being brilliant, his French never scoring below eight, a diligent reader, charismatic, educated, a modern person, and well liked?

'A thousand pardons, Gusti Kanjeng.'

'I'll tell you, Raden Mas, two years ago a retired Java Doctor came to see me. He sat right where you are sitting now. He was just a Mas. He made the same suggestion that you have. My answer was the same. Who do you think the Bupati of Serong is? You are a Raden Mas. Even so, my answer is still the same.'

My blood boiled. I raised my head and looked at him without bowing: 'I came here to meet with an educated man, to have a discussion with a fellow educated person, to exchange thoughts, not to deliberate over the greatness of anybody. I thought you were genuinely concerned about what I had suggested, as was indicated in your letter. Did you think I came here just to admire you?'

I had stood up. I looked him straight in the face. His eyes were glowing with rage that a Native dared stand up before him.

'Perhaps the retired Java Doctor was willing to endure being humiliated by you but I am not. There is no law compelling anybody to crawl on the floor before you and make obeisance to you like a slave. Good morning.'

'Raden Mas!' He called me back.

I stopped and turned around. I saw that he had got up from his chair. I went back and said: 'If you are angry, you can bring a case before the courts charging me with violating protocol.'

'That would be easy, Raden Mas. But, in any case, a meeting that began with good intentions, should not end badly.' He held out his hand.

I took his hand. I could feel my hand shaking with anger, and I could feel his shaking as he restrained his.

'As an idea, your proposal is good, but . . . '

'I looked forward to meeting the Bupati of Serang as an educated Native, not as a Dutchman's *bupati*.'

'You forget that it is not whether people are educated or not, but rather what they do, what position it is that they hold. You forget that I am *Bupati*.'

I left him in his *pendopo* bearing his own pain brought about by his own arrogance. I left Serang straight away. Perhaps the old Java Doctor had been even more pained than I. Fine. And this was the result of my first foray.

It took me several days to get over my anger. Fortunately another letter arrived from Ter Haar, which boosted my spirits. It was from Bali.

My friend, now that Denpasar has been taken, the Dutch have decided to move against Klungkung. This means they intend to conquer all of Bali.

Here, standing on the Balinese earth, it is only the spirit of heroism that I feel. I came to Denpasar so I could have a chance to follow the army's movements. They banned me from following. But eventually, with the help of a Lieutenant Colijn, I was given permission to join a brigade that was ordered to go to Klungkung, which is about fifty kilometres from where I am now.

They had to march over the bodies of men, women and children for two months just to make six or eleven kilometres and then fight for another thirty-two days to actually take Denpasar. How many more thousands will die over the fifty kilometres to Klungkung, not to mention in the battle for Klungkung itself?

Denpasar is deathly silent. The dead no longer move. Those inhabitants, men, women and children, who are alive have moved to the east of the town, about four and a half kilometres away, where they have built a fortress on a hill surrounded by deep gorges. They call it Gelar Toh Pati – the place where we lay down our lives in battle.

My friend, the battalion that attacked Denpasar was almost wiped out. They had to continually bring in reinforcements. The troops' morale was collapsing. Lieutenant Colijn never stopped going around encouraging his men. Take whatever you can get from these people, he told them, their lives, their possessions, their women! Pillage everything there is to pillage!

I should tell you how the Balinese fought. I can't tell you all that much as this war is different from that fought in Aceh. The army's soldiers were marching along. The place seemed deserted except for the trees and beetles. Then, all of sudden, soldiers were falling to the ground everywhere, covered in blood. Their bodies were pierced by spears and keris. But nobody ever saw where the attack came from. The Balinese are like chameleons who can blend in with their surroundings. No one ever sees them when they attack.

The army attacked Gelar Toh Pati from three directions. They were almost all killed, including their commander, a captain. They had to call in more and more reinforcements. The Dutch decided to postpone their final assault. They had learnt from some Balinese traitors that the Balinese position was too strongly fortified. Toh Pati was four kilometres long, with several layers of embattlements. The Dutch decided to call in extra troops from outside the army, from the Mangkunegaran Legion.

To take Klungkung, the Dutch were forced to bypass Toh Pati. It might be several more years before they can overrun it. A remarkable people, the Balinese, to fight so fearlessly against a modern army like this. You can truly be proud of these people.

Praise of the Balinese danced and swayed before me. He was too clever a writer. He had aroused my sympathy for this people whom van Heutsz wanted to subjugate. If all the Indies had fought back like the Acehnese and the Balinese, perhaps today we would be as strong as Japan. The island of Java had run out of men, mobilised by the kings and the Dutch army, and killed on so many battlefields.

'Sandiman!'

He was washing the bicycle. From my window I could see him leave a rag on the handlebars and go to the well and wash his hands. He came inside to report, nodding, like a military man.

'Perhaps you too were once a Legion soldier?' I said, fishing about.

'What legion do you mean, Tuan.'

'Mangkunegaran, of course.'

'Yes it's true, Tuan, for five years.'

'What was your rank?'

'Very lowly, Tuan.'

From his quite un-Javanese attitude, I guessed that he had, in fact, held a high rank. He could tell me a lot about the Legion.

'Have you heard that there is a war going on in Bali?'

'I've heard, Tuan.'

'Have any of your family been involved?'

'Yes, it's true, Tuan. You have not guessed wrongly.'

'Did you resign properly from the Legion or did you desert?'

I watched him closely at that moment and so I began to suspect he was a deserter.

'I will not tell anyone,' I said, encouraging him. 'You can be honest with me. You could be in trouble if it was anyone else.'

'Thank you, Tuan.'

'Then you have heard the rumours that the Legion will be sent to Bali?'

'All of them know about it.'

'And so you don't agree?'

'More than just don't agree, Tuan. And it's not just me. Our duty is only to defend Mangkunegaran. The war in Bali has nothing to do with the defence

140

of Mangkunegaran. We didn't join the Legion to die in Bali. We often discussed this. People said that Balinese and Javanese had the same ancestors. Why should we be fighting each other?'

'If you were forced to take sides between the Dutch and the Balinese, who would you choose?'

'I wouldn't choose either. But neither do I want to fight against Bali.'

'Good, Get the bike ready. Can you ride it?'

'Not yet, Tuan.'

'Then learn.'

I pocketed the letters from the others who had responded positively to my call. I left for the first address – the Patih of the district of Meester Cornelis. As far as the Bupati of Serang was concerned, I struck his name off the list. I crossed off the other three *bupatis* as well. All the *bupatis* would behave the same way. I would have to look one level lower.

And I was right, the Patih of Meester Cornelis was much more polite. He invited me to sit in front of his desk.

'*Bendoro* Raden Mas?' he asked in Malay. 'I have discussed Raden Mas's letter with a number of other *wedana*. They have also discussed it with others outside my district. Congratulations, Raden Mas, most of them are also in agreement. And if the *wedana* agrees then his subordinates will also support the idea.'

'Thank you very much indeed, Tuan Patih. And what about yourself? What do you think?'

'What do I think? I've heard that you have had quite a bit of experience with the press. I think Raden Mas knows better than I. You must know a lot about what is happening in the world and here in the Indies. You will know what is best for us here. But yes, there must be efforts to advance our people, to improve their lives and their way of life. An honourable goal, Raden Mas, to build schools, educational hostels, and to explain to the Natives their rights under the law. Of course, you intend also to publish your own newspaper.'

'That will depend on the decision of our first assembly, Tuan Patih.'

'Good, good. There is something else you should know, Raden Mas, if you care to listen . . . '

There was a wealthy man, of only lowly official position, who had long dreamt of starting an endeavour such as this. But because of his lowly position, he had always held back from starting. He was a charitable man who was always prepared to help a good cause.

' . . . try contacting him. One man like him is worth a thousand like me, even though I have a higher position.'

The person he was referring to was the Wedana from Mangga Besar, Thamrin Mohammed Thabrie.

A *wedana*! My thoughts dashed about trying to guess what kind of

141

education he might have obtained. At the most he would have finished primary school, wouldn't be able to speak Dutch, and would know very little about the ways of the world. So I didn't take the Patih's suggestion seriously.

'And you yourself, Tuan Patih, are you prepared to help with getting this organisation of ours started?'

'Contact the Wedana of Mangga Besar first. If he agrees, then everything will be much easier.'

That's all he would say. I couldn't get anything more out of him. I asked to be excused and he escorted me to the front door.

I went about on my bike visiting the other people on my list, each time trying to find out more about Mohammed Thabrie, who certainly seemed to be held in very high regard by the Patih of Meester Cornelis.

'The Wedana of Mangga Besar? A big landowner,' said one.

'Thamrin Mohammed Thabrie? A very pious man,' said another.

'It's true,' said another, 'he once paid for the building of two mosques.'

'A very generous man,' said someone at another address, going on to explain how he had been helped out of some difficult circumstances, which is why he still had his present position.

It seemed he was quite well known among the *priyayi*, not only as a *wedana* but also as a human being.

I stopped at a street stall just near his house in order to complete my information.

'He has houses everywhere,' said the stall owner. 'People say there are more than a hundred. And there is his *delman* business. And some say he even owns a shipping company which he has given to someone else to manage for him . . . '

Perhaps he's someone like Nyai Ontosoroh. He's sure to be a very interesting person. According to the Patih of Meester Cornelis, he is the key to the successful founding of the organisation we wanted.

My spirits rose again. His *pendopo* was spacious. There were two other people waiting. They were seated on a divan.

'Assalamu . . . '

A young man emerged from around the corner, still carrying a broom.

'Is Tuan Thamrin in?'

'Yes, Tuan, please take a seat.'

I went and sat down. I took the opportunity to observe the various people waiting to see the *wedana*. It seemed that *wedanas* were very busy people. I had plenty of time to look over the *pendopo*.

It was different from any other I had seen. Over the entrance there hung not only a picture of the Queen but also of the former English Lieutenant-Governor of Java, Sir Thomas Stamford Raffles. From whatever angle I looked at the picture, it looked exactly like Raffles. What was the relationship between the master of this house and Raffles? No other house would ever be decorated with pictures of Raffles. Or perhaps it wasn't Raffles at all?

And while I waited I reflected. Why was this man so influential? Because of his wealth? Because of his good deeds? Because of his intelligence? It must be because of one of these, or all of them.

My turn came one hour later. As the last guest came out of the office, he invited me to go in. Before me stood a Eurasian, wearing a *pici*, a Chinese jacket and a Samarinda *sarong*. His eyeglasses perched on the ridge of his nose. He welcomed me with a smile and greeted me warmly in Betawi-accented Malay: 'Ayoh, come on in, Tuan.'

I walked across to him and he held out his hand.

'You must have something important to discuss. I don't think you have ever been here before.'

I observed his brownish hair, now greying. He was still smiling. He invited me to sit down.

'Tuan Thabrie?'

'You're not mistaken. What can I do for you?'

I began to explain how I had come to be visiting him. He said he was sorry but he didn't understand Dutch. We continued the discussion in Malay.

'So it was Tuan Patih of Meester Cornelis who suggested you come see me,' he mused. 'Yes, he often comes here, but never says much. Tell me what this is all about.'

And so I told him about the plan to set up an organisation, and about its philosophy and aims and objectives. He pushed across a box of Cuban cigars, as was the practice among all the rich Europeans.

'If Tuan Patih thinks it is a good idea then I certainly will also agree,' he said humbly.

Behind his glasses, I could see his rather European-looking brown eyes. I think he often found people staring at his eyes. He took off his glases, wiped them with a handkerchief and put them back on.

'So you want to establish a *sarekat*?'

'*Sarekat*! What's that, Tuan?'

'You're a Moslem?'

'Of course, Tuan Thamrin.'

'Do you pray?'

'I'm sorry, Tuan Thamrin, no.'

He smiled and nodded, then: '*Laa syarikaa lahuu*,' he recited fluently, a quote from the Ifitah prayer, 'there is no other united with Him, with God. Sarekat, Tuan, means a union, an association based on having a common interest.'

'What's the best name, Tuan, *orginasasi* or *sarekat* compared to *perkumpulan* or *persekutuan*?'

'Of course sarekat is best. Firstly because it is an Arabic word, the language of the Koran. Secondly, because it reminds people of their *ikat*, their bond.

143

Thirdly, because it is shorter and simpler than *perkumpulan*. Fourthly, because it has nothing to do with *kutu* – lice. To unite is more than just gathering together, isn't it, eh? And *persekutuan* implies a gathering of people who share the same *kutu*, heh?' he laughed happily, admiring his own joke.

'We've just begun and you've already been able to pick such an exactly right, perfect word,' I complimented him. It seemed he too was pleased to be commended that way.

It was a very pleasurable meeting, with plenty of cigar smoke and a generous spread of refreshments. He was always quoting from the Koran to show that he was a Moslem. And that too was his right. His world and his personality united in this.

Once, when the converstion slowed a little, I had to ask: 'Perhaps I'm mistaken, Tuan, but isn't that a portrait of Lieutenant-Governor Thomas Stamford Raffles that hangs above that door?'

'Yes, you're right.'

And it struck me then the similarity between Thamrin and Thomas. Then: 'And you yourself bear quite a resemblance to him.'

'And so I decided to put up that picture.'

'Raffles is famous as a wise and knowledgeable man. Perhaps also because of that resemblance you are as wise as he.'

'Allah willing.'

'And your first name starts with the same letter. Thomas – Thamrin.'

He laughed, then shifted the conversation to another topic: 'I am willing to work for the sarekat, Tuan, a sarekat that does good works, and I'm willing to give money as well, providing, providing it does nothing to violate the law.'

That day I went back to see the Patih of Meester Cornelis.

'If he agrees, Raden Mas, then all will go smoothly. Many people are in his debt. Once he says "yes", the others will say "yes, yes". You can prepare as many invitations as possible and copies of the Constitution and Aims and Objectives. Don't use Dutch. Malay, Tuan. Only a few Natives can speak Dutch. You can give me one hundred invitations.'

'We'll have to find a place that can take that many people.'

'This *pendopo* can take over two hundred.'

I agreed, and he was very pleased that his place was going to be so honoured.

'You're right. This *pendopo* is going to be honoured indeed. The sarekat we will found here will be the very first Native modern organisation. And you and I are the initiators.'

He was very satisfied with my comments. The conversation then turned to Thamrin Mohammed Thabrie.

'Yes, he does look like a European. But his heart and soul are genuine Native. He was brought up and educated here in Betawi. His education?

144

Well, perhaps he had a little more schooling than his playmates.'

'Why has he hung a picture of Raffles in his house?'

'While Raffles was living here in Betawi, he lost his wife. She died, Tuan,' He hesitated to continue, but he went on anyway. 'She was buried in Jati Petamburan.' He stopped, he wasn't going to continue after all. 'Ah, it's just a coincidence. His father looked just like Raffles. At least his face, anyway . . . the more you move among the Betawi, the more you'll learn about him.'

And as I mused on this, I remembered the rumours about how the Bupatis of Kedu had been descendants of Governor-General Daendels. Ah, what does it matter who people are descended from? What matters is how a person treats his fellow human beings.

As soon as I arrived home, I instructed Sandiman to duplicate two hundred invitations. He worked until two in the morning. He seemed to be very enthusiastic.

'I was hoping that something like this would happen in Mangkunegaran, Tuan.'

'Why didn't you start something?'

'No one knew how to start.'

'Now you know.'

'Now I know, Tuan, but who must make the first move? If it was only someone like me who initiated something like this, who would listen? And who should be invited to join is also a problem. If a criminal – whatever he had done – received an invitation, attended, agreed and said he was willing to join . . . then what, Tuan? So in Mangkunegaran we just sat and talked. May I attend also, Tuan?' he asked suddenly.

'Of course. We'll go together.'

It was a beautiful day for me, the day God led me to chair that meeting in the Patih of Meester Cornelis's *pendopo*.

There were many more there than had been invited. Some had brought their children. There were primary school children. Some brought their wives. There was no lack of babies either. The laughter of children, the cries of babies as they suffered the heat, babies silenced with their mother's nipples.

The Patih of Meester Cornelis sat in a place of honour but did not speak. Thamrin Mohammed Thabrie, ever humble, sat among the crowd, in one of the middle rows.

Tasty snacks and drinks were continuously being served. I was the only speaker. No one else tried to speak.

I talked about many, many things, drawing from all I had learned from the people I had known, and from my reading. There were two things I deliberately avoided talking about – the Acehnese War and the Balinese War.

'And we will call our organisation Sarekat Priyayi because it is the *priyayi* who are most educated and most advanced. All *priyayi* can read and write. So does everyone agree?'

For the umpteenth time, there was no answer. Instead everyone kept looking in the direction of the Patih of Meester Cornelis.

'And the sarekat will use the Malay language because all *priyayi* speak Malay. Do you agree?'

And still no one answered. Perhaps I was repeating the experience of the old Java Doctor, crying out to the desert-dry hearts of all those present.

The Patih could see I was in trouble. He stood, came across and positioned himself next to me. He asked my permission to speak.

'Heh, all you who have come here tonight. You are not in audience tonight with a *patih*, or a *raja*, even though this is a *patih*'s *pendopo*. Tonight there are no *raja*, no *patih*, no *wedana*, and no *mantri*. Everyone is equal here tonight. So, if you agree, say that you agree, if you don't, then speak out and say so. Now, who agrees with the formation of the Sarekat Priyayi?'

No one answered. Thamrin Mohammed Thabrie also sat silently in his seat.

'Tuan Thamrin Mohammed Thabrie, Wedana of Mangga Besar, perhaps you agree?'

Thamrin suddenly stood, his tall body towering above those around him. Everyone looked at him. 'Not only do I agree, I put myself down as its first member.'

'Nah, now we have a real answer. Who else agrees?'

Everyone stood up, including all the little children, except the babies asleep in their mother's arms.

'I also agree and put myself down as member number . . . you all agree, don't you? Then, perhaps I'm member number two hundred and ninety.'

And for the first time, I heard someone laugh.

'Do we agree the Sarekat's language will be Malay?'

The *pendopo* echoed with shouts of agreement.

'So our organisation is now formally founded? Legitimate and valid?'

'Yes! Yes! Yes!'

'Now they're all trying to out-bray each other, Tuan,' he whispered to me.

'It doesn't matter,' I whispered back.

'Good. Tomorrow we'll apply for registration from the government. Now all those wanting to become members must write down their names and addresses. Also their ages and occupations.'

Sandiman circulated notebooks, one for every row of those present.

In half an hour, amidst the buzz of many voices, we collected four hundred and eighty names, including those of four year-old children, who at that moment were at home asleep in their mothers' arms. That was also good. There was not a single woman's name.

It was easy to guess who would be chosen president – Thamrin Mohammed Thabrie. I became Secretary. And the meeting broke up with everyone feeling relieved and satisfied. The sky was overcast. It was a pitch-black night. The thunder cleared its throat and the lightning tried to flash away its headache. The rain poured down without let-up. Sandiman was busy duplicating. As soon as the sheets were dry, he addressed them and they were posted that night, to the major towns in Sumatra, Borneo, the Moluccas, and especially Java.

Membership applications flooded in over the next few days, from Java, Madura and elsewhere. But Sandiman was clearly unhappy about something.

'There's something bothering you,' I said. 'What's wrong?'

'Nothing, Tuan. Only, well, yes, how can I say it? The Sarekat Priyayi, Tuan, I don't have the right to join.'

'You're already a member, you've put your name down.'

'But I've never felt myself to be a *priyayi*.'

It was a statement that at once surprised me and annoyed me.

'Why didn't you say anything at the meeting?'

'What should I have said, Tuan. I'm just an ex-soldier. Are soldiers *priyayi*?'

'So what class are soldiers?'

'How would I know, Tuan? This name means the soldiers in Mangkunegaran will hesitate to join.'

'Ah, you, such an important idea. Why didn't you say something earlier, at the meeting?'

'I don't actually know what is the meaning of *priyayi*, Tuan.'

And I didn't really know what the real and accurate meaning of the word was either. It has generally been used to refer to those in Government employment who came from the local nobility. But who was included and who left out had never been made clear.

'So what is my status as a member, Tuan. Am I a *priyayi* or not?'

'And if your membership is declared valid, will you then know what is meant by a *priyayi*?'

'Declared valid or not, I will still not know, Tuan.'

'Then it makes no difference either way, you remain a member.'

'But I still don't feel right about this, Tuan.'

'If you spice up something enough it will taste good in the end, won't it?'

He was still unhappy about it, I perhaps more so. Our organisation would not be able to recruit from the lower classes because of that word *priyayi*. The traders will be wary too. There was nothing that we could do now. That name had been accepted by the meeting. It had already come into effect. The Government had also registered and published it in the *State Gazette*. The organisation now had legal status, and a legal identity – like that of a European.

And so it was that the year 1906 passed, it too producing something new to savour.

8

The work of the Secretary of an organisation is like that of a weaver. Ideas from the eight directions of the wind have to be woven together with those from the middle direction, the ninth direction, from the direction of the Secretary himself. The result: a tapestry woven out of suggestions – a reflection of what actually exists in society. And as the Secretary of a legally registered organisation, with the same status as a European citizen, my room to move and to make connections expanded dramatically. It was as though each step I took no longer came down on colonial ground. It was as if I had become legal owner of this earth. Experience, knowledge, wisdom and, most of all, enthusiasm for life all combined to build up a giant entity, stronger than the sum of the strength of all its members. Its self-confidence was enough to drill through to the centre of the earth.

On the other hand, my income started to dwindle. I was living off my savings. Only the weak-hearted and weak-kneed hope for free blessings. What is there that is free? Everything has to be paid for first or paid back later.

The proposal to reach out to a wider audience by publishing a paper was agreed to by the organisation's leadership. Our capital? Every proposed member had to pay, in advance, dues for either a quarter, half or whole year. They immediately became owner of a share. A company was formed. A lawyer quickly had it registered with the Ministry for Justice. The weekly magazine *Medan* – Arena – began publishing, owned and operated by Natives. Not by the Dutch, not by the Chinese or any other newcomers. By Natives! What had to happen has happened! United you can achieve anything. Anything!

Alone in my room I found tears coming to my eyes. I had discovered a new world: the accumulation of capital using money donated by my own people, people who found it hard to make ends meet. These donations took food from their plate but they were still willing to give. We had accumulated some capital. A new world, a new birth.

And in my diary I engraved the following words: Who can predict how a baby will grow up? To become a prophet or a criminal, or just another inhabitant of this world, blank, contributing nothing?

And it was the old way that we had used. The *priyayi* way. It was as the girl in Jepara had said: Once a *bupati* had set an example, all his underlings would copy.

Four *bupatis* had subscribed to *Medan* – worth more than all our money capital. Within only three months we had gained one thousand five hundred subscribers from all over Java, and from the main towns in Sumatra and the Celebes. A print-run of two thousand was not enough.

At the very least, Nyo, even though it is just a beginning, you have started your work as a propagandist. There is no need to regret not having become a doctor. You are the first Native to start, wrote Nyai Ontosoroh from Wonocolo after she had received the first few copies. She paid for a two-year subscription. But she wasn't a very successful subscription agent.

She also wrote: *Your magazine mainly publishes explanations of laws and regulations. Many priyayi need this so as to be able to more confidently violate them. You yourself have been a victim of the law. At the very least there are both just and unjust laws. Regulations just reinforce the laws. Don't you remember what happened when you yourself were the victim? Be careful! Don't end up strengthening injustice as a result of your work.*

And her other letter: *What? We all know that you began this endeavour with the best intentions. You think that is enough? A pure heart and good intentions, and the ability to carry out your intentions, are exactly the qualities sought by bandits. A pure heart, good intentions, and the capability to carry them out, Nyo, Child, are not enough. No, nowhere near enough. There has never been a lack of people willing to use Jesus to oppress, has there? Be careful!*

The majority of our subscribers were those who wanted to know the laws and regulations better so that they would not make mistakes and would be promoted more quickly. Now there was a new challenge from Mama. More letters arrived asking for explanations about new or different laws. Mama challenged me again: *It can't be avoided? There's nothing else to do but service these requests? Ah, there are many things more important than these laws and regulations.*

Our subscribers' need for legal explanations kept growing and growing. The Patih of Meester Cornelis couldn't handle all the work any more. We had to hire a European lawyer for two hours a week. Sandiman worked himself half to death noting down lawyer Mahler's answers to all the questions that came in. Luckily he was a friendly and helpful person.

My husband is interested in the work you are doing, wrote Mir Frischboten. *If we were in Betawi he would very much like to help you out of the troubles you're having in keeping up the flow of advice. He would be so happy to help, con amour, and not just two hours a week but whenever he could.*

And Mahler's fee came to one-third of the business's profit.

The equivalent of one-third of your profits? wrote Mama, *you're crazy. The Government wants its officials to implement its laws properly, to carry out its own regulations as they should, so why should you be paying out one-third of your profits? It seems like a joke to me, even though I don't know all the details. Or is it you that is becoming the joke? This is the Government's business. It should pay, not you.*

In the meantime *Medan*'s circulation spread further and further throughout Sumatra and to the big harbour towns of Borneo, the Celebes and the Moluccas. The subscribers from outside Java brought their own demands. They wanted us to use the kind of Malay they had learnt at school. They wanted a language that knew where heaven and earth was, not a bazaar language that floated about without roots, disoriented.

With much effort the printers were able to meet our demand for a larger print-run. The circulation reached over two thousand. The new subscriptions took it over three thousand and the printer was unable to handle the order. And the new subscribers were not coming from among the *priyayi*. That market seemed to have become saturated. They came from Native traders and businessmen who had picked up Malay in their business dealings.

Thamrin and Patih refused to switch to school Malay, especially seeing that the new subscribers were traders and not *priyayi*. And then the village heads began to subscribe and the Eurasian employees on the private plantations. Finally the Europeans were forced to start subscribing.

Then people began referring civil cases to us. Mahler had to be paid even more because he was now working four hours a week instead of two.

I have telegrammed our company in Amsterdam, wrote Mama from Surabaya, *to ask them to check out this Mr Frischboten. Perhaps he can replace Mahler. But you need a bigger publication. Have you thought about publishing a newspaper?*

Our own newspaper! Like in a fairy-tale. Publishing every day! We were being run off our legs just trying to get a magazine out.

There's more and more work to do? A good sign. Hire more people. Or is your aim to make yourself rich from this endeavour? wrote Mama again. *Attend to all the cases that involve injustices. You're the only one that they dare trust. You're being honoured, Nyo. But if you continue your work explaining these laws, you'll just be working for the Government free of charge. It will no longer be a joke. For a person like you, it will be a tragedy. A newspaper! There is more to life than just laws and regulations.*

Most of the requests for help concerned abuses carried out by the railway, the plantations and Government officials, as well as the abducting of wives and girls by officials who abused their authority. Mahler began working six hours a week. And *Medan* became an angel of mercy for the Natives of the Indies.

We took on new people, including an old friend, Wardi. Even so, work piled up higher and higher.

Thamrin kept coming and asking about our program for establishing schools and hostels. We convened a meeting of the council. The decision –

the establishment of a special body to carry out these tasks and another to administer financial assistance to qualified students who could not afford to pay for more schooling. These three bodies were to be administered by a Funds for Advancement Foundation which was registered a week later in the office of the solicitor Mr Willhelmsen. Thamrin donated from his own pocket an amount equivalent to the cost of two pilgrimages to Mecca as well as two hectares of agricultural land.

A month later those in charge of the foundation were arrested by the police for losing on the gambling tables of Gambir Market the money that had been entrusted to them.

I kept on with my work. And as time went on I learnt from all the letters just how much people needed help to cope with the injustices done to them. There were even such letters from Government officials themselves, who held some power in their hands. It was just like it was half a century ago in the time of Multatuli. I began to understand more fully just how persecuted the Native people were, by the Government and its officials, by other criminals, and by dishonest traders.

Mei, how wonderful it would be if you were alive today!

I think 1907 would have flown by, except for something that happened that I will always remember.

That afternoon I was sprawled out, exhausted, lazily enjoying a cane rocking-chair. There was a small table beside me. Sandiman was just putting on a recording of Verdi's opera *Rigoletto*. I'd started the practice of setting aside three hours a week to listen to European music, copying what had been the practice of Mama and her children.

Perhaps because this had been our practice in Surabaya, Verdi always took me back to old memories, to Mama and her business, to Annelies and to all the happiness that had ended with tragedy.

It was true that I didn't yet appreciate European music as fully as I did *gamelan*. European music stimulated in me many different thoughts. *Gamelan* music instead enveloped me in beauty, in a harmony of feeling that was without form, in an atmosphere that rocked my emotions to an eternal sleep.

Just as the phonograph was playing 'The Last Rose of Summer' and I had, by coincidence, opened my eyes, I saw a two-horse carriage pull up in front of the house. A young Eurasian girl alighted and then helped out a young boy. Then a Native women descended who, in her turn, helped down a European. And the European man used a crutch.

Marais! Jean Marais! He had come from Surabaya to visit! And that Native woman – wasn't that Mama! I jumped up out of the rocking-chair. Mama! Yes, it was her. I ran out to welcome them.

'Mama! Ah, Jean! Who would ever have guessed you were coming? No letter, no news of any kind!'

A touch on my back made me turn round.

'Uncle,' the Eurasian girl greeted me. 'Have you forgotten me already?'

'Ai, is this Maysoroh? Oh, it is you May!' I shouted out. 'You've grown into such a young lady!' And she kissed me on the cheek as was the custom among Europeans.

'This is Rono. You've probably forgotten. Rono Mellema.'

I stopped for a moment, trying to remember who Rono Mellema was.

'Rono!' I cried. 'I remember now.' I lifted him way up above my head and took note of his eyes. His eyes were somewhat bluish, like Robert's.

'And what about you, Child? It looks as though things are better for you now,' said Mama.

'No complaints, Mama. No complaints.'

She spoke so sweetly and gently. I don't know why I was so moved by this great woman, whom I had been fortunate to meet during my life, a goddess always extending her hand and helping with her wisdom in times of trouble.

Limping along, Jean Marais spoke his words of friendship in French: 'You've become a great man now.'

'Ayoh, come on in,' I invited them, while putting down Rono.

Sandiman ran about back and forth bringing in their things. And I didn't understand why the two families were both visiting Batavia together. Mama perhaps wanted to get back her loans to me? But Jean Marais? Perhaps he was going home to France?

'You'll stay here, of course?' I asked.

'Where else if not here with you?' replied Mama in Dutch as usual.

We all went inside. As we entered the living-room, everyone stopped, except Rono Mellema who flopped himself down on a chair. They were all nailed to the floor before *Flower of the Century's End*. I too stood there silently, joining with them in their feelings.

'It's a pity she could not be here with you, Child,' said Mama, her voice filled with sadness. Then she looked away from the picture.

'Enough, Ma.'

'You put up her picture even now? Doesn't it torment your thoughts?'

Jean Marais came up to me and put his two hands on my shoulders. He spoke in a deep voice: 'We are so happy now, and you . . . why don't you put the painting away?'

'I'm happy too, Jean, truly, Come on, these are the rooms. You choose for yourself.'

Sandiman put their things in their rooms. Mama examined the house and its furnishings, the paintings and other wall decorations, and then went into the kitchen to talk with the housemaid. I didn't know what they were talking about.

152

Back from the kitchen, she asked straightaway: 'So you're still single? How come? You're in good condition. You need a wife and children, at least two or three. Or perhaps you're keeping a mistress somewhere?'

'No, Ma.'

'Enough. Forget that picture. Get married. It's not right for people to live alone. They should live together with someone,' then she went into my room to continue her inspection.

My heart started pounding. She would see the picture of Ang San Mei! And, yes: 'Come here, Child!' she called out from inside my room.

I hurried in. Mama was standing in front of the picture.

'Who is this Chinese woman?'

'My wife, Ma.'

'I have never seen her. You never told me about her.'

'She died, Ma.'

'Child!' she cried out, 'you always have such evil luck. You must marry again quickly. Such a pretty child, even though narrow-eyed and skinny.'

'She left me no children, Ma.'

'And why didn't you ever tell me about her? Did she die or did she leave you? Don't hide anything from me, Child.'

'What is there to hide, Ma? She died without children.'

I began to recognise again the voice, the look in her eyes, the loving expression of her face. Seven years had aged her slightly, but her energy and friendliness had not changed.

'Be frank with me Child, don't hide anything from me – she ran off and left you?'

'No, Ma, truly she didn't. She died.'

'She wasn't faithful to you?'

'She was more than faithful, Ma.'

'There is something you're hiding from me.'

'What is there that I must hide from you, Ma?'

'There's something. You hang the other picture in the sitting-room. You hang this in your own room. There is some secret between you and her.'

I didn't understand what she meant. And I was at an even greater loss as to how to answer. But Mama's sharp eyes never missed anything. So I told her everything. She listened attentively to every word while keeping her eyes on Ang San Mei's picture. Then: 'So she was the fiancé of the young Chinaman? What an amazing girl! To leave her own country to die in another people's. Of her own free will. So what makes you so downcast, Child? You did everything you could for her.'

'I'm not downcast at all, Ma. And anyway I have something else now.'

'So you'll be marrying soon?'

'No, Ma, but I'm very happy now with my new work.'

Like a mother with her child, she rubbed her delicate head up against mine.

153

'You mean you want to follow my example, work and do nothing else, without rest? You think I was happy in my work? You were wrong, Child. You didn't see everything. I had two children. Both are dead now. And now I have a grandchild. No one can say I have not worked hard enough, Child. Even so, Child, for a woman without a husband, without a partner-in-life who is beside her always, life begins to seem more and more empty.'

Then I understood. Mama was talking about herself, using my case as the opening. She had married Jean Marais.

'Congratulations, Mama!' I offered my hand to her.

Her eyes shone with happiness.

'So you understand, Child. Don't get the wrong idea.'

I went out to congratulate Jean Marais. He was sitting in the lounge-room, scrutinising the painting, his own work of several years ago.

'Even now I feel that the painting needs nothing changed or added to,' he said, when he saw me entering.

'You two didn't tell me. Congratulations, Jean.'

Mama came in and sat down too. She righted her husband's crutch which was leaning across the arms of one of the chairs.

Maysoroh came back into the room after having tidied up and also sat down with us.

'You have such a big moustache now, Uncle,' commented May in French.

'Yes, May, I'm an old man now.'

'Old? You're handsome with that moustache, Uncle. Who said you're old?'

'So, should I propose to you then?' I asked.

She let out a little cry and pinched me on the thigh. She was blushing with embarrassment. Mama was laughing elatedly. Jean just bowed his head shyly.

'And what would be wrong if you did?' asked Mama.

May's father, Jean Marais, looked the other way.

'I'm going home, Uncle,' said May, continuing in French. 'To Paris.'

'Is that why you won't speak Javanese, or Dutch or Malay?' pressed Mama.

'You're going home to Paris, May?' and I looked back and forth between Mama and Jean.

'Yes, Child, we have married and now we are going.'

'So Mama will be honeymooning in France?'

'No, Child, it's not for a honeymoon. You see, Child, for so long now I've read and I've heard about a country where all stand equal before the law. Not like here in the Indies. And the story also tells that this country holds high the ideals of liberty, equality and fraternity. You know the story. I want to see the country of that story, in reality. Does there really exist such beauty on this earth of mankind?'

Mama knew, of course, that French imperialism was just as evil as any other. France too had betrayed her own revolution over and over again. But

I didn't want to spoil the atmosphere.

'Mama!' I cried.

'Yes, Nyo, we four will be moving to France.'

'See, Uncle, you heard for yourself.'

Rono Mellema was secretly watching me – perhaps enthralled by my moustache – as if I was some freak at the night market. Or perhaps he was just lost in thoughts of his own.

'And why are you so quiet, Rono?' I asked in Javanese.

'I'm going too,' he answered in Madurese.

How happy and contented this family seemed. And their departure for France was made possible by Mama's business success.

'Wouldn't you also like to go to France, Child? And marry May there?' asked Mama.

'Oh, Mama, you!' cried May, giving her a pinch.

'See your daughter, Jean, how happy she is to be near her boyfriend.'

'Who said he's my boyfriend?' parried May, pinching Mama again and again. She was blushing again.

Jean Marais didn't say anything, as if his mind was off far, far away. And I too suddenly came over shy when I saw this very pretty girl steal glances at me.

Her skin was not too white, perhaps a legacy from her late mother. Her hair was long and wavy. The front wave in her hair was fixed with an emerald-studded gold comb. Her earrings and pendant were diamonds and emeralds in a gold setting. They were once worn by . . . ah, what's the point in bringing all that back? She was also wearing the perfume that Annelies used to wear. Perhaps this had all been arranged by Mama to bring back certain memories.

I knew then that Mama had dressed her before leaving the ship to come here to my house so that I would see her as . . .

'Say something, Jean,' Mama said in Malay and then repeated in rather awkward French.

Mama was learning French!

Jean Marais didn't answer.

'We've talked about you often, Child,' Mama began again. 'About you and May.'

'Those concerned have never said anything,' said Marais. 'You're the one making all the fuss.'

Maysoroh stood and ran off to her room, slamming the door behind her, like someone wanting to hide from the world and secrete herself away.

'She'll be trying to listen from behind the door,' said Mama.

Mama wanted me to marry Maysoroh, and May knew about this. Marais didn't seem to want to take sides.

When I glanced across at Jean, he had turned to look at the door.

'I'm too busy with my work, Ma. I've never thought about getting married again.'

'Listen, Child. We'll be leaving soon. We don't know when we'll be back. If you truly have no desire for this, fine. But if you do, then Jean is here now. Don't waste this opportunity.'

'Give me time to think about it, Ma.'

Mama seemed disappointed. She was well-intentioned. I myself had no objections to marrying Maysoroh. May would do whatever her father asked her. It would all depend on what I decided. But my thoughts wouldn't keep on this track. I was worried Mama would ask me to repay the money she had sent me. And I knew better than anyone that my reserves were just about depleted.

'I have not returned all Mama's money yet.'

'Listen, Child, your magazine is already popular, except they say there's not enough in it. There's too much emphasis on one topic. That's your opinion too, isn't it, Jean?'

'Yes,' he answered, and then went silent again.

'I've suggested to you that you start a newspaper. Have you thought about it?'

'No Native has ever tried to start a newspaper!'

'Then you will have the honour of being the first.'

'Too much capital is needed, Ma.'

'I'm with you too, Child! How much do you need?' she asked, daring me. 'There's no need to return the rest of what I sent you before. How would three thousand guilders be? Enough?'

I fell into silence, pondering, embarrassed at having all this witnessed by Jean.

'Enough. Good, then you agree. Then you can start working on it.'

'Yes, I believe you can do it,' Jean proposed. 'You've got the ability. You've had experience with papers. You'll succeed in anything you try.'

'Well, anyway, I failed at becoming a doctor.'

'That was just bad luck. Actually a blessing in disguise,' said Mama. 'If you had become a doctor then today you might be working in the middle of Borneo or on some government ship somewhere. You wouldn't be editing *Medan*. And there would be no Sarekat Priyayi.'

I was glad everyone had forgotten the topic of marriage. But it wasn't for long. Mama started again: 'Our ship leaves for Europe at two o'clock tomorrow afternoon. We will alight at Amsterdam, then go to Huizen. Then we will catch the train to Paris. We will leave here tomorrow morning at nine in the morning.'

'If you go to Huizen, Ma,' I asked, 'then could you get the most beautiful bouquet of flowers for her, and a red ribbon with "From Betawi" written across it in silver. Just that, Ma.'

156

'Of course, Child. You see we don't have much time for talking. If you think I'm pressuring you it's just that I'm thinking about how little time we have. So now, with Jean here, you must say something, so I know you won't suffer in your loneliness. Or must I speak for you and you just listen?'

How aggressive she was now. Was this her real character? Turned into a matriarch as a result of her success? Was it true that she was just interested in my happiness? Or did she want to free herself of a stepdaughter? Was this really the last chance to decide this and did we really not have time to discuss things first? And why was it that I, a writer, from whose pen hundreds of thousands of words had flowed, was now unable to produce even a single word?

'Very well,' said Mama finally. 'Nah, Jean, see, he does want Maysoroh as his wife. He is embarrassed to ask you for her hand. He will make your daughter happy. Look upon me as his mother. And, in any case, you already know him quite well.'

She has become so aggressive!

'Let him speak for himself,' Jean's words were in French.

'Speak, Child. Or do you still find it difficult to speak?'

It seemed as if all the good intentions in the world were being heaped upon my head. I had known May since she was little. I used to take her by the hand when we headed off to school, and then we'd catch a *bendi* together. And it had to be admitted that May was a healthy, active, attractive girl with a beautiful, perfectly formed body. This would have been obvious to even those who weren't connoisseurs of beauty, who weren't philogynists. How old was she now? Seventeen. With no experience, spoiled, an only child, and with a great love for her father. Jean gave her all his love – something that guaranteed she would also have a pure and simple heart free from any difficult complexes. But what must I say to an old friend who I suddenly now confronted as a prospective father-in-law? And why was I about to carry out Mama's wish without thinking it through properly first?

'First of all, I ask your forgiveness, Jean. For several years we lived together as friends. It's true that I find it difficult to talk to you now. I would be enormously grateful if you were to allow me to crown my life by taking your daughter as my wife. Don't be angry that these are the only words I've been able to find.'

Jean Marais turned, drawing in a deep breath. He looked old. And I don't think there was anything he could do. He seemed to be totally dependent on Mama. His business had gone bankrupt. I regretted now that I had bent before Mama's will. How embarrassing it would be if my proposal was rejected – perhaps it would ruin relations between Jean and Mama. I had behaved very rashly and without principle. Why I had become like this – just a shadow in the presence of this extraordinary woman? Why am I so helpless before her? Why have I allowed myself to create more burdens for Jean?

Was I basically just an opportunist? Or was it because of my debts to her?

'She is my only child,' Jean said suddenly in French. 'Maysoroh has been with me since she was little. She lost her mother when she was a baby. You know that.'

'You don't intend to return to the Indies, Jean?'

'I don't know. Why am I thinking about myself?' he rebuked himself. He stood up, unsteady on his one leg, and cried out: 'May! May! Come here darling.'

But Maysoroh didn't come out, neither did she answer.

Mama stood up and walked across to knock on the door, speaking in Dutch: 'Come out, Darling. Your father needs you.'

The door opened warily. I no longer looked at the door but at Jean. Perhaps these were difficult moments for him, the time when other hands were about to seize his beloved daughter away from him. He watched the door with eyes guarded by a worried frown.

'Why won't you come out, May? What are you afraid of? Come on, Darling,' Mama greeted May and guided her across the room and sat her beside me.

'You don't regret your words?' asked Jean.

'If you don't, neither do I, Jean.'

'May!' Jean spoke his daughter's name lovingly, 'You have known him since you were little. Heh, don't bow down your head like that. Lift your head up so Papa can see your face and eyes.'

And I myself avoided May's gaze. I still saw her as a little child, who came weeping to me after I had argued with her father. I had cradled her in my arms. And then she made me go back to make up with Jean.

'You know, May, that just now, he has asked permission to marry you. I have not yet answered. It is all up to you. I am not compelling you to answer yes or no, or even to answer at all. It is all up to you, nobody else.'

Maysoroh was silent. Would she refuse me? Would I suffer the shame? And if she did say 'yes' what would be her reasons?

'You can answer now, tomorrow or later after you settle in France,' Jean added.

The atmosphere was gloomy and silent. No one spoke. Mama stood up and went out into one of the back rooms.

'I'm not proposing because of pressure from anyone, Jean,' I said, trying to change the atmosphere.

'Of course not. I agree that you need a good wife, Minke. Tomorrow we leave for Europe and I have a feeling that I won't be returning to the Indies. There is not much time left. It's important we make good use of what time we have together now.'

'I understand, Jean.'

'What about you, May?'

'I want to study in Paris.'

'So you won't reply to this proposal?'

'Not yet, Papa. Don't be angry, Papa. Don't be disappointed in me, Uncle. I'm allowed to study, aren't I?' she said slowly and cautiously.

Everthing went dark. Maybe Jean watched my face go from white to red with shame and embarrassment.

'You won't regret your decision, May?' Jean asked again.

'Papa, my darling Papa,' I watched May rise, go up to her father where she cuddled and embraced him. 'I'd like to have Uncle as a husband. Really, Papa. But not now.'

'Tell him yourself.'

'You heard, didn't you, Uncle?'

The sun shone once again on my universe. No, I would not have to suffer the shame I imagined. I looked calmly at May. She would be my wife. She came across to me and knelt down in front of me in the Javanese way, with her two hands resting on my right hand.

'I'd like to be your wife, Uncle, but not now. Please forgive me.'

I stood and pulled her up also and sat her down on a chair.

'Jean, May, thank you for this answer. Neither of you must think that my proposal today is a result of the prodding of anybody else. I have done it all of my own free will. And, May, if tomorrow or the next day you change your mind, please let me know. If later when you're living in France, mixing with many new friends and your views change, remember, there is someone here who always awaits your letters.'

We had a merry evening that night once the question of May and I had been attended too. Mama as well as Jean, and I also, all wanted to talk only about the future. May stayed silent most of the time.

The evening ended with these words from Mama: 'So don't worry about anything, Child. I'm looking forward so much to reading your paper – a paper that will defend your fellow Natives, your people. You can't just close down the weekly, of course. It has built up a good name among those looking for explanations of all the laws and regulations. But I don't consider that to be your real work, Child. A daily, Child, a daily! I will look for a lawyer to help, someone who isn't two-faced. What I've found out about Frischboten is quite encouraging. Perhaps he'd be willing. And, Child, remember this. You must telegram me in Paris if three thousand guilders are not enough.'

It was midnight when I went to bed. I was filled with happiness. So many good things seemed to be flowing in my direction. And all because I had dared to begin. Everything else would come my way too. All things need a beginning. And I had set off on my beginning.

Even so I was ashamed of myself. Near this woman I had once again become just a shadow of a personality. Perhaps Mr Mellema had also been bowed down and subjugated by her iron will. Maybe he too had just become a reflection, unable to resist. Mama should have been a man. I understood too that Jean Marais had become putty in her hands.

As was my habit in the evening, I stopped to look at Mei's portrait before I went to bed. And the picture wasn't there. I looked under my bed. It wasn't there. I found it lying on top of the wardrobe wrapped up in cloth. Mama had done it. Not under my bed. On top of the wardrobe!

Mei, you replaced Annelies, *The Flower of the Century's End*. Now you would be replaced by Maysoroh Marais. Don't be angry . . . You were never the sentimental type anyway, were you?

And I put her picture back in its place. I examined her face. Like a being from another universe. Her smile (I had asked the artist to paint her with a smile), the way her eyes shone out from the corners of her eyes, it was as if all her life she had never confronted the world clearly, as if she was just glancing out at it half-heartedly. Everything seemed to be enveloped in a pallid morbidity.

I felt ashamed as I examined my heart. Had I really loved her – in the way people and the stories talked about love? Do you have to study how to love too, love in the way that everyone talks about but never has been clear to me? Can a wife die because of a lack of this kind of love, and then become just a picture which is worshipped like an idol, as I have done with the *Flower of the Century's End* and now Mei?

Oh God, teach me to understand love as other people understand it. Because, it is said, love is the source of everything.

They had left: Jean Marais, Mama – now Sanikem Marais, Maysoroh Marais and Rono Mellema. To France!

My house and my heart felt empty.

Sandiman and Wardi agreed with the proposal to publish a paper. Thamrin Mohammed Thabrie wasn't talking with anyone. He was still very upset about the embezzlement of the foundation's funds. So was the Patih of Meester Cornelis.

This scandal had eroded many members' faith in the Sarekat Priyayi. People started to say that the organisation had been established simply to enrich certain individuals. We issued a special statement, inserted in the magazine, presenting an account of the use of the funds – almost all anyway. We could not state how much we were paying Mahler. But people didn't care. They needed and wanted to read *Medan*. They weren't interested in the explanations we gave about our financial situation.

I suggested we hold a conference. But no one ever supported me. We found it impossible to get people to pay their membership dues any more. Quite a large number of people stopped sending in their payments for shares. I had to start to pay for expenses out of my own money. The organisation was in trouble. And most of the *priyayi* showed more interest in dancing girls, dance parties and gambling. The dues stopped coming in altogether. Our *priyayi* members all returned to their old ways.

On the other hand *Medan* was spreading rapidly. It had plenty of life left in it. People referred more and more of their problems to the magazine. People demanded we cover more matters, and still more again. People wanted to learn more about the world, as well as hoping that we would struggle for their interests. Not through an organisation any more but by trying to rally public opinion behind them when they were confronting exploitation and oppression by either white or brown colonial authorities. To do this they needed a publication that would tell the truth.

The people did need a Native daily.

'The time to publish a daily has arrived,' I told Wardi and Sandiman. 'It's a pity we can't get the organisation involved. It has lost its ability to act. I will publish the paper myself.'

Wardi agreed, but didn't think it was possible. He didn't really respond too much to the proposal except just to smile.

'Actually I might not be able to keep helping the weekly for much longer either,' said Wardi.

'I understand. The weekly can't provide anyone with a decent livelihood. It's just a labour of love.'

He didn't stop helping me but he wasn't as active as before.

Things kept moving along. The reading public of the Indies was following another major development.

Governor-General van Heutsz had announced openly his intentions to bring into the Indies all the independent territories of the archipelago. He was demanding that the independent principalities in Aceh, the Celebes, the Moluccas and the Lesser Sundas sign what he called the Korte Verklaring, the 'short agreement'. This document was an agreement that they would all accept the authority of the Netherlands Indies government. These pockets of independence were called 'Landschap'.

The newspapers were all saying that the barbaric and uncivilised practices going on in these territories could no longer be tolerated by the Netherlands Indies authorities, who represented Christian and European civilisation in this region. The laws of the Netherlands Indies must be enforced in these territories, and this would also bind their people and their leaders to the Netherlands Indies.

Behind the Korte Verklaring, which indeed comprised only a few sentences, stood the ranks of the army with their rifle and cannon and sword. War would soon be ravaging these countries that had not yet bowed down before the Dutch. The military graveyard in Kotaraja, Aceh, was a reminder

161

of how terrible a colonial war could be. Now there would be more such wars in the Celebes, Moluccas and the Lesser Sunda Islands.

Van Heutsz wanted to see his dream of a united Indies become a reality before his term as Governor-General expired the following year – even while the Bali War, which he had started in 1904, the first year of his term, had not yet ended! Though, of course, the kingdom of Klungkung was starting to break up from within. But the King of Klungkung himself stood firm.

Ter Haar had been able to write five more letters to me before news reached me that he had died of heavy wounds incurred while accompanying the army in one of its attacks on the Toh Pati fortress. I don't know what kind of weapon killed Ter Haar. It must have been a Balinese blade or spear that killed him. He had a great sympathy for the Balinese people, but he was never able to get close to them. And he always accompanied the army. It was hard to know exactly how to classify his death. He clearly wasn't a hero. Neither was he an oppressor. He died only because he wanted to know the outcome of the Balinese fight to defend their nation and people! Just because he wanted to know!

One of his letters gave a little background to what had happened in Bali: *During the time of the great Empire of Majapahit in Java, Prime Minister Gajah Mada appointed four rulers. The first, Sri Juru, was crowned the King of Blambangan in East Java. The second, Sri Bhimacali, was crowned King of Pasuruan in West Java. The third, Sri Krisna Kepakisan, was crowned King of Bali. The fourth, Princess Kaneja, was crowned Queen of Sumbawa, in the Lesser Sunda Islands.*

Sri Krisna Kepakisan, King of Bali, had originally been the main adviser of Prime Minister Gajah Mada. Following his coronation, he left for Bali with one hundred and fourteen Javanese knights, including Arya Wang Bang and Arya Kutawaringan.

The area called Gelgel was chosen to be the centre of the new kingdom. They built a palace, Swecapura palace. That kingdom has continued on down to the current king, I Dewa Agung Djambe, who held court at Asmarapuri palace in Klungkung. Four hundred and fifty years! Asmarapuri itself had become the capital in 1710 and governed over the eight smaller principalities of Bali, each of which had their own king as well.

But in 1892 the Dutch managed to incite the principality of Buleleng to break away from Asmarapuri. Buleleng was soon Klungkung's enemy. Now, in 1908, the Dutch had managed to persuade another king, the King of Gianjar, to join the opposition against Klungkung. It was his soldiers who surrounded and overran Toh Pati fortress. And so now, with Toh Pati taken, the Dutch were in a position to march on Klungkung itself. Dutch soldiers were landed on Kusamba beach. Klungkung was attacked from three directions. And Gianjar, which had betrayed the mother kingdom, also took part in the attack.

The Colonial Army and Gianjar's soldiers had to march seven kilometres to reach Klungkung. Meanwhile the King of Klungkung issued orders that every man, woman and child, weapon in hand, must fight until no one was left standing. The sound of the gong that had been named Ki Sekar Sandat reverberated over and over again. And the sacred keris, I Pacalang and I Tan Kadang, both of which had for so long protected the kingdom, were drawn from their sheaths. The kingdom was ready to fight . . .

In his later letters, Ter Haar had written:

Van Heutsz was growing impatient with Bali's refusal to accept defeat. If Bali was nearer to a foreign country, as Aceh had been, this war would be able to go on for ten years, and still the Dutch would not be guaranteed victory. This courageous and isolated people received no outside help at all. I'm not sure that van Heutsz will see his dream realised. The Balinese on the island of Lombok remain loyal to the king and they will not surrender so easily as their brothers of Javanese descent.

The war would go on. One by one my fellow countrymen would fall on the field of battle, unable to resist the steel of colonial bullets. How different was van Heutsz from that other colonial hero, van der Wijck. In order to conquer North Celebes, he set village against village. Each village usually had between fifteen to forty men armed to defend it. Bribing the village chiefs with cigars, he bred enmity and conflict among them. Village after village fell into his hands without his having to use more than a few score middle-level army troops. And so he obtained fame and glory as the man who conquered North Celebes.

Van Heutsz with bullets and the Korte Verklaring, van der Wijck with cigars. There were many ways, it seemed, to steal someone's country. And the objective was always the same – to win the race being run by all the colonial powers of the world to see who was the greatest thief, the greediest, the best at sucking up the riches of the earth and of its peoples.

It made me sick.

Then one day: 'It would be ideal, of course, if the Indies was unified,' said a journalist, 'But won't it mean a greater burden for the Government?'

Van Heutsz didn't answer. Instead he made the following pronouncement: 'Those who resist will pay dearly for their resistance.'

'What do you mean "will pay dearly"?'

'As it was after the Padri War and the Java War. West Sumatra and Java were subjected to a system of Forced Cultivation.'

'But the people of the Sunda Islands, and of the Moluccas and Central Celebes, and of Sangir and Talaud are not known as farmers.'

'They will soon learn to be very fine farmers.'

Then came another idea, no less sharp than the first: 'If the Korte Verklaring was inspired by Christian values then why was it military methods that were used? Why weren't they helped instead with priests, teachers, engineers and money?'

But the Government only knew the methods it had used ever since first setting foot in the Indies.

'This is the only way they will come to understand the good and honourable intentions of the Government. Crime and sin must no longer be allowed to flourish in these small states, which have not yet subjected themselves to the authority of Her Majesty. Financial help? The people of the Indies have always been corrupt. Corruption is a part of their mentality, whether *dukun* or trader, whether peasant or king. They do not understand the value of money. They only understand the needs of their own lust. Only the power of the Netherlands Indies can educate them. Only the army understands their character.'

These were the words, such impressive words, that were on everybody's lips – in official discussions and over coffee. Sometimes spoken out in the open, sometimes whispered as a rumour. Once, when van Heutsz was speaking to the press, I was the only journalist – and the only brown one also – who did not ask a question of van Heutsz. I was taking notes when the interview had finished.

Then the Governor-General turned to me: 'Ah, Mr Minke. I'm glad you didn't fire any questions at me. I was worried.' He laughed. 'It's usually the last question that is the most difficult to answer!'

Seeing that I wasn't going to ask a question, he reached out with his eyes to the white journalists. He spoke again: 'Gentlemen, this is Mr Minke – writer, journalist, failed medical student – and now helping the Government with his weekly paper, *Medan*, which has been explaining and strengthening our legal system here. I almost didn't recognise you with that handsome moustache.'

His friendly laugh was overdone. His voice struck me like a bolt of lightning. Mama's warning had been affirmed by none other than Governor-General van Heutsz himself. In my heart, I felt so ashamed and humiliated.

'Thank you, Your Excellency.'

'I know you have an important question.'

'Very simple, Your Excellency,' I answered. And the following question seemed to emerge from nowhere: 'The Government's desire to eradicate barbarism and sin from these areas is truly noble. The people living there will receive protection and progress and also lose their independence and freedom . . .'

'Don't forget, Sir, the people there were never independent, let alone free. It was only ever the few among the rulers who knew independence and freedom. The rest were their slaves,' van Heutsz hit back.

'There can be no doubt about that, Your Excellency. And how would Your Excellency compare their situation with that of the Javanese people who have lived under the rule of Holland and the Tricolour for three hundred years, but still live in barbarism and darkness and have lost their independence and freedom as well?'

The Governor-General roared with laughter until his shoulders shook. But his laughter did not arise from a tickled sense of humour.

'Gentlemen. Java and Sumatra cannot be used as comparison. These two territories are special, they are the mother territories. If you want to make a comparison, use Ambon or North Celebes. The people there have progressed so much, it's almost impossible to tell them from Europeans. You gentlemen are no doubt able to testify to their loyalty and bravery. As for Sumatra and Java, the problem has always been that their nobility are always plotting. When the nobility had been put in order, then the landlords started. They were put in order, now it's the *kyai* and the peasants. Ah, Mr Minke, you yourself once spoke about the peasant troubles in Sidoarjo? If only the people of Sumatra and Java would stop making trouble like this, I'm sure that even in as little as five years, they would catch up to the Ambonese and the people of North Celebes.'

His adjutant signalled that the interview was over. But van Heutsz didn't seem satisfied with the explanation he had just given. He asked the journalists: 'Have any of you heard about the peasant rebellion calling itself the Samin movement?'

No one answered.

'They began their rebellion at the beginning of the Aceh War. They've been in rebellion now for a quarter of a century! They too are going to be taught a lesson in the near future.'

The interview was over.

I cycled home slowly. It was a beautiful, cool evening. The sky was full of sparkling stars. Night-time quiet had settled down upon the town of Betawi. Everywhere there were lights and lamps. The gas-lit street lights and the oil lamps of the street peddlars shone all along the streets. It was only in my heart that no light shone. Pitch darkness reigned there. I did not deserve to be able to walk upon the earth beneath my feet, to enjoy the beauty of the sky above me, or the respect of the people who moved about me. Mama had warned me. And now the Governor-General himself had said it. I was helping the Government with my magazine *Medan*, while across to the east, my fellow countrymen, the Balinese, were laying down their lives as they faced the rifles and cannons of the army – sent there by none other than van Heutsz himself. Where could I hide my shame? What was the meaning of all my efforts of these last two years?

I felt small and without meaning. A Troenodongso, fleeing wounded by an army sword, understood things better than this so-called educated man. He had fought back, wounded and defeated. But he had never helped the Government as I had been doing during the last two years. Neither had Mama. Nor Panji Darman. And Jean Marais himself had been ashamed that he had fought in the Aceh War. And now I, yes I, had indeed aided the militarist, van Heutsz.

Was I no more than just a dog?

Speak! Why are you silent, conscience, come on, speak!

Very well. I am more than just some street dog. And I will never be just a dog! I will be myself. Fully, not a dog. Never! Believe me. Never!

Heh, you, riding the bicycle! Your dislike for the Governor-General is just because he's Dutch? But look at the army – most of the soldiers are your own people. Would it make any difference if the Governor-General was a Native and most of the soldiers were European? What do you think? What's your position? Or what if the whole of the army was made up of your own people? A Native Governor-General would have the same goal – a 'unified' Indies. If you think van Heutsz is vicious, then what is your opinion of Sultan Agung who did exactly the same thing? Without even ever thinking about such an ideal as unifying the archipelago?

These thoughts were painful thoughts. I pedalled faster. I leave you behind here in the middle of the road, you feral thoughts! Leave me alone!

I was still feeling ashamed and guilty when I arrived at the printers later that night. Sandiman and Wardi were waiting for me.

'They won't print our paper,' Sandiman reported.

To hell with the paper, I cried out. But out of my mouth came: 'Very well. We have no right to force them to print for us. They have no enforceable legal commitment to us. There is nothing we can do. We'll have to look for another printer tomorrow. Let's go home.'

Three weary people walked out of the printers.

From behind us came someone's sneering laughter.

'Don't turn round,' I said.

But the laughter became louder and was even more obviously being put on. It seemed we were being deliberately provoked into looking round. It was only I who turned. Behind us stood a Eurasian, tall and heavily-built, with a big, thick moustache. He was flexing a long cane stick held between his two hands. He wore a cap pulled down over his forehead. His eyes were bulging out and his teeth were bared at me.

'The last Days of Pompeii are upon us,' he muttered in Dutch.

The word 'Pompeii' reminded me of a book that I once owned and had lent to Robert Suurhof: *The Last Days of Pompeii*. He had never returned it. And that grumbling voice . . . The hairs on the back of my neck stood up. Could it be him? I looked again. He was following us. And yes, it was Robert Suurhof.

I quickened my pace and headed for my bicycle. Wardi and Sandiman, who knew that something was wrong, followed on behind me. And I found my bike lying on the ground without a single spoke of its wheels left unbroken.

This is what I get for helping Governor-General van Heutsz, my heart wailed.

If you knew all that had happened today, Mama, you would withdraw all your offers of help. And Panji Darman had long ago warned me about Robert Suurhof. And now there he was, threatening me behind my back.

That night I couldn't sleep. Even *Flower of the Century's End* and Ang San Mei's picture could not give me inspiration. They had both become lifeless for me. I had asked Sandiman to report the attack on my bicycle first thing in the morning. It was Wardi's job to find a new printer, a routine task.

And what about *Medan*? Would I continue with that shameful work? And Ter Haar had never once said anything about my magazine. He had only ever written about the struggle of the Balinese. Perhaps he had never had any respect for what I was publishing. Why was I only beginning to understand now? After he had died on the blade of a Balinese fighter?

When I awoke the next morning, I found that Sandiman and Wardi had left. I began to reflect over the contents of this magazine whose publication was now under threat and which were themselves under question. And what had Robert Suurhof to do with the printers? And why should he try to stop the publication, when van Heutsz had said it was helping the Government?

I had not yet found the answer when Wardi returned. All the European and the Chinese printers refused to accept *Medan*. Only one Arab printer was interested and he wanted a two-year contract.

'Do we have to have a press of our own?' I asked.

'The Arab will do the job without a contract but in that case his price is very high.'

Even with all the new questions I had, I was not prepared to let this magazine die after I had kept it alive for so long and with so much effort.

'Accept the offer,' I said, and Wardi left to arrange it.

Sandiman returned about an hour after Wardi left. He had been taken by the police to the scene of the crime, and was ordered to watch the arrest of the worker who had did the damage.

'The police will be here in about an hour to take the bicycle as evidence.'

'Sandiman!' I called to him, taking no notice of his report. 'Would you be willing to go back to Solo to meet with your friends and your brother in the Mangkunegaran Legion?'

'If the purpose was clear, Tuan.'

'You yourself said you had heard the rumours that the Legion was going to be sent to Bali to fight there. Well, the rumours have become even stronger now. It seems likely that the Dutch will give the order soon. They are going to have to expand the war to Lombok. The people there are loyal to Klungkung. The Dutch need many more soldiers.'

'Yes-yes, I understand, Tuan. I will leave straight away.'

'And what will you do there?'

'That which you're asking me to do?'

'And what is it that I want?'

'To stop the Legion from going.'

'Good. You can leave tomorrow.'

Our conversation was brought to a halt by a suspicious-sounding rumble. It became louder and louder and the louder it became the closer it sounded. The two of us swung round to face the street. There appeared a big four-wheeled box, which stopped in front of the house.

'An automobile!' I shouted excitedly.

Immediately we both descended the front steps and headed for the horseless carriage. But before we made it to the gate, the car was surrounded by people. It was shaped like a normal carriage, except there were no horses. Its wheels were made from wood. Its hood was folded back. Smoke and dust was still spewing out of the back.

This was possibly the first car to arrive in the Indies from England. And whose was it?

A European, in a yellow-green civilian uniform, wearing a cap of the same colour, and civilian shoes, alighted. Another European, sitting behind the wheel, stayed put. The one who had alighted came through the gate into my front yard.

'Does Mr Minke live here?' he asked in Dutch. 'Ah, it's you yourself? What luck,' and he gave me a letter from the palace summoning me to an audience with the Governor-General in Buitenzorg, and suggesting I try out riding the automobile.

The automobile raced along faster than any train. I felt I was in a box that had been thrown down from the heavens by San Hyang Bayu, the God of Wind. Everybody and everything in the car was shaken by its vibrations. Ascending hills gave it no problem. And when going downhill it raced even faster. Unlike a horse, it did not have to worry about breaking a leg because of a too-heavy load. The view along the road was also different than that from the train. And the wind rushed past with such gusto!

People made way for the automobile as soon as they heard it coming from far away – carriages, buffalo carts, pedestrians. Everyone stopped to admire, even the buffaloes and work-horses. Only once did a surrey race off, diving into the paddy-fields. There were even more admirers once we entered Buitenzorg. Everyone wanted to be the first to report what they had seen.

The automobile came to halt in the palace gardens. The Governor-General, wearing civilian clothes, was seated by himself on a white painted cane chair. I alighted and greeted this wild beast who I was meeting now in his own lair. He held out his hand.

'Ha, Mr Minke! How did you like travelling by automobile? Good, heh?'

'A most exquisite experience, Your Excellency, a true product of the modern age.'

'It won't be long before there are many travelling the streets of Batavia and Buitenzorg. You'll no doubt be getting one yourself.'

'How would that be possible, Your Excellency?'

'How would that be possible? Why wouldn't it be possible! Anyone can order one and have it brought out here. Without exception.'

'Huh.'

'Please, be seated. Why are we standing like this?'

As soon as we sat down I thanked him for this honour and for his being prepared to make time to receive me.

'Yes, it's nice to be able to chat quietly in the evening like this. How do you like to be called? By your pen-name? Or your real name?'

'My real name, Your Excellency.'

'Ah-ha, this is not an official function, you can drop the "Your Excellency".'

'Very well, Sir.'

'I'd like to have a heart-to-heart talk with you, Mr Minke. The Government has high hopes that the educated Natives will help it carry out its work, its work in implementing the new Ethical Policy, a policy based on the Netherlands repaying its debt to the Indies. You can see for yourself how we have moved many people from Java to Lampung so as to alleviate the poverty on Java? The roads and railway system of Java are now among the best in the world – something which you should also remember. Then there are the forests – they are the most beautiful, giant plantations in the world. There is all the work done in expanding the irrigation system so that now we can get more than one crop per year from the same land. There is still a need to do some research into the education question. Especially as concerns financing it. And if the result of educating Natives is simply to produce a question factory like yourself, then, that, of course, would be disappointing to the Government.'

'But, Sir, all my life I have only ever asked you two questions, once when you were a general and once as Governor-General.'

'Yes, but questions asked in public, and such sharp questions,' he smiled, and smacked his lips a little. 'Yes-yes, perhaps you didn't realise just how sharp your questions were. The Government's efforts will have been of little use if all they produce are such cutting questions as yours. And of not much use to the Natives either.'

He did not want to be disturbed while he unified the territories of the Indies. He was determined to murder without having to face any accusers. He wanted everyone to say that he was doing the right thing. And that the destruction of those who resisted was also right. He had lauded my efforts to help the Government. Now he was showing his displeasure that I had asked a question – just one question. A wild beast that wanted to have everything its own way. Like the kings of my ancestors.

169

Like the Native rulers he himself had criticised.

'Do you understand what I'm saying?'

'I'm trying to understand, Sir.'

'Ah, you are too intelligent not to understand,' he laughed good-humouredly. 'But I have to say that I am truly grateful for the help you have given us through the publication of *Medan*. Why do you seem surprised? No need, Sir. I am sure we can be friends. Don't you agree?'

'Of course, Sir. Why not?'

He stood up and held out his hand. As a sign of friendship, I also stood and shook hands with him. What was the purpose of this ceremony anyway? A Governor-General wants to be the friend of a powerless Native? My mother's words came back to warn me – watch out! And Ter Haar's voice echoed within me too – you are now in the wild beast's lair. Be careful. You may unexpectedly meet death itself, gentle or brutal, perhaps in the form of the caresses of friendship, like now. It would mean the same thing – death. Killers only had one thought – to kill those who did not support them.

'Every day you advance further, Mr Minke. With more and more influence in society, among the *priyayi*, the merchants, the businessmen. I have already expressed my thanks to you publicly, haven't I? Now I want to suggest to you that you be careful. It is not so hard to be careful. Everyone can. As a person with influence you should be careful in the way you use it.'

'Thank you, Sir, but I truly don't feel I have any influence over anyone.'

'Nah, it's strange if you don't understand your own power. That is where the danger lies. You might make a mistake and use that influence wrongly.'

'Thank you, Sir. I'll remember what you have said.'

'And what are your plans for the immediate future?'

And I became very nervous when I remembered what I had just asked Sandiman to do.

'I don't understand your question, Sir.'

'You must have some bigger plans.'

'If this is what you mean, and if the Government has no objections, I will be starting a daily newspaper.'

'Excellent!' he laughed happily. 'It's not unexpected. You've had great success with your weekly. I'm sure you'll have even greater success with your daily.'

'I hope that will be the case, Sir.'

'Good. Perhaps you will not believe me, but I set aside time especially to read your writings, both those in Dutch and in Malay. You don't think you could write in simpler Malay, do you?'

'Thank you, Sir. Then perhaps you could give me some comments on my work?'

'I've told you what I think. If I praise your magazine over and over again, isn't that a form of comment? You are the pioneer of Native publishing. You

170

have experience. You won't find it so hard to start up the first Native daily. Tell me, do you need any help?'

'Thank you, Sir, but no.'

'In short, you can rest assured that the Government will continue its policies to advance the Native peoples – emigration, irrigation and education. What happens next will depend on the Government's next decisions. You know, it's an out-of-date idea, the idea of fighting the Government. An idea that always leads to disaster. It's impossible to win. One million ignorant people cannot drive or move along a train, Sir. But one modern human being can do it.'

For how long was I going to be lectured by this Governor-General?

'I can understand and accept all of this, Sir.'

'In the villages you will see the village crier with his cymbals shouting out the news. Now all we need is a newspaper. The news no longer need seek out listeners along the streets. It arrives without fanfare in your house.'

'Yes, Sir.'

'All you need to do is write a little commentary and within hours, thousands, tens of thousands of people have been filled with whatever you want. This is all possible only because of modern science and learning . . .

'And organisation, Sir.'

'Yes, the organisation of work. You are the most advanced of the educated Natives. You stand in the front line, listened to and copied by others. You no doubt understand your position. Your influence will help determine the progress of your people in the coming years. What do you need to start up your new paper?'

'I'm in the process of working that out, Sir.'

'What about finances?'

'I'll work that out later, Sir.'

Van Heutsz gave a friendly laugh.

'It seems you're very sharp. The others seem to be concerned first with getting the money, and only then work out exactly what they want to do. If you need capital the Government would be happy to help, with all or part.'

'A thousand thanks, Sir.'

I could hear Mama's whispering – they will make you their propagandist and you will do it voluntarily. He will use your influence, and you'll work for them without payment. Be careful, make sure your abilities, influence and experience don't end up serving other ends.

'How is the Sarekat Priyayi?'

'Not as it should be, Sir.'

'Every beginning is difficult. But once you've started, half the job is done, says a proverb. No doubt you have come up against the problem of the conservatism of the *priyayi*, who are only concerned to protect their jobs. Their ambitions go no further than their promotion. You will just have to work harder. What do you think of Multatuli's writings? Outstanding, don't you think?'

'Yes, we can say at least, that he has a unique way of looking at things, a unique style.'

'And you like his works, yes? I don't think anyone can truly understand the Indies without having read Multatuli. And if you don't understand the Indies then you don't know what it is you have to do for the Indies. In the past many people criticised and ridiculed his works. They were backward colonials. He understood the Indies and the Netherlands of his time. He understood the spirit of the times. But, Mr Minke, the Indies has changed since the time of Multatuli. As has the Netherlands itself.'

His two-hour lecture soon passed except for the exhaustion of having to listen. And, of course, every important person needs a listener. All the powerful are the same. It's when they start talking that they feel greatness, and even more so when they're not listening to others.

'Times have changed, and so has the colonial outlook. Today's colonial outlook recognises the need to help the Natives to progress. And it's also right and proper that this advantage should not be denied the smaller principalities whose people are oppressed and kept ignorant by their own rulers. The Indies were once united by Majapahit. Then they fell apart again. Now the Government is able to unify the Indies again. More concretely, over a wider area, and with greater stability. And under the protection of a legal system which protects the Natives and their property.'

'Who is not convinced that Your Excellency is succeeding and will succeed even further.'

'Thank you, Mr Minke. But it is not the Governor-General who is doing this. It is the times themselves. These are different comments than those you made the other day at the interview, Mr Minke?'

'It was a matter of whose point of view I was looking at things from.'

'So where were you looking at things from then? From the point of view of the principalities?'

'More-or-less, Sir.'

He laughed again.

'You're staying at a hotel?'

'Of course, Sir.'

'You should move to Buitenzorg.'

'Do you think that's necessary, Sir?'

'Ah, just a suggestion. So it's easier to see you.'

This wild beast had now invited me to move closer to his lair. So it would be easier for me to come in and out of his lair. So I could join in his depravation? Or was I to be his prey? Or, a third possibility, he wanted me to be a witness to his success. And I answered as Ter Haar would have, but silently of course. I have never needed to make others my victims, *Meneer*

General, *Meneer* Governor-General, and I have no desire either to be turned into a wild beast.

The colonial press was overtaken by a wave of incredible jealousy because of van Heutsz's meeting with me. They refused to publish my articles in any of their publications. The European printing firms would not touch me. And there was an ex-convict mixed up in all this – Robert Suurhof.

There was no other way. We must publish our own daily.

Good-bye colonial press!

9

Mama was able to come to an understanding with Mr Frischboten. He would open a practice in Java, while also helping our paper. His retainer would be paid by Mama's business in the Netherlands. Later he agreed to be paid in Java from the earnings of our publishing enterprise.

One day Mir and her husband arrived at my house in Buitenzorg. They had not told me when they were arriving in Batavia. And now there they were standing at the front door.

Mir was wearing a silk dress decorated with pink flowers. Her skin was whiter than I remembered. Her cheeks were red. She now wore her hair tied in a bun with a red ribbon, not loose and flowing like before.

'I'm so happy to be back in the Indies.' She held out her hand. 'And most of all to see you again. This is my husband.'

'Welcome. Lawyer Frischboten? Welcome. Welcome. Please sit down.'

'I'm also happy to be back in the Indies,' her husband spoke in a deep sonorous voice.

We relaxed immediately and I felt as if I were talking to old friends.

'Where's your wife?' asked Mir.

'I have no wife, Mir.'

The two of us launched into a hectic discussion of times past and Hendrik Frischboten sat there watching us without wanting to interfere. I found out then that Mir's sister had married a Canadian and had moved with him to Canada. Her father had gone to French Guyana to become a plantation administrator. European birds, they flew wherever their hearts took them. Wherever they landed they found themselves masters.

'You were born in the Priangan, I hear?' I asked Hendrik.

Lazily he indicated an answer of 'yes'. And he did look a lazy man. His body was covered in folds of fat. His face was round. His round cheeks hung down like those of an old man. And contrasting with all this was his very pointed chin. There were lines also going from the ends of his mouth down to either side of his chin. He had the black eyes of a Native with eyelids that didn't seem to want to open all the way.

On no, I thought, he's a lazy one. Mama may have made the wrong choice.

174

'It's a pity you didn't let me know when you were coming. We haven't got a house for you yet. If you don't mind why don't you stay here until we find a house for you. And also . . . '

And I told them that our paper would soon be ready to be published. It would be printed at No 1 Naripan Street, Bandung.

'I have family in Bandung. That's even better for us. We have a house there,' said Hendrik.

'No shop talk,' forbade Mir. 'We didn't come to see you for that.'

'Anyway, you two will stay here for the time being, yes?'

'That sounds like a good idea. Hendrik, you don't have any objections, do you? So we can have a bit of a holiday first.'

'No objections whatsoever,' he answered lazily, 'as long as it's no trouble.'

As he spoke I asked myself how could such a pretty and energetic girl like Mir end up with such a sluggish man for a husband?

They would stay in Buitenzorg until things were ready in Bandung. That afternoon, while I was out, summoned to an audience with the Governor-General, they returned with their things. It wasn't much, two suitcases and a box of books. When I arrived back from the palace, which was only a few score metres away, I found Mir sitting by herself under the *pendopo*. Hendrik Frischboten was off having a walk somewhere.

She seemed very pleased to see me. She wouldn't let me go in to change clothes.

'You seem so alone here. Why don't you get married?'

'There's a time for that, Mir. Why do you always ask about that?'

She looked at me without blinking, then: 'I wish my husband could grow a moustache like yours.'

'You've changed, Mir. Do you remember when we had that talk about *gamelan*? About gongs?'

'I remember. That's all in the past now. After listening to Madame Marais . . . ah, what a woman . . . all that talk about the Theory of Association, about *gamelan*, it was all garbage, it was all mixed-up nonsense. I'm so glad to be able to meet you now that you are so important. Even the Governor-General wants you for a friend. Who would have ever guessed?'

'What are you talking about?'

'A Native woman. That Mama of yours was able to convince my husband to work for you. My husband, a lawyer, was able to be won over by her proposals! You have been so lucky, Minke.' She was lost in thought for a moment. Then she quickly continued: 'She has had such success in her business despite all the misfortunes that have befallen her. And it's no penny farthing affair that she runs either!'

As interesting as all this talk about Mama, about her husband, and about me was, I felt that there was something strange here. As she went on more and more of her sentences become unconnected, her thoughts seemed to

175

wander. She seemed to have lost her concentration. There was some unresolved problem troubling her within.

'You don't have any children yet, Mir?'

She shook her head, and then went on to something else again: 'It's strange how the world turns things upside down,' she said, seeming to be thinking hard about something. 'Before, when we met, I was the senior and you the junior. Now we meet in another place like this and you are my employer, our employer.'

'We are not employer and employee, Mir. We are working together.'

'It's the same, Minke, only the name differs.'

'Your regret your decision?'

'No. I'm glad to have returned to the Indies. And all the more happy to see you turn out as I had hoped, surpassing all my expectations. You have flown up into the highest layers of heaven, by yourself, without the aid of anyone. So inspiring.'

'You're wrong, Mir. I have had a lot of help. So many good people have helped me, including you, and now both you and your husband. No, nobody can grow and develop without the help of others.'

She gazed at me with eyes that pleaded for my eyes not to leave hers. Mir was indeed no longer the girl I once knew. She was someone's wife who was dreaming of other things.

'Why are you looking at me so strangely, Mir?'

'I'm worried, Minke. You've just come from the Governor-General's palace. It seems you're close to him.'

'Not quite right, Mir. I'm a subject of the Netherlands Indies, aren't I? That's all.'

'Do you remember what my father and I once hoped for you? That you would be a leader of your people? Now, with this friendship with van Heutsz . . . we came to work together with you, like you said, not to be just an employee, just as you're not our employer.'

'I don't understand what you're getting at, Mir.'

'If we came here just to be an extension of the power of the Government and not to help you . . . '

'It that's what you mean, Mir, there's no need to be concerned. Van Heutsz needs my friendship so as to know what I'm thinking. He thinks I represent the thinking of the educated Natives. He's copying Snouck Hurgronje's behaviour towards Achmad Djajadiningrat.'

'So you really are still travelling your own road?'

'Why wouldn't I be?'

'You're not keeping something from us?'

'There is one thing, Mir. Deep down inside I'm also inspired by your decision to leave Europe to work together with us here.'

'You're being serious? You're just not saying that?'

'Take my hand, Mir. This old friend of yours will never deceive you.'

She shook my hand. And sat back down. But she still seemed to be trying to put her thoughts together.

'I wanted to talk about other things too. It seems this is not the right time or place,' her voice was faint like a lone cry in the desert.

She had some problem. Perhaps a problem with her marriage.

'Why haven't you brought your children, Mir?'

'We haven't any yet.'

'What about stepchildren?'

She shook her head. The electric light shone down on her thin, sharp European face. Her head was shaped with beautiful curves. God had not allowed there to be too much in any one place, nor too little anywhere else. The pointed tip of her nose shone with the reflection of the light. More independent and older now, she had grown more attractive. Four or three years older than me. Maybe only two. Maybe she was the same. Her skin was red from the tropical sun she had sailed under from Port Aden to Batavia. It was also covered with that unpleasant blonde hair Europeans have all over their body.

'Why are you looking at me like that? I'm too fat?'

'No, Mir. You're just as slim as before.'

'You're just saying that. I've put on three kilograms.'

'Three kilograms is just enough to fill you out. You're just as slim as before. A bit taller, that's why.'

Her conversation was also different now. She used to be always trying to work out what I was thinking. Now she was seeking attention for herself.

She gave a little laugh for no reason. I joined in to be sociable. Just then Hendrik returned from his walk, a cane in his hand.

He nodded. Mir rose from her chair, went across to her husband and patted him on the front of his shirt, which was wet from perspiration.

'Change your shirt, Darling. You need time to adjust yourself to the Indies climate.'

Hendrik nodded to me and went inside with his wife.

I was left sitting in my chair reflecting on how harmonious and close were European husbands and wives, the man not making a slave of the woman, the woman not enslaving herself to the man, as was the case with my people. How beautiful would such a marriage be. I would never find the kind of woman I hoped for from among my own people.

'You're not finished your work yet?' asked Mir. She had sat down again, her husband beside her in his clean shirt.

'It's not work, Mir. I was just thinking about something.'

'Minke went to medical school,' Mir said to her husband. 'You can ask him about your health.'

'A failed medical student, Mr Frischboten,' I parried quickly. 'And I have never gone back to my studies.'

The lawyer didn't respond to his wife's comment nor to mine. He just nodded mysteriously.

'You like going for strolls, Meneer.'

'Yes.'

'Doctor's advice. Hendrik must do a lot of walking, the faster the better,' added Mir.

'Ill?'

'No, Meneer, but I need a lot of exercise.'

I was beginning to understand a little about the dynamics of this family. And the little I could understand indicated that there was something wrong there. The harmony and closeness was perhaps just an outer skin covering whatever was wrong.

'At the very least the atmosphere in the Indies will be a good influence. Isn't that right, Darling. Hendrik was born in the Indies.'

I hope it isn't a mental problem, I prayed. Working together with him in that case wouldn't be of much benefit. But Mama would never suggest a person who had mental problems. From his sagging cheeks I guessed he might be suffering from some kind of nervous exhaustion. He wasn't old, forty at the most. And the exhaustion was even more evident in his eyes.

'You can rest here in Buitenzorg for as long as you want before starting work,' I said. 'There's no hurry. If you need to rest, take even one or two months. There's no problem. Whatever you need.'

'Thank you, Meneer. I would never get the chance to rest before starting work in Europe.'

The evening's conversation ended. I listened to them say 'Good evening' and watched them walk off to their room. Such rapport, such harmony. But was the reality different?

Sandiman arrived with a student from the medical school. He had come to my house in Betawi several times. He was moon-faced and he had spent most of his time gazing at the *Flower of the Century's End*.

'I'm sure you haven't forgotten me,' he said in careful Dutch.

'Of course not. But your name . . . I'm sorry, really, but I've forgotten. Forgive me.'

'Tomo, sir, Raden Tomo.'

'Oh yes, Raden Tomo,' I said, even though I had never known his name.

'I've come hoping to discuss some business with you, and, of course, to visit you in your new home.'

'Thank you, Sir, and this is all it is.'

'It's a very big house, much bigger than the one in Betawi.'

'Just a coincidence. This building was empty.'

'The news is that it was gift from the Governor-General?'

Whaaat! The rumours have spread that far!

'The Governor-General owes me nothing. He has no reason to give me a gift.'

'They say the Governor-General once thanked you openly and in public. Is that true?'

'Yes, that did happen. In a meeting with the press. But it's going a bit far to try to connect that with my new home.'

'But you are his friend, aren't you?'

'It's the Governor-General who wants to be friends. I am just a Native subject of the Netherlands Indies.'

'From your tone I would say that you're not too happy to be thanked by him and to have him seek you out as his friend?'

'You can make your own judgement about that.'

Raden Tomo was quiet for a moment, thinking, then he glanced around the room.

'You don't hang that picture any more, Sir?'

'Why? Did you like it?'

'Just asking, Sir. I am here on other business.'

'I hope I can be of help.'

Meanwhile Sandiman was watching us suspiciously.

'How is the Sarekat Priyayi?'

'Not so good, Meneer Tomo. It hasn't lived up to our expectations. I went after the wrong membership. Its members are the *priyayi* – static, no initiative, no life in them. Their only ambition is to spend the rest of their life undisturbed working for the Government. I shouldn't have chosen them. But what can be done? It's a mistake that has already been made.'

'Perhaps that mistake has given you a new perspective on things?'

'Yes, I've thought it over, I do have a new view on these things now.'

'May I ask what it is?'

'If the organisation became rigid and lifeless it was because that's the kind of members it had. We should have sought out the young, idealistic people to recruit, definitely not *priyayi* who have become mummified in Government service, but independent and free individuals . . . '

'So what will be the fate of the Sarekat Priyayi?'

'It sounds as if you're interested in organising?'

'Since that day, two years ago, that you first proposed the idea to us, I have followed what you have been doing and the fate of the Sarekat. I've thought a lot about why the organisation has not even been able to carry out the things it advocates in its own consititution.'

'Or perhaps it's my fault. I'm such a bad organiser. Isn't that so Sandiman?'

'A stone house cannot be built without stones, Tuan,' he answered cryptically. 'And a wooden house cannot be built without wood.'

'A stone house can be built without stones. It just means that you have to make the stones first,' I answered. 'If you have a capable engineer, he will be able to build the house. I'm not such an engineer. I even failed as a doctor.'

'Why don't we stop talking about failure?' said Sandiman. 'Tuan Tomo wants to talk about new initiatives.'

'Yes, Meneer. It seems that you don't expect much more from the Sarekat Priyayi. It won't offend you if I talk about the new initiatives – an organisation being founded by young, idealistic youth?'

As far as I was concerned the Sarekat was dead. Whether that was fair or not is beside the point. There was no reason to mourn. A deformed baby will usually miscarry.

'You cannot force things.'

'Thank you, Meneer Minke. If such a new initiative did get off the ground, would you have any objections to helping?'

'As a person with ideals it would be my duty to help.'

'If Tuan Minke promises help,' Sandiman emphasised, 'you will surely receive it. Once promised it will never be withdrawn.'

'Of course, I must believe you,' whispered Raden Tomo. 'The stories about your relationship with the Governor-General have been exaggerated, perhaps?'

'It sounds as though you would like those rumours to be true?'

'Well, Meneer Minke, I think that if you go with the stream things are always easier.'

Sandiman's eyes almost popped out.

'It seems that Meneer Sandiman doesn't agree. I expected so,' Raden Tomo tried to explain his views. 'Everything that wants to grow must adjust to the situation. It is the situation that must bring things forth to grow.'

'Excuse me,' Sandiman rose and left the room. He didn't reappear.

'It seems he definitely doesn't agree. I think my opinion is sufficiently scientific, based on the laws of life.'

'At least you have an opinion.'

'I didn't come to this opinion lightly, Meener. In fact, I base it on my observations of what happend to the Sarekat. Are you still willing to help?'

'I've given my word.'

He returned to Betawi satisfied. Sandiman was disappointed however. He came out and sat down across from me.

'The reports about your friendship with the Governor-General are also rife in Jogja and Solo. They say this house was a gift from him and that you have received a European housekeeper, a man and wife. Is it true, Tuan?'

'You're beginning to distrust me, Sandiman. We have worked together all this time on the basis of mutual trust. You left for Jogja and Solo on the basis of that trust. How could you distrust me now?'

'Because I also have the right to look after my own security, Tuan.'

'Am I the sort of person who could betray you?'

'At the very least, Tuan, I could meet disaster because of your orders, while you would be protected by your friendship with the Governor-General.'

'It's fully within your rights to disagree with what I say and do, Sandiman, or what anybody says and does. You think that I should have refuted Tomo when he said it was better to float with the stream rather than resist authority. Well, I think he's right, at least as far as organising goes. Once the roots and stalk are strong, they will be strengthened by storms and cyclones.'

'I do not agree, Tuan.'

'You have the right to disagree, but do not force others to agree. Tomo doesn't have the right either to force you to agree with him. At least he's put a lot of time and effort into coming to his opinion, and into studying what has happened.'

Sandiman was not satisfied.

'So how did things go in Solo? That's our work, not Tomo's.'

'I am not sure that I should report, Tuan.'

'In that case, you needn't report now.'

He looked angry. He excused himself to go back to my house in Betawi.

Outside my life, big things continued to happen. The last period of van Heutsz's rule was laden with violence. In central Java, centred in the village of Klopoduwur, a peasant rebellion, calling itself the Samin movement, was also suppressed with arms. After a quarter of a century of rebellion these fifty thousand simple peasants finally knew defeat. They threw away their weapons, sharp and blunt, and drew a new, more powerful weapon from its sheath – social resistance, the refusal to obey all Government laws and regulations. They refused to pay tax. They refused to do *rodi*, whatever the authorities called it, however they tried to disguise it. They gladly thronged into the gaols and gladly thronged out of them again. They cleared forests and put up buildings without seeking permission. The Government didn't know what to do. In the end they decided to let the Samin peasants live the way they wanted as long as they didn't threaten the Government, the authorities and their agents with armed force.

In Klungkung, Bali, the army launched a massive attack. Villages fell one after the other – Kusamba, Asah, Dewan, Satera, Tulikup, Takmung, Bukit Jimbul. The King of Klungkung, of Bali, I Dewa Agung Djambe, along with his wife and children, all his family and his people, dressed themselves in white ready to die. They came out of the palace and their houses and encircled the city – six kilometres in all – to await the army.

In Minangkabau, in south-west Sumatra, another rebellion broke out. The people there refused to pay taxes and do *rodi*.

The independent principalities, the enclaves, the pockets of power that the Government called 'Landschap' one by one fell into van Heutsz's hands without offering any resistance, without there being more wars – in Sumba, Sumbawa, the interior of Timor, Central Celebes, Borneo . . .

The resistance in Tapanuli, in North Sumatra, was announced as over when Si Singamangaraja was killed. Dutch power had begun to be consolidated in Tapanuli around 1876. The colonialists' obituaries for Si Singamangaraja were full of insults and slander, and were spittle in the face of all Native youth. They were being faithful to the colonial way – slandering those who had been defeated, who were powerless, and especially those who had already become spirits. The most strongly voiced slander was that Si Singamangaraja was no better than any other Native leader – they were all unable to keep themselves from stealing women. They said that not long before he died he stole the maiden Natingka, the daughter of King Pardopur, the fiancée of Radja Nawaolu. When they hate there is no slander too great; when they are pleased there is no praise too great.

And in my own life, the daily edition of *Medan* began to appear in Bandung. There were more rumours that the paper was also a gift from van Heutsz. While these slanders remained rumours I had no way of refuting them. I could not refute them openly in the paper, as that would mean mentioning the name of the Governor-General as the representative of Her Majesty.

'That's the Indies for you,' Mama wrote from France. *'The papers don't dare print the truth, afraid they will be closed down or suspended, while the greedy* priyayi *are mummified in their jobs, as you said yourself, and those in power know only how to punish. Life is dominated by rumours. Anyone can become a victim without any chance of defending themselves. You must stop this, Child. Make your paper the only one in the Indies that works only for justice, for truth, for your people. Frischboten is an honest lawyer, he will do all he can to help you. On first impression you make not like him, but don't be put off by what you see on the outside. He knows the Indies well. He too once said to me that the Indies is a factory that only produces* priyayi, *bureaucrats and tyrants. It has never produced a single leader, except when they produce themselves, outside the Government.*

I could no longer question Frischboten's reliability. Together we had solved the problem of the News Agency's refusal to sell us their cable reports on important domestic news. They would only sell us international news. And our Native readers weren't so interested in international news. We couldn't afford to hire reporters of our own yet. In order to obtain local news we struck out on an unusual path. *Medan* opened its pages to all Natives, whether they held official positions or not, who wanted to report the problems they were facing, the troubles they confronted. Any problem, any trouble. Frischboten was ready to deal with all his strength with the cases that came in. People could get free legal advice. And underneath the name of the paper, on the front page, I printed the following explanation: 'Open to any Native to present his opinion or to report his troubles'.

Within three months our office at No 1 Naripan Street was continuously full of people coming from all over the place to report the troubles they were suffering – oppression, theft of their property, injury to their body by the colonial authorities and local elite, both white and brown. Sometimes it involved a conspiracy between the two of them, white and brown. Our administrative office in Bogor was also always full of village people asking for justice. Often it wasn't only legal justice they were after but natural justice. They became the source of news for *Medan*. Within three months we had won the public's confidence. And after three months Sandiman also turned up again.

He came to Buitenzorg one evening: 'Yes, I have to admit, I have succeeded in no longer distrusting Tuan.' He started work in Bandung together with Wardi.

He had gone back to Solo and Jogjakarta to carry out the tasks I had given him even while he distrusted me. The paper had restored his faith in me. He had contacted his brother in the Legion. They were making preparations to depart for Lombok. But the Legion's officers all came to an agreement that they would not go and fight their brothers out there across from Java.

In such busy times I would have forgotten altogether about Maysoroh had she not written so often. Once she wrote:

'Mama is already far advanced in her pregnancy and is going to give birth again in a few days. She hopes to be able to read the latest edition of your paper before the baby arrives.'

It appeared that the last batch of papers I had sent had not reached her. Perhaps it was because one of Rotterdam Lloyd's ships had recently sunk. *Rono Mellema is going to school now,* she wrote another time, *I had to enrol in a one-year course in French in order to be able to enrol in Gymnasium. I was so bored having to sit through all the classes so I left and have taken up violin and music lessons.*

Her fourth letter was an event in itself:

Om, *I'm beginning to feel at home now in Paris. The Indies seems like an unending jungle compared with what it is like here. We like to stroll along the Place de la Concorde and in the Cité, which people say is the heart of Paris. Everywhere there are palaces and gardens. Everywhere there is music and laughter. Everywhere there are cars and electric trams.*

Om, *I don't think we'll be coming back to the Indies. Mama says that things are so much quieter here, no evil and barbarity. What about our relationship, Om?'*

What about our relationship? What about it? My whole life was now dedicated to my two beloved children: *Medan*, coming out daily, and its older brother, coming out weekly. Even with these, the readers were still not satisfied. We also brought out a Sunday edition, the first in the Indies. This was something even the colonial press had never done, white or brown, let alone yellow.

The paper must be something that nourishes the Natives and gives them energy to fight for truth and justice. Within three months we overtook the circulation of *Preanger Bode* and Betawi's *Nieuws van den Dag*.

My heart full of pride, I would often shout within myself: My fellow Natives, my people, now you have a paper of your own, a place where you can air your grievances. Do not worry. No more will evil escape being shamed and exposed before the world! Now you have *Medan* where you can state your opinions, explain your views, somewhere where every one of you can come to seek and find justice. Minke will take your cases before the court of the world!

About our relationship, May, I answered, *it is up to you. I am bound to the land and the people of the Indies. It is to the Indies that I have dedicated myself. It is only in the Indies that I can achieve something meaningful. In another country I would perhaps be nothing more than a dried-out leaf being whisked along by the wind. You can decide, May.*

And, like a thunderbolt I received a letter from Ter Haar who, it turned out, had not died but only been severely wounded and had collapsed at the feet of Lieutenant Colijn: *Within the next few weeks, my friend, I will be leaving the Indies forever. I will try to call in at your office in Bandung. I make sure that I follow your paper every day, even though I cannot yet appreciate the Malay that you use. The printing is also quite good for the Indies, especially remembering that it is not being done in Betawi. It's a pity though that you use such big type, you lose a lot of space that way. Why don't you use smaller print? It would make the paper look much better.*

He asks for smaller print. He is a true Dutchman, not a Native. He does not know and does not want to know that the Natives cannot afford to buy spectacles. Many *priyayi* are forced to retire at forty-five and cannot afford to buy them.

Jean Marais wrote: *We've now received several issues from your first year of publication. As it happens I have a friend here who is a journalist. He was totally amazed that there were Netherlands Indies Natives capable of publishing a newspaper of their own. He thought that you and your people were still eating each other. Then he found out that you were among the top students in medical school. He asked whether there were proper grammar schools in the Indies. I told him that there were not. All he could do was stand open-mouthed in bewilderment. I did the same.*

I happily translated some of the news items for him as well as your editorial.

He said – and please don't be offended – that they weren't proper news reports like those to be found in the European papers. He said that they were more like short articles. I said that these were the types of reports that people needed in the Indies. They tell you what has happened – when, what, who and why – and there is also commentary. It wasn't so important whether the comment was correct or not. The Native readers would always forgive you. The comment gives them something to discuss as well as something to curse. He said he was sorry for them.

But he ended up using material from Medan. *He even used material from* Medan *to write about how there had been a rebellion in the Philippines and how it had been suppressed by the Americans. There are still no signs of rebellion in the French colonies of Africa, Asia and America. You are doing more than just publishing a newspaper, you are beginning the rising up of a people. If this wasn't the case then people wouldn't be reading your paper and it would not be able to survive. You are pioneering the way even if it is just the beginning. You should be very happy. I am proud to have a friend such as you.*

Ai, my heart swelled as big as mountain. The goings-on of this beloved child of mine had made it into the French press – it didn't matter how or exactly what was said. It's always harder to reply to praise. Whenever I'm insulted or challenged there is a kind of automatic machine inside me that reels out all kinds of responses, replies, attitudes, actions already tied together with a string of words. The only words I have to answer praise are 'thank you'. And I did have a lot to thank Jean Marais for – for teaching me French and for bringing me to an understanding of what were an educated person's duties and responsibilities towards his country and people. He too was the one who taught me to distinguish between colonial Europe and free Europe. And it was free Europe that created the colonial mentality even while it retained its own stature. The colonial was condemned for all time to remain colonial.

Nyo, wrote Mama, *I am so happy to be able to pass on to you two pieces of news. Firstly, you now have a pretty little sister. Jean has called her Jeannette. It's right that she doesn't have a Javanese name because she looks just like a Pure-Blood. Jean is also very, very happy to have another child. Secondly, Child, I am so proud to read your newspaper. Even though I feel it is not very tightly edited, I enjoy it very much and am now able to follow what is happening with my people. I would never be able to read that kind of news in the colonial press.*

Congratulations, I'm so proud of you, my son. Now you have begun to be the kind of person you yourself always wanted to be. You have found a way to truly express your thoughts and feelings. But I worry about your safety. The Indies is like the wild jungle. Do you remember someone called Darsam? Without him our business would never have flourished. Without him we would have been at the mercy of all kinds of bandits – white, brown and yellow. Have you thought about this, Child? Don't ignore this. There will be many people – white, brown and yellow – who will not like what you are doing. Frischboten will be a good friend. You can rely upon him at all times. Involve him in everything. And don't put any faith in your friendship with Governor-General van Heutsz. He may treat you well now but the moment his shirt is soiled by you or because of you, he will not hesitate to bring disaster down upon you. Don't forget this, Child, don't ever forget.

They are all the same, the priyayi, *whether white or brown. Their mouth speaks only for their pockets. If you know what is in their pocket then you will know everything there is to know about them.*

If you can't get on with Frischboten, then telegraph me straight away. We've also got to know a good Dutch lawyer here in Paris. He's going to open an office in the Indies. His mother is French. He has lived in poverty ever since he was a child. He understands what it means to be poor.

Om, wrote May, *May I have permission to study singing?*

Of course, May, do not feel bound because of me. With Mama beside you, you will grow into the woman you want to be. She is a goddess who understands the inner workings of people's souls. Follow her guidance and accept her advice and you will never regret it.

Mr Minke, wrote Ter Haar, *please forgive me that I will not be able to visit you in Bandung or Buitenzorg. I haven't been able to find anyone to take me, so there is no way I can get there. I will sail straight to Europe. Before I leave the Indies allow me to say one more thing. Never let your very good newspaper ever be used to further personal ambitions. Your paper and yourself now belong to your peoples, the peoples of the Indies.*

I belong to the peoples of the Indies! Honoured and enslaved together! Like other people I too like to be honoured. I accepted the honour. But I also accepted my fate as a slave, the lowliest of slaves serving the peoples of the Indies.

I, Sandiman, Wardi and *Medan* – newspaper and magazine editions – laboured on like the wheels of a locomotive.

And another letter arrived from Maysoroh:

Om, on this peaceful night tonight, I am writing to you to thank you with the most sincere of hearts for all the help you gave Papa and me during those difficult times in Surabaya. What would have happened if you hadn't come to us? Papa often tells of all your kindness to us, how you always respected and helped us. I listened to all Papa's stories with my head bowed with emotion. Through these stories your goodness has become one of the most beautiful things in our lives, something we will never forget. How can we ever repay you? Mama often talks about selflessness. And that is what rules your heart, says Mama. And that too is what I think, you are a great and good man. May you have a long and happy life. May God always bestow upon you happiness, safety, and success . . .

I put the letter away without finishing it. What did it mean when a young woman opened a letter to her fiancé with such excessive praise? Such letters always ended with the sharpest of barbs.

Your Excellency, the honourable, Tuan Chief Editor, began a different letter.

'Your excellency, the honourable' – what was this all about? But I didn't get a chance to smile. This letter did not end with a barb but with the raging cry of the helpless. I read on:

Would perhaps it be possible for Your Honourable Excellency, if Your Excellency should so be willing, to consider my most unworthy case and to accept my humble request for assistance in my difficulties. I have a daughter named Marjam, nine years old, attending Angka Satu school. In third grade. One day it seems that she was sleepy at school. The tuan teacher struck her. My daughter was unconscious for four days and nights. Then she died. Then even while we were in mourning, my wife and I, the tuan teacher came to our house and threatened to have me exiled because of the base and contemptible behaviour of my daughter, totally improper behaviour, he said, which only caused difficulties for the teachers that the Government has brought all the way from Holland . . .

My blood boiled. I jumped up out of my chair. The letter was from Bandung. I immediately hailed a *delman* and set off for the address on the letter. The house was gloomy. The master of the house was an employee of the forestry service. When he found out who I was, he fell to the floor to make obeisance as if I was my slave or servant. I forbade him. And he said that the teacher would be here any moment now.

And it was true, a few moments later the teacher arrived. He spoke rudely, in Malay, and sat himself down without waiting for an invitation.

He was a Pure-Blood Dutchman, heavily built and with arms covered in thick, blond body hair.

'Is this the teacher you wrote me about?' I asked in Sundanese.

'Who is this?' the teacher asked the master of the house in Malay.

But our host was too afraid to answer. It was I who answered in Dutch: 'I am the person who is going to take you to court. I am going to bring charges against you. You are not a teacher, you are a murderer!' I accused him, pointing at his nose. 'Liar and bully! Get out, or run away!'

The big-bodied man shrunk up, bending like some old doll. He picked up his briefcase, stood up, and walked towards the door, looked back again, and then disappeared from sight.

'We won't let them get away with this. Come on, stand up. No one bows down to people here. Don't be afraid of the court. Come with me now.'

'Where to, Your Excellency?'

'There are no "Your Excellencys" here. To my office, so we can start things rolling.'

He refused, afraid that he would lose his job and pension.

'So you're not prepared to lay charges?'

'I'm truly scared, Your Excellency.'

'Even so I am going to have papers drawn up so that you can have him charged. You will be called before the court anyway.'

'Please don't involve me.'

I found Hendrik Frischboten back at the office attending to someone, and I gave him the man's letter about his daughter.

'Let's take this case up. I've met both the man concerned and the teacher,' then I went back to my desk and finished reading Maysoroh's letter:

My violin teacher, Om, has suggested I study singing. He says my voice is more beautiful than the sound of a violin. So I am studying singing as well now. It's only now I realise that singing has to be studied too.

I know you do not tire of reading about what I am doing here. Forgive me if it does bore you. Papa is always telling me that I should remember and honour all those who have ever done good to us, whether it is the people around us or across the world – my teachers, and the world's great writers and thinkers. And there is one name which I will honour and remember for all my life. You know the name, Om? Yours, my fiancé's.

Why is there no end to all this flattery? She can have everything she wants in Paris. The Indies is just an untamed jungle and I am just one of its millions of monkeys. Why is there so much of this praise and flattery?

And so I am also very happy and proud to be able to tell you, Om, that I have decided to become a singer. As a singer I will be of no use to you, or to the Indies. On the other hand, Om, if I am a success, at least I will be of use to France.

Mama says, Om, that you should be a happy man because you are needed by your people. And happy too would I be if one day I was also needed by France. You will pray for my success, won't you, Om, and not try to stop me?

You who are so experienced, who understands the inner feelings of people, I am sure will be prepared to let go of that little dream we once dreamt together. Om, forgive this Maysoroh, Om. Forgive her. She will never forget you, the person, his goodness. I do not regret the tears I have shed strengthening myself to write you this letter.

Every day I put flowers next to your picture, Om, so that I see you and the flowers as one, just as you and your goodness are one. Forgive me, Om, I who have other and my own dreams . . .

How I had tormented her. It took her days to get up the courage to write that letter. May, you are a daughter of France. It is now up to France to determine who you are to be and what will be your future. Only one thing stands firm in my life now – *Medan*, in all its forms of publication. *Medan* must grow, must spread its wings like the *garuda*, and the Natives from across the Indies will find protection in their shade. From a circulation of two thousand it grew to four, then five thousand. No colonial paper had ever reached that high.

The colonial papers snarled open their snouts and started howling their complaints. One attack followed another. The paper importer from whom we bought our newsprint, Jacobsen van der Berg, suddenly stopped selling to us. Very well. We were forced to buy from a Chinese importer at a higher price. Then finally we had to arrange to import paper ourselves, from Stockholm. While this was happening we opened stationery shops, which became our sales agents. Then the News Agency started offering us only the uninteresting wire stories. It's lucky our readers weren't so interested in international news. Anyway, they were patient enough to wait until we were able to quote the news from the foreign press. We had to take on more and more people. One of the big Dutch trading companies, the Bormsumij, offered to sell us paper again after we started importing ourselves but we politely refused.

The reports of injustices and the calls for help kept flooding in. *Medan* had been accepted as a reality, as the defender of the Natives. *Medan*, as a newspaper, had a dual role because of the needs and the social situation of the Natives. But there were also strange letters that came in, such as:

Don't interfere in this matter because you may find you're unable to defend yourself.

Workers on a cocoa plantation had banded together to bring accusations against the plantation manager, a Mr Meyer, that he had been brutally mistreating their families. He was even worse than Vlekkenbaaij in Tulangan. It became obvious from the fact that Meyer found out that the workers had banded together that he was in league with the local prosecutor who had received the workers' complaints. The prosecutor froze the case. It was then that they turned to us and Frischboten took up the case.

If Mr Meyer does not desire to stand trial before the courts, we would be very happy to bring him before another court – Medan *and its readers, whose prosecutors and judges, European and Native, are almost infinite in number.*

The local prosecutor was forced to bring him to trial. Meyer went to gaol.

Fine, we accepted these dual duties gladly. And it was not I, but life in the Indies itself that demanded it be so.

There was one letter that we used which turned out to be fake. I was trapped and had to have dealings with the law. There was great uproar when I refused to go before a Native court. As someone with noble blood, a Raden Mas, I had the right of *forum privilegiatum*. I could not be handed over to a Native judge and prosecutor to be done with as they pleased.

Hendrik Frischboten threw himself into the case. My defence depended on being able to find who wrote the false letter. We succeeded and the case was dropped. When we discovered the culprit we also learnt that there was someone else behind the plot, manipulating things like a *dalang* – Robert Suurhof.

Don't put it off, wrote Mama, *find someone like Darsam. You'll regret it if you forget about this.*

Every day more and more people came seeking help. Frischboten advised them in Malay, Sundanese and Dutch. He, who first looked as though he was lazy, lacking self-confidence and energy, turned out to be fired by idealism when it came to defending truth and justice.

'Don't worry,' said Frischboten, 'heap all the problems of the Natives onto my back. In every colony, no matter in what part of the world, you find only evil and crime, coming also from the colonisers themselves. The colonials are often more evil than the most primitive Native to be found in the jungles of Papua. You mustn't believe too much in school education. Every good teacher may still end up producing evil bandits who have no principles whatsoever, an outcome even more likely when the teacher is also a bandit.'

And all the cases we dealt with seemed to prove what he said. The crimes committed by Europeans were generally more extensive, bigger and worse.

'In the colonies today it is like it was five hundred years ago when those who had power did what they liked – enslaved, oppressed, killed, stole and destroyed. All in the name of "peace and order". The modern states of Europe are no longer so barbaric. Or at least they don't let things go to such extremes.'

Om, wrote Maysoroh again, *I have received your letter. One evening Papa and Mama were sitting reading the newspapers. I said I was sorry but could I disturb them for a minute. Papa put down his glasses and his newspaper. Mama too. Jeannette was asleep in her lap. I was hesitant as how to start, then Mama began: Is there something wrong, May?*

Her question made it easier for me to begin, and so I began: No, Ma, I answered. Would you both like to hear a letter I wrote to Om in Bandung. And I read them my letter to you. And then I read them your answer, finishing with the words: May, you are a child of France. It is up to you what France makes of you and your future.

Mama asked: You mean you're breaking off your engagement? And I answered with a question: Will I be sinning against him, Ma, if I break off the engagement?

Mama didn't say anything. We both know that it was her, wasn't it, Uncle, who wanted us to face our life and spend our futures together. It seemed to her that our futures would be simpler if we were together.

Mama seemed very sad for us. She was the one most affected by this. I'll put the baby to sleep first, she said, you talk to your Papa. She went and did not come out again. Papa said: It's all up to you both. I have no right to interfere, darling May, said Papa.

I was so worried that I had made Mama unhappy. So I went after her into the baby's room. She was lying down on the bed cuddling the baby to sleep. And I sat on the edge of the mattress facing her. Are you disappointed, Mama? I asked carefully.

Finally Mama spoke, slowly: May, perhaps it was I who was wrong. I entered the real world when I was sold by my parents to a man who was foreign to me in every aspect – his person, his language, his people, his ways and his customs. What I did for you two I thought was a much better thing than that. And so I thought I was doing right. It's only now, today, that I realise that it was not right at all, not the right thing to do for either of you. Please forgive this old woman who did not realise what she was doing, May.

Om, to hear Mama speak with such remorse made me almost cry, I could hardly breathe because of the lump in my throat. This very, very wise woman was asking forgiveness of me. And who was I? What was I? The words became stuck in my throat and: Who am I, Mama, that you should ask forgiveness of me? Mama sat up and caressed my hair as if I was a baby, and said: If I had given birth to you myself, I would still ask your forgiveness. Have you spoken with your Papa? I nodded. Whatever you decide is best, said Mama again, best for you, will surely also be best for your Papa and for your om back there in Bandung.

I never replied to her letter. And I never wrote to her again.

I know you will not be broken by this, wrote Mama, only old branches can be broken. The young ones bend with the storm. Only the stupid ones try to resist.

Ah, Mama, I have encountered no storms. None. Or is it not yet? Maybe the storms will come one day, but not now. I am in the midst of my triumph . . . even though I know that every triumph has its end. But not yet, Ma.

And in Klungkung the army began to enter the six kilometre area around the city that was defended by the Balinese heroes, all dressed in white and prepared to die. There was no one among the people who did not fight. The battle to overthrow the kingdom of Klungkung lasted over forty days and was followed enthusiastically by every newspaper reader in the Indies.

Klungkung fell, but Lombok rose in rebellion.

10

Raden Tomo's emissary came to Bandung to demand delivery of the promise I had made. He and his friends had established the kind of organisation suggested by the retired Java Doctor. And by myself as well. The name of the organisation was Boedi Oetomo. An approximate translation of Jamiatul Khair, meaning 'of noble character', one of the most progressive of the Arab self-improvement associations. He also brought a Constitution and a Statement of Aims and Objectives, all written in reasonable Dutch. He asked for space in *Medan* to publicise the new organisation.

'We'll be glad to. Just send us the materials. Eh, why have you given your organisation a Javanese name? Is it only for Javanese?'

'That's right. Only for Javanese, because we are Javanese. We know each other's language and customs. We have the same origins, the same ancestors, one civilisation and one culture.'

'Then why is the Constitution written in Dutch?'

'We can put it into Javanese later, that's no problem.'

'If this is an organisation for Javanese why hasn't it been written in Javanese first and then translated later into Dutch for others?'

'Ah, that's just a technical matter.'

'And why are you speaking in Dutch to me, then?' He didn't answer. 'You are a medical student, aren't you? What grade?'

'Third.'

'So a non-Javanese cannot become a member?

'No, sir.'

'What about a Javanese who cannot speak Javanese?'

'That's probably all right, Sir.'

'Why "probably"? Why isn't it written down in the Constitution? And what about non-Javanese who can speak Javanese? And what about those who are not Javanese but their families have lived here so long, they live and behave like Javanese? And what about a Javanese only one of whose parents was actually from Java? And how do you you actually prove someone is Javanese or not?'

He appeared confused. My questions were just another version of the questions Sandiman had once asked about the Sarekat.

'What does the Boedi Oetomo actually mean by "Javanese"?'
He didn't answer this either.
'In the eye of the BO or you yourself, am I a Javanese?'
'Of course you are Javanese. And we also hope you will become a member.'
'But I prefer to use Malay and Dutch to express myself. Or just Dutch. I hardly ever use Javanese. What about that?'
'You are definitely at the very least a Javanese. Not only will you be accepted as a member, but we would like to have you as an active member.'
'Forgive me. I was just asking, that's all. In any case, we will definitely publish your material.'

After he left, I discovered that Sandiman and Wardi had been listening to the conversation.
'And you, Sandiman, you've been putting your mind to work to find a way to help the Balinese and the people of Lombok,' I said.
'Yes, Tuan, while he and his friends are all busy getting ready to become Javanese, whatever that is. Meanwhile Javanese are sent to Aceh, to Bali, all over the Indies, to fight the other peoples of the Indies. Then the Ambonese, the Menadonese, the Timorese and others from the eastern islands are brought here to fight the Javanese. And in Betawi there are Javanese concerned only with putting their own little house in order, he grumbled.
Wardi didn't give his opinion.
'They are educated people,' I said.
Sandiman cut me off straight away: 'So we should expect more of them. What are they really after?'
'Mas' Wardi complained, 'I think Mas Sandiman is right. I have just received a letter from Den Haag. Some students from the Indies have formed a new organisation – the Association of University Students of the Indies.'
'Maybe that's right. Indies! Yes, "Indies". That's right. What's the point of isolating yourself as a Javanese? Except it's a pity that no one is pushing forward Malay as the language of the Indies.'
'They say it's Sosro Kartono, Kartini's elder brother, who founded it. Yes, they have chosen Dutch as their language.'
'I think he has the right idea about the peoples of the Indies. I think he may have what it takes to become a leader in the future. A leader of the peoples of the Indies.'
I read out the covering letter from the BO leadership, signed by Raden Tomo himself.
We are beginning with members of the same culture. We think that is better than a multi-peoples organisation. Since the Sarekat, I've noticed that you've given up the idea of 'one people' and have become more concerned with the idea of a 'multi-people' grouping. I've been worried that you won't be able to keep your promise.

Sandiman and I had a good laugh that he should have such a worry. The three of us joined the Boedi Oetomo.

Medan also became a forum for the BO. In a short time we had made Boedi Oetomo famous throughout Java and in the trading cities of the islands as well.

We had our different views about the Boedi Oetomo, but then again it also developed differently than any of us had imagined.

During the holidays several of the medical students at STOVIA, who were members of BO, travelled around propagandising for their organisation. And they were tremendously successful in Solo and Jogjakarta, and in the Mangkunegaran and Paku Alaman areas. In Mangkunegaran they sowed their seeds in ground already prepared by Sandiman. With the aid of the Mangkunegaran Legion, these seeds became like a spark blown by the wind to set aflame the palaces of Solo. And once a prince announced that he had joined BO, then his family, subordinates, servants, and friends also joined. In the other towns, in the villages, once people heard that Prince Mangku-negaran and Prince Paku Alam had joined, then they too, without hesitating for a moment, followed in the footsteps of those they exalted so much.

For me it all seemed like a miracle that didn't make sense. Village heads, their assistants, teachers, were all prepared to pay the membership fee of one *ringgit*, the equivalent of a fortnight's pay! Even the office assistants, who had no guarantee of ever being promoted to clerk, sold their valuable belongings in order to get the money to join.

The sarekat never had so many propagandists. It never woke up from its sleep. Meanwhile the BO propagandists travelled round Java calling out to the people: join the BO because only Boedi Oetomo can give your children a European education. Without a European education they will never be able to become a *priyayi*! In these modern times, those who do not receive a European education will never be more than tillers of the soil. So we call upon you to donate some of your money so that we can build Dutch language schools! The Boedi Oetomo will arrange everything!

Such stupid propaganda! It wasn't true and it could lead many people astray. I and Wardi, and others who had received a Western education, an education much wider than the BO could ever give, had refused to become *priyayis*, to become Government employees, wage addicts, slaves.

In other towns the propaganda was different – with the BO, we, the Javanese, will be able to work together to make a better future. We will raise the level of our civilisation and culture. We will raise the dignity and honour of the Javanese people. Not all of your children can get a place in the Malay primary schools, let alone the Dutch ELS. We will build our own schools using our own resources.

It was this propaganda that met with success. Boedi Oetomo branches sprang up like mushrooms all through Central Java and in some parts of East Java as well. And while the propagandists were at work in the towns and villages of Java, other students organised what they called the first Boedi Oetomo Congress. It was held in Betawi.

Mighty speeches thundered forth. Boedi Oetomo will soon found Dutch language schools teaching the Government curriculum!

When the congress finally adjourned, Tomo and his friends received a warning from the STOVIA director. Which would they choose – organisation or study?

But the warning had no effect. It had no strength. The BO's idea of the 'educated *priyayi*' had people in its grip. It seemed as if the competition for official jobs might be much more intense in the future. The *bupatis* and the princes became worried about the future of their children and so they all hurried to become members. Their target – to seize the leadership of the BO to make sure the current leaders would present no threat to their children. In Betawi, the STOVIA students soon moved their organisational activities outside the school complex. Reports started to come in confirming the bitter rivalry between the *bupatis* and the princes. And the Dutch administrators watched from the tops of the trees.

The formation of both the BO and the sarekat had been inspired by the retired doctor's speech at the STOVIA. The sarekat was born and died in the midst of the *priyayi*. The BO was born among the students of the STOVIA to give birth to the new *priyayi*, and, though only newly emerged from the womb, it had already achieved a high profile in a society caught up in the grip of the dream of the new educated *priyayi* of the future.

When the sarekat died, it's legacy was *Medan*, which grew to become a tower of strength like a banyan tree. That was my assessment. It was a major publication that in just a few years had overtaken all the colonial press. BO was already planning the founding of its first schools in Betawi. The cavalcade of students who lined up to enrol was bigger than that for the army. The sarekat was never able to start even one school!

More time was needed in order to understand this new development. Van Deventer, the Dutch champion of the Ethical Policy, came out with his decision – Boedi Oetomo represented the rising up of the Javanese youth. The Indies elite listened. BO was allowed to continue to live. And, amazingly, it was none other than the Eurasian writer Douwager who started writing in Holland in support of Beodi Oetomo. The sarekat had died without even leaving behind a grave.

The BO would suffer the same fate. Its first year was exciting. People were impressed by its vitality. But while it remained imbued with the *priyayi* spirit, it would never be able to shake off the rigidity of mentality that would forever stalk it.

My attempts to understand what was happening were not motivated by envy. The sarekat had died. That was that. Tomo was trying a different strategy, floating along with the current, in accordance with the laws of life. He had succeeded with this beginning. But it was doubtful if it could last for another five years. Except, yes, except if he was willing to accept as members people from other classes, who were not *priyayi*. The *priyayi* themselves were a caste with a way of thinking that always sought security in the authority of the Government. The entry of other nobility besides the princes of Mangkunegaran and Paku Alaman and of the *bupatis* made me certain that the ideals of the young founders of the BO would not have a long life.

It was easy to understand why the BO had rejected the idea of a multi-peoples organisation. Linguistic and cultural chauvinism had made them feel superior to the other peoples of the Indies. And the other colonised peoples also had their own chauvinism. Even the Betawi Malays, whose origins were very uncertain, considered themselves superior to the Javanese. So what would become of everything in the future?

And those who thought like me – who favoured bringing together the different peoples of the Indies – what organisation could we join? An organisation that was an Indies organisation! That was what we needed.

I came to a conclusion, that by separating itself off from the other colonised people of the Indies BO had limited its possiblities. The Indies was not Java. The Indies comprised many peoples. The proper organisation must have a place for them all. Even the island of Java was inhabited by different peoples. The Indies as a country of many peoples was a fact of colonial life. Van Heutsz was simply finalising the process of consolidation.

I had just come to this conclusion about the BO when a letter from their leaders arrived, asking if I would be willing to help strengthen their organisation by joining their Council of Leaders.

It was easy to guess what lay behind this offer. Tomo and his other student friends were not able to spend enough time on the organisation because of their studies. They also needed my publications.

I went to Betawi to meet them. I thanked them very much for their invitation. I explained my ideas on what kind of organisation the Indies needed. They laughed at my ideas, politely. In the end I had to retreat, my credibility damaged by my own failure with the sarekat. And they still offered me the position on their council.

My answer was also a polite laugh, and in the same manner I excused myself without leaving an answer. You, Sirs, I thought, will have to learn to understand reality. The Indies has many peoples, not just Javanese. No one could prise me way from this idea now. Perhaps it was not just personal ambition that was driving van Heutsz to implement his dream about unifying the territory of the Indies. Perhaps he was just the unconscious instrument of history.

And with these thoughts on my mind, I inspected the *Medan* kiosks in Kotta, Sawah Besar, Gambir and Meester Cornelis.

I went to see Thamrin Mohammed Thabrie at his house but he was not home. The Patih of Meester Cornelis was also out. I was told he had gone to see the Bupati about the Rawa Tembaga dispute.

I went back again to Thamrin's house that night. He seemed to be happy to see me. He didn't ask me into his office, but we sat outside under the *pendopo*. He wore a white Chinese shirt and a Buginese *sarong*. His *kopiah* was pushed back a bit from his forehead so I knew he had just been praying.

'Like Tuan, I too am grateful that the sarekat left us a legacy,' he said after avoiding any discussion about organisations. 'It's still going. And now you've added a daily.'

The *pendopo* was well lit with electricity, but the light wasn't as red as with an oil lamp. His face and smile were beaming as was usually the case with people who surrendered all their wordly troubles to God and gave thanks for every happiness, no matter how small.

Now was the time to discuss the failure of the sarekat. 'There was something wrong with our organisation, Tuan. What is your opinion?'

'It was to be expected, given the nature of our membership.'

'Yes, it looks as if we went after the wrong membership.'

'It was an expensive mistake we made.'

'Yes, very expensive. You no doubt have heard about BO?'

'From your paper.'

'It's also active among the *priyayi*, present and future. And it's only for one people – the Javanese.'

His opinion was the same as mine. The BO would suffer the same fate as the sarekat.

'But this is different, Tuan. The princes of Mangkunegaran and Paku Alaman and some *bupatis* are helping.'

Thamrin laughed. And I didn't disagree with him. I deliberately did not tell him of Sandiman's news that the *bupatis* and others were plotting to achieve their own aims. Whether this was true or not, time would tell. Sandiman and his brother had been able to influence the Mangkunegaran Legion. There was organising going on underground. And it had gone beyond just refusing to leave for Bali and Lombok. They were now dreaming that Mangkunegaran and Paku Alaman could become the centre of Javanese culture, of the Javanese nation, a beacon for the whole of the island of Java, with the Legion as its defender and its greatest pride.

'In our organisation the highest *priyayi* we had was a *patih*.'

'Let's not talk about it any more.'

'Agreed. Tuan. Except I still can't stop myself from thinking about the sarekat's death. What do you think, Tuan, is it possible to have an effective organisation without recruiting the *priyayi*?'

'You still haven't given up, have you?'

'Because Boedi Oetomo's mistakes are obvious from the outset. Firstly, they are basing themselves on the *priyayi*. Secondly, they are denying the reality that the Indies comprises many peoples. What is your opinion?'

'I don't think the real issue is whether you base yourself on one people or many. You have to identify what can unite people. You have to find those things on which unity can be based.'

'You're right! And you find those unifying elements within and among the various peoples, Tuan.'

He didn't go on but waited until refreshments were served. He invited me to partake. He was still reluctant to continue the discussion.

'And what is it that can unify us?'

'Religion. Islam.'

His answer astounded me. He didn't include anything to do with education. I asked a few more questions but he wasn't really interested. He didn't want to be disappointed a second time. So I took my leave, carrying with me his ideas – religion and Islam.

Back in Buitenzorg I became absorbed in thinking about these ideas. The Prophet had united his people. The vast majority of the people of the Indies were Moslem. And yet a feature of the modern era was that the non-Christian peoples of the world had been defeated by Europe. Was it only because they had not yet modernised? What was the use of unity without modernisation, without education? You might share some superficial feature, but what else would there be? The kind of strength you can gather that way – assuming you can actually build a strong organisation – would just turn into a heavy boulder, unable to be lifted, unable also to move forward, until one day someone comes along and destroys it with dynamite.

Being educated, having a progressive outlook, these also must be among the principles that guide the organisation. Islam and being educated! Only modern learning and understanding can show the way!

Boedi Oetomo succeeded in its first year. It succeeded in isolating itself from the other colonised peoples of the Indies. It ignored the reality that the Indies comprised many peoples. If an organisation was formed that was based on religion . . . but there are many religions among the colonised peoples of the Indies. There are those who have no religion, following the old beliefs of their ancestors. What was it that could really unify our peoples?

Once again, for the umpteenth time, I was groping in the dark.

A big event took place – in Surabaya. Who would ever have imagined that such a little incident could evolve into such a major affair, just because of a principle!

A Chinese merchant had gone to a big European firm to buy some goods. There was a misunderstanding. The Chinese merchant was humiliated and thrown out. People had forgotten that since the formation of the Tiong Hoa Hwee Koan in 1900 the Chinese had emerged as a powerful force. They had advanced dramatically in commerce, leaving behind the Natives, Arabs and other Orientals in all fields. This new unity and solidarity had not only strengthened them but also isolated them more from the other colonised peoples.

Within just a few weeks something wondrous happened. All the Chinese merchants in Surabaya – followed later by those in other towns – refused to patronise the European merchant houses. The big European trading house where the initial incident had taken place went bankrupt. Soon afterwards several others also had to close up. These bankruptcies were followed by chaos among the banks. The business world was thrown into turmoil and confusion. The impact was felt right down to the lanes and alleys of the villages.

'It's a boycott,' said Frischboten. He explained the teachings of Captain Boycott. It's not just the strong who have power, but also the weak, providing they organise. 'And only through organising can the weak show their true strength. The boycott is the concrete form of the power of the weak.'

His words burned through me. I was set aflame. Everything could be won merely by organising the weak. So simple! I could do that, I thought, tomorrow, the next day, even now.

'There is only one thing that is necessary – unity of mind,' added Frischboten. And he did not come forward with any other conditions. He didn't talk about religion, being educated, let alone having official positions. Just the united outlook, the unity of purpose of the weak. And the weak have much in common, precisely because of their weakness, that can unite them.

I wrote an editorial on the boycott and sent it straight off to the printers.

I had to study further this boycott movement of the Chinese. I needed to make connections.

I needed to gather enough material so that I could prepare a handbook about boycotts as a weapon.

And I began to think that the boycott, this new weapon of the weak, could not only be used against the big Dutch firms but also against the Government itself. The Samin movement, a movement of peasants, had already tried this. The Government was never able to get one cent out of them. This fanatical group of rebels had been able to defy completely the will of the Government. If all the people of the Indies united, if there was a total boycott of the Government, maybe the Dutch would then also have to close up shop, and move out!

Three days after the editorial was published, suitably modified, there was more news – the Mangkunegaran Legion had been transported out of Solo by train. Destination – Bali and Lombok. But they refused to board the ship in Surabaya that would take them to Bali. The Dutch failed in their attempt to pit Javanese against Balinese. And there was more boycott news – the Samins were rebelling again.

I received two letters about the mutiny on the same day and at the same time. One of them read:

We know, respected Tuan Editor, that in Bali there are more women than men. The men of Bali are spoiled. They are kept ready to go forth as heroes into the battlefield, perhaps never to return to their wives and children, or their lovers. Just like the fighting cocks of Java. And it is not uncommon either for the women to be ready and willing to die riddled by bullets. Because when the army's cannons start roaring, respected Tuan Editor, even the spirits flee. Satan himself could not compare with the army for its brutality. Its cannon send shivers into everyone's hearts, including Hanoman's, the king of the monkeys in the Ramayama story.

I myself, Tuan Editor, have three daughters. If we go to fight our brothers in Bali, let alone to fight the women of Bali, then that would be the same as waging war against our own daughters because do not these girls have the same dreams about life whether they live in Bali or Java? The girls of Bali will fight us with the same resolve and bravery as the men, their husbands or lovers or fathers. And if I did fight them and was able to return home to my family, what could I tell them? Even to explain the beginnings of the story would be too difficult. So we refused to be put aboard the ship, let alone to be landed in Bali and Lombok as fighting cocks for the Dutch.

We are ready to receive our punishment. We will not go. We remain in Surabaya, or go home to Solo.

We respectfully request that this letter be published without name.

The second letter said:

Your Excellency Tuan Editor, allow us to express to you the inner feelings of our hearts, the units of the Mangkunegaran Legion. We have deliberately and consciously refused to be sent to war. We refuse to be made to fight against our brothers in Bali. If we do not do this now, Your Excellency, then there will be no end to the Javanese being sent all over the Indies to fight their brothers. Already too many of our people have died in Aceh, in Sumatra among the Minangkabau, in Sumatra among the Batak, in the land of the Bugis, then in Bali and now they want to send us to Lombok . . . If we talk about clearing the jungle, building the rice terraces, the fields, digging the mines, building roads, starting plantations, yes, Javanese hands have done all these throughout the Indies. There is not a single steel bridge outside Java which was not built by Javanese hands. But making war . . .

These letters were not really meant for me, but for all the governed people of the Indies.

The Chinese merchants' boycott, the revolt of the Mangkunegaran Legion, the social revolt of the Samin peasants – none of these would have been possible without organisation. Even the peasants must have an organisation, an organisation of their own kind. Peasants! The so-called lowest class in society! They had organised, and rebelled! And we who have received an education, we are still learning how to organise and have not, or, at least, have not yet for certain, mastered how to do it. I myself had tried and failed. So what was it that unified them?

It's four years since the retired doctor made his call for us to organise. It's a pity he didn't talk about the question of the basis for unity, didn't discuss the question of there being many peoples in the Indies. Boedi Oetomo chose to organise only one of the peoples, the Javanese. It was only I who was left groping, feeling my way forward in the darkness.

A messenger from Boedi Oetomo came to our office in Bandung with an invitation for me to attend its second congress, to be held in Jogjakarta.

'You're having two congresses in one year?' I asked.

'We have no other choice, Sir. BO has been growing as if it had been whistled up out of the earth. And it hasn't been one year yet. This will be our second congress in seven months!' he answered, glowing with pride. 'The congress won't be complete if you are not there, Sir. And anyway, Sir, BO's success is also partly due to all the much valued assistance you have given it.'

'You have come here as an emissary of the BO but why are you speaking Dutch to me?'

'Just a matter of being practical, Sir.'

'So Javanese is not a practical language according to BO?'

'It seems you want to repeat your questions from last time.'

'And they still haven't been answered either.'

'We're not here to argue, are we?'

'Of course not. It's just that this organisation of yours is a Javanese organisation. And Java is called Java because of its culture, not just because of the island it's found on. Tell me, I would be very interested to know, which has the higher status – the editor of a newspaper or a doctor or a candidate doctor? If my status is higher you must speak *kromo* to me. Isn't that the rule in Javanese? I'm not looking for an argument with you. I'm just interested in knowing, because the Javanese are so sensitive on matters of social caste.'

'I promised last time that these matters that you have raised would be taken to a plenary of the Council of Leaders. Forgive us that we haven't done that yet,' he went on, still in Dutch.

'Good. And at the congress, will Javanese be the official language?'

'We will discuss all these matters, Sir.'

'Good. I accept your invitation.'

'Thank you very much, Sir. All your transport, accommodation and daily needs will be taken care of by the BO.'

'No need, Sir. Add the money to your funds for building schools in Jogjakarta. There's still no BO school there, is there?'

He went home to Betawi. A few days later I left for Jogjakarta. This was December 1908.

Seated in the train, which was by now fourteen years old, I could not help but be amazed at how the BO had been able to gather the money to hold two congresses within seven months. The nobles and merchants of Solo and Jogja, both known for their miserliness and their usurious activities, must have been convinced to make generous donations. Was it really true that they made donations?

And I was even more amazed at Sandiman. It was he who had blazed the trail into the hearts of the Legion soldiers, and the princes and the merchants too. It was a pity, though, that between him and me there stood the Javanese devil – of social hierarchy – separating each Javanese from all Javanese, and all Javanese from each, and everyone from each other.

He should be my friend, not my subordinate. Ayoh, you, devil of Java, get away!

At Kroja everyone alighted from the tired-out train to change to another. We continued on to Jogjakarta. At Kroja a new passenger boarded and sat next to me. He wore Javanese dress, a clean, white, buttoned-up top, his own *destar*, and a *kain* with big broad pleats. He wore black leather slippers and carried a black wooden cane with a carved ridge coiling round it.

As soon as the train started off he took out a copy of *Medan* from his bag. He browsed from page to page, unable to concentrate properly.

'Tuan is going to Jogja?' I asked in Malay.

He looked at my European clothes, giving a friendly nod. From the way he looked, and the fact that he was in first class, I could tell he was a VIP.

Suddenly his smile disappeared. His eyes blinked open wide, and he asked hesitatingly: 'Excuse me, perhaps I'm mistaken,' he spoke in Dutch. 'You studied at the medical school?'

'That's right, Sir,' I answered in Dutch also.

'Ah, I was right. And you've forgotten me?'

'Ai-ai, so it's you?' I cried. 'How could I ever forget you?' while I groped around trying to remember who he was. 'So you're the doctor in Kroja?' I asked, making a guess.

'For two years now.'

He'd been a doctor two years. How was it possible for a doctor to travel first class?

'On the way to the BO Congress?'

'You too?'

It turned out he had been two years ahead of me. He owned large areas of paddy-fields at Karanganyar and would inspect them after the congress was over. When I asked for his address, I found out that his name was Mas Sadikoen, a member of the Kroja BO leadership, and a doctor at the Government hospital. He spoke enthusiastically about his organisation and explained that, providing no unexpected obstacles arose, they would be starting a Dutch language primary school in the next year.

'Our main problem is finding a qualified teacher,' he said. 'If you can help us find one, we will pay him one and a half times the Government salary.'

'Advertise.'

'Yes, I think we will have to do that. Heh, I'm glad we've met like this. I can thank you for everything you've done.'

'What have I done to deserve such thanks?'

'Your paper. It's helped a lot of people in Kroja too. And I should also beg your forgiveness that I was unable to do anything to help your wife. I was assigned to the hospital to do my practical while your wife was ill. You didn't have much time to wait upon her.' But then he looked at me carefully and said: 'You were a medical student. How could you let your wife develop such extreme complications? You were studying medicine. You should have recognised all the symptoms.'

'Both of us were too busy.'

'Who isn't busy?'

'Let's not talk about the past?' I suggested.

A little piece of my sad past had returned to visit me. Seated beside me now was someone who – for I don't know how many hours – had looked after Mei. And his words sounded like accusations. He had sat me in the accused's chair as a husband who had not been good to his wife. And worse still, as an educated man who had not been correct, not paying enough attention to the person who was closest to him.

'Yes. It's better not to talk about unpleasant things of the past. But there was something your wife said to me that I have never been able to forget: "Why are you humouring me, Tuan? I am not going to get well again. I have seen what I have wanted to see of the world. I have done what I have wanted to do." She spoke in quite good Malay. She had no regrets about her situation, she was ready to face her death. She spoke as if to herself, as if she was coming to terms with the course of her life.'

The longer he spoke the more I was drawn back to think about the past. And I didn't like it. My relationship with Mei had ended when God had intervened in our lives. And death was not my responsibility.

'Did you know that your wife was colour blind?'

Colour blind? Good God, and I had never known that. Colour blind! So she had never seen the beauty of the world's colours! How little this life had given her. Colour blind! The world had not given her health, nor a long life, and neither had she ever seen its colours. Yet she had given everything she had to the world. I bowed my head in remembrance of her soul, the soul of a wife I had never known well enough.

My travelling companion kept on talking. 'Do you know what the people say to the rich and powerful in Kroja when they need to frighten them? We will tell His Excellency Honoured Lord Editor of *Medan*. And so they are freed from the oppression they were suffering.'

'Yes, let's be grateful the Indies now has a Native paper,' I answered. 'At the very least we can say that things will not be worse because of it.'

'I was amazed, though, to read your article on the boycott. You gave people information that turned upside down everything that educated people, especially the *priyayi*, believed. Do you think it's proper that this kind of information be given to the public? You're teaching people to use it, even though you don't make clear against whom.'

'Boedi Oetomo esteems democracy, doesn't it?'

'We have never discussed it.'

'But you agree with it, don't you?' I pressed him. 'Modern organisations are born out of democratic choice and consent, aren't they?'

'Of course, and we know that democracy does not need boycotts.'

'Democracy means that everyone may know everything we know. Are you worried that other people may know what you know?'

'That's not the issue. You are giving a weapon to people who don't need it.'

'If they don't need it then they will store it away. If they need it they will use it.'

'For what? To fight the Government?' he chipped in. 'Anyway, aren't you the golden boy of the Governor-General van Heutsz?' he turned to look out the window.

Once again I heard the clitter-clatter of the train and felt its rattling. And my body was conscious once more of swaying from side to side on the seat. As soon as he pulled his head back inside, I asked: 'Do you still remember Tanca?' He nodded without looking at me. 'The science of medicine can also fall into the wrong hands, into the hands of people not worthy of it. He used it not to save life but to kill.'

He was startled out of his *priyayi* world. His eyes were open wide and he was gazing down at me as if I was his subordinate. He felt that a *priyayi* was so much superior to a free worker and such a comment implying that a *priyayi* could be unworthy seemed to offend him.

'Do you think it is appropriate to say such a thing to a Government Doctor?'

'Of course it is, Koen. Wasn't Tanca after all first mentioned to us in the midst of medical students and witnessed by our teachers, themselves doctors? Do you consider our teachers to be of lesser status than a Government Java Doctor who has not yet graduated? I'm just talking in general now. You're angry?'

'You forget that I am an employee of the Government. You, being such a special friend of the Governor-General, should know better how to speak to an official of the Government.'

'Very well. So we should consider this congress as the Congress of the Government's *priyayi*?'

'Be careful. The princes and the representatives of the Government will also be there.' He was sounding more and more like a *priyayi*. 'It's lucky you're not one of our leaders. This democracy of yours could ruin all our efforts to educate the country's children. In just another twenty years – may God give us the time to achieve our victory – BO will change this people and awaken them.'

This big-mouth was putting up his embattlements now – the *priyayi*'s arrogance. And these were the corps of people I had tried to unite, and were now united as Javanese under the banner of the BO. I closed my eyes and pretended to be about to drift off into the world of dreams. But the thought that it was not right that I leave this argument unresolved made me open my eyes again. I added: 'Government *priyayi* and the princes are no better than anyone else who is not a *priyayi* or a prince.'

'Yes, people have to be educated to know who are their betters. You're from a *bupati*'s family, aren't you? You were taught to know the difference between a street urchin and someone who has been to school? Those who have a schooling have been taught to honour the *priyayi*, the officials, the *raja* and their families!' 'His face was turning red with anger.

'And what honour do they who are neither *priyayi* or prince have? Do they have no dignity and honour at all? Are they just garbage?'

'If everyone had honour and dignity, then there would be no honour at all.'

'If one is to be honoured and the other not, then it means one has stolen the other's honour.'

'There is no question of stealing anything,' he answered nervously. 'We were born into a world where there are already *raja* and their families, where there is already a Government with its *priyayi*. There are those who are honoured, and those who have no honour, and there are those who are humiliated, because that is the world. There are men and there are women. There are the high and the low. There is the earth and the sky. There are the poor and the rich. You were taught in school too that for everything there is a plus and minus . . . '

' . . . And that humankind moves from minus to plus and that is called

205

struggle? Or have you forgotten, Koen? Or has BO forgotten? It is not the intention, is it, of the BO to maintain things as they are? So that the poor remain poor, the ignorant remain stupid, and the sick just lie waiting for death to arrive?' And because I had now begun to study the Islamic religion in a more systematic manner, these additional words also came out: 'And our prayers, what are they if not also movement from minus to plus? Do you know what is the meaning of prayer? A request to God, a movement from the most minus to the most plus.'

And I closed my eyes, pretending to yawn. From underneath my eyelids I could see him bite his lips, take out his copy of *Medan* and then start reading.

I was still restless. Was this the face of the educated Native? So what was the point of an organisation if not to move from minus to plus? If Sadikoen was representative of the BO then it would just become a salon club without a salon.

I heard Sadikoen ahem. Once. Twice. It seemed he now had a reply and was trying to wake me up. But I chose just to listen to the clatter of the train and feel it trembling. He didn't know that without Sandiman the Boedi Oetomo would quickly meet the same fate as the sarekat. How could it be otherwise when the raw material was just the same old stuff? If the only difference was that its leaders were from among the young *priyayi*?

The Boedi Oetomo was also propelled by the so-called 'demonstration effect', everyone was infused with the spirit to copy whatever was done by their superiors, everything that the rich and powerful did was turned into a fashion, even their way of life. As soon as someone powerful joined the BO all his followers and underlings followed suit. And wasn't that also the way the religions were spread in Java, and wasn't it also in that spirit that the *raja* had handed over themselves and their peoples and their countries to the Dutch?

I gave thanks that my meeting with Sadikoen had been productive, had led me to thoughts that now made easier my struggle to understand the mistakes of the past and find a way forward for the future. There were no mistakes that could not be corrected.

As usual the carriage was not full. This was especially the case for the Betawi–Surabaya express. The fare was too expensive for anyone without position or a major business, especially for first class. There were even very few Europeans.

From underneath my eyelids I saw Sadikoen stand up and walk away. Perhaps he was going to the toilet. Not long afterwards he returned with a man wearing overalls, who just stood there beside Sadikoen, with a bit of a bow in the way he stood. He clasped his hands before him. He didn't dare sit down, only because the *priyayi* caste system classified him as being of lower status.

Sadikoen ahemmed twice to wake me up. I opened my eyes, pretending to rub away the sleep and: 'I seem to have fallen asleep.'

'For quite a while,' which was obviously not true, said Sadikoen. 'Ah, this is one of the brakemen. He wanted to talk to you. He is also a member of the Kroja Branch of the BO.'

'Your servant's name is Ja'in, *Bendoro*,' he said in High Javanese.

I glanced at Sadikoen. He didn't feel uncomfortable at hearing *kromo* being spoken to me.

'Why don't we just use Malay?' I asked

'Very well, Bendoro.'

'Sit here, beside me,' I invited him.

'Forgive me, Bendoro. I'm happier standing like this. I'm used to working standing up. And please don't be angry with me for seeking an audience with you, Bendoro. I am also a subscriber to *Medan*. Happily Bendoro Doctor told me that Bendoro was also on the train. When else, if not now, would I get such an opportunity?'

'What is it that you want?' I also stood.

'Please sit down, Bendoro,' he begged.

But I remained standing. Sadikoen was watching each of us closely.

'Many of my friends, either individually or together in groups, subscribe to *Medan*. We like it very much. Truly, Bendoro. *Medan* is not just something that entertains us, it has also become our leader. Bendoro has been able to help my fellow railway workers three times now. The publication on the law as well as the extremely interesting Sunday supplement have all helped us a lot.'

Such praise had become by now extremely boring. Yet I had to listen. It usually ended with either some biting criticism or with some pathetic request, depending on the opening. The more the praise, the more biting the ending. And I had to listen and pay attention just like Multatuli's Droogstoppel, because, who knows if one day I will need his voice? His services? His agreement?

'Bendoro, *Medan* has published a newspaper and a magazine explaining the law. I would very much like to request *Medan* to publish a special magazine for us, the railway workers.'

'A special magazine?'

'Yes, Bendoro, like that published by the Railway Workers Union.'

'But you can follow what's in the union magazine.'

'It's in Dutch, Bendoro. We can't read Dutch. And it is only for union members and we Natives aren't allowed to join.'

It was only then that I learned that the union was organised along racial lines, joining up only Dutch and Eurasians.

'Give me time to think about it, Ja'in,' I answered.

'*Medan* won't lose money, Bendoro. All the railway workers have a decent wage. They also want to advance. And if Bendoro will not hold out his hand, then who else will?'

No one else will help except *Medan*. Once more someone is hoping that a new project will be begun. And once it is begun, in the spirit of dedication to one's people, then one after another from that people come more demands even more substantial and with even more worth. Each time you take up one of their demands, another comes forth. If you had decided to simplify your life and be a doctor, perhaps in a hospital or on a ship, or in an army barracks, your work would never have been as exciting as this. You have chosen. Every word that comes from you, whether written or spoken, challenges your abilities, and pushes you to limits where the law too always makes its own demands.

Ja'in continued his stories about the lives of the railway workers, their joys and sorrows, the fact they had little hope for advancement in their work because all the senior positions were reserved for Europeans. Their only distraction was their endeavour to advance themselves generally, to learn and understand more about the world and its ways. They would never have an opportunity to advance in their work beyond what had been determined officially.

The brakeman bowed hurriedly and excused himself, making his way quickly out of the carriage. Not long after the conductor entered checking tickets.

Mas Sadikoen handed over his ticket without looking at the conductor, who accepted it while bowing in deference. '*Ndoro* Doctor is on his way to Jogja?' asked the conductor.

'Yes. Mmmmm. Could you check on Madam Ndoro?'

'Very well, Ndoro. Have a good trip, Ndoro Doctor.'

The conductor left throught the same door as Ja'in.

Mas Sadikoen was still looking at me.

'You're angry at the way I answered his questions?' I asked, without bothering to defer to his *priyayi*-ness.

'Could be. I have to say, at the very least, you have strange ideas that I need to understand better.'

'You're looking at me if I were some monkey lost in the night market.'

'Could be. I still don't understand you. Everywhere you go you're famous and people look up to you. People come to you to ask your help, to appeal to your heart.' All of a sudden he changed the subject: 'Eh, in Kroja there's this Indo. He's been wanting to meet you for some time now. Actually he has a house in Kroja but is rarely there. At the moment he's on leave from his job in Jeddah. He works in the Dutch Consulate there. A real Indo, everything about him is Indisch. Would you like to meet him?'

'He also wants something from me?'

'Maybe he's like everyone else.'

'Why doesn't he just go to the BO?'

'He's an Indo. He asked to join the Kroja branch but was rejected. He went to the Betawi Committee, but they rejected his application too. He's also going to Jogja, not to attend the congress but to protest.'

'So what does he want with me?'

'He has some suggestions and would like to discuss things with you. He's a very interesting chap. I can assure you that you won't find him boring. He's called Hans. I don't know Hans who. I met him playing cards.'

And he studied me, as if I was one of his patients. The train raced on, rattling and shaking. Paddy-fields, crops and villages all chased after each other. But it was the telegraph poles that sped by the fastest.

'This Indo is truly an extraordinary person. He prefers to be called *Pak Haji* "Father Haji". Wherever he goes – at least wherever I have seen him – he wears the Moslem *fez*. He calls himself Haji Moeloek.'

'He may incur the anger of the Moslems,' I said.

'He has gone on the pilgrimage himself twice already. I said he was an employee at the Dutch consulate in Jeddah. You mustn't forget that his Dutch is as good as – in fact, better than – any graduate from a religious school on Java. He will be returning to his job in Jeddah next month.'

'He must be a person with many experiences,' I said.

'His stories are always fascinating.'

'Good. Then I would like to meet him.'

The brakeman didn't appear again. It wasn't until the train had stopped at Jogjakarta that I saw him again. He was waiting outside the ticket gate.

'I wish you all the best at the congress, Bendoro,' he said, then went off to his work.

The second congress of the Boedi Oetomo was the first big meeting I had ever attended. The main auditorium of the teachers' college was packed full. There was the president of the Betawi BO, Raden Tomo, who spoke in Dutch, never having had a Javanese education, unable to express himself in Javanese. God have mercy on us! The *bupatis* and the princes paraded their smiles. Six soldiers of the Mangkunegaran Legion silently stared at all around them. The old retired Java Doctor, who was now the president of the congress, had unilaterally renamed it Boedyatama. The *pendopo* at the front of the building had been extended on all sides by several metres of temporary roofing. It was truly an event to be remembered for the rest of your life.

Of course, the front rows were taken up by the high nobles and the senior officials of the Netherlands Indies Government, as well as the Sultanate and Residency of Jogjakarta, including the Resident himself. They were all seated in rows according to their rank. There was the retired Bupati of Karanganyar, Tirtaningrat, who was the Life President of the Tirtayasa organisation and the first Javanese to establish a traditional organisation and school on his own initiative. There was also the Bupatis of Blora, Temanggung, Magelang and Jogjakarta city as well as several other senior district officials, and many teachers and high school students, prospective new-style *priyayi*. Almost everyone, except a few people from outside Java, wore traditional *priyayi* clothes. The nobles of Jogjakarta wore locally-woven clothes. The *priyayi* from outside Jogjakarta wore white blouses. Not everyone wore *keris*, as they would at a reception. There were many who ventured to wear leather slippers, either black or brown, except those who wore full European dress. And everyone carried a briefcase, as if they were on duty in a Government office.

The columns around the auditorium were decorated with the Tricolour and leaves of the *beringin* tree. There were also decorations all around the building made from green woven banana leaves.

There were three rows of chairs along the sides for the journalists who had come from all over Java – Native, Dutch, Malay and Chinese. I also sat with the journalists. Among them was my old Surabaya friend Kommer, and I noticed that Douwager, that protégé of Multatuli so often mentioned in Mir's letters, was also there.

Together and amidst all these people, assembled with one purpose and one spirit, I felt a part of them all. I felt so proud. The humming hubbub from the auditorium felt like the rumbling of my own heart. And the colours that abounded everywhere reflected my own joy at the occasion. The trembling in the atmosphere was the trembling in the crucible of my own soul. Everything loomed so large. Even the strangeness. It was as if slithering along the floor, crawling and bowing down were now alien to the ways of the Javanese. Amazing!

The President of the congress, the retired Java Doctor, in the manner of the priest who, in the *wayang*, had just descended from meditations on the mountain, explained the meaning of the name Boedyatama. Then he gave this advice – master the Dutch language, because it is a weapon. And then followed more consciousness-raising. Before there were only two classes – the *priyayi* and the peasant. Now there is a third group – the middle class.

Go to school! To school! one of the students of the Native civil service schools exhorted. He spoke school Malay, and most of the people there didn't understand. Foreigners had come to our country and they had all become wealthy. Not because of their own cleverness, but because of the ignorance of our own people. To school! To school!

Study and copy how the Europeans do things, admonished a Java Doctor from the Surakarta palace. Then the debate started. The issue: Most of the Javanese felt they did not need to learn anything new, that they did not need the Europeans. Rather it was the Europeans who needed the Javanese. After all wasn't it true that it was the Europeans who had come to Java?

Raden Tomo spoke: The Government has now set up many primary and vocational schools. We are grateful, but they are still not enough. Indeed it would be too great a burden for the Government if it were to build all the schools we need. We must ourselves take on the responsibility of advancing our children even while waiting upon the compassion of the Government as it increases the numbers of schools and courses.

And the opening speeches then concluded. The Java Doctor from Kroja did not speak. He sat in the ninth row.

Back at the hotel I made only a few notes. They all assumed that it was the natural role of the *priyayi* to lead. This was the thinking that led me to found the Sarekat Priyayi and the same thinking that took it to total disaster.

And who would have guessed that on that very evening I would receive a visit from a *bupati*! The Bupati of Temanggung! And he did not require me to bow and scrape before him. He went straight to the matter that concerned him. He had also founded an organisation – a local organisation, called Sasangka Purnama. It was a traditional-style organisation. It had no constitution or organisational rules. He was dissatisfied that his organisation was unable to grow outside Temanggung.

This was a remarkable *bupati*. He had come to listen to the opinion of another person, who wasn't even a *priyayi*. What was even more amazing was that he understood that there were other subjugated people in the Indies besides the Javanese, such as the Arabs and Chinese. And he could understand and indeed agree with the need for a multi-racial organisation.

The congress moved quickly to adopt a Constitution and organisational rules. There were thirteen candidates for the position of Central President: five *bupatis*, two doctors, four teachers, a major in the Pakualam palace regiment and an architect. I knew only Dr Tjipto Mangoenkoesomo and the Bupati of Serang, Djajadiningrat.

While sitting in the auditorium during the counting of the votes, everyone was busy introducing themselves to each other. A young man come up to me and invited me to go and eat at one of the Jogjakarta street stalls with him. He looked like an office assistant. He was still very young, and he wore his *destar* the way the clerks do. He was barefooted, his traditional blouse was held together by discreetly placed pins and his widely pleated *sarong* was held in place with clips. He said it was important. While gulping down coffee and savouring the aroma of frying *tape* and newly harvested *duren*, he took out a sheet of paper from his coat pocket, as yet unadorned by a pocket watch. And he never said a word. Just like any *priyayi* meeting with his superior, he just bowed his head with his eyes fixed below. He paid for our drinks, excused himself, and then disappeared who-knows-where.

My hands shook as I read the paper he had given me – a secret document from the Governor-General's office. Van Heutsz was instructing that efforts be made to ensure that the Bupati of Karanganyar was chosen as the President of BO, as he would ensure that BO would remain in reliable hands.

And so I realised just how far the iron hand of the Government could extend.

I set the paper alight with the glowing tip of my cigar. It was impossible that the young clerk could have composed the document himself, written as it was in Dutch and in the style of an official instruction. He was not one of those falsifiers of documents who sought to create a sensation in the press, which was one of the first things that a new reporter learnt about. No, he was perhaps a clerk in the office of a Resident, who knew just sufficient Dutch to cope with his tasks and that was all. And so it was clear as day what was going to happen – the Bupati of Karanganyar, Tirtokeosoemo, would push aside all other candidates, even Tomo, as well as the retired Java Doctor.

And indeed that was how it happened. A language teacher from a Java Teachers' College, Mas Ngabehi Dwidjosewojo, was elected Secretary. This was another victory for van Heutsz. Tjipto Mangoenkoesomo, a doctor in Demak, was elected Treasurer. The Javanese character of the congress was preserved amid a flurry of self-congratulation on the refinement of Javanese customs and the greatness of *wayang*. Everyone came to the same heart-felt conclusion – the Javanese were a great and unique race, superior to all others.

Many of the speeches contained the suggestions and questions of the dwindling number of visitors. Could Sunda and Madura be considered Javanese? Yes. In that case, Javanese could not be the organisation's offical language. Malay was then adopted as the language for those who did not know Javanese. What about Javanese who lived outside Java and Madura? Could they also become members? No one answered. What about those Javanese who had been given official status as a Gazetted Dutchman? No one answered. What about somebody who had only one parent who was Javanese – an Indo, for example? No answer. What about the Chinese in the Sultanates and surrounding areas who had completely adopted Javanese ways? No answer again. And Europeans who had mastered Javanese language and culture, like Mr Wilkens, who was also attending the conference? There was no response except for everyone to turn and look at Mr Wilkens. It was as though Sandiman was speaking through many mouths. Perhaps they were the mouths of Mangkunegaran soldiers in civilian clothes.

Everyone agreed that the BO should have its own press. A teacher, in the style of the traditional Javanese comic, eloquently defended the importance of the work of teachers. Without teachers everything would revert to the ways of the jungle. But all they had as a guide was what they were taught in the basic schools for teachers. These might be adequate for training teachers, but even then they only taught the same old things over and over again. Meanwhile the world marched onwards. Every hour it advanced. Here it is day. In America it was night. Humankind never slept, it never stopped moving forward. Someone nominated His Honour Mr Douwager as a candidate for editor of the proposed BO newspaper.

'I have the honour of nominating His Honour the Editor of *Medan*, who is here with us today . . . '

212

I felt truly honoured by the applause that followed. It was an honour too for Native journalism. This was a reward for all the effort and struggle, and devotion all this time. So my eyes were not just moist – actual tears welled up and a few ran down over my cheeks. These were beautiful moments for me. Then Douwager spoke up in Dutch: Natives are not yet ready to run a daily paper, a magazine or any publications.

The whole audience went silent. One by one everyone walked out, myself included. The congress did not give me a victory in this matter. Kommer visited me at my inn to express his condolences.

'It was you, Kommer, who taught me to use Malay.'

'But you are a great man now.'

'What are you doing these days?'

'The same as before,' and there was disappointment in his voice. Perhaps he had been experiencing misfortune lately. Perhaps in his work, perhaps in other things.

I closed my notes and brought the evening to an end with the following remarks. Boedi Oetomo was born in Betawi. In less than one year the young founders had been pushed aside. BO had been carried away to Jogjakarta where it had fallen into the hands of old men . . . all on such a grand scale.

11

Bogowonto Inn was full. My room was cramped, with three other congress participants crowded in there as well. There was no escape from the aggravating, musty smell. There was nowhere better available. All the hotels were full. There weren't even any easy chairs at the inn. They made no effort to rent or borrow extra chairs. Even though its only purpose was to provide a place for me to rest my body, the inn was a very unpleasant place. There were bedbugs everywhere and the bed sheets looked as if they hadn't been washed for ages. The mattress was filthy. And the pillow . . . God knows how many different types of saliva had dripped over it!

When Haji Moeloek and Mas Sadikoen arrived, I had to take them to the food stall next door. And Sadikoen was right – from the very first moment this Haji Moeloek came across as an interesting character. He wore a *haji*'s hat and European clothes, complete with shiny black shoes, which were clearly not locally made. His watch-chain seemed very large and reminded me of a ship's anchor-chain. His whole appearance was very Indo. He wasn't so tall though, just two or three centimetres taller than me, and a bit broader.

'Mas Sadikoen has told me about you,' I began.

He laughed happily, the laughter of someone who wasn't sure about his own strengths. 'I am really happy to be able to meet you, Tuan,' he said. 'I have been wanting to discuss something with you for a long time now, if you would agree to hear me out.'

'It must be something quite important,' I said. 'Otherwise Mas Sadikoen wouldn't have gone out of his way to bring us together.'

'It's like this, Tuan . . .' He broke off. 'But first I should tell you a little about myself. I was born in Parakan, and was brought up and educated there as well. I went to primary school in Salatiga, but I always loved Parakan better. I went to the HBS school in Semarang, and another five years in HBS in Holland. While I was in Holland I attended an agricultural school where I studied about plantations, and then I came back to Java. After ten years of going from plantation to plantation, I became pretty bored with it all. So I became a sailor, and sailed with the ships of the Semprong Tiga line. We used to take the people going on the pilgrimage, sometimes from the Indies, sometimes from South Africa . . . Yes, even from South Africa.

They are the descendants of Moslems who were exiled from the Indies a long time ago. There were some Indians as well.'

'You are a Moslem yourself?'

'Just a muallaf,' so I knew he was a recent convert. He laughed and glanced at Sadikoen. 'Isn't that so, Doctor?'

'What does "muallaf" mean?' Sadikoen asked back.

Haji Moeloek ignored his question and went on: 'It's like this, my friend the Chief Editor, I have been thinking about this for a long time, weighing up the issues, assessing them again and again. Perhaps I am in error, perhaps my evidence is flawed, full of mistakes . . . and if I am in error I ask you to forgive me, and if there are mistakes I ask you to correct them, Tuan.'

'What do you mean, mistaken and in error?' I asked, not understanding what he was talking about.

'In my opinion, Tuan, being in error means that from the very time you had the idea you were wrong. A mistake, on the other hand, is when you had the right idea but got things wrong when you put your ideas into practice. Am I right?', his enthusiasm for his subject had still not waned.

'Well, if that's what you mean, you could very well be right.'

'So, Tuan. The influence of Europe on the Indies Natives is not direct, is it? Europe and the Indies are two worlds which are completely different both in form and content. And because Europe is superior, Indies Natives have had to accommodate to this new victor. Isn't this so, Tuan?'

'You are not in error.'

'Are we all right speaking like this, Tuan, or do you prefer Dutch?'

'Malay is fine.'

'Very well. You don't mind either, do you, Doctor?'

'Why would I mind?' Sadikoen asked back.

'What would you like, Ndoro?' asked the woman at the stall.

'Curried goat, if that's all right with you gentlemen,' I suggested.

'I'm sorry, I've had enough goat lately,' Haji Moeloek answered. 'I've got high blood pressure, and goat is too fatty.'

'Do you have grilled chicken?' I asked the woman. 'Good, grilled with *kecap*? Three!' and to Haji Moeloek, 'Please continue.'

'So, Tuan, the Indies Natives take what they need from Europe via the Indos, who are quite a small group. I am not mistaken, am I? Where there are no Indos, European influence is usually blocked. In my opinion, which of course is not necessarily correct, it is the Indos who have introduced European civilisation into the lives of the Natives. I am not in error, am I?'

'If that is what you think, and also what you say, then, of course, you are not wrong,' I said.

He laughed happily.

'So, Sirs, I cannot really continue until you have said whether you agree or not with what I have said so far.'

'How can we agree or disagree?' accused Sadikoen, 'I have never thought about this issue before. It's your idea. You keep going.'

'You yourself are an Indo, so of course you should understand the situation of your people best.'

'Look. Take music, for example. The Indos learnt to play European musical instruments, to play Indo songs. And then Natives learnt from the Indos and went on to spread the skill among their people. Am I wrong?'

'You are correct,' I said, encouraging him.

'And it's the same in other areas. Clothes, for example. Crafts. And indeed as far as clothes go – don't the Natives have an extremely poor culture? All the terms that are used in tailoring, they all come from Dutch. And didn't the Native tailors learn them all from the Indos? Even the word "pisak".'

'What does "pisak" mean?'

'That's the join between the left and right leg of a pair of trousers.'

Sadikoen burst out in laughter. I didn't know what was so funny.

' "Pies-zak" ' Haji Moeloek repeated in Dutch for my benefit. He went on. 'And it was the Indos who first put windows in their houses, to be followed then by the Natives. You gentlemen are not offended, are you?'

To be honest, what he had been saying wasn't very pleasant to listen to. It was as if the Natives had no achievements to their credit at all. But what could I say, for I had no reply to his argument?

'Even the idea of parting one's hair came from the Indos. And we ourselves just copied from the Pure-Bloods.'

That was going too far! Now even the parting of our hair was not a genuine Native custom!

'And it's the same with having a forelock.'

He was getting worse and worse.

'But it's also in relation to more important matters that the Indos have acted as disinterested go-betweens between the Europeans and the Natives. Perhaps one day, when the Indies catches up to Europe, people will erect a monument in memory of the Indos' role as unpaid passers-on of civilisation. Perhaps they may even be remembered as the civilisers of the Natives themselves,' he laughed happily. 'What do you think?'

'To be honest, I don't think I can voice an opinion one way or the other as yet,' I said, a bit cranky. 'Are you finished?'

'Of course not, Tuan. Look, there are also many Natives now learning to paint. And once again their unpaid teachers are all, without exception, Indos. See, the Natives only have five colours, mixing them a little here and there. Now the Natives have learnt twenty colours, both primary colours as well as combinations. It is the Indos who have also pioneered setting up social organisations. Ah! Yes, but the time will come where my people's role as go-betweens will end, when the Natives can deal directly with the Euro-peans – namely when European education has become widespread in the

Indies. Heh-heh, Tuan, do you know that the human being's lips are now used for something that Natives never used them for?'

Now what was it with these idle lips?

'You see, before the Indos began to have their impact, the Natives never did, and indeed couldn't, whistle.'

Sadikoen laughed indignantly. I let out a bit of a laugh, piqued. Haji Moeloek on the other hand really enjoyed his laugh, feeling that for the first time he had provoked a reaction from us.

'See, Tuan,' he went on more provocatively, 'I am talking about this period we are in now, while the Indos are still needed as civilisers, who don't force people to learn new ways and aren't paid for it either. This is a time when their pupils come to them of their own free will, voluntarily. Have you had enough of my talk yet?'

'Oh, what will you all drink? I'm sorry, I forgot to order drinks. Miss! Miss! Coffee? Tea? Lemon?'

'For me, tea please, my friend Editor Minke, strong tea,' said Haji Moeloek.

'I think I'll have the same, please,' Sadikoen added.

'Three strong teas, please! Will the chicken be long?'

'Maybe another hour, Ndoro.'

'Do you have cigars?'

'Of course, Ndoro,' the woman presented three cigar boxes each with a different brand of cigar.

Sadikoen didn't smoke cigars. He wanted cigarettes.

'What about if we continue, Haji Moeloek?'

'Yes, Tuan. It's true that the Natives have enriched their vocabulary with words gained from mixing with Indos, and this includes the names of the different tools that are used today. But the more important thing, Tuan, is that written Malay, that is Malay written in Latin script, was also pioneered by the Indos. The publishing of Malay newspapers and magazines was pioneered by the Indos. There was one Malay publication that was started by someone else, but that was in Singapore and he was an Arab. And his Malay was written in Arabic script. The Malays and the Natives of the Indies have in fact not pioneered anything. You, Tuan, have that honour, of being the first Native to start up such a publication, by and for the Natives, and in Malay! It is only proper that you be congratulated.' He held out his hand and I shook it happily.

'That is why you are such an interesting person. You, a Javanese, who started publishing in Malay! And Malay is the language of the Indos. We use it among ourselves and when we converse with the other peoples. May I ask why you didn't publish your newspaper and magazine just in Javanese? You didn't choose to publish in Batavia and Bandung by chance, did you?'

And I explained to him about the multi-racial and multi-national character of the Indies. He listened to me intently, nodding, pondering, like a truly fine play actor.

'You're not going to say that my ideas have also come from the Indos, are you?' I asked.

'Yes, I have misjudged you. You didn't choose Malay by accident, and you aren't copying my people. Your ideas go much deeper than that. With ideas like that, you must have your own view of BO then?'

So I explained to him my views of this organisation.

'I have tried to raise these concerns with the Council of Leaders of the congress. Their answer – we will give them our consideration' said Haji Moeloek. 'After hearing your views, Tuan, I am even more glad that I use Malay. I very much agree with and support your ideas on this.'

Once more he offered his hand.

'And what about what you were talking about earlier, Tuan, what were you getting at?' I asked.

'So, my friend, Mr Minke, you see the first Malay language paper was published in Surabaya. That was the beginning of the history of Malay language publishing in the Indies. The paper was called *Bientang Timoer* "east star", yes? It was also started by Indos. Just think, that was thirty years ago, when the Natives couldn't even read the Latin script yet! And the Indos pioneered such papers purely out of their love for Malay, Tuan, yes, that was it! That's what it's like with me, Mr Minke. There is no language that I enjoy more, that gives me more pleasure, than Malay. It is such a beautifully free language, you can use it anywhere, under any circumstances, without feeling any loss of dignity.

'You see, Tuan, in the matter of writing short stories, it was also the Indos who pioneeered writing in Malay, long before the Malays themselves began trying. The Indos had already begun! Yes, the Indos are indeed the pioneers of the Indies. This is not just boasting, is it, Tuan Minke? They wrote out of love for the language, never tiring, without pay, seeking profit from no one. There are still no Natives writing stories in Malay. Just recently, and also out of love for the language, the Chinese have begun writing in Malay. And still the Natives have not tried. I hear that you yourself still write your prose in Dutch. If that is the case then you too must understand what is involved in writing stories. You squeeze everything you can out of what is in your heart, holding nothing back. Isn't that the case?'

'More-or-less.'

'I'm sorry, Dr Sadikoen, I know nothing about medicine.'

'This is all very interesting, Tuan Haji.'

'Thank you. Yes, well, you shouldn't be surprised if I lecture you about the accomplishments of my people. Just look, the Pure-Bloods ignore our writing, it has not even occurred to the Natives to have a read. And so it has been all this time. You see, even until now, there has been no writer

218

to outclass Francis. No one can rival him. What is your opinion?'

'Perhaps. I last read Francis in 1898 when his book *Nyai Dasima* was published. But I've forgotten what it was like.'

'His books should be studied more, and not just by the Indos. It was *Nyai Dasima* that was published in 1898, and that is considered his best work. You don't mind me mentioning your rival, do you?' Without waiting for my reaction, he continued, 'But now there are fewer and fewer people who want to write. There is no pay, and little honour in writing. People enjoy reading the stories but don't want to know who it was that strived so hard to create them. So, Tuan, what I would like to know is whether or not you would be willing to publish Francis's stories if he were still alive. Either in book form or as a serial in your paper?'

Seeing that I was hesitating in answering, he quickly continued: 'Yes, the answer is not as easy as the question. Your paper doesn't have much space. In any case, I put this to you simply as a suggestion. It's not just a matter of whether to print or not to print either. It is a matter of honour – a way of recognising the so far unrecognised contributions of the Indos. Such a person as yourself, with such broad vision, must surely agree with me that the mark of a civilised people is their ability to repay debts of honour.'

At first there had been just the three of us at the food stall. Now two other people, who looked like traders, sat down and ordered. They also listened to what Haji Moeloek was saying.

From behind the stall wafted the aroma of our almost-ready chicken. Our glasses of tea had been drunk to their last drop. Sadikoen had begun to nibble on crackers, forgetting that he was a Bendoro doctor who would never be seen eating at such a small stall as this back in Kroja.

'You are frowning,' he went on. 'To put it more clearly, we are hoping, maybe in the name of the Indos, that you will be able to publish occasionally some of the Malay stories of the Indo writers. If possible Francis. Francis has already died. Other writers are Makarena, Melati van Java, Don Ramon, Hendriksen de Baas, Barelino . . . '

He mentioned several other names that I had never heard of. I studied this lover of all things Indo. Perhaps he was just making up these names or they were the names of people he had met on his way here

' . . . and if you can't get hold of their writings, perhaps you would be prepared to publish some of my writings. Heh-heh, I sound just like a trader in the markets, don't I?' he laughed at himself.

'Why don't you publish your writings yourself, as a book?'

'I'd have to sell two or at least one house to get enough money to do that. And anyway, I only have one house, and it took me a long time to save up the money for that.'

'But the honour and fame is more important than a house, isn't it?'

'That's not it, Tuan. For me perhaps the house is not so important. But for my son it is important. With one hectare he can grow a few things, enough anyway. And for my grandchildren it is important too.'

'You never mentioned that you also wrote.'

'Now I'll tell you. My novel is about life on a sugar plantation and around a sugar mill, Tuan. It's about how the Indos emerged as a group, how they mixed with the Pure-Bloods and the Natives, how they built their own world . . . how they loved . . . '

Troenodongso suddenly came to mind.

'And the peasant uprisings . . . '

'Exactly. They are also in my story.'

'And the concubines . . . '

'Of course!' He laughed boisterously. Sadikoen stopped crunching on his crackers, covered his mouth and joined in the laughter.

'Do you know Arabic?'

'I can read, speak and write it.'

'Why don't you translate it into Arabic and publish it in Jeddah?'

'The Arabs are only interested in stories about other Arabs,' he shook his head.

'Why don't you put it into Dutch?'

'Perhaps I could, but I would have to do it in the Indies, so I would still have to sell that house.'

'Let me read your manuscript. I will try to publish it, if it's good.'

'You can publish it as a serial over a two-year period,' he said enthusiastically.

'So it's not a small work then.'

'Its title is *The Tale of Siti Aini*. No matter where I go, I always take the manuscript with me, so that I can work on constantly improving it. I also see it as a contribution from the Indos, and not just from this worthless person, Haji Moeloek.'

He shifted the conversation away from the life and activities of the Indo community. His description of that life was so completely different from that of Mama's in Surabaya – an incredibly boisterous life full of unfathomable events, confusion, conflicts and other jumpings up and down on the stage of life.

'I'll go and get the manuscript, ' he said.

'But the chicken is almost ready,' I said, trying to discourage him.

'It will only take ten minutes,' he said, crowing.

He left and straight away the grilled chicken arrived, golden brown and glistening in oily *kecap*. And out of the holes left by the skewers wafted the most mouth-watering smell, an aroma more wondrous than could ever come from any incense.

'His manuscript is, of course, more important than grilled chicken,' I hissed.

'I think he should have been more polite. Please forgive my friend,' said Sadikoen. 'Now you have to let your chicken get cold while we wait.'

And the beautiful white rice with the steam rising up out of it set my intestines dancing. And perhaps even the worms in my stomach were cursing that they had still to wait for their meal.

'Why aren't you at your congress?' I asked Sadikoen.

'I thought more about this question of movement from minus to plus. All movement towards a better situation is positive, whether through prayer or action, but boycotts . . . '

'Ah, so that's it?'

'There was no need for you to publish your editorial. I don't know what van Heutsz would have thought of it. Have you seen him recently,' he pressed me. When he saw me shake my head, he went on, 'I don't think he would have liked it. He will think you've gone too far. At the very least you will get some kind of reprimand.'

'Yes, I'm waiting for a reprimand. But that's his mistake. As time goes on, people start to take bolder and bolder steps. And not everyone just returns to where they started out. He should understand that.'

'Nothing but trouble will come of this.'

To be truthful, his warning worried me. The question had become more and more an issue in public debate. I had received several letters asking for further explanation. There was even a young woman who came to see me, escorted by her maid. She arrived, explained in fluent Dutch what she wished to discuss and then asked for a further appointment. She didn't give her name but announced her title – Princess of Kasiruta. A princess, and with such a unique beauty! As regards the boycott, Princess, I said to her, I will write about it further at another time. Would you mind, Princess, if I ornament that article with the dedication: For the Princess of Kasiruta! She smiled so sweetly, caressed by my offer. And she was unlike a Javanese girl – her movements and the way she talked were so free, so relaxed. And now Java Doctor Sadikoen was warning me that only trouble would come from my boycott editorial.

'Now about BO. I purposely stayed away today. Everything is going as planned. BO wants to get rid of all the bad ways. It will keep those things which are good. Everything will stay within reasonable bounds. We want to achieve things by accepting things as they are. We're not fantasising about things that can't be achieved, we're not kidding ourselves.'

'You mean BO is pursuing realistic policies?'

'More-or-less. Yes.'

'But humankind is able to create new conditions, a new reality. We are not fated to swim forever among the realities that are here now.'

'We are not dreamers, not fantasisers.'

'Everything that is worthwhile in human civilisation has not only originated from but indeed been inspired by dreams, by imagination . . . Do you think the automobile and the locomotive were created by "accepting things as they are"? No, they also came from dreams and imaginings.'

Haji Moeloek returned with a big parcel. His face was red. It looked as though he had been running: 'I hope the chicken isn't cold,' he apologised.

'Ayoh, let's eat,' I set the program.

And three chickens, that two hours before had still been running about on their own two feet, still tidying up their ruffled feathers, still competing with their fellow roosters, now disappeared, destroyed, dissolved in our mouths among the glistening *kecap* and saliva, then to descend our throats to meet the waiting worms in our stomachs.

As I savoured the deliciousness of the meal, I remembered what some of the students at the medical school used to say. The measure of a man's pleasure was fifteen centimetres. And so it was with this meal. As soon as the chicken had passed through our throats, the deliciousness disappeared to who-knows-where.

'It hasn't disappointed you, Ndoro, has it?' asked the stall woman.

Haji Moeloek held up his thumb. Mas Sadikoen nodded slowly, while swallowing the last bits he had in his mouth. And I growled like a cat, spied by a rival.

Now Haji Moeloek opened up his 'merchandise'. A tall pile of exercise books sat before me. His handwriting was large and beautiful, in black ink. I observed that there were no crossings-out anywhere. He must have been a first-class scribe at one time or another.

'You may study this manuscript, and I am sure you will not be disappointed.'

'I will study it.'

'This is what I will leave behind me when I die. Next week I sail again. Give me a receipt. If you publish it, send it to the Dutch Consulate in Jeddah.'

While it was true that his self-introduction had been rather tedious, it turned out that this man was not difficult to get along with. In fact, it was a pleasure to know him. He did not hide what was in his heart. Perhaps it was because he was an experienced man of the world. I gave him a receipt.

'Perhaps one day people will look back and remember that the Indos did indeed make a contribution to the advancement of the Natives.'

'But you don't use an Indo name here. People will think you're a Native.'

'One day people will know he was an Indo, and not just any *haji*, but someone who wants to be buried not far from the grave of the Prophet. I'm not upset that the BO won't accept me as a member because I am an Indo. But neither is the BO capable of writing what I have written.'

'I get the impression that you have actually written quite a lot.'

He laughed. His already wrinkled face shone.

'That's right, using many different pen-names.'

'You'd probably be famous by now if you hadn't used different names.'

'It's a pity but I just prefer to disappear amongst it all. Perhaps it's not so much a preference as such, but just a tendency that I have,' he laughed politely. 'It's enough to see that my writing has made someone else happy. Then I am happy too, Tuan.'

'But you would like to join the BO?' asked Sadikoen.

'So I could disappear into BO too. That's closer to the truth,' he answered.

'And it makes you even happier to be able to leave behind some mysterious signs, though,' I added.

'Perhaps you're right. But only one person will know who is the author of *The Tale of Siti Aini* – Haji Moeloek. Witnessed by you two gentlemen. No one else will know.'

The meeting ended, leaving a deep impression of a strange man who wished to leave the world a legacy without anyone knowing.

I didn't meet Kommer again until after the congress. When the congress ended, I wasn't chosen as the Editor of BO's new magazine. Neither was Douwager. My suspicions about the whole thing grew stronger.

From Jogja I went to Solo to hear the latest news about the soldiers of the Mangkunegaran Legion. Several officers were detained but no other action was taken. On the other hand BO began to grow dramatically. The merchants of Solo were also giving assistance.

From Solo I went to B – . It was a boring trip, mainly through dust. And something amazing happened. I was received by my father without having to crawl along the floor. I was allowed to sit on a chair the same height as his.

'I may be transferred to a more difficult area,' he complained. 'To where the big rebellion by the followers of Samin is going on.'

'But the Samin are no longer in rebellion.'

'Yes. But the results are the same. The rebellion may have waned, but that hasn't helped the local treasury. In fact, there is less money coming in now than before. They dare the authorities to gaol them and stir up turmoil everywhere. And imprisoning them just costs us more. The prisoner doesn't have to pay anything. It's the Government that has to bear the cost.'

'But they have no leader any more, Father.'

'Yes, he's been exiled to Bangkahulu, they say. But it hasn't had any effects. His teachings still inspire them.'

'Does Father really need to be bothered by all this?'

'Indeed this is precisely the matter that I will have to solve.'

'Well, what's wrong with them going on like they are now? They are not criminals, or thieves, or robbers.'

'That's precisely the problem. They don't do any harm to anyone, nor do they desire to. They just want to be left alone to live their own way.'

'Why don't you just let them then?'

'But refusing to accept the authority of the Government is itself criminal.' He was silent a moment and he watched me. 'Everyone says that you are often summoned by His Excellency the Governor-General. Couldn't you raise this matter with him?'

'They just want to live their own way. I don't think I should raise it with him, Father.'

'That means not being a *bupati*.'

'That's not my intention, Father. Leave the Samin people alone, and Father can still be a *bupati*.'

Father stood up, and said: 'Don't you know that what you have said amounts to conspiring against the Government?' His voice had become hard.

'I don't see that. While they don't make any trouble, they don't need to be the subject of any report, do they?'

'You don't understand. If I do that, I will end up with the poorest region in the world.'

'Father hopes for a medal from the Governor-General?'

'Which *bupati* doesn't?'

'Perhaps Father even hopes to be blessed with the title of "Prince"?'

'That is the greatest hope of all *bupatis*.'

'And a gold umbrella?'

'You are making fun of your parents.'

'The Governor-General doesn't need any of those things,' I said slowly and cautiously.

'They are the measure of a good *bupati*. For you too if you are made a *bupati*. How many in all of Java have been made a prince? Five at the most.'

'That is why I do not wish to be a *bupati*.'

'It is only if God wishes that you become a *bupati*. If God chooses you to become a *bupati*, then a *bupati* you will be. You will have no power to refuse, that would be rebellion. It's strange that someone should not want to be a *bupati* – to govern over thousands of people, to be honoured, to be bowed down to . . .'

And I remembered all of a sudden the speech that Multatuli had made to the Bupati Kartawijaya in Lebak, who was also honoured and bowed down to, but was also the object of curses, hatred and revenge.

'I am fortunate then that God has not made me a *bupati*,' I said, even more slowly.

'Is it true what I am hearing? What would you do if the Government issued a decree appointing you?'

'I would refuse.'

'And where do you get the courage to refuse?'

'From the knowledge that I do not need medals, the title of "prince", or to be bowed down to,' again I spoke slowly and cautiously.

Father let out a deep sigh, mumbling, then: 'That's what happens when you don't know your place,' he whispered. 'Go on, go and see your mother.'

I left my father without bowing in obeisance. I could feel his gaze follow me and stick to my neck. I strode slowly but confidently out to the back area. I found my mother sitting in a chair chewing betel nut. She didn't see me arrive. I immediately went up and squatted down beside her, kissed her knee, and said nothing.

'Who is that coming up to me, surprising me like that?'

'It is I, Mother, Mother's favourite son.'

She held my *destar* with her two hands and turned my face to hers.

'Greetings, my son, Mother feels she has received a blessing and inspiration from your arrival.'

'Forgive me, Mother, for not sending word.'

'You came by train?'

'Yes, Mother.'

'Bathe first.'

I went off to bathe. When I came out of the bathroom, all fresh and neat, my younger brother and sister were waiting for me to say hello.

'Eh, you all,' I said, 'Come on over here, don't just stand there. Ah, and you, when do you marry?'

'Ah, you, my brother, you've just arrived and already teasing.'

'But this means I'm in favour of it, or do I have to go out and find someone for you?' I smiled.

She looked away and ran off, embarrassed.

'And you, how are you going at school?'

'Thank you for your interest, Brother, I am progressing.'

I left them to go and see mother.

Mother waved to me that I should sit. There was a little tobacco protruding from the corner of her mouth. She looked older. There were more grey hairs than white.

'I've been thinking about you all this time, Child, all this time, about you. Are you happy now?'

'Yes, thank you, Mother.'

'Your voice is bright and clear now, not like the last time we met. Thanks be to God, Child. Around here everyone is talking about you. You're a journalist, they say, putting out thousands of newspapers, going all over Java, all with your name on them. That's good, Child. You wanted to be a doctor, but it didn't happen. Then you wanted to be a *dalang* and that didn't happen either. Now you are a journalist. Is that something like a trader, Child?'

'More-or-less the same, Mother.'

'So no one bows down to you except your servants?'

'And my servants do not bow down to me either, Mother.'

'So there is no one that you rule over, Child?'

'No one, Mother.'

'So are you doing that which is the task of a *sudra* or *brahman*?'

'Both at the same time, Mother, serving others and also teaching through my newspaper.'

'You will not regret that you did not become a *ksatria*?'

'No, Mother, never.'

'Regret is a torture, Child. Try not to make any more wrong choices. Do you have any more ambitions, Child?'

'Well, I have lost all desire to be a doctor. But I still wish to be a *dalang*, Mother, please forgive me.'

'There is too much that you desire, Child. And you want to be a *dalang* as well. Do you know enough stories yet?'

'I still lack one, Mother,' I told her of my ideas about the multi-racial nature of the Indies, that I wanted to build an organisation that reflected that reality, but that I had not yet found the means for unifying the peoples. I also told her about the merchant, Thamrin Mohammed Thabrie, and about the power of the Chinese businesses that had been able to destroy the big European firms, using that power available to the weak, the boycott.

'So you do not yet have all the stories that you need.'

'Give me a sign, Mother, and your blessings.'

'You know better than I what you need, Child, and I give my blessings. Be somebody who is good.'

'A thousand times thank you, Mother.'

'Have you ever heard the *kedasih* bird singing to its fellows?'

'I have, Mother.'

'And the thrush also?'

'Yes, Mother.'

'They are always singing to each other. Sometimes they are without a friend, because they've been injured or in an accident, and they cry out for their lost friend. Sometimes their companion will never answer again. Whenever you hear the lamenting of a *kedasih* or a thrush and there is no answer, it breaks your heart, and you realise how lonely life can be. And you, Child, do not become like a *kedasih* who sings alone, only knowing laments. You need not make everyone feel pity for you like that. There was one *kedasih* who sat in the old *kapok* tree outside and called out and called out, every two hours. It sang its call to its friend over and over again. Yes, Child every morning. For two months. Then it was never heard again. It never returned to sit on the branches of that tree again. It was never seen around here again. It was heartbreaking, Child.'

'Mother told me about that *kedasih*, Mother.'

'So you remember. Don't become a *kedasih* that does not sing, that does not make music. Don't become a *dalang* that has no stories. A *dalang* can survive without puppets, Child, but not without stories . . . '

I left B – with my spirits refreshed, with my mother's blessings, and with an instruction – don't end up singing alone in your own house. At the very least there should be a wife who can answer your music, the music of your heart.

And in my bag I carried Haji Moeloek's manuscript. I read it during my journey and it invigorated my thoughts, my heart.

And there was one more thing that I was taking home – the knowledge that the merchants of Jogja and Solo, though renowned for their miserliness, were willing to donate money to help advance our society, yes, for an organisation that would bring us progress in the days ahead.

And there was one name that shone out brilliantly in the Boedi Oetomo – that of the Secretary, Mas Ngabehi Dwidjosewojo.

12

There was a pile of letters waiting for me at the *Medan* office in Bandung. Three of them were from the Princess of Kasiruta. Her palace Dutch gave the impression that she was not used to writing letters. Or that she had been brought up to be always courtly and formal.

She had sent me three letters while I was away. She wanted to meet me. Perhaps she wanted to know more about boycotts. Perhaps there was something else in her heart.

A messenger delivered my reply to her.

Not a second after the messenger left, a thick-set youth appeared before me, about two centimetres shorter than me. He wore a buttoned-up blouse, a tightly-woven *sarong* and a very neat *destar*. He might have been a district level *priyayi*. But a closer examination, especially of his movements, revealed that he was a village boy who was wearing his very best clothes.

'Your servant's name is Marko, Ndoro,' he said with his head bowed and his hands clasped in obeisance. 'If Ndoro is willing to accept me . . . I have come to serve.'

'Heh, Marko. I've been waiting for you a long time now. Come over here closer. Lift your chin up, straighten up your chest. A fighter doesn't go about bowed down like that.'

He smiled and lifted up his chin. His face shone. His eyes were sharp and bright. More than that – he was handsome.

I stood up, went over to him and tried to strike him in the face. He ducked, jerking his head back. I lifted my leg to kick him in the stomach, and he jumped away.

It didn't seem that Wardi had chosen wrongly. He could duck and swerve beautifully as if he was dancing, without his arms or legs moving away from where he stood. Perhaps because I hadn't practiced for a long time I quickly became tired doing this and I still couldn't hit him. I stopped. I stood panting in front of him.

'Good,' I said. Without asking where he came from or where he lived, I gave him my first order. 'Make sure the office is cleaned every day.'

A few minutes later he was no longer the district *priyayi*. His blouse and *sarong* were off, so too his slippers, which he probably didn't own anyway. Now he was wearing yellow cotton shirt and trousers – just like any villager come to town. He went skilfully about cleaning the walls, the furniture and the floor.

'What else, Ndoro?'

'Get dressed again, and come and see me.'

I had just got through one more letter and he was before me again. Without hesitation he sat down.

'This office must never look dirty.'

'I am your servant, Ndoro.'

'Call me Tuan. And speak Malay. Do you know Malay?'

'Yes, Tuan.'

'Your job is to look after security here. Any other work will be on my orders alone. Where did you meet Wardi?'

'Which one is Ndoro Wardi?'

'Stupid! The one who brought you here.'

'I don't know his name yet. I only know Sandiman.'

'Have you known him long?'

'I've been travelling around with him for these last three months.'

'Can you read and write?'

'Javanese, Tuan, in Latin and Arabic script.'

I threw him a page from *Medan* and told him to read it aloud. He read out a passage on the Boedi Oetomo congress. It was clear from the way he read that he understood very well what he was reading, although his 'd' and 'b' still had a heavy Javanese accent.

'So what is your opinion of this article?'

'The language isn't quite right, Tuan.'

'Where did you go to school?'

'I taught myself, Tuan.'

'You've never been to school?'

'Just village school, Tuan.'

'Did you graduate?'

'Yes, Tuan. I have my diploma here with me, if you want to see it!'

At that moment the Princess entered, accompanied by her maid. I stood and told Marko to leave. In a leap he was out of the office.

'Good afternoon, Princess. Please be seated.'

She was wearing silk. She carried in her hand a yellow umbrella, decorated with pictures of flowers and made from silk. She carried herself freely and confidently, with no sense of shyness. Her maid waited for her outside the office. She hung the umbrella on the arm of the chair and sighed.

She was tall and slender and her skin was an attractive ebony colour. For a second she reminded me of *The Fower of the Century's End* except for her colour. Perhaps she had Portuguese blood.

'And so what about this boycott matter, Tuan?' she asked in Dutch, very politely.

'You really need to know, Princess?'

'I will take the idea back to Kasiruta,' she answered.

I studied her rather narrow face and her pointed profile.

'What use will it be for you in Kasiruta?' She smiled and I didn't understand why. 'It will be printed in a few more days,' I said.

'That is why I have come to see you, Meneer. They have forbidden me.'

'Who are they?'

'The Assistant Resident of Priangan.'

'The Assistant Resident?' suddenly I remembered Mir's letter asking whether it was true a *raja* from the Maluccas had been exiled to Sukabumi or Cianjur?

'Princess has the appearance of an Indian?'

She smiled and gazed at me without embarrassment. It was only when I started to study her face and figure that she turned away, embarrassed.

'Is Princess living at Sukabumi with her family?'

'Yes.'

'But Princess is in Bandung.'

'Not for long, for sure. My scholarship will expire when I graduate and then I will join my family. At the moment I am trying to get permission to return to Kasiruta. The Assistant Resident has rejected my request three times now. So I have come to you to ask for help. Whatever else is the case, it was not I that was exiled.'

'Please wait a minute,' I said. I went to fetch Frischboten. But he was out. 'Our lawyer is out at the moment. Now tell me just what were the reasons given by the Assistant Resident of Priangan for not granting your request.'

'He just said: It's a great pity, Miss, but it just isn't possible at the moment. Just that, nothing more.'

'Very well. I will go and see the Assistant Resident.'

'Thank you very much, Meneer.'

'How long has Princess been in Priangan?'

'Three years. Ever since my graduation from primary school.'

It almost came out of my mouth – it will be two more years before you are allowed to return to the land of your birth. But I didn't have the heart to tell her. And it was only a guess anyway. It was said that there were only two terms of exile in the Indies – five years or forever.

'Can Princess speak Sundanese?'

'During these three years I have learnt only to speak it.'

'Can Princess speak Malay?'

'Of course. School Malay as well as the Malay of society.'

'And why do you want to take my writings about the boycott back to Kasiruta?'

She now looked at me with suspicion in her eyes. Her hands seemed to grope for the umbrella hung on the arm of her chair. The idea of taking back the material on the boycott was no doubt her family's idea, and she knew the purpose quite well.

Suddenly she changed the subject: 'And what if the Assistant Resident still refuses?'

'Would the Princess then permit me to raise this matter with His Excellency the Governor-General?'

'People say that it is indeed only you who are able to do that.'

'And if, for example, permission is refused, then won't the Princess lose her faith in me?'

'Just for you to ask is enough to put me in your debt, Meneer, and it will never be forgotten.'

'Could you tell me how it is that people are saying that it is only I who can bring this matter to the Governor-General's attention?'

'Forgive me, Meneer, but it is said, I don't know whether truly or falsely, that you are his favourite.'

These rumours had long been irritating me. What could I do, they were spreading further and further each day. I told her the truth of the matter, that the rumours were not true.

The conversation ranged over many things. It was good to talk with a girl who was confident, free and dared to voice her opinions. And as a woman she was also perfect – her face, her breasts, her waist and hips, her thighs and legs, all her body. She was completely in control of herself. It was clear she had a great deal of self-respect. Perhaps she had received some kind of good, strict European education. She was a flower among all womankind. European ways seemed to have become a part of her character. But that was just a first impression.

And my old nature began to reassert itself! Ahoi, you philogynist, you connoisseur of female beauty! You have greater rights to this flower than anyone else on earth. Mother, I have heard your message. I will wed this flower.

'But you mustn't hope that you will be able to return to Kasiruta in the near future, Princess. You can speak Sundanese and Malay. Would you be willing to help me?'

'What is there that I can do to help?'

'I have long had the desire to publish a magazine for women. Until now there has been no one able to work on it. In the meantime, how would you feel, Princess, about helping edit such a magazine?'

Her eyes were full of questions. Then: 'I have never done work of any kind. How could I help edit a magazine?'

'Do you agree, Princess, that the treatment of women is an important question?'

'But I don't know anything about such things.'

'Of course, you will have to be helped to begin with.'

She went silent, thinking.

'Of course Princess is unable to answer straight away,' I said. 'Let me help you answer. Princess agrees to help us, and has no objections, and is not repelled by the idea of being helped.' I looked at her for some time.

She didn't retreat from my gaze for a long time either, then she looked down.

'You should go home now, Princess. I will visit your house later on and bring with me news of what our lawyer says about your case.'

She hesitantly rose from her chair, and bowed, saying goodbye. I escorted her to the door, and handed her over to her maid who was sitting sleepily in the corner.

'Heh,' I said in Sundanese to the maid. 'Take your mistress safely home now, all right?'

'Your servant, Master.'

Princess van Kasiruta, carrying her yellow umbrella, walked ahead of her maid. Neither of them turned to look back.

Back in my office my heart cried out to me, telling me: You have been victorious! Victorious! She knew that your gaze was a gaze of admiration for her as a woman. You also know now that she is under your influence. And then Ter Haar's warning came to me: Do not use your publication for furthering your own ambitions! Then quickly came a reply: This is not a matter of personal ambition, this is just something between a man and a woman.

Then Wardi and another man came into the office from the print shop. The other man was an Indo. I did not know him.

'Mas,' Wardi began, 'I've brought an acquaintance of mine. Let me introduce him.'

He was none other than Douwager. I suddenly remembered Mir Frischboten.

'You have been in South Africa and England?'

'How did you know that?'

'But it wasn't reported where you were wounded. You have come straight from England?'

Without anyone to do the formalities, we all sat down. And I sensed that he was somewhat anxious, Wardi too.

'No, Meneer. I have not come straight from England. I have travelled to many other countries on my way here. In India I was arrested and gaoled for quite a while. When I was released I had to promise never to enter a British colony again. Then I came straight home to the Indies.'

I almost told him that Mir was in Bandung. But I didn't. What was the point?

232

'I've brought Edu here, so that perhaps you two can come to agreement on one or even more things. Go on, Edu,' said Wardi, calling him by his nickname.

'I have heard from Wardi that you have an idea about the need for an organisation that has an Indies character. Like Wardi, you don't fully support the Boedi Oetomo. I too don't support the idea of organisations based on a single race or ethnic group. Could you explain to me your ideas on this question?'

For some reason or other, his request made me feel uneasy. There was a kind of arrogance in the way he asked his question. It was he who said that Natives could not yet run a newspaper. Perhaps, from the moment he set off from his house, his intention has been to come here to give me a lesson of some kind. And in any case, what business is it of an Indo what kind of organisation Natives build for themselves? If he wanted to, he could join up with one of the big Indo organisations like Soerja Soemirat.

I looked quizzically at Wardi. He hurried to offer an explanation: 'Mas,' he began, gently, 'let me explain to you what has happened,' he looked at Douwager to keep him quiet. 'After seeing the situation in South Africa, Edu came up with some ideas that might be of use to us. In South Africa, you see, there are three peoples – English, Dutch, Natives – as well as various Asian aliens such the Slameier exiles from Java, Indians and Arabs. The war over who would rule South Africa was indeed won by the stronger army of England. But even with the British victory, it is the Dutch who still hold power over the Natives and the other coloured peoples. The Natives remain a subjugated people.'

'Everyone knows that, Wardi. The Natives remain oppressed.'

'Yes, that is the fate of a people who have not progressed.'

'It's not a question of not having progressed. The Natives are not allowed to progress, they are not educated to advance themselves. These are two quite different things both in substance and appearance,' I said.

Wardi went silent and Douwager took over. It was probably their intention to try to draw some comparison between the Indies and South Africa. I knew what Wardi was like. He had began to think about bigger things, the question of power, for example. It was likely that his relationship with Douwager was connected with his interest in that. He had also spoken about the Dutch farmers in South Africa who had founded their own republics free from the authority of either the English or their own homeland – the Oranje Vrijstaat and the Transvaal Republic.

'Yes, it's true that the Dutch settlers actually established their own colony there, whereas they haven't done that in the Indies.' He had reached the final part of his argument. 'But there are more similarities than differences. In both South Africa and the Indies, the Dutch have established their authority, one in conjunction with and one independent of the mother country . . . '

233

It seemed that Wardi and Edu had formulated an analysis of two kinds of power that ruled in each of these far-apart places. In South Africa it was a power that ruled independently and in the Indies it was a power that was still tied to Holland. It was easier for the Dutch in South Africa, they thought, because there were more of them. In the Indies they were a very small group. But there was a group that were greater in number than the Dutch, and virtually just as advanced. They were the Eurasians, Indos. And if to them were added the educated Natives . . .

I remembered the story of how Multatuli had been accused by the colonial newspapers of wanting to be a white emperor ruling over the peoples of the Indies, independent of the Netherlands!

'I'm not finished yet, Mas.'

'Good, please continue.'

It seemed that both Wardi and Douwager had sensed that I was not happy. Wardi continued carefully:

'We think that the ideas Edu has worked out based on these observations can be used to have a more successful go at reviving or building something like the sarekat, which we have to admit has failed. You'll listen to him, won't you?'

'Please go ahead.'

'Now, you explain your ideas, Edu.'

'Yes, my friend,' Douwager took over, 'I have heard from Wardi about the failure of the Sarekat Priyayi. We are of the same opinion, actually – namely, that it failed to unify the educated and advanced groups. The sarekat tried to organise those who had received their positions from the Government, a layer of people who are actually satisfied with their lot. This would only have led, even if the organisation had kept functioning, to consolidating the *priyayi* in their positions and strengthening their privileges. As soon as it became clear that the organisation could not do that, especially as it required of them new responsibilities, they dropped it. It collapsed.'

'And it was the original intention of the sarekat to unite the educated and advanced groups,' Wardi explained, 'but it didn't turn out that way.'

It seemed that both of them were hoping that I would try to defend myself. But I didn't say anything.

'Anyway, the key thing is that the idea behind the sarekat was correct. Indeed it still needs to be carried out somehow. The real question is, exactly who are the educated and advanced groups in the Indies?' Douwager continued. 'Not the *priyayi*. It is my observation, my friend, that in the Indies as soon as a person receives a position with the Government he ceases to act as an educated person. He is immediately assimilated into the *priyayi* mentality – inflexible, greedy, corrupt and with an insatiable appetite for others to bow down to him. I think the people we have to try to unite are not the *priyayi* but perhaps those who do not hold any position with the Government.'

234

'Those who hold no position, Mas, we can call them "the independent people", not servants of the Government, their ideas and activities are not fenced in by any allegiance to the Government.'

No Government position, free and independent people – this concept awakened my consciousness. The two of them were right.

'Continue, Mr Douwager.'

'The further away from any Government position a person is the more free their spirit becomes, the bolder their ideas. This is because their thinking is more flexible and dynamic. They can be more productive and creative. They have more opportunity to take initiatives. They're not closed off and haunted by the fear of being dismissed at any time.'

'It's very rare to come across an Indo who does not work for the Government.'

'Forgive me, my friend. If you use the word "Indo" there always seems to be a racial connotation. Perhaps it's better if we use the word "Indisch" meaning "of the Indies". The word Indo doesn't seem to really carry any political meaning. But Indisch does have that connotation.'

'I don't understand what you mean.'

'This is precisely the matter which we wish to discuss. From what I have heard from Wardi, you hold the view that the Indies is made up of many peoples and that is its character, multi-racial?'

'Yes, I told him that this was your view, Mas.'

'In my opinion, this is where we have slightly different views. The Indies is not multi-racial in character. The Indies has only one people, the Indisch. This idea means that every Indisch, every citizen of the Indies, no matter what his racial origin – Arab, Javanese, Indian, Dutch, Chinese, Malay, Buginese, Acehnese, Balinese, Mixed-Blood Chinese, even a Pure-Blood European who lives and dies in the Indies and is loyal to the Indies – they are all a part of the Indies people, Indisch.'

It was a startling idea, except that he was an Indo. It was another case of wanting to lose one's identitiy, like Haji Moeloek. But it was only an idea. The reality was that such a thing would never happen in this century. Who would be willing to merge their identity into this 'Indisch people'? Would the Natives or the Indos be willing? Or the other peoples?

'And what is the language of your Indisch people to be, my friend?'

'All the educated and advanced people use Dutch, of course,' said Douwager without hesitation. 'It is not only the language of society and organisation, but it is also an internationally recognised language in the world of education and science.'

'So you ignore the languages of the twenty-five million Javanese and the two million Malays, not to mention the other people who use their languages?'

'Yes, to set out on this path will mean we face many difficulties. But however that may be, this is the path that we must tread. It is only the educated and advanced thinking people who can lead. The others must follow.'

'What is your opinion about the Samin movement?'

'The Samin? Yes, there are one or two educated Europeans who admire them, but without educated leaders they will not get anywhere. They are a movement produced by the end of an age.'

'The end of an age?' Wardi asked, amazed.

'The teachings of the Samin mix beliefs that are more-or-less religious with politics.'

'Religious beliefs and politics?' I cried.

'Europe has separated politics and religion.'

'But Saminism is not a religion.'

'Before humankind knew the kind of politics we have today, my friend, religion was politics, as it is with the Samin movement now. And the followers of Samin also believe that their politics is their religion and vice versa.'

'But Saminism is not a religion!' I repeated hotly.

'No, you're right, it's not a religion. But that's where it is heading, and where it would have been already, if they hadn't lost their spiritual leader so quickly. In the past that was always the way men built power and the way they went about using it. That's why some people say, and I agree with them, that the Samin movement is a product of the end of an age.'

'You are going too far, Meneer, to think that, or even to agree with such an idea.'

'Hasn't the boldness of Europe's intellectual tradition now been passed on to the world? And also pioneered by Multatuli? Wasn't Multatuli himself prepared to die in misery and in exile in the name of intellectual integrity? And are you yourself not an admirer of Multatuli, if I am not mistaken?'

'But your ideas mean challenging the enemy before we can stand on our own two feet!' I exclaimed. 'You have to take into account the social reality in the Indies.'

'Every beginning is difficult. But fundamental ideas need not always be checked against reality. Reality must be made to conform to a fundamental idea, or the idea will be destroyed by it.'

'But that is not the way to unite people. It is an invitation to conflict and strife amongst ourselves,' I said, in all honesty. 'Your ideas about organising are not right. You will end up isolating yourself from the real developments. Perhaps what you suggest could take place in Europe. But here in the Indies? What about you, Wardi?'

'Yes, I agree, his views are too extreme on this,' he replied. 'You never mentioned any of this to me, Edu.'

'What is it exactly that we wish to discuss? About our own personal views on different things or about the question of organisation? If it's one's personal views on things, it's best just to write them up and publish it oneself. If we're talking about organisation then we are talking about common interests, and we shouldn't be aiming to become prophets over or among our fellow countrymen. What is the common interest that binds together the peoples of the Indies?

'Every new opinion and idea always attracts its opponents,' Douwager went on. 'Such new ideas are themselves born out of opposition to existing ones with all their deficiencies. What we need is not an organisation that has thousands of members but that can't do anything. What we need is a small organisation that can lead because its ideas cannot be refuted, and therefore they have to be accepted without conditions, an organisation that can be the brains of the Indisch nation.'

'If that's the case, then it should be enough to set up a salon for intellectuals, Mr Douwager, as is also the tradition in Europe. Indeed the world still does value the intellectuals and scholars who have been prepared to die to defend the truth. Is there a scholar among us three, or among the people of the Indies?'

A worker from the print shop came in and handed me a proof of the next editorial. I excused myself to Douwager and checked over the proofs, stamping them as ready for printing. I asked the worker to summon Sandiman.

He left. Sandiman arrived.

'How is the Sunday edition?'

'Everything has gone to press, Sir. You can take a holiday tomorrow, Meneer. Monday even, perhaps even Tuesday.'

'Thanks, Man. Has Mr Frischboten arrived yet?'

'He's in his office. You can leave Bandung now if you like, everything's under control.'

'Good, Man. I'll leave now. If you don't see me around again, that'll mean I'll have left.'

'Have a good rest, Tuan.'

Sandiman left, and I apologised to Douwager that I couldn't continue the discussion just then. He left. And I went to see Frischboten.

He explained that it would be impossible for the Princess to leave Java without special permission from the Governor-General. He needed to give no justification for any decision he would make. The Governor-General had special rights and was not bound by the law. The Raja of Kasiruta had been exiled through the use of these special powers. That his daughter had not been involved in whatever had brought about the decision was irrelevant. Such a practice came from the backward custom of the peoples of the Indies themselves that held that with blood ties went shared responsibility.

So I didn't need to go to see the Assistant Resident. If it was possible, I should go straight to the Governor-General . . .

Haji Moeloek entered just as I was about to leave my office. He was displaying a row of teeth that was no longer complete. He was obviously happy.

'You see, Tuan, my ship is not leaving until the day after tomorrow, so I thought I would come and see you. Who knows, you might have a present for me. An opinion on the manuscript that I left you, perhaps?'

'Oh yes, your manuscript. I have read it all. I liked it very much. It really brightened me up when I read it. It turns out that you are a wonderful writer. You obviously have a lot of experience.' He smiled, this time not showing his teeth. 'I promise you that I will publish it as a serial in *Medan*. As you said I think it will take at least two years.'

'It doesn't matter.'

'What about payment, Haji Moeloek?'

'Just a copy of the paper will be enough, my friend.'

'Ah, your real name. Could perhaps you tell me?'

'Haji Moeloek is name enough, Tuan.'

I looked at him in amazement. He opened his mouth wide and again I could see his uneven rows of teeth, incomplete and stained black from cigarette tar. His attempt at laughter failed, because what came out was not what he intended. 'I am very happy to hear that you want to publish it, Tuan.'

'In the name of Allah, Tuan Haji, I promise I will also publish it in book form.'

'Such a great blessing. *Allhumdulillah*. Praise be to God! I'm so happy that I can leave the Indies with such beautiful news. I'm going back to Betawi today. If you are also going to Betawi, you're very welcome to join me. I have hired an English motor car, Tuan.'

'A taxi?'

'Yes, I hired it in Betawi.'

It was obvious that Haji Moeloek was rich. And it was then that I realised that not only London had taxis now – so did Betawi. The first automobile to enter had now been followed by others.

I told him that I would be very pleased to come with him but that I still had something to attend to. He said he was happy to wait and would even take me where I wanted to go.

And so it was that he escorted me to see the Princess van Kasiruta.

It was half past four in the afternoon. The Princess was boarding with a Dutch family, named Doornebos. I told her everything that had been explained to me by Frischboten. It was different than when we met in the office. Now she sat with her face turned away as if she didn't want to look into my face.

She was wearing an evening dress made from brown-coloured silk, as if to go with her enticing black skin.

'There is no use in going to see the Assistant Resident, Princess. I will try to see the Governor-General himself, tomorrow or the day after. Don't be discouraged. I'm going down to Buitenzorg right now.'

It was only then that she decided to look up at me, and at Haji Moeloek.

'Don't forget our request for your assistance, Princess.' I added.

'So you will be going down to Buitenzorg by car. Would it be all right if I went with you as far as Sukabumi?'

'Of course,' said Haji Moeloek, as fatherly as he could be, and that was the first time that I heard him speak Dutch. 'Come on, we can leave as soon as you're ready.'

'Is it all right if I have ten minutes to get my things together?'

Haji Moeloek took out his gold pocket-watch, looked at it and replied openly: 'Why not? Please do. We will wait.'

As soon as the girl left, he whispered: 'Indo girls aren't usually as refined as that.'

'She's not Indo. Native. Princess van Kasiruta.'

'Ah, this is the first time I have met a Native Princess,' he murmured, 'I thought she was Indo.'

'She has been exiled with her family to Priangan.'

'A boring story. All stories that are not about a free and liberated life are tedious. It's as if there is nothing else to tell about in this colony except exiling and oppressing. Other people travel the world, enjoying life, smiling and laughing, full of joy. Here there are people exiled in their own country.'

Princess van Kasiruta emerged carrying a leather suitcase.

Haji Moeloek quickly took the case from her, and we all climbed aboard the automobile.

The driver was a young Indo, hunched up, and, it seemed, a rather surly-spirited type. He sat calmly beside Haji Moeloek. I sat in the back with the Princess.

The sun had begun to set and the car pulled up on the side of the road. The driver alighted and lit the automobile's carbide lights. Then we continued the journey but at a reduced speed.

'Why are you so quiet, Princess?' I asked.

'What is there to talk about?'

'Many things, if you have the desire to. How many times has Princess ridden in an automobile?'

'This is the first time.'

'Do you like it? Our ancestors never rode anything like this.'

She let me listen to a little laugh as an answer.

Haji Moeloek turned round to the back and asked: 'So, Tuan, what do you think of what I had to say that time about the Indos? Do you agree that they are a group that has made a contribution but has not been recognised for it.'

'If you were to put your ideas down on paper in detail, I'm sure it would provoke a lot of discussion. You would need to polish your analysis a little,

239

adding things here and giving up things elsewhere. Why don't you write your ideas down?'

'Maybe that's the best thing to do,' he said. 'Perhaps I also argue a bit too hard sometimes. Forgive me, Tuan,' he faced the front once again.

'So, if His Excellency the Governor-General still refuses you permission to return home, you will surely be willing to help us with the magazine, Princess,' I said, trying to influence her. 'Everything is always difficult in the beginning. But things always get easier later. And don't forget – in Malay, Princess.'

'I think I would like it very much. But of course it is my father who will decide.'

'Fine. You will be able to speak to your father about it in a moment.'

After one hour on the road, we stopped in front of a simple dwelling on the side of the main road. As soon as the car had entered the front yard of the house, it was surrounded by a swarm of people. Everyone inside the house also came out, amazed to see a car stopping at their house.

Carrying her own case, the Princess ran off and went inside the house. She didn't come out again. An old man with glasses wearing a *kopiah* on his head, dressed in a velvet shirt and black velvet trousers and carrying a cane, came out and invited us in.

My friend just listened when I spoke up to introduce myself in Malay. The old man nodded. With a movement of his hand, he invited us to sit. Then he went into a room and didn't come out for some time. Haji Moeloek kept glancing at me, perhaps protesting at having to wait here for so long. I pretended not to understand. It's true, isn't it, that sometimes a long wait can bring its own blessings?

The old man came out again, still with his cane, but this time his *kopiah* was pushed further back on his head. And he seemed to have changed. His face shone, and he went straight into Malay: 'So you are the Chief Editor of *Medan*, Son. Thank you, Son, thank you. I never expected it. I hear that you will seek an audience with the Governor-General tomorrow or the next day. Good luck, Son, good luck. And could you ask him also why was it that we were exiled secretly like this? You have no objections to asking about this, do you, Son?'

'I will try, Tuan Raja.'

'Just say *Bapak*. And who is your friend?'

'Haji Moeloek, Tuan Raja,' answered Hans.

'What if you were to stay here tonight?'

I looked at Haji Moeloek, who happened to be looking at me at that moment. The light from the kerosene lamp reflected off his tired face. 'Ah it's a great pity, Tuan Raja, but my boat is about to leave and everything has to be readied tomorrow.'

'Where are you going, Tuan Haji?'

'Jeddah, Tuan Sultan. Please forgive us, our time is almost up. We have to continue our journey.'

'What a pity. And you, Son, where are you heading.'

'I am going home, Bapak. Buitenzorg.'

'Give me your address.'

And I gave him my address.

The automobile lurched off northwards. Haji Moeloek now sat in the back with me and tried once more to convince me of the contributions of the Indos. After he was convinced that I was not paying much attention, he changed the subject to that of the big sugar plantations. He obviously knew many of the big men in sugar.

'They are all millionaire moguls, no doubt, you too, perhaps, heh?'

'No, not me. They are indeed like emperors with their enormous wealth. Who is surprised? Sugar from Java is in demand right round the world. The Europeans are hard at work trying to make sugar from beet, but they will always need sugar from Java. As of the beginning of 1909, Tuan, sugar exports will go up 10 per cent. Formosa has still been unable to catch up to Java with its exports. It's because the Dutchmen's administration is better than any other. They calculate down to the smallest item.'

'It's not easy for someone to become rich through trading.'

'Merchants are the only rich people there are, Tuan.'

'No, that's not right. Others become rich through avoiding tax, specu- lation, squeezing and exploiting people and through deceit. And the Tax Office doesn't monitor these last three. So every wealthy person means another tax avoider.'

'Those American billionaires, Tuan, do you think they are the same?'

'There are no exceptions anywhere in the world, Tuan Haji. Tax evasion, speculation, exploitation and deceit.'

'Such a guess is tantamount to making an accusation.'

So I repeated to him all that I had learnt from Ter Haar, what had happened in the Harmoni Club, and also Ter Haar's explanation of what van Kollewijn had said.

'But that's not business, Tuan, that's politics.'

'Yes, business that is politics, and politics that is business. A two-headed beast that has brought nothing but misery to the colonised people, Tuan Haji. You have heard of the Ethical Policy? That is what the Ethical Policy is all about! And the political targets of their efforts are the Natives, and the Natives remain forever destitute and poor.'

'I have never heard any of this before.'

'And the people in the sugar plantations who deal with the Natives directly, Tuan, are usually Indos. I'm sorry. They are the trusted tools of the sugar companies who ensure that no Native can ever better his income even when he deserves it.'

'That touches on my own role too.'

'Perhaps. So if you write about the contributions of the Indos, don't forget about the other side as well.'

'Why don't you expose this in your paper?'

'That time will come, Tuan. And you will be able to follow what is happening from Jeddah,' I said, convinced that it would happen.

'Are you serious? You will be the first to do anything about this since the sugar companies were set up half a century ago. And you will shake the shareholdings of the big business houses back in Holland who have been financing the sugar companies all this time. You will make many enemies.'

'Let's just wait for the right time.'

'Before we separate, Tuan, let me shake your hands as a sign of respect for your courage in doing what one day you will do.' He held out his hand. 'As long as you remember that the sugar houses are more powerful than anyone else in the Indies.'

And just then the automobile stopped in front of my house. He couldn't stop and said goodbye. And I expressed my regrets that I wasn't able to see him off at the harbour.

The automobile roared on its way.

I stood paralysed at the door. Mir Frischboten stood before me in her evening dress.

'I'm staying in my old room tonight,' she said.

Hendrik had not mentioned anything about Mir coming down to stay when I spoke to him in Bandung. Perhaps they had had a fight.

'Why do you look so surprised? Didn't you see Hendrik before you left?'

'He didn't say anything about you coming down,' I answered as I hesitantly walked in through the door. And I had even more doubts about what was going on, because she was dressed up more than I had ever seen before. 'Everything's all right at home?'

'Yes, of course.' She looked at me with shining eyes and smiling lips, both of which served only to confuse me more.

'Did you tell him that you were coming down here?'

'Of course. You seem to be really worried.' She went into the kitchen and brought out a tray with a cup of coffee and a dish of my favourite *emping* crackers. She set them out on the table and went inside again.

Usually I drink my coffee as soon as I get home. But this time I hesitated. So I just sat back in the lounge chair letting go of my tiredness as my thoughts groped about trying to solve this new mystery.

'You're too tired.' She came out again, pulled up a cane chair and sat down beside me. 'Whose car was that? The Governor-General's?'

'No. It was a hired car. Haji Moeloek hired it.'

'He must be very wealthy. Why aren't you drinking your coffee?' She picked up the cup from the table and offered it to me. She took it back from me after I had drunk a quarter of a cup. She put it back on the table. 'You came straight from Bandung of course.'

'I'm meeting your husband at the station later. The last train.'

'You needn't trouble yourself. He won't be coming.'

'So you're really by yourself here.'

'Maybe for a few days. I've been under some stress lately.'

'Have a good rest then. I'm going to bathe.'

After bathing I found her reading a book. She spoke in a voice that was just as friendly as before: 'Dinner is ready. Let's eat.'

We went into the dining-room. She was behaving like a newly-wed.

Suddenly, in the middle of dinner, she spoke out: 'Perhaps because I was brought up on Indies food, I become hot like this. All the Natives always look hot. I prefer Indies food.'

'Do you eat local food or European at home?'

'It depends on Hendrik. He prefers European. It's more practical. You don't have to cook different dishes,' she said.

'You're not meaning to say that Hendrik is cold, are you?'

'How is Hendrik going? Does he like his work?' she moved quickly to turn the conversation.

'He more than just likes it, he's completely absorbed in it.'

'That's what I thought. It was like that in the Netherlands too. He never took a holiday. At home he never stopped working either. Sometimes it made me angry inside. A bit angry from time to time doesn't matter, does it? We always got on well together, we never argued.'

And so it became clear to me that there was something not quite right with their marriage. That was the impression I had got when I had first met her husband. European women, and especially men, did not usually discuss their personal affairs openly like this. Mir wanted to talk to me about something.

I finished my dinner quickly. And Mir copied my example.

I hadn't sat down in the lounge chair for more than a few moments before Mir had sat beside me again in the cane chair.

'I would like to talk to you, Minke, as a friend that I knew even nine years ago. You'll listen, won't you, Minke.'

'If it's to do with any argument with your husband, I can't, Mir, I'm sorry, forgive me.'

'We haven't fought. Truly. What is there for us to fight about?'

'What's the trouble, Mir?'

Slowly Mir Frischboten raised her head, and looked at me nervously, then she spoke slowly, also nervously: 'The trouble started a year after we married.'

'It couldn't have been money troubles, Mir?'

'No. The problem was with Hendrik. He worked like a horse. There was no way of stopping him. It seemed as though work and study were the only things in his life. He no longer looked after himself or his health. He was working beyond what his body was capable of.'

She stopped. She looked at me with her big eyes as if anticipating some response from me. Seeing that I was waiting for her to continue her story, she shook her head, bit the lower right corner of her lips, and then wiped them with a handkerchief.

'You don't know if you want to go on, Mir?'

'Yes, all of a sudden, I'm not sure any more,' she answered softly.

'Do you want me to leave the room for a few minutes?'

'No, no need for that. I'll continue. One night I found him sitting at his desk. His hands were lying in his thighs. His eyes were closed. He wasn't thinking, or working. His body was empty of any strength at all. You're too tired, I told him, go to bed. He turned his face towards me, and stared at me with a hopelessness in his eyes, and he said: "Go to sleep, Mir". Then he got up and left. He went outside, and probably spent all night, until morning, wandering around.'

'He had some problem that he wasn't telling you about, Mir.'

'He didn't need to tell me. It was I who knew it best. He had lost confidence in himself. He felt humiliated whenever near me. I had tried to encourage and support him so that his confidence would return. But he just turned in on himself more, and drowned himself in his work and study.'

'You didn't take him to a doctor?'

'There were four doctors, none of them could help.'

From her rather roundabout story, I guessed that Hendrik had become impotent. But I pretended I didn't understand.

'Look, I'm thirty years old already, probably the same age as you.'

So my guess that she had been three or four years older than me had been wrong.

'I married late,' she went on. 'My husband wants to have children, but he has already given up all hope. He no longer believes that he will ever have any children. Twice he has offered to divorce me. But that is impossible. I love him. He is such a kind and simple man. He believes that his work is for the good of others and he loves his work. And too, he loves me with all his heart.'

'You must tell me more clearly, Mir, just how can I help?'

'Perhaps you know a *dukun* who can help cure his trouble.'

'You mean his losing confidence in himself?'

'It's so terrible happening to such an honest and pure person. Even if it were someone else, it would also be a very sad thing.'

'A *dukun*?'

'Or some herbal medicines, perhaps you know of them?'

'Are you telling me that your husband is impotent?'

She turned the other way, then nodded: 'You must know, Minke, it's not

244

only he who suffers, but me even more so.'

'I understand, Mir. As for the *dukun* and the herbal medicines, I've never even thought about those things before. It will take a little bit of time to find out what's the best thing to do. How badly is he afflicted?'

'Totally.'

'Totally! That means you will never have a child by him.'

'You know better than I. You were a student doctor.'

'I'll find out about the *dukun* within the next fortnight, Mir. You go to bed now. Good night.'

I went outside and shut the front gate, then came back in and went around closing the window shutters and locking the doors. Miriam was no longer to be seen in the sitting-room. I put out the lights and went into my room. Tomorrow was Sunday and I would visit the palace. Perhaps the Governor-General would not be in Betawi tomorrow. Suddenly I heard a rustling noise. I quickly turned the electric switch behind the door.

Good God! It was Mir standing before me in the middle of my room.

'You've come into the wrong room, Mir.'

'No. I have come to the right room,' she said firmly.

'I will try to find out within the fortnight, Mir. Be patient. Go back into your room. You are the wife of my friend.'

'I don't beleive in *dukuns* or herbal medicines, Minke. And that's why I have come to you!'

'Mir!'

'Give me what my husband cannot give me. Give me your seed!'

'Mir Frischboten!'

'Do you have the heart to refuse to help a friend?'

'I understand your problem, Mir. But is this the way out?'

'I am not leaving this room. I'm staying.'

'I will move into another room.'

She jumped forward and grabbed my hands. 'Don't shame me. We have been friends for a long time.'

'Why me, Mir? There are many Europeans in Bandung.'

'I'd rather die than suffer the shame. You can kill me now. Or I will kill myself. What's the difference?' I could hear her panting breath, gasping, her face was white, and through her grip on my arm, I felt her hands shivering. Spots of sweat began to soak through her evening dress despite the coolness of the evening.

'Mir, don't do this. What will people say later?'

'No one will ever know unless you tell them.'

I shook her shoulders: 'Get hold of yourself, Mir, for heaven's sake.'

'I've thought this through fully. I would come only to you,' she stared at me with glassy eyes. 'You are my friend. If you don't agree, it will be the same as sending me to my grave.'

'You haven't given me any chance to think about it.'

'If you go through that door, if you leave me here, you will be humiliating me.' Her hand would not let go its grip on my arm. Her eyes shone with fear and tension.

And in my mind's eye, I could see Hendrik Frischboten, who had been so good to me, and to all people who needed his help. And before me I saw my good friend from nine years before.

'You're afraid.'

'Yes, I'm afraid,' I answered.

'I'm afraid too,' she said.

'You're not afraid, Mir, you're frightening.'

'You don't appreciate my openness with you. I don't believe you want to humiliate me.'

'That's never been what I intended, Mir.'

She hugged me with her body, refusing to let me go, shivering with fear of the humiliation that might yet befall her. The hissing of her gasping breath deafened my ears.

'You mustn't think I am some kind of cheap street woman. Far from that. Am I so low in your eyes?'

'No, Mir. You are a very courageous person.'

'But you hesitate, as if I am a woman without any honour.'

I almost told her that Douwager was in Bandung. But I didn't. Then I thought of telling her some beautiful story that might get her to think about something else. But no such story came into my mind. I tried to pull her out of the room, but she wouldn't yield at all: 'Don't throw me out. Don't shame me.'

And now I faced one of the more complicated problems of life, one that lived below the surface: the real physical desires of a person are only known by the person involved. She had come in honesty and with bravery. I was dazed and silenced . . .

'Mir! . . . ' I couldn't finish what I was saying.

The next afternoon I was received by van Heutsz under a pergola in the middle of the lush green lawns.

'You haven't written any short stories for a long time now,' he reprimanded me. 'Your short stories are a much more valuable and long-lasting contribution to writing in the Indies than your piece on boycotts, for example, will ever be. Are you going to let your pen-name disappear forever?'

'Managing the newspaper takes up all my time and energy, Meneer. Things are always happening, day after day. I never get the chance to properly digest everything that is going on.'

'Yes, I can understand that. Do you really think, Meneer, that your piece on boycotts was necessary? But, of course, you did think it was necessary, that's why you wrote it and published it. In any case, it seems that you have come here with something you wish to discuss?'

'Only a question that I wish to ask.'

'You have run into trouble because of that piece on boycotts?'

'No, Meneer.'

'No or not yet?'

'No, and hopefully never, Meneer.'

'Yes, hopefully you haven't sown the seeds of some new kind of chaos. What is your question?'

I told him of Princess van Kasiruta's wish to return to her homeland. He listened intently, and watched me without blinking even once. Perhaps this wild beast was angry. But it was he who invited me to be his friend. He will not swallow me up, at least not yet.

Suddenly van Heutsz clapped his hands. An adjutant arrived, dressed in uniform, all white with gold braid. 'Summon Mr Henricus.'

The adjutant saluted, then left.

I knew exactly where Mr Henricus lived. It was just a few houses away from my house. If he was already dressed, he could be here in just a few minutes.

'Why does the Princess want to go home? Isn't Java a much more pleasant place for her than back home? Meneer, this is actually an issue that is the Governor-General's personal concern. It truly surprises me that you have brought this matter to me.'

'So I should withdraw the question.'

'It's best that you don't continue with it. Do you remember the time at the Harmoni Club? The territorial integrity of the Indies! Not even the tiniest island can be left out!'

'I am sorry, Meneer.'

'It's best that you should know what are the limits, Meneer. In a little while, in a few more months, my term as Governor-General will end. There will be a new Governor-General. Perhaps he will be better than me. Let's hope so. But perhaps instead he will be worse. If that happens, you will have a lot of difficulties. What seems to you to be a very simple matter, and then flows out of your pen, could be taken very seriously by my replacement. I hope you will remember that?'

'Of course, Meneer,' and I fully understood that he was giving me quite a serious warning.

'It's important to know the limits. Simple people can become incurable drunkards just as a result of not knowing how far they should go. And tell me, Meneer, where did you get to know the Princess?'

And I told him how one day she had visited the office to ask for help. And as time went on I began to realise that I was being interrogated.

'Oh, I see,' he said. 'And, tell me, what do you think of her? I mean as a bachelor. Attractive?'

'The Princess is indeed attractive.'

'And so what about if you were to marry her? Perhaps that is a possibility?'

So now I could believe more firmly that Governor-General Rosenboom had also done the same thing to the girl from Jepara. And now van Heutsz wanted to prevent any trouble coming from the Princess by getting her onto the bridal bed.

'Why don't you say something? She is well-educated and would be a good partner for you during your life. People say that you seek a well-educated wife.'

'Your question has startled me, Meneer, coming out of the blue like that. And in any case, that sort of thing must be decided by both parties, and not by me alone.'

'So you agree, yes?'

'I have not really thought about it or given the matter any consideration.'

'Of course, of course. But you have, haven't you, thought about this. If that hadn't been the case, you would never have brought this matter to me. Even one of my Residents, no matter how moved he was by her family's plight, would never dare raise this matter with me.'

I could see Mr Henricus and the adjutant in the distance. They were headed this way.

'You didn't come here simply out of the desire to help her, did you? You have other intentions, yes?'

'Even if that were so, I would not need an order from the Governor-General.'

He laughed happily and stood up to greet Mr Henricus and the adjutant. They moved back and began to whisper between themselves. Then Governor-General van Heutsz turned to me: 'Excuse me a minute,' and he continued his conversation with Henricus without me being able to catch one word of what they were saying.

It wasn't three minutes before they had finished. Henricus bowed respectfully to van Heutsz, nodded to me, and left again.

Van Heutsz sat down opposite me again. 'Nah, what did I say?' he said suddenly, smiling all the time. 'You do already have ties with her family.'

It sounded like an irrefutable accusation he was making.

'I have no ties with them,' I refuted him.

'How can that be! If that's the case then why are the Princess and the Raja awaiting you back at your house?'

'Waiting for me at home?' I asked, amazed.

'Would you like to wager that they are not there?' he asked, challenging me.

'Yes, I'll wager you!' I cried, becoming more amazed with every minute.

'What for? I'll tell you now. The Raja and the Princess are waiting for you at home. They are no doubt waiting to hear what my answer is. Yes? Ah, my friend, neither the father nor daughter will return to their homeland while I am Governor-General. My replacement will surely make the same decision. Go home now. Don't let them wait any longer. And I suggest to you that you propose to the restless, homesick Princess.' He stood, and held out his hand to me. 'Good afternoon, may you have success with your proposal. I am sure you will meet with success.'

He turned away in military style and marched off towards the main building without looking back.

I stood and bowed respectfully at his back. After he marched away a few score strides, I turned and headed out of the palace grounds.

As soon as I emerged out of the grounds, I could see a part of the front of my house. I didn't go straight there. I decided to walk the long way round, through the markets. And the problems of the Frischbotens suddenly came to mind. Then, as if it had all been pre-arranged, like on stage, the following occurred.

'Tuan!' came a cry from a young Chinese, dressed in black pyjama top and pants.

I stopped and looked at him, and the youth smiled.

'Tuan used to be with Encik Teacher Ang?'

My knowledge of the enmity between the Old and Young Generation groups amongst the Chinese made me wary.

'Have you forgotten me? Pengki, Tuan?'

'Pengki?'

'Yes, I was the one who took you from Kotta station to my house to see Encik Ang who was sick.'

'Eh, it's you Pengki? I can't recognise you any more!'

'Where is Encik Ang now, Tuan?'

'She went home, Pengki, back to homeland. Three years ago. You're not in Betawi any more?'

'No, Tuan. I've been here two years now.'

'You're a trader, Pengki?'

'No, Tuan,' he said, guiding my eyes with his own to a big sign hanging outside a shop. It was in Chinese with a translation in Latin script underneath: '*Sinse* – Chinese doctor.' 'I work there, Tuan. I am helping out there while studying to become a *sinse* myself.'

A *sinse*! Perhaps he has his own way of curing Hendrik.

'Please come in,' he invited me inside.

With a prayer that I would find something that would help behind the glass wall, I entered the little shop. Inside there were rows of ceramic jars, all with labels, written in Chinese.

He offered me a seat on the wooden waiting bench. He sat down beside me.

'Have you been studying medicines for long, Pengki?'

'For these last two years, Tuan. Helping out, you know. Perhaps, you need something?'

'Yes, Pengki. That's why I have come in. Perhaps you know of a medicine that can help my friend?'

'It's better if you can bring your friend here, Tuan. Then the *sinse* can examine him. What's the matter with your friend?'

And I whispered in his ear. And in the flickering light of the kerosene lamp, I didn't notice any movement at all in his face.

'Let me call the *sinse*.'

He went inside and came out leading an old Chinese man with a long white beard.

'Yes, I can help, Tuan,' said the old *sinse*. 'But I can't prepare what is needed just like that. I must find out first what is the cause of the problem. All I can do now is give you a letter which your friend must take to the place where he can be examined. That is, if your friend has no objections.'

So they have their own rules too, I thought.

'Very well, give me the letter.'

The *sinse* went back inside, then wrote something on a piece of paper at the table. He came out again and gave the letter to me, without any envelope.

'Does Tuan know the bamboo house in front of the markets?' I nodded. 'Your friend must go there. Any time before five in the afternoon. On any day.'

'What kind of examination, Sinse? Can you cure many?'

'Such an illness can usually be cured. It is usually just a result of weakness. Except if there is something actually physically damaged that cannot be repaired. And weaknesses, if they've been allowed to go on for too long . . . well . . . If your friend cannot bring himself to come to that house, then there is nothing we can do to help.'

What kind of medicine is it that is practiced in a bamboo house without any guarantee of cleanliness? It is more properly classified as a kind of faith healing or something like that. But that is what is needed by the Frischboten family at the moment. Those who are dying of thirst in the middle of the desert will fight for even a dirty drop of dew. They will head off towards any mirage.

I strode off to the post office with the letter and sent a telegram to Hendrik in Bandung summoning him to Buitenzorg.

Van Heutsz hadn't been joking. I found Mir Frischboten entertaining the Raja and the Princess in the sitting room. Mir was very happy to see that I had arrived back. She met me at the door and took me in to meet my guests. She excused herself and then withdrew into another room.

Both father and daughter stood to greet me.

'Forgive us, Child, for coming here without informing you first,' the Raja began.

'That's all right, Tuan Raja, and please stay here the night.'

'I thank you in anticipation, Child. It was indeed our intention to stay here tonight.'

'It is an honour, Bapak. Mrs Frischboten will prepare the rooms. She is the wife of a friend who is also staying here at the moment.'

As soon as I sat down, the Raja asked: 'You have just had an audience with the Governor-General, Child?'

'You are not mistaken, Bapak.'

His eyes shone, full of curiosity about van Heutsz's answer.

'Are you allowed to leave Sukabumi, Bapak?' I asked cautiously.

'If I get permission, Child, from the Bupati.'

And so I understood how Mr Henricus knew that he was at my house.

I looked at the Princess, who was still sitting, head bowed, as she had been ever since I arrived.

'Tired, Princess?'

'Oh, no,' she answered, somewhat nervously.

'Let me check if the rooms are ready. Excuse me,' and I went out the back.

Mir Frischboten, helped by two of my domestic servants, had prepared two rooms. Their things had also been placed in their respective rooms. My servants told me that my guests had brought with them one basket of fish and another of jackfruit.

I came out again with Mir and invited them both to rest in their rooms. Only Princess went into her room. The Raja remained seated.

'You are not tired, Tuan Raja?' asked Mir in Malay.

'No. How far is Sukabumi anyway?' He forced out a polite laugh, then quickly wiped away his smile behind the tense corners of his mouth.

It seemed that he did not like Europeans.

Mir looked across at me, appealing for guidance. I nodded. She stood and excused herself, saying that she must go and prepare dinner.

'Is she your wife, Child?'

'No, Bapak. As I said before, she is the wife of a friend. She is staying here while she seeks out medicine for her husband.'

'I have never before been received by a woman, even if European.'

'Forgive us, Bapak. That is the European custom these days. They don't distinguish between men and women, that is, both are considered equal.'

He still didn't seem happy about it, although he did his best to suppress

251

his real feelings. His forefinger kept tapping on his knee, and his eyes were full of unease. So he had been struggling with his feelings all the time Mir had been looking after them.

A few moments afterwards Princess came out again, wearing Sundanese dress, and sat down where she had been before. And I knew then that I would never regret it if I married her. But why did she become so formal and stiff when her father was here?

The Raja looked at his daughter for a moment, then at me, then at his daughter again, and back to me.

'So Child is still a bachelor?'

'I have been too busy with my work, Bapak. Indeed I have even asked your daughter for help in starting a magazine for women.'

'Yes, she has told me.'

'So Bapak has given her permission?'

'And what is the use of such an endeavour, and is it a good idea for a woman to be doing such things?'

'Of course it must be a good thing, Bapak, otherwise I wouldn't have asked her.'

'Of course, you have good intentions, Child, but the situation is not good.'

'And if the situation is to be better, Bapak, someone must work to improve it. That is why I have asked the help of your daughter. There is no point in allowing the situation to go on forever if things are bad, whether for us or for others. There are things that need to be made better. Yes?'

'Mixing with just anybody . . . '

'With me, Bapak. Do you include me as "just anybody" too?'

'I didn't mean you, Child,' he said quickly. 'Don't be angry. Everyone knows who you are, Child. Where you are from and what you have done But the others?'

'No one would dare bother the daughter of a Raja, Bapak.'

'Yes, that would be true, if we were back in Kasiruta. Bandung is not Kasiruta. In Bandung every race is mixed up together . . . like . . . ah, what can I say?'

'You weren't intending to say "like rubbish", Bapak?'

He coughed.

'At the very least, Sukabumi is much quieter, Child. People still know how to show respect to each other. It's a bit like Kasiruta in that way. The only thing that is missing is the sound of the drums at night.'

Mir came out and invited everyone to the dining table.

And dinner passed without a single word being spoken. We also refreshed our palates with fruits in silence.

We went back into the sitting-room. Mir didn't accompany us. Princess remained silent as was the custom for a woman in the presence of a male who was not a close relative. She remained seated in her chair, with head bowed. Her father never once encouraged her to speak.

'Nah, Child, could I perhaps now enquire as to the answer of His Excellency, the Governor-General?' he asked carefully.

'Do you know Mr Henricus?'

'No, Child.'

'While I was with the Governor-General, he came and whispered to him that you and the Princess were waiting for me at home.'

'They could find out and tell the Governor-General so quickly?' whispered the Raja. Then suspicion came over his face. 'How did you find out if Mr Henricus only whispered to the Governor-General?'

'After Henricus left, His Excellency told me.'

'My God, so His Excellency is angry with me?'

'No, he is not angry. In fact, he laughed.'

The suspicion drained away. He sighed with relief. The Princess remained seated quietly. It looked as if she was under orders.

'So my daughter will be able to go home?' he whispered to his daughter.

Princess raised her head and looked me in the face.

'You hear that, my daughter!' he now spoke aloud to her.

'No, Bapak,' I rejoined. 'His Excellency has not granted his permission.'

'He spoke about us, didn't he?'

'No.'

'About what we had done wrong, perhaps?'

'No.'

'It's a pity you didn't ask what it was that we had done wrong, Child.'

I explained to him about the Korte Verklaring and van Heutsz's intentions to unify the Indies. He would take action against all sultans, *rajas* and tribal chiefs that he did not like, especially those who defied his will. There was no power that could stop him, except God Himself. I then told him about the *exorbitante rechten*, the extraordinary powers that had been vested in the Governor-General, the greatest powers vested in the hands of the greatest of the colonial officials.

He listened intently, and he didn't reject anything I said, or ask any questions.

'This year there will be a new Governor-General. Perhaps his policies will be different. Perhaps then you might have some chance, Bapak.'

'This year. I think things will be the same.' Then he spoke in a language I didn't understand, quickly and high-pitched, to the Princess. His daughter nodded, keeping her head bowed all the time. 'Is that all?'

'He also spoke about the Princess,' I said. At that moment the Princess lifted her face to look at me. 'About the possibility of her marriage.'

'My marriage!' the girl gaped wide-eyed at me.

'Why is he interfering in my child's affairs? It is nothing to do with him!' hissed the Raja. 'We are Moslems.' His face was red with fury. He grabbed

253

his cane and was squeezing it with all his strength.

'This matter is, of course, your prerogative, Bapak. Don't be angry. And don't let others know of your anger. That will only bring more problems.'

'Yes, yes,' he answered, then spoke rapidly and in a high-pitched voice to his daughter again.

Princess stood, nodded to me, and went into her room.

'And whom does His Excellency intend my daughter to marry?' he asked cautiously. Seeing that I was not answering, he continued in a growling voice, 'They tore my daughter away from me, and put her with a Dutch family in Bandung. They are trying to turn my daughter into a Dutch woman and an infidel. Now they want to decide who she marries. That's going too far, isn't it? God's curse be on them!'

'Not so loud, Bapak.'

He was silent. His eyes dashed about, looking over the room. Then he moved closer and whispered: 'Tell me, Child, who is it?'

'He didn't say. He just said that the Princess of Kasiruta had reached marriageable age. He didn't want the Princess to go home, that would only cause trouble.'

The Raja whispered a prayer. I bowed my head, participating also in his anxieties. Suddenly he raised his head, looked at me for quite a few moments and asked: 'You are a Moslem, Child?'

'Of course, Bapak, otherwise you and your daughter would not have been prepared to stay here tonight. Don't get too upset by all this, Bapak. There is still time to think it all over.'

'Has anything like this happened before?' he asked, half-hoping for something that would save them.

I told him about the girl from Jepara and her father, how such a young and brilliant girl finally passed away at such an early age. He followed every movement of my lips. Then came his voice, like a moan: 'I will not allow such a thing to happen to my daughter. Oh Allah, protect my daughter!'

'We have no power in this matter, Bapak. Even so we do have some time to think things through. The most they will do in the short term is pressure you about her marriage or keep asking who she will marry. I will help you all I can in this matter. Ayoh, Bapak, it's already late. I'll show you your room.'

He stood, leaned on his cane, and limped off towards his room . . . '

As I stood before the door to my own room, I became lost in my thoughts. In my mind's eye I saw Mir, and behind her, my good friend and her husband, Hendrik Frischboten. Lay no more claims upon my soul, Mir, Hendrik. I opened the door. I was right. Mir was asleep in my bed.

She awoke to greet me.

'We can't go on like this, Mir,' I said. 'Tomorrow your husband will be here. I sent a telegram summoning him. I have hopes that the Chinese *sinse* can help him.'

'He's just a *sinse*,' she said, belittling the idea.

'You yourself have already lost hope.'

'I have never heard of such an illness ever being cured.'

And I too didn't really believe it was possible.

'Maybe, but you two have never tried this before. You must give it a go. Who knows? The Chinese are an ancient culture, and with everything written down too,' I said, humouring her.

'That's just a hope, not a reality. It's late,' she embraced me, and in a moment I was gasping for breath again because of her kisses.

The next day I escorted Hendrik Frischboten to the bamboo house across from the Buitenzorg markets.

'In the name of our eternal friendship, my friend, rid yourself of all prejudices,' I said.

He was reluctant to go. He had no faith at all. We had to force him to go. Mir was on my side. It was as if she had suddenly developed an unqualified faith now in the *sinse*. And so it was that the two of us, bearing a thin, valueless piece of paper with unintelligible Chinese writing on it, entered the bamboo house.

An old Chinese man, just like in all the pictures, with a long white wispy beard, greeted us. He was wearing a black cap. He was no more than one metre sixty tall. He stood straight and firm, despite looking dried-up and thin. His lips were blue, which was a sign that he smoked opium.

After reading the letter from the *sinse*, he nodded and spoke in broken Malay: 'Which one is it, Tuan?'

I pointed to Hendrik Frischboten.

Without asking for any names, he guided Hendrik into a dark and stuffy room. I went too. Like a doctor, the *sinse* ordered Hendrik to undress. Bowing again and again to me, he also asked that I leave the stuffy room. He emerged from the room, dressed and neat again, after three-quarters of an hour. We walked home, via the other *sinse's* shop. Hendrik handed over a letter that he had brought with him from the bamboo house.

Pengki nodded as he read it. While he made up the mixture he said: 'If you do not feel humiliated to come at the times he has indicated, Tuan, you will be cured within a month. It's just a problem of a weakness in the nervous system caused by not looking after yourself.' As he handed over a bottle of liquid substance, he added, 'And you must drink this as indicated also. Three spoons a day. This bottle will be enough.'

How confident was this boy from yesterday afternoon in his people's medicine!

'How much do we pay, Pengki?'

'When he is fully cured, you must come and tell us. That's all. There is nothing to pay.'

'No, Pengki, that's not right.'

'This is our way, Tuan. Only if you are ever writing to Encik Teacher Ang, please pass on my regards to her. I often think about her. If I get the chance to return to my country to study, I will come and get her address from you.'

As we walked home and I asked Hendrik how the blue-lipped *sinse* had examined him, he just shuddered.

'He stuck needles in you?'

'So you know their way?'

'I've heard stories.'

'There were needles around my navel, and others down both sides of my backbone, below my waist. I think there were six. I was so afraid I would get infected. But the strange thing was that there was no pain. It was a different feeling, not really pain, more a kind of prickling or smarting feeling.'

'How far did he put the needles in?'

'I couldn't really tell. It felt as if they went just below the skin. But I don't know. Perhaps they went in as much as the thickness of a finger.'

'Crazy.'

'Yes, well let's see how good this crazy doctor's medicine is. I have to go every three days, he said.'

'You must go.'

The next morning the three of us caught the train back to Bandung. The Raja and the Princess had left earlier. When Mir had fallen asleep in the corner, Hendrik whispered: 'That old opium-addicted doctor has amazed me.'

'You're not going back then?'

'No, on the contrary. I think I can already feel a change.'

'Are you sure? So quickly?' I cried out, so surprised that my cry woke up Mir.

'What's the matter?' asked Mir, with a startled look on her face. 'What are you talking about?' she asked anxiously.

There was no one else in the carriage besides us. Hendrik Frischboten kept glancing at me and I also kept watching him. After a while he moved across to sit beside his wife.

'Why were you so startled, Mir? We were just talking about that strange Chinese doctor.'

'Oh, Hendrik. I thought you two were arguing,' cried Mir, while she embraced her husband.

I stood up and moved away. What did Hendrik's glances mean? He knew? But was pretending not to know? My knees almost gave way, and I had to hold onto the back of the seat. I hadn't totally recovered from my own shock when Mir had woken so startled and worried.

Hendrik took hold of my shaking body and sat me down next to Mir. He moved back to where he was sitting before. I felt a cold sweat all over my body.

Watching the two of us sitting there silently, Hendrik smiled and asked: 'Mir, why don't you thank him. It is because of Minke that such happy things are happening to us now.'

Showing just the slightest hesitation, Mir bent over and kissed me on the cheek. I could see that her eyes were glassy, as she held back both tears of happiness and worry. 'Thank you very, very much, Minke.'

Then she turned to look outside the window and didn't look at us again. My head was full of unanswered questions. We were almost in Bandung when Hendrik spoke: 'I will come down and stay at your place in Buitenzorg every three days – so I can visit the *sinse*. Is that all right?'

'Of course,' I said.

Hendrik and I went straight to the office from the railway sation. Mir went home by herself. Did Hendrik know what had happened back in Buitenzorg? I felt so ashamed whenever I was near these two very good friends of mine.

Fifteen days later I received an invitation from the Raja and his family to visit them at Sukabumi. They also invited me to stay the night. As soon as I arrived and after the formal greetings, I bathed. Then the Raja took me out onto the grounds at the back of the house. There were tables and chairs and a whole range of Moluccan cakes. I neither recognised nor liked any of them.

'Child,' he began, 'the Kontrolir has visited us, just as you predicted. He kept asking about the Princess. When will she be married? Do I have anybody in mind? If not, then shouldn't I be looking for somebody to marry her? What do you think I should do, Child?'

'Bapak no doubt has already formed a view on this. Have you plans for Princess to marry? Do you have a prospective husband in mind?'

'Of course I always intended that she marry a fellow countryman from Kasiruta. But she is not allowed to return home. And for some time now, while we have been in Java, I have not known what to do. We have been very isolated here.'

'Yes, it's a difficult situation. What about if the Princess were to marry someone who wasn't from Kasiruta?'

'But who? I don't know of anyone who is suitable and soon the Kontrolir will be here again asking about her.'

Anyone in my shoes at that moment, if he had been educated properly and was a gentleman, would have felt just as I did – that I shouldn't be there with the Raja, because, in fact, I had hopes of becoming his son-in-law. I felt as if I was part of a plot to force him into allowing me to marry his

257

daughter. It truly wasn't right or proper that I use this opportunity.

'Perhaps you should ask the Princess herself? Who knows, perhaps she herself has given some thought as to who would make a good husband for her?' I asked.

'How deep could her understanding of this kind of thing be? She is just a child, and a girl, too.'

'Well, she has had two years of European education in Bandung and seven years while she was in Ambon. Perhaps she has a better understanding of these things than her ancestors did.'

'It may be true that she knows many things that her ancestors did not know, but neither does she know anything of what they knew. She knows better the ways of the Dutch than those of her own people, those of her father.'

'From what I can see, Bapak, she is a person who is very polite, knows her place, knowledgeable and, more than that, educated. She knows how to carry herself and has always seemed to honour and respect her parents.'

'The Dutch education! She only prays when she is here with me! I don't believe she prays when she is staying with the Dutch family in Bandung.'

'No one knows better about such things, Bapak, than God himself. People do the best they can in accordance with their opportunities, needs and abilities,' I said, repeating the teachings of the religious scholar Syech Ahmad Badjened. 'When it comes to the relation between God and human beings only God really knows how deep it is. It is something between God and that individual. No one else will ever know, not even that individual's father or mother. Someone might always be seen to be praying but may have no real relationship with God, and, on the other hand, someone who is never seen to pray may be very close to Him,' another quote from Badjened.

So, as if I was someone who was learned in religion, I began dropping names from the great religious works. Then I ended: 'But I believe Bapak knows more about this than I.'

'Yes, I have known all that since I was a child,' he said.

'That is why it is important that the religious books be taught to the young, so we may all benefit from it when we ourselves have to make such decisions.'

He nodded his agreement, listening intently as if he were my devoted student. After I had been silent for some time, he began again in his aging voice: 'I have been giving this whole matter serious thought ever since the Kontrolir's visit. I have been weighing up all the possibilities and considering who would be a good husband for the Princess. No name or face has come to me, Child, except one. Just the one, Child. But there is one thing that worries me about him. Just the one thing, nothing else. I am afraid that perhaps, without me knowing it, my daughter could end up as the second or third wife.'

'She is the daughter of a king, a Princess, with a European education, and beautiful. It would indeed be totally inappropriate for her to be married as a second, third or fourth wife.'

'So you have the same opinion as me?'

'I agree with you totally.'

He seemed happy, pleased.

'It's a pity, however,' he continued, 'a prospective husband should properly come to me and formally ask for permission to marry her. If you were in my place, Child, perhaps you would also feel the same way?'

'Of course,' I answered quickly.

'In the eyes of others will it not be a humiliation for me, as a father and a king, to have to go the man myself and ask him to marry her?'

'Everything is determined by our situation, Bapak, whatever may be our real desires. A man travelling the desert does not sail a ship, and he crossing the oceans does not ride a camel.'

Again he was very pleased with how I answered. He went silent for a moment, inviting me to take some refreshments. He stared up at the sky that was beginning to fade. His eyes wandered all about. He took a pinch of tobacco and started to roll a cigarette. Quickly I fetched a box of cigars that I had brought from Bandung as a present.

He laughed happily and thanked me several times. He put down the leaf he was using to make the cigarette, and tried to open the box of cigars. I took out my pocket-knife and opened it for him. He smelled the aroma of the cigars and laughed with satisfaction. Everyone knows that smokers of home-rolled leaf cigarettes don't like cigars. Cigars were just a status symbol.

'It's been a long time since I have smoked a cigar, except for that time at your house, Child.'

'If Bapak really likes them I will make sure you are sent some more.'

'Thank you very much, Child, thank you.'

Then came the sound of the *magreb* drums telling us it was time for eventide prayers. He ahemmed and stared at me.

'It's *magreb*, Bapak.'

'Why don't you sit in the front room, while I pray, Child.'

'No, allow me to be Bapak's *makmum*.'

After *magreb* prayers, we sat down in their far too small parlour. Indeed the whole house was too humble for that of a king, even a king in exile. It was clear that van Heutsz was totally unconcerned about their welfare. (It was only later that I found out that they lived far better in exile than they ever did back in their own village.)

He didn't resume talking for some time. I myself was preoccupied with my own thoughts about the Princess. I was still not in a position where I felt I could honourably propose to the Raja.

'Of course,' he now spoke up, 'the Kontrolir came here as part of carrying out instructions from the Governor-General. Isn't that so, Child?'

'A Kontrolir would never do such a thing without having his orders,' I

259

answered. 'And as well as that, the Governor-General himself already told me his views about the Princess.'

'Yes, after you told us about that, I started to think . . .' He couldn't go on and seemed to be gathering up courage, 'I thought . . . ' He stopped again. 'Forgive this old man who cannot understand what goes on up there, Child . . . But I thought, forgive me, Child, please don't become angry with me, but I thought, yes, how good it would be if you, Child, were to become Bapak's son-in-law.'

If was as if the whole of humanity's happiness suddenly fell upon and enveloped me. I couldn't speak. What had I dreamt the night before that I should be given such happinesss? Had I done so many good deeds that I should be so blessed?

'Why don't you say something, Child? I hope you do not feel insulted or humiliated?'

'*Syukur Alhamdulillah*, yes, Bapak, thank you for showing such trust and belief in me. But should you place so much trust and faith in me, having known me for such a short time, Bapak Raja?'

'I have seen no one more worthy. Moreover, you already know her and she already knows you. Indeed I know she has both admired and respected you, Child, from afar. And even more so now that she has met you.'

'But what will people say, Bapak? You, a Raja, have been exiled by van Heutsz. And everyone sees me as the friend and a favourite of the Governor-General.'

'I have also given thought to that matter, Child. Through your newspaper, Child, you have helped many people who have been oppressed and exploited by those in authority and with power. None of that can be wiped away because of your relationship with the Governor-General. I have thought about all these things. The issue now is only what you yourself think about the idea. I have visited your home. I know you have no wife and live a proper and God-fearing life.'

His last statement opened the door to a new life for me. The Raja wanted us to marry as soon as possible.

In a meeting with van Heutsz a week later, he greeted the news by saying: 'There is no one who will be more pleased than I to see you married to the Princess van Kasiruta before I leave the Indies. Congratulations. She is a woman worthy of you.'

And exactly one week later we were married. It was a big event with many guests. Father and mother came. Several *bupatis* and other lesser officials also attended. One of van Heutsz's adjutants arrived by automobile to deliver a giant wreath of flowers and presents for my wife and me. All my friends came, including Mir and Hendrik.

There is nothing worth telling about the party. There was nothing extraordinary about it. For someone who had been married so many times already, it left no deep impressions on me. None. It was as if weddings had become a routine experience. Even so there were a few things that I will remember, at least three.

Firstly, my father-in-law, the Raja, was very depressed and saddened that there could be no one from Kasiruta at the wedding. Princess also seemed to be affected the same way. For at least a week they suffered this emptiness, an emptiness that would never be filled. They were far from their homeland, from their people, from the sea and air of their coast, from the beating of the Moluccan drums.

Secondly, I became the object of gossiped insults: Even his wife came as a present from van Heutsz, people were saying. It was an insult that did hurt. And it hurt even more because it spread throughout the community and there was nothing I could do about it. It would not have been proper to use the paper to rebut the accusation. There was nothing I could do but suffer in silence. And the insults didn't stop there. They found their ultimate form when people started talking about me as Prince van Kasiruta. That at least was the name that lasted longest. Others like Nalasona, or Dog Heart, were transformed by my friends into Nalawangsa, or Heart of the People. Other names like Haantje Pantoffel, which means The Shoeshiner, referring to van Heutsz's shoes, didn't last long either.

The third thing that happened was something that I would remember for the rest of my life.

It was like this. Mir and Hendrik Frischboten came up onto the wedding dais to congratulate us. Then after all the guests had arrived, I went down to talk to them. When I got to Mir and Hendrik, they both stood up.

Hendrik looked strong and fresh and his eyes shone. He shook my hands for the second time. He wouldn't let go, indeed he was gripping my hand with both of his: 'On this day of your happiness, I can also tell you our good news,' he looked at Mir, and she nodded in agreement. 'It appears that your help is already bearing fruit,' and again he looked at Mir, but she turned away. His words were like lightning striking on a clear day. Beginning to bear fruit?

'My help?' I asked.

'One day I will go back to that opium-smoking doctor and give him a present – not just one or two ounces of opium, but a kilogram! And for your friend Pengki too, the *sinse*'s helper.'

I shook his hand happily.

Again he looked at his wife, who then also shook hands with me. It seemed to me that Mir's eyes were glassy with emotion.

'Say something, Mir, don't just stand there staring.'

'Thank you for all your kindness and help.'

'It's a pity that we're in public like this, Mir. You should give him a thank-you kiss.'

His smile was so open and sincere, a smile that should have freed me from my pangs of conscience.

13

In all of the Indies I was one of only a handful of Natives who followed the official reports on the Indies economy. This information helped me greatly in understanding what was happening in my country.

Europeans dominated all major commercial activity. The lesser commerce that flourished in the ports and harbour towns along the Javanese coast was being gradually taken over from Natives by Chinese traders. Even the Arab traders were rapidly being pushed aside by the Chinese. The Chinese merchants were moving inland as well. There seemed to be only a few places left in Java – Solo, Jogja, Kudus and Tasikmalaya – where the Natives were able to hold out.

It was this information that made me realise why the Native merchants of Solo and Jogja, otherwise known for their penny-pinching, were suddenly willing to make large donations available from their treasuries to Boedi Oetomo. If BO hadn't come along, then the money would have gone to whatever other organisation seemed to suit their needs at the time.

The *batik* trade was centred in Solo and Jogja and was still in Native hands. The trade in *batik* amounted to several hundred thousand guilders annually. Then there was also the trade in silver and gold crafts. The Native merchants would fight tooth and nail to defend the *batik* trade from the Chinese. On the other hand the manufacturers of woven hats in Tangerang had all been successfully taken over by the Chinese, who now exported them to Latin America, as well as to France. Solo and Jogja were ready to fight to ensure that the same fate did not befall them.

What my religious teacher, Syech Ahmad Badjened, said was true: Trade is the soul of a society, Tuan. No matter how arid and empty a land might be – like Arabia, for example – if its trade flourishes so will its people prosper. Even if your country is blessed with rich and fertile land, if its trade is dead and deflated so too will everything be and so its people will remain poor. Small countries have become great because of their trade, and great countries have fallen because their trading life has withered.

This Arab, who had no Western education at all, had a wealth of practical knowledge and wisdom that was most definitely worth studying and respecting. He had also sent his sons to the university in Turkey where they had learnt to master several of the modern European languages. Thamrin Mohammed Thabrie agreed with Badjened's views. Indeed he enthusiastically added his own comments.

'The traders are the most dynamic people among humanity, Tuan. They are the cleverest of all people. People also call them *saudagar*, people with a thousand schemes. Only the stupid wish to become employees of the Government, people whose minds have already gone to sleep. Look at me. While I have been an employee all I have ever had to do was follow orders, just like a slave. It's no coincidence that the Prophet, May Allah's blessing be upon him, began his career as a trader. Traders understand the realities of life. In commerce people are not concerned with people's social status. They don't care if someone is of high or low rank or even a slave. Traders must think quickly. They bring to life that which has become frozen and bring into action that which has been paralysed.'

What interested me most at this time were the big *batik* businesses in Solo and Jogja. It wasn't only the people of the main islands of the Indies who needed *batik* but also those in the eastern islands, in the Moluccas, as well as in Singapore, Malaya and Indochina. Even in Siam there were thirty thousand people who spoke Malay. And there were those in South Africa! And in Ceylon! And Jean Marais, who could create such things of beauty, had to live in straitened circumstances simply because he did not have the talents of a merchant!

This year Europe and the United States were importing a lot from the Indies. Trade flourished and many villages were thus awakened from their slumber. More and more money left the towns for the countryside. In the Government there was talk that *rodi* should be abolished and replaced with a head tax – at least in those villages where money was starting to circulate widely. Things were more prosperous than five years before. The factories in the towns called out for people to leave their paddy-fields and gardens to sell their labour in the towns.

Who could escape from the tentacles of trade and commerce? No one! From the time of the womb until old age we are all caught up in the never-stopping traffic of commerce – from the nappy to the shroud.

I couldn't get these ideas out of my head. And then I thought: What if we established an organisation to unite all those people who were active in commerce, the most progressive and independent people in society? It could be a real power. From the village clerk to the Governor-General, everybody's lives and livelihood were tied up with commerce in one way or another – from every piece of fruit to every granule of sugar. And then there was the boycott!

So I began to visit and talk with Hendrik more often. He was a good and patient teacher. He spent the little free time he had explaining to me what I needed to know about economics and the law, but after a couple of months

264

passed and his time became even more pressed, he suggested I order some books from the Netherlands.

Whether the books arrived or not, I had already made up my mind. Those who were not tied to Government jobs, those who were independent, those who traded, who struggled for a livelihood standing on their own two feet, dynamic people with a practical knowledge of the world, these were the people who had to be united.

One afternoon Thamrin Mohammed Thabrie received me in his *pendopo*.

'So you agree, Tuan Thabrie, that such an organisation should be established. One that is multi-ethnic, that has Malay as its official language, that is not based on the *priyayi* but on the traders, on those who struggle for a livelihood independently – the free people – and that is based on Islam?'

'Of course I agree. It will then have a broader base than the Sarekat Priyayi. The only problem is finding people honest and responsible enough to look after the finances. The finances will be the life-blood of the organisation, just as they are the life-blood of home and household.'

'Why don't you take on that task yourself, so we know the finances will be secure and handled effectively.'

'Good, I will look after them myself.'

And so it was that the Sarekat Dagang Ismalijah (Islamic Traders' Union) or SDI was founded, with a Constitution written in Malay with Dutch and Sundanese translations. It was headquartered in Buitenzorg. My religious teacher, Syech Ahmad Badjened, was made President, mainly to look after commercial and religious affairs. There were several other Badjeneds on the National Council, including his son who had graduated from the university in Turkey.

The Assistant Resident of Buitenzorg welcomed this development warmly. We rented a building. We bought the furniture. The SDI now had its own headquarters.

Sandiman received orders to return to Solo and Jogja, where he had recently been active on other matters, to propagandise for the SDI. But he wasn't enthusiastic about the idea. He had questions about the SDI similar to those he had asked earlier about the Sarekat Priyayi.

'Am I a trader?'

'Ah, trader, or not a trader,' I explained, 'everyone who does not depend on the Government for their livelihood, but upon their own efforts, they are all traders. Maybe they trade in services. They are civilians, independent people, free people. OK?'

'Very well, Tuan. And tell me, Tuan, can I truthfully be called a Moslem?'

'You have never acknowledged any other religion, have you?'

'It is true that Islam has always been the religion of my ancestors, and of my family, including me.'

265

'So that means so-much-a-percent Islam, definitely Islam.'

'Is that all that is required of me, Tuan?'

'Has anyone said it is not enough?'

'That's not the question, Tuan. As a propagandist it is very likely that I will face questions such as these in my work. And I will be working in my home territory where everyone knows me. I am familiar with just about everyone in Solo, even though not always as close friends.'

'Of course there will be many who know more about Islam than you. You are a propagandist for the organisation, not for the religion. You can learn from them about religion. You must work out your own method of propagandising for the organisation.'

As soon as the SDI was registered with the Government and its notarisation published in the *State Gazette*, Sandiman departed for places unlimited, and for a time unknown. We inserted pamphlets into *Medan* which meant that news of SDI travelled to Singapore, Malaya, Indochina, Europe and Haji Moeloek in Jeddah, even though I still hadn't published his *Tale of Siti Aini*. News spread far and wide. And so it had to be, because *Medan* was still the biggest circulation paper in the Indies, next to *De Locomotief*.

Douwager entered my office, all agitated: 'Have you given enough thought to this idea of setting up the SDI? Has it properly taken into account the concept of an Indisch people?'

'The term Indisch will frighten many people.'

'Only because it has not been explained enough.'

'People will be reminded of the Eurasians, and then of Christianity.'

'We will call the Eurasians Indo. That which is of the Indies as a whole we will call Indisch.'

'Trade and Islam provide a broader and more compelling basis of unity than Indisch. It's not that I didn't give your suggestions consideration. I did. It was just that they don't seem to have a solid basis, they're too vague. At least I couldn't see what they are based on. Your concept seems more of an ideal, not something that is already emerging out of reality. Of course, today's ideals can become tomorrow's reality, but today we have to work out what to do on the basis of today's reality.'

'I'm not saying that I think the foundation of the SDI should not go ahead and I certainly am not going to oppose it. It's just that I want to know whether or not all our discussions – at least fifteen now – have proved that all the peoples of the Indies have to unite into an Indisch nation, a single people? Isn't it true that such a thing has to be struggled for, and therefore an organisation is needed to struggle for it?'

'I agree – all these things are needed. But not in the way that you have tried to convince me. Whether this new nation will be called Nusantara or

Indies or Insulinde, as Multatuli suggested, I don't know and it isn't my concern. That all the peoples of the Indies will slowly or quickly become a single people is, for me, not just likely but a definite certainty. But the method, Meneer, that is the point. And it won't happen just because there is an organisation to lead the struggle to attain such unity. The proper preconditions have to exist as well, such as commerce.'

'Commerce!' Douwager pursed his lips, holding back laughter.

'Commerce brings the peoples closer together.'

'The Europeans came here for the purposes of trade, Meneer, but always distanced themselves from the Natives. Indeed they often traded in Natives.'

'The Europeans didn't come here with the intention of trading with us. They came here with cannon and rifle.'

'Whatever it was they used, they were still here for commerce.'

'If I were to rob you at gunpoint, taking all your clothes and just leaving a handkerchief to cover your embarrassment, and then I left you one and a half cents, would you call that trade or commerce? And that is exactly what the Europeans have done here in the Indies.'

'You forget that these days rifle and cannon are also instruments of trade and commerce,' said Douwager, rejecting my argument. 'All around the world the conquered peoples are being turned into the producers of goods for the colonialists. And in some cases the people themselves become objects of trade.'

'It makes no difference. Commerce only takes place voluntarily between two willing parties. If an exchange takes place that is not voluntary then it is criminal theft and not a commercial transaction that has occurred.'

'But in this modern era there are many ways to force people to sell or buy something. Even in the most advanced country of America, huge advertisements surround everyone, like great waves in the ocean, creating new desires and wants so that people are blackmailed, and threatened – if you don't buy and use this or that product you'll suffer this or that, or you will lose out in some way or another. Sooner or later people start to believe it all, and are forced or tricked into buying something as a result of being confused and impotent. And it's the same with clothes. People are forced to buy and wear new clothes. If they don't everyone will say they are behind the times.'

Seeing that I was silenced and caught up in his comments, he continued with his harangue: 'We need to arouse an Indies nationalism. We need a political party, not just a social or commercial organisation. The Indies has never had a political party. That's what I have been talking about all this time,' he stopped, giving me a chance to think about things for myself.

I thought of Ter Haar, who had first introduced to me the concept of nationalism. But then I didn't understand. Now Douwager was confronting me once again, but more directly, with this problem.

'I can't answer you at the moment,' I said. 'The questions of trade and Indies nationalism are questions I will, of course, respond to later.'

Then I went on to tell him of the commercial situation in Solo and Jogja and Tasikmalaya, as well as the collapse of the Native bamboo firms of Tangerang, about matters relating to Sugar and land, about everything that can be brought alive if touched by trade, even the peaks of mountains, and about how money was now circulating more and more in the villages. I told him how there was talk of the abolition of *rodi* and how this would provide more room to move for the Natives. And how all of these things had to be pushed in the right direction, so that it was the Natives who would emerge triumphant, to be carried in the direction of progress, science, knowledge, and to discover themselves.

And it was Islam, I went on to explain, that had always fought and opposed the occupiers ever since the Europeans first came to the Indies, and that would continue fighting as long as the colonialists held power. The softest form this opposition ever took was the refusal to work for the Dutch, and so the Moslems became traders. This tradition had to be marshalled, brought alive, it mustn't be allowed to run amok without direction. This tremendous and powerful tradition could be turned into a force that could bring many good things for all the peoples of the Indies.

We could probably have continued and finished this discussion that week if it hadn't been for the controversy that exploded in Bandung. The source of the explosion was *Medan* itself. Marko, without my knowledge, had quietly been writing and putting in various news reports, most of them innocuous. Then suddenly there was that earth-shaking article.

Over the last few months Marko had shown extraordinary abilities. From being a cleaner and bodyguard, he had taught himself to set type. He started with the headlines but was soon a competent setter of text as well. Then he started to teach himself how to write reports. And he started to put his reports into the paper without telling me and without Wardi and Sandiman cottoning on to what was happening.

One day he handed over several articles to me. They seemed to have been written in a hurry. They were quite good, but it would have been dangerous to publish them, so I put them away in a file. He never asked about them. I thought then that he realised that they could not be published. He handed in seven or eight more articles of the same dangerous kind over the next few weeks.

After the seventh time, he came and asked me straight out why his articles hadn't been published.

'I respect very much your spirit, attitude, mentality and knowledge, Marko. But you must realise that if we published these, the whole enterprise

268

would be closed down without us achieving what we all hope for. There will be a time when your writings will be able to be read by the public, but not now.'

'Then can I have them back, Tuan?'

'No, Marko, they're too dangerous for you to keep.'

'Then allow me to burn them in front of Tuan?'

'No. These articles speak of values that everyone should know of.'

'Then what, Tuan?'

'I will keep them myself. Listen to me Marko. Governor-General van Heutsz has gone. If he was still here we could perhaps rely on him to intervene on our behalf if we got into trouble. None of us know what the new Governor-General, this Idenburg, wants. Everyone is saying that his main task is to increase Government revenue. He has never summoned me. You know that yourself. Neither did he invite me to the ceremony for his installation. You know what that all means?'

'No, Tuan.'

'So I will tell you. If the rumour about raising state revenue is true, then it is likely he will take strong action against anything that gets in his way. People are saying now that van Heutsz wasted too much money on wars. His debts must be repaid with these increased revenues. And the army, with all its unproductive soldiers, must be reduced in size. Do you understand?'

'Of course, Tuan. But none of my articles were about Government revenue, I swear it, Tuan.'

I couldn't help myself bursting into laughter on hearing how simply he looked at things. He didn't appear insulted. And indeed it wasn't my intention to insult him.

'But your writings inflame hatred of the Government and its officials.'

'But that's the feeling everywhere, Tuan. And it can be proved.'

'Of course that's the general feeling. But you would never be able to prove it in one of their courts of law. I am not saying that you are wrong, Marko. But the Government will always side with its own people who have helped it rule all this while. So you have to choose how you want to deal with the Government – as a part of a great wave or as a turtle that can be the plaything of the rulers?'

'Do I have to answer, Tuan?'

'Only if you want to.'

'I choose to be part of the wave, Tuan.'

'That's easy,' I said, 'then throw yourself into the organisational work. Make yourself and your friends a part of a great mountainous wave.'

And indeed he did throw himself into the organisation, like an ant who knew no tiredness. But his hatred of the officials seemed to have become a permanent part of his character. Perhaps he had suffered at the hands of officialdom even when he was a child, without ever being able to defend himself. And so it was that his article appeared that day in *Medan*:

A youth from a well-off family, though not of the nobility, had graduated from the HBS. He quickly obtained work in the office of a local business. His name was Abdoel Moeis. Twice every week he could be seen leaving his house, in white short-sleeved shirt, white trousers, white shoes, white felt hat, riding an English bicycle to the local tennis courts. And there he played tennis with his European and Eurasian friends, no different from those Europeans except that he, like them, had his own personality.

A local Native official of some importance was infuriated by the sight of this youth with his European ways and clothes. Abdoel Moeis, who knew nothing of this person's fury, continued with his ways.

It seemed he was not interested in knowing that in many places the local Native officials banned Natives from wearing European clothes, even if they had become Christians. People must continue to wear the clothes of their ancestors. Such a law or custom had never been formally decreed in Bandung.

And because this Native official could no longer restrain his fury at the young man, he ordered his underlings to teach the impertinent boy a lesson.

One day on his way home from tennis, Abdoel Moeis was stopped by a group of men. All the conversation that followed was in Sundanese.

'Who gave you permission to wear shoes?'

'There is no ban on shoes,' the youth answered firmly.

'But His Excellency the Bupati of Bandung and his Minister don't even wear shoes.'

'That's up to them. If you like wearing shoes, why shouldn't you wear them?'

These underlings began to lose their tempers and began to move threateningly towards him. One of them threatened: 'Come on then, insult Their Excellencies again!'

The youth Abdoel Moeis did not show any fear. He answered spontaneously: 'So if they don't wear shoes, I'm to blame?'

'Shut your mouth!'

And so the attack began. How did it all end? With his clothes torn and ripped apart, his bicycle lying bent and ruined by the side of the road, his shoes vanished to who-knows-where, he crawled in the dusk light to the local police station. The police ignored him. The youth crawled out of the police station, and was then helped by passers-by to the hospital.

Marko's piece was clearly an expression of his hatred for the officials, as had been his previous articles. The actual incident with Abdoel Moeis was secondary to these feelings.

The police felt they had been slighted. Commissioner Lambert came to my office, and threw a copy of *Medan* on my desk. He pointed to the report, which had been circled in red ink and asked: 'You permitted the publication of a report such as this?'

'Correct.'

'Who wrote it?'

'That is none of your business.'

'Very well. Don't you realise that this report is an insult to the police?' His face had gone a deep red, and he refused my invitation for him to sit down. He stood with his fists on his hips, as if he was facing a burglar or thief.

'So you do not believe that the report is true and that this incident took place?'

'You have insulted the police, I said.'

'And you know that this incident did in fact take place.'

'You have put a slur on our name.'

'And you have insulted the facts,' I accused as I began to stand up, fists on hips, in the same style as he. 'Mr Uninvited Guest who does not even know how to behave politely. Get out!'

He was shocked that he, a European and a ranking servant of the law to boot, could be challenged this way by a Native. But this lasted just a second, then he recovered his composure and roared: 'Do I need to teach you a lesson with my own fists?' while waving his huge right fist at me.

It seemed that the roar of Commissioner Lambert had been heard in the printery. All the workers came out. Marko was there too and he walked straight up to the European, and said in Malay: 'I myself helped carry Abdoel Moeis to the hospital. I myself saw him ignored by the police. So what are you going to do?'

'And this incident here in my office,' I said to Marko, 'make sure it is written up and published in *Medan* too.'

'Of course, Tuan,' replied Marko without turning around.

'There is no point in you having a fight here, Tuan,' I went on to say. 'It would be better if you returned to your office and prepared a case against us. That would show that you know the law.'

Seeing that there were so many people there, Lambert swung around and stormed out of the office. Everyone followed him out on the street cheering and goading him merrily. They returned to their work in high spirits indeed. We didn't actually publish a report on Lambert's visit to the office. But Marko did do some more research on the background to the Abdoel Moeis affair.

Marko's next report made the accusation clearly – it was the Chief Minister of Bandung, the Bupati's right-hand man, who ordered that Moeis be beaten up. Marko also knew that the Minister himself had received the order from the Bupati. But we didn't mention that in the report.

After that second report, all sorts of opinions began to emerge in the community. There were those who blamed Abdoel Moeis. There were those who blamed the Minister. The most sickening thing was that once again all the *priyayi* came out in support of the Minister. There were a few readers from the villages who wrote in to say that Abdoel Moeis's behaviour was not correct (but at least they didn't express support for what had happened to him). For them, to wear European clothes was to deny the traditions and religion of their ancestors. They opposed every example that eroded the authority of their ancestors.

Support for Abdoel Moeis mainly came from among those Natives with an education. There were only a few. What are shoes anyway? Just clothes. If people change the clothes they wear does that mean that their soul and body suddenly turns into something different? If someone went for a swim in the river naked, does that mean he no longer has ancestors and no longer has a religion? And no matter what clothes he wears, doesn't he remain naked underneath it all anyway?

The police did not press charges against *Medan*. Instead they began investigations into the attack on Moeis. Three people were arrested. Then the opposite of what was expected happened. The Minister himself laid charges against *Medan*. Based on my *forum privilegiatum* and the fact that I was only so many degrees removed from a *bupati*, I refused to appear before a Native court.

Meanwhile the three who were arrested were brought before a Native court where they admitted that they were under orders from his Excellency the Minister. The court was forced to adjourn. The Minister himself, as a high official and a noble, also had *forum* rights and could not be brought before a Native court.

Hendrik Frischboten urged us to continue our reports on the affair.

And with these reports the Indies began to learn that shoes are not sacred objects, they are not symbols of the gods or of the priests like in *wayang*. They do not have to be worshipped. Shoes are nothing else except a means to protect your feet from broken glass, sharp stones and dog shit. Wearing shoes is not the same thing as becoming European or Christian. They are not a symbol of how close you are to the Dutch authorities, so the Native rulers do not need to be offended and infuriated when they see another Native wearing shoes. They need issue no orders to have people beaten up.

This was such a small incident! Such a minor affair! But it made so many things clear. And the impact! Even while the trial of the three was still under way, the shoe shops were besieged by young people wanting to buy shoes. And so Bandung was full of youths defiantly striding the streets in their new shoes, knives hidden in their belts, ready for any attack ordered by the Native authorities. But nothing happened. A week went by and there were no reports of any new attacks.

The three thugs were sentenced to a three-month gaol term. The Minister was publicly reprimanded – by the *bupati* who had given the orders in the first place.

Marko was furious that the Netherlands Indies Courts were only able to pursue the matter that far. This village boy, who had been with the paper for just a few months, not only did not regain any confidence in the authorities but, indeed, had his hatred against them further inflamed.

A little while later I started to urge him to learn Dutch. He needed a weapon that would help him explode at the right time and place and in the right way. Without an understanding of Dutch he could become a volcano that destroyed his comrades together with his enemies at one and the same time. He took my advice and began to study with Wardi.

It was such a moving thing to watch those two, as unlike as heaven and earth in both education and origins, sitting there facing each other. One taught, the other studied, but leaving behind altogether the tradition of obeisance and hierarchy of their ancestors. This village boy did not crawl along the ground, and neither did Wardi feel insulted to be near him. Even though he was a Raden Mas like me. They were friends. They sat at equal levels, like older and younger brothers, in the European way. And indeed it was one of *Medan's* tasks to eliminate these stupid differences, which were made so much of by the servants of stupidity. So grow, my friend, Marko, grow!

The Minister suddenly withdrew his charges against *Medan*. But *Medan* did not withdraw and has never withdrawn its accusations against the Minister.

Douwager came to express his congratulations and to continue the discussion we had been having.

'Look, Minke, in the outside world man has already subjugated lightning and thunder, putting them to his own use, to power electric engines, locomotives, ships and other giant machines. Electro-chemistry is creating even newer miracles. And in Bandung, the city in the Indies with the most Europeans, people still can get in an uproar over whether it is proper or not for Natives to wear shoes! And what are shoes anyway? Just leather and thread! How far removed are these shoes from that nationalism which hides behind the stars above!'

'So you have changed your mind? You understand then that the time is not yet right for a nationalist party?'

'We still have much work to do just to create the right foundations.'

'This is now your firm opinion? In that case why don't you help us with the SDI then?'

'But I'm not a Moslem.'

'Consider the SDI as an organisation that is preparing the ground for the rise of nationalism, Douwager.'

'But nationalism cannot be founded on religion. Religion is universal, for everybody. Nationalism is for a single people, it helps define one people from another.'

'The conditions for the rise of nationalism will not emerge by themselves,' I said. 'Everything has to be fought for and built beforehand. And if so many people agree with this method, of building the SDI now, isn't that then the best way to do things? This is also an education in democracy for all of us. And isn't it democracy that will accustom people to choose for themselves how to organise according to their own needs?'

'But you do agree, don't you, with my argument, that a nationalist approach is the correct one?'

'Absolutely, Douwager. It's just that the time is not yet right.'

And it was then that I had to admit to myself that all this time my attitude towards the Indos had been unfair and dishonest. Racial prejudice, ancestry, had created in me a dislike of them. These children of the lowest caste of Native women and Native society had been able to rise to levels in society and positions of authority that were out of bounds for a Native. That's how I had felt. It was Haji Moeloek who had began to soften my attitude. But in Douwager's case, in his particular case, I found that I still could not bring myself to soften my attitude.

In all the towns along the northern coast of West Java the SDI had branches with memberships of between forty and a hundred people. In the mountain towns it was more stagnant. In Tasikmalaya, Garut and Sukabumi there were quite fantastic developments. Garut entered the history books with the first ever public meeting to propagandise the SDI. The first ever public meeting! An important breakthrough, yes, even if it was held at the request of the Assistant Resident.

I had an excellent new helper with all this additional work – Princess, my wife. So now I was not only no longer a *kedasih* bird that sings alone, but was in charge of an organisation that had gained an indefatigable new worker.

Princess threw herself into helping with the work of the SDI Secretariat. She was a first-class administrator. She would work late into the night correcting the manuscripts of my writings on the boycott, which were then distributed to all the branches throughout Java. Throughout all of Java! Outside Java we still only had branches in Palembang, Pangkal Pinang, Medan, Banjarmasin, Poso and Benteng on Togian Island.

Sandiman was no less remarkable. As soon as he was back in Solo he was once again harvesting the ground that he had earlier prepared, and indeed, harvested during the heyday of the Boedi Oetomo. Within fifteen days he had won over a big *batik* merchant in the hamlet of Lawean called Haji Samadi. And a huge branch sprang up in Solo as if whistled up out of the depths of the earth.

Sandiman continued on to Jogja and there too he met with success. Then he started visiting all the district capitals of Central Java and speaking to all the Native merchants, whether they were Javanese, Madurese or from Banjar. After that he shifted across to Surabaya, where he also had brilliant success. The Surabaya branch was not as big as Solo, but it was the fifth biggest after Madiun and Tulungagung. These two branches sprang up by themselves.

There was no chance of a response from Bali. Because of SDI's Islamic name, the courageous fighters of Bali could not be incorporated into the new organisation. The cannon and rifle had only just fallen silent in Bali. The clouds of gunsmoke had not yet been swept away. The tinkling percussion sounds of the *gamelan* had not yet resumed the people's celebrations of the quiet cool Bali evenings. These people, now conquered, had nothing for their offerings to their gods. And from the Colonial Army's barracks came only cackle and laughter at the expense of the vanquished.

From all the towns of Java where Native commerce still flourished came letters requesting that the local group be formally registered as a branch. The massive correspondence that was required was, of course, looked after by Princess. There was even more of this work following a visit from Thamrin Mohammed Thabrie.

'We must hold a conference to decide what we should do next, Tuan Thamrin,' I began as soon as he had sat himself down in a chair.

But he already had his own answer to that issue.

'Tuan Minke, living in Betawi I'm too far away from SDI Headquarters here in Buitenzorg. It's not good for the organisation. I think I should concentrate on looking after the Betawi branch, and hand the Treasurer's responsibilities back to the Leadership Council.'

So the Treasurer's work shifted to Buitenzorg.

The SDI President, Syech Ahmad Badjened, organised the Buitenzorg branch, right down to the setting up of sub-branches throughout the district. He no longer only taught religion. He also emerged as one of the key propagandists in the Buitenzorg area. I also became a propagandist, but outside the Buitenzorg region.

Then came our first test. The problem arose because of our Arab members, who did indeed have the right to join and become members. They were Moslems, residents of the Indies and, more than that, they were indeed free and independent people, traders and merchants. Their deficiency was related more to Douwager's concept of the Indisch nationality: a resident of the Indies, who, regardless of his race, lived in the Indies, sought his livelihood in the Indies, and was loyal to the people and nation of the Indies. The Arabs almost met all the requirements that Douwager had set out. It was in relation to the last bit that people had their doubts. It wasn't just a matter of their being Arab, it was more a question of whether they, like the Indos too, even if they agreed to the concept of an Indisch identity, could ever fulfil the requirement of loyalty to the Indisch people as a whole.

275

So the story unfolded this way.

In the program the SDI Congress had prepared, it stated that the SDI planned to act to advance Native commerce. The aim was to free the small traders and small producers from the arbitrary actions of the landlords and money-lenders, and to accumulate as much capital as possible so that new businesses could be established, to ensure that Native businessmen would not fall prey to non-Native capital. The money from the SDI's enterprises would be used to help the development of commerce, handicraft and educational activies.

Not long after the congress, a Native leather merchant came to visit the SDI headquarters in Buitenzorg. He brought a complaint that all the leather trade in West Java was being monopolised by members of the Buitenzorg branch of the SDI. He had no business left at all. He could only sell in the market if he was prepared to sell below cost price.

'Excellency,' he asked in Sundanese, 'was it to kill me and my family that the SDI was formed? All my friends are suffering the same fate as well.'

'How has this happened?'

'The members of the SDI have boycotted us, Excellency. It is the Arab leather merchants.'

'What do you mean, boycott?'

'They won't accept leather from us and they won't sell us any of the materials we need. All of a sudden they started approaching the village people directly and buying leather from them at just a slightly higher price than we could offer. We can't get leather any more.'

I went to Syech Ahmad Badjened's house but couldn't get in, let alone actually see him. The gate was locked from inside. I couldn't even see the front yard of his house.

Then there was a visit from a merchant who traded in produce.

'Excellency, I have come here as the representative of many of my friends, all produce merchants like me,' he said, also in Sundanese. 'We are unable any more to hire wagons to transport our produce. We can't get our produce on the train. All the wagons and space on the trains has been contracted by the SDI members. All of us are willing to become members, Excellency, two of us already are members. But are these others acting on your orders, Excellency? And if so what about our livelihood?'

I was quite worried by this new development. The whole purpose of the SDI was to encourage trade and commerce, but the reverse seemed to be happening. I was buffeted by feelings of guilt. And once again all I found was a locked gate at Badjened's house. I didn't know where he had gone.

The next day several members of the Leadership Council hired a carriage and travelled down to Betawi to see Thamrin Mohammed Thabrie. No Badjened came along with us. Our discussions that day went on deep into the night. Eventually we had to stop. We all had to work the next day.

276

The decision – the Buitenzorg problem would be resolved by holding a conference of the Buitenzorg branch after a campaign to increase many times over the number of non-Arab members. If this test could not be passed, then the whole SDI project would fail.

We didn't have too many propagandists. I too went down among the villages. But we succeeded. People from the branches outside Buitenzorg also helped explain what the Arab merchants were doing. People flocked to join the SDI.

The theory was formulated in some circles that it was the Arab merchants' long-term plan to use the SDI to fight the Chinese. The Natives were being used as pawns. All this could be traced back to my writings on the boycott. The weapon was being turned against its creator. This had to be stopped. It couldn't be allowed to continue. The Indies did not belong just to the Arabs. It was by no means certain that the Arabs would remain loyal to the Indies as their motherland. They may very well decide to go back home after they become rich or even half-rich. That was what the Europeans and Orientals often did.

We were able to hold the Buitenzorg Branch Conference. The Native delegates were in a majority, but the Arab delegates were such good speakers, it was impossible to refute their logic. The conference began at five in the evening and went all night, stopping only for *magrib* and *isa* prayers. It went on until nine the next morning, and still there was no decision.

What was going on? What was this all about? Could I cope with all this? Did all organisations have to go through experiences like this? I had never heard of anything like this happening in the Boedi Oetomo. In the SDI, the members all shared the same interests. But apart from these general interests that we all shared it seemed there were other, private and often hidden interests amongst us. It seems that amongst all peoples there are special interests that flow from our specific situation. This is true even when we come from the same house, let alone when we come from different peoples and nations. And besides this, there are also the private dreams that everyone carries with them.

I had committed myself to the task of building an organisation. I was to be a *dalang* whose story would be written by building a multi-peoples organisation as the first step towards the creating of a single people, a nation – I was *brahman* and *sudra* at one and the same time. In my imagination I had often worked out and mulled over all the things I would have to do. But it was turning out that there was no work more complex under the sun. My *wayang* characters were not made of dead leather that could be painted and decorated however I liked. They were alive, indeed a part of life, all reacting and responding to each other. I had merged the work of *brahman* and *sudra*, teacher and student, speaker and listener, messenger and propagandist. I was a peddler of dreams for the future, a psychologist and psychiatrist without a diploma, someone who tried to organise things while being out amongst those being organised. And all this in my own country, amongst people who ate and drank from the same earth. It felt, even so, that I was about to fail. I bowed my head in respect to those organisers who had succeeded, especially those who had worked successfully away from their home, in other people's countries.

The Islamic Traders Union was meant to advance Native commerce as a means of strengthening the position of the Natives. Now there was this power emerging within the SDI itself that wanted to push aside the interests of the Natives. Having Islam as the basis of SDI was turning out to be providing the opportunities for dispute. Thamrin Mohammed Thabrie's only advice was that we continue the discussions until we reached consensus. But both sides were there precisely to refuse to unite in purpose and instead to defend their different interests.

Was it going to be necessary to freeze the Buitenzorg branch and set up a new one? Wouldn't that set a bad precedent for the future?

A member of one of the other branches – from Banten – came to see me after the conference had been going for a full week.

'Sudara . . .' and to be honest I was amazed to be called 'brother'. It had never happened before.

'Are you offended to be called "sudara"? We in Banten always use sudara to speak to each other.'

'It is a good word, sudara,' I said and immediately started using it myself. He nodded happily.

'My name is Hasan.'

I grew wary as soon as I heard his family name. It must have shown in my face.

'It is true that I am from the family of the Bupati who so disappointed you that time. I myself hold different views than he. I myself was also extremely disappointed when I heard of that incident three years ago. It was a pity that I didn't hear about it sooner. I am here to offer an opinion on the troubles here, if I may.'

'Every suggestion, and especially those from members, is especially welcome. Please.'

'Our organisation is a Native organisation, Sudara,' he said, as if he was standing before the conference, which it seemed was never going to end. 'Indeed it is based on Islam, where everyone is a brother to the other. Which means that no Moslem should make things difficult for another. I don't know exactly what the law is if one Moslem causes trouble for another. It is a difficult problem. And it will always be so. Brothers with the same mother and father are often at each other's throat until their dying days. This has been so since the days of the Prophet Adam, may peace be upon his soul. If one Moslem fights with another, therefore, we cannot claim that they are

278

no longer brothers in Islam. But we have another measure – this is a Native organisation . . . '

I took him into the conference and introduced him as a delegate from the Banten branch who wanted to make a suggestion as to how we might proceed. In a clear and challenging voice, and in beautiful Malay, he challenged the conference like a lion in the desert: 'This organisation arose upon the earth of the Indies as a Native organisation, not as an organisation of all those peoples who wanted to do their worst for the Natives. There is no one, no matter of what race, whether a member of the SDI or not, who has the right to exploit or do harm to the Native people, be they trader, farmer or craftsman. If any branch sets off in its own way and deliberately starts taking action causing harm to the Natives, it is not a branch of the SDI because it is violating the Constitution of the organisation which we all have agreed to. The central leadership has the right to withdraw all recognition to such a branch. Indeed all the SDI branches around the country would have the right to take common action against such a wayward branch. I am sure, my brothers, that the central leadership will not hesitate to take whatever action is necessary.'

The Arab rebellion from within weakened and finally died out. This incident taught me a very simple but fundamental lesson. Finding a compromise and achieving consensus were not the only things that might be necessary – sometimes it was necessary to fight for the implementation of basic principles without being afraid that you might lose a member, a brother or even a branch or two!

We had passed our first test successfully. And all the Badjeneds left the organisation. Just in the way that I, Wardi and Tjipto had left the BO.

Medan's circulation continued to grow. Our imports of paper and writing utensils increased as well. The incident over the Arab members of SDI monopolising the hire of freight space on the trains accelerated the implementation of our plans to publish a magazine for the rail workers. And it turned out that its readers were very loyal, clever and critical, rich in experience, and full of interesting suggestions.

Our magazine for teachers was also warmly welcomed. They used much of their spare time to read and to write for the magazine. This meant that whether we liked it or not the magazine used school Malay. The material we published about the experiences and theories of educationists from around the world gave our teachers an idea of how the advanced peoples had been moulded and how they moulded themselves, how the younger generation was made aware of the nation's concerns and of the problems and challenges of the future, how the sciences were taught and practised in and out of school, how the forms and content of social intercourse changed as science and industry developed . . .

The women's magazine had begun publishing even earlier. This was something we were especially proud of. It was the first of its kind. When the Queen Mother Emma awarded it a medal, puh! how the stupid ones who had missed the train growled! They united to oppose us, to try to sabotage us at every turn. This was no surprise. Success always caused the backward types to unite against those who were succeeding. Princess, along with three other women, helped with its publication. She often headed off to Bandung to oversee things at the printery herself. So we more often than not stayed at the Frischbotens' house in Bandung. Princess and Mir were soon the closest of friends, although she never knew about the problem that the Frischbotens were facing. She never knew about what had occurred between Mir and me. Mir on several occasions wrote short articles for Princess.

In the midst of this activity and expansion Mir Frischboten and I were constantly worried by a gnawing question: Whose child was it that was growing now in Mir's womb? How would the baby turn out? Who would it look like? Me, Mir or Hendrik? Would it be Native, Eurasian or White?

I sometimes caught Hendrik stealing glances at his wife and sometimes at me. Why? Were these suspicions of mine just that, unjustified suspicions? I could tell from the look in Mir's eyes that she was worried and I often found her too gazing at Hendrik and me in turn. As for my own anxiety, my heart could vouch for that.

And Princess? There were still no signs that she bore within her any seed from the love between us. Every day she drowned herself in her work. And she enjoyed it. In facing all the paperwork around her, it was as though she disappeared into some other dimension, becoming blissfully ignorant of the world around her. Sometimes she even forgot that she was my wife and that as my wife she occupied a specific place in society. When she was concentrating all her thoughts on some problem or other and all her ideas and hopes on succeeding with it, her forehead would cloud over, and her eyes though wide open would see nothing that was before them. It was just her inner eye that was trying to capture the essence of something that was there in that other dimension. And if you heard a deep sigh and saw her breast heave you knew that she had been unable to penetrate that high wall that stood arrogantly before her mind's eye. Then she would look around with her big eyes for her husband. And if she found him, I would hear her quick but gentle voice: 'Mas, I can't seem to solve this problem.'

So I would go over to her. And she would then set off explaining what the problem was. We would become involved in a discussion. But I would be more caught up in admiring the perfect proportions between her big eyes, her sharp pointed face, her pointed nose and her full lips.

'Mas, you're not listening!' she would accuse me in Dutch, which was the language we always spoke.

If I squeezed those full lips of hers, she would reply with a pinch. 'That's a bad habit, squeezing people's lips!'

People said that full lips were a sign that their owner enjoyed the sensual pleasures. What about thin lips? I've never heard anyone comment about that.

And she knew that I wasn't hearing anything of what she was saying. All I could hear was the thumping of my passions inside me. Only after the pinching had gone on for some time could we actually get back to the discussion.

One day, or one evening actually, the following conversation took place.

'Here is a strange article, Mas. It's completely different from what you've always said. It says that the Sarekat Priyayi was not the first Native organisation in the Indies. It says that the first was called Tirtayasa and was founded in Karanganyar at the close of the last century. It already runs a school for girls, a co-operative and a mutual credit group.'

I explained to her the differences between modern organisations and traditional associations. Tirtayasa had indeed been founded at the end of the last century by the Bupati of Karanganyar, Tirtokoesomo. Its members were his own subordinates. It was not founded on the basis of a common decision and common interests, but on the basis of the authority of the Bupati. It was he who was now President of the Boedi Oetomo.

I continued that the key feature of modern life is the emergence of responsible individuals capable of making their own decisions and not simply acting all the time on the instructions of their superiors. Individuals now stand as autonomous persons in society. They are not just a component of society, as an arm or a foot is to a body, but a part of society that actually participates in deciding what will happen, and this lecture, which, if the truth be known was meant as much for me as for her, went on and on and became more and more involved. And she bowed her head, listening attentively, aware of her ignorance before her teacher who was no less attentive and no less ignorant.

These convoluted discussions became more and more frequent as well as longer and longer. And it wasn't long before it was no longer a situation of an ignorant student and a bossy teacher. We became comrades in discussion and debate. At first she just asked questions, then went on to rejecting some of my notions, and soon we had real debates taking place. In the end, however, it had the same outcome – she had to acknowledge the supremacy of her husband. And she was always willing to surrender, not to a bossy teacher, but to her husband who loved and cherished her – to a husband who was always full of passion for her.

Life was beautiful. Love, work, passion and debate seemed to form a never-ending chain into the future. Month after month passed by unnoticed.

Then one day I was visiting the Frischbotens in Bandung. I found Hendrik pacing up and down nervously in the front room.

'What's the matter, Hendrik?' We no longer used Meneer or Sir.

'This way,' he said, and he guided me by the shoulder into the house. We came into a room that was divided in two by a white sheet curtain.

'Is that you, Hendrik?' came Mir's voice from behind.

'Yes, and Minke's here too.'

'Is it you, Minke?' came Mir's voice again.

'It's me, Mir. Good evening.'

'Sit down there both of you. Don't go,' she was silent. I could hear her panting and gasping. Silence. Then there came a piercing cry. Why did Hendrik bring me into his wife's labour room?

'Don't lift up you hips, *Mevrouw*,' came the voice of another woman, 'the baby could tear you. Be careful, don't move your legs. Keep them still and they will stay beautiful, no varicose veins.'

Then came the panting and gasping again, then the cry. Then came Mir's voice calling out: 'Are you two still there? Oh, God!'

'Patience, Mevrouw,' came the other female voice. 'Isn't that better? Ah. Take a deep breath. Concentrate all your strength for the push.'

Suddenly: 'Minke, is your wife pregnant yet?'

'No signs yet, Mir.'

I glanced at Hendrik, and he was obviously anxious. Then I thought those unanswered questions again.

'Why don't you talk to me, Hendrik?' Then suddenly Mir stopped and let out a groan.

The normally-large room became claustrophobic with groans and cries. The white ceiling with its green ornamental iron flowers seemed to be moved by her cries.

'Can you imagine how painful this is, Hendrik?'

'More than you think, Darling. Hold on.'

But Hendrik wasn't as in control here as he was when as a lawyer he was dealing with all the cases of injustices and abuse of power that he confronted in his work. He was at a total loss of how to deal with the birth of his child. His child? Whose child? His child or mine? Perhaps within me, my manhood was crying out that it would be mine, my seed, my flesh and blood.

'The pain is more frequent now, yes, Mevrouw?' asked the woman in a rather mumbled Dutch. It was the voice of a recently-arrived Pure-Blood. 'yes, yes, it's every ten seconds now. Come on, take another deep breath – get ready to push with all your strength. Come on, Mevrouw, now!'

'Oh, God!!'

'Keep going, Mevrouw, don't stop. Don't lift up your hips or legs.'

The groans, cries and the gasping for breath stopped.

'Don't, Mevrouw, don't lift up your hips. Take another breath. It won't be long now, Mevrouw.'

'Hendrik!'

'I'm here, Darling.'

'Minke, are you there too?'

She didn't know that I couldn't breathe either because of the way I too was feeling her pain.

'I'm praying for you and your baby, Mir.'

'You're not praying for me, Hendrik?'

'Of course I am, Darling.'

Her voice could no longer be heard from behind the curtain.

'Yes, that's the way, Mevrouw. Good, good, don't speak now. Concentrate all your strength on pushing down. Don't hold back now, push, Mevrouw, that's it, push, push, push.'

'Uh-uh-uh-uh.'

I knew that Mir was now biting her lips, holding back the cries of pain. Uh, woman, it is with pain that you give birth to new life on this earth. I thought of my mother giving birth to me, no doubt the same as Mir was experiencing now. You risk your life for a baby that for nine months now you have been waiting and longing for. Mother, forgive me for all my sins. Bless the birth of this new being. Accursed are all those who say that mothers who die become ghosts with no real name of their own. Accursed are they. I curse them. They are low indeed, those people who are unable to appreciate the pain and suffering and risk of death their mothers went through to give birth to them. Ah, you, Mir, parts of your body will be torn and bruised by this birth. You will lose the beauty of your years of maidenhood, you will perspire the sweat of pain, cry out in pain, almost unable to breathe, all for your baby. Ya Allah, keep her safe and forgive her all her sins. Forgive her all her dreams, the unworthy ones and the grandiose ones. Without woman there would be no humankind. Without humankind there would be no one to praise your greatness. All the praise that reaches You, Allah, does so only because of the blood, sweat and cries shed by woman who, with body torn, brings new life into the world.

And I remembered the words of the girl from Jepara before she died, when she expressed her hopes that her sons would be educated to respect womankind. And you, Mir, stay safe. Do not die, because life is beautiful. Push your new child out into life. And do not die! No! Do not die!

The shriek of the baby from behind the curtain pulled me out of my reverie. A new human being had arrived. I straightened my posture and took a deep breath of the fresh Bandung air. From behind the curtain I could hear someone working hard at breathing.

'A boy!' came the voice of the midwife.

'Oh, God! Is he all right?' asked Mir.

'As healthy as a fish in water, Mevrouw.'

'Does he have everything?'

'He's perfect, Mevrouw.'

'Thank you, Oh God!'

'Quiet now, Mevrouw, everything is over.'

The baby was crying, unconcerned at anyone else's problems, demanding whoever was about to pay it attention, and give it love. All I could do was listen to it crying ... and who did this shrieking baby look like? A cold sweat broke out all over my body.

Hendrik stood up. He didn't move across to the curtain. He turned round, looked at me, and then sat down.

These were the most important moments in the life of my friendship with my good friends, Hendrik and his wife.

Whose child was it? I felt I would have to shout out the question to the baby at any moment.

'Meneer,' suddenly Hendrik was using the formalities with me again, 'You too are shedding tears?' and tears hung from his eyes too.

He took out his handkerchief and wiped his eyes. I did the same.

'Would you like to have a child too, Meneer?'

Lightning out of a clear blue sky would not have caught me more unready. I grasped for something amongst all those feelings and thoughts I had been having. I answered quickly: 'The great honour of womankind appears in its full glory at the time of birth, Hendrik. That's what moves me. Go on, go in and see her. I will wait here.'

He looked at me for a moment, then stood and strode over to see his wife lying in bed behind the curtain. I sat and waited but with my ears pricked to hear what was said.

'Hendrik, here is your child, the child you have been longing for.'

'As white as cotton, Meneer!' added the midwife. 'Congratulations, Meneer, congratulations, Mevrouw. No, Meneer, don't squeeze his nose like that, his bones aren't strong yet. A true Roman nose. No, not really, more a classical Greek.'

My heart felt empty and blank. And only two people knew why. It was not my child. I wanted to run, to run away from that room.

'Minke, aren't you coming in?'

'Of course, Mir, if you're ready!'

'Come on in, I'm ready.'

Hesitantly I too entered behind the curtain. The European midwife was washing the howling baby in a big washbasin. Her assistant was gathering the dirty towels, stained with the blood of the baby's mother. The baby screeched again and again. Mir was lying down with a blanket over her. Hendrik was combing his wife's hair. And – I don't know what the smell was – but I could hardly breathe, something was pressing in on my lungs.

Mir summoned me over close with a gentle wave of her hand. I held her hand, which was warm, and said: 'Congratulations, Mir. I join with

284

you in happiness over the birth of your child.'

'Hendrik's child too.'

'Congratulations to you too, Hendrik,' I held out my hand to him.

'Thank you, Minke.'

'Well, everybody seems safe and well. I must get back to the office, if I may,' and I left without waiting for an answer.

As soon as I got out of their house, it was as if I was running, carrying with me the blankness and emptiness that was in my heart. It was not my child. How I longed for a child at that moment! I now experienced the agony that Hendrik had once experienced.

'Quickly!' I ordered the coach driver.

And the coach raced off in the direction of my office.

I stared down at my desk. With my thoughts still on the baby, on Hendrik and Mir, I began examining the letters that lay waiting there. The one on the top – didn't I recognise the way he wrote the letter 'r'? Whose writing was it? But my memory wouldn't work for me. I tore open the envelope. The handwriting, with that peculiar way of writing 'r', was the same inside. I had known that handwriting for a long time now.

'Meneer,' it read, 'Governor-General van Heutsz has left for good, he and his pension. You are now without a protector anywhere on Java. There is no more special-friend-of-the-Governor-General status for you. Be careful, Meneer. Don't disturb things. Stop all your activities. Disband the Islamic Traders Union. Listen to this warning. If you don't, be assured, Meneer, that something will happen to you.'

There was no signature. It closed with a line of big block letters: DE KNIJPERS – the Pincers.

I was not in a mood to deal with this or any other kind of threatening nonsense. I called Marko, and showed him the letter.

'Read it!' I ordered, and he read it. 'Understand?' he nodded. 'The Dutch isn't too difficult, is it?'

'I get the meaning, Tuan.'

'So. What do you say?'

'No problems, Tuan. Don't worry.'

'What if they have guns?'

'No, Tuan. If they had guns they wouldn't need to send a letter like this.'

'How do you know?'

'They would come straight here and take action.'

'How do you know that?'

'From experience, Tuan. If they have guns, they are Government people, or people close to the Government, and they would be in uniform.'

'This is your responsibility, Marko.'

'Of course, Tuan.'

'Even if they have guns?'

'No problems, Tuan.'

I went on with my work, reading through the mail. There was nothing there that was at all interesting. Everything felt empty. What was it that I wanted? I handed all the work over to Wardi and told him that I couldn't work that day.

I returned to Buitenzorg by train.

The emptiness and blankness began to smother me inside. The scenery that flashed by could not claim my attention.

'Mir did not give you a child.'

'And not Mei either.'

'And Annelies, neither did she.'

I bit my lip until it felt it might drop off. Was I indeed infertile? I had never had myself examined. I had never been sick all this time. I had never even had a cold. But such a frightening thing as . . . could I be impotent? Had the infliction that Hendrik suffered now befallen me?

I found Princess examining the latest SDI mail.

'Home already, Mas? Are you ill?'

I didn't answer. I grasped her head in my hands and kissed her with all my might. It felt as if the blankness and emptiness inside me was driving me insane. How I longed for a child of my own.

Princess groaned in protest.

'What's the matter with you?' she protested. 'Let me go. There is a letter for you, for you especially.'

'Who cares about any letter!'

'Listen to me,' she said, still trying to get loose from my grip. 'We had guests earlier. Three Indos. They were looking for you. They didn't give their names. They made threats. They called themselves De Knijpers.'

'Who cares about the Knijpers?' I answered. 'Listen!'

'What, Mas?' she answered, as I covered her with kisses.

'Give me a child, Princess,' and then I embraced her.

'Who have you just met to make you like this?'

'Give me a child,' and I dragged her inside.

14

Branches of the Islamic Traders Union mushroomed in all the coastal towns outside Java. Its membership grew to over five thousand. We received several journalists in the office who wanted to discuss this development. Then reports started appearing in the press of the European capitals about how a new bourgeois organisation was emerging in the Indies that was the precursor to a future Indies nationalist movement – a movement that wouldn't be long in developing.

I have heard about your activities, wrote Mama from Paris. *You are becoming more and more important to your people. You must be more and more careful. You are moving closer and closer to danger. Don't forget what I advised you once, make sure you have people who can guard you properly. Don't forget, Child. This worries me.*

Marko had brought in several people from his village to help him with his work. There was no other way. I received more threats as soon as SDI began to get international press coverage. On the other hand the rich merchants in Solo and Jogja brought more and more contributions of money to the national headquarters for use by the Leadership Council.

I bought a two-storey timber building, made from teak, in Kramat Street in Betawi. I turned it into a hotel, called *Medan*, which was used by people staying over in Betawi on their way to making the pilgrimage to the Holy Land. We used the ground floor as a shop to sell office and school supplies and as the central distribution point in Betawi for all the *Medan* publications.

During certain hours Thamrin Mohammed Thabrie would be there to look after SDI business. After only two weeks, he received an order from his superiors to withdraw from all involvement with the SDI. He was faced with a choice – his job or the organisation. He had served the Government now for twenty-five years. Almost overcome with emotion, he said he was sorry but that he would have to resign from his positions to become an ordinary, non-active member. It was a real loss for us. But what can be done? The organisation should not be dependent on just one or two people.

The Leadership Council decided to buy or rent some ships. But the Government quickly indicated that such a thing would not be allowed. Even the shipping companies owned by the Arabs and Chinese, which had once transported the soldiers of the Colonial Army on their way to war, were now being closed down by the very same colonial power. They had to sell their ships in Hong Kong and Singapore at very low prices. Meanwhile the Royal Shipping Company, known as the KPM, step by step consolidated its monopoly over inter-island shipping in the Indies.

Others urged us to buy a printing press, but I knew better than anyone that most of the printing presses in the Indies stood idle for much of the time. The market for reading material in the Indies was now almost saturated.

Our plans to set up schools also faced difficulties. Half of the members wanted to set up religious-based schools, the other half wanted schools that provided a general education, and the two points of view just didn't seem to be able to reach a compromise. What was the use of calling the organisation Islamic if we didn't educate our children in Islam? But a general education was no less important, in fact it might be more important, not just in terms of meeting the higher standards of today's world but also so that we could understand Islam better.

There was no agreement, so we used the contributions that came in to fund some of the other non-government schools that had been set up by Natives and were already running. These included the school founded by Nyi Raden Dewi Sartika in Cicalengka, Bandung, as well as the Boedi Oetomo schools, and those too of the Jamiatul Khair. And we also used some of the money to fund our legal aid work.

Still the SDI was unable to set up its own schools.

Meanwhile fighting had broken out in several towns between gangs of Indo youths, under the banner of the Knijpers, and SDI youth, mostly Marko's people. Marko himself had been involved in one fight. The Knijpers had attacked an SDI group with knuckle-dusters. One of Marko's youths suffered a broken rib. Meanwhile the Knijpers disappeared without a trace.

None of the papers, including *Medan*, reported these incidents, hoping that the fighting might not spread. In a report issued by the SDI leadership we argued that the Indos weren't simply motivated by prejudice but were fighting to prevent any real advance in the position of the Natives.

I received a visit from Douwager, who expressed his concern and regret that this fighting – which he referred to as ridiculous and indefensible – should be occurring.

'It's a fact of life now, Mr Douwager,' I answered. 'If the Indos had been united in the way that you hoped for then I think the first thing they would have done is to act to oppress the Natives, just as they have done in the Transvaal Republic and the Oranje Vrijstaat in South Africa – oppression for oppression's sake. It reflects their psychology – they hate having Native blood flow inside them, something that happened to them that no one ever

288

consulted them about. It's a part of their mentality that is affected by their frustrated desire to be Pure-Bloods.'

'That's a bit extreme,' he answered unhappily. 'The world is not heaven and there will always be evil people, from all races. Not just from among the Indos. Anyway, we should be using the term Indisch, not Indo. I thought we had agreed to use the term Indisch for all the people of the Indies . . .'

'I was talking about the Indos in particular.'

We found no way out of our disagreements.

I was worried that I had become blind as to what was going on in the Government. What was being discussed in the Governor-General's circles? The officials of the State Secretariat never visited me any more. Idenburg himself never summoned me.

I could not afford to let this ignorance continue any longer.

When Sandiman arrived back in Bandung I ordered him to find work as a waiter or gardener at the palace. He had no success. Marko also failed. Then the Patih of Meester Cornelis offered his nephew for the work. He worked there for three months and was then caught looking through some papers. They found out he understood Dutch. He was dismissed. The Patih was also pensioned off and he returned to his village.

Through Wardi I asked Douwager to act as intermediary with the Knijpers to see if he could cool things down a bit. It turned out that he had already tried. And it was from him that I found out that their leader was Robert Suurhof. And it was also confirmed for us that the group wasn't just motivated by racial hatred. It was receiving funds from some mysterious organisation about which we couldn't find out anything, except that its task was to ensure that no one except Europeans would have any success in establishing major businesses. So it became clear why it was only the Natives who were arrested whenever there were fights.

The Knijpers were active throughout West Java wherever there were active SDI branches. The smaller the town, the more afraid people were of the Knijpers, who were brought in from Bandung and Betawi armed with knives and sickles. Among them were also to be found Ambonese, Menadonese and even Javanese.

There were no signs yet of the problem spreading to East and Central Java. The Solo SDI branch announced that if the Knijpers turned up in Solo the Mangkunegaran Legion would act against them without mercy. They were prepared to move to wipe out the Knijpers, whatever loss of life was involved. They sent a group of Legion soldiers to me in Bandung offering to start a campaign to get rid of the Knijpers. There were more and more fights, but still there were no reports in the papers. No matter how many they mobilised the Knijpers were always outnumbered. Then soldiers in civvies started to help out their fellow Indos.

I had no choice but to seek an audience with the Assistant Resident about these developments. I gave him a list of the incidents, the dates and places.

'The SDI, Your Excellency, in accord with its Constitution, has never intended to contravene the law or cause trouble. We only aimed to raise the welfare and prosperity of the Natives, thereby assisting the Government in raising revenue. So we hope that Your Excellency will be prepared to intervene to bring to a halt the activities of the Knijpers. We promise not to start any fight, and indeed we never have started any of the fights. We have only been defending ourselves!'

The Assistant Resident for Priangan region just nodded and listened. He never said a word. He just shook my hand when I arrived and shook my hand again when I departed.

We had to find our own answer to this problem. Wherever there were SDI branches we began self-defence classes. *Pencak Silat* classes sprung up everywhere, but with the proviso that no weapons were used.

The Government did not move to help us. We had to help ourselves.

There was one big battle near the Bandung railway station one day. I had just arrived on the train. Marko was there to meet me and ordered me to move away behind the train and to leave the station by some other exit. The Knijpers were waiting at the exit gate shouting as if they were insane: 'Where's Minke! Where's his snout! Drag him out!'

The Knijpers didn't understand the situation they were in. They didn't realise that I had good relations with the railworkers because of the magazine we published for them. The railworkers moved to disperse the Knijpers, who then went on the attack. A huge fight ensued. Using all sorts of railway equipment and tools, the railworkers defended themselves and soon were also on the attack. Blood was flowing everywhere. Some police arrived but just stood there open-mouthed not knowing who to act against. They weren't going to attack the Knijpers, but neither could they move against the workers who were only defending their workplace.

So the fighting continued. One by one the Knijpers were put out of action as they came into contact with a spanner or a crowbar. The fighting ended as the Knijpers started grabbing up their fallen comrades.

This incident wasn't reported in the press either but it did bring an end to the activities of the Knijpers.

The SDI could breathe easily again. Except that we never came forward with any further proposals, like the one to buy ships, that could threaten European control over big business.

Whenever I had the chance, when things were quiet, I would try to understand why Mama's businesses never suffered this kind of harassment. Perhaps because the SDI was a big movement while Mama just worked quietly away without frightening the Europeans?

290

Frischboten couldn't answer this question either.

'This is a new phenomenon,' he said. 'There's nothing like this discussed in any book. We have to study it more closely,' he said, 'and we must study it carefully. If we come to the wrong conclusions we could end up in big trouble.'

He had asked me several times to come and visit them at their home. Mir missed me, he said. And it was true, I hadn't been to see them for quite some time. Mir's greetings were always like a spear that pierced through my heart. I knew she didn't mean any harm. But it was a torture I could hardly bear: 'Is Princess pregnant?'

My wife still showed no signs of being with child. And so I now faced a personal problem of my own: Was I a failure as a man, despite being a lover of women – a true philogynist?

It was only the huge amount of work I had to deal with that made me forget these personal problems. The SDI was another new child that I had to look after. It needed never-ending care and attention and protection.

There were no more reports in the international press about SDI, but it kept on growing and growing, turning into a giant tree with fifty thousand members. No European organisation had ever grown to that size in the Indies.

The art of self-defence flourished throughout West Java, just in case it become necessary once again to confront the Knijpers. We continued to assist some of the non-government schools. Requests for legal assistance in overcoming cases of injustice flooded onto Frischboten's desk. *Medan*'s circulation continued to increase, though not in leaps and bounds, but steadily. A comradeship started to develop among the membership. Native commerce blossomed wherever there were SDI branches. Rivalry among Native traders was replaced with co-operation.

And the activities of the Knijpers had stopped as if whisked suddenly away by a whirlwind. That meant that they would re-emerge later in some new form.

In any case, the organisation had passed its second test without injury.

I conducted several tours around Java to observe the organisation up close. Either Sandiman or Marko always went with me. Neither of them would let me travel by myself. So I was like a maharajah inspecting his realm. Everywhere I went the people came out to pay their respects and honour me. That's what it was like! Multatuli had once dreamt of becoming a white emperor in the Indies. But he never had the chance to witness how the people greeted me. Everywhere!

Don't lose your balance! I cried out to myself, reminding myself of the dangers. Behind honour, there lay in wait annihilation. Behind life, death. Behind greatness, ruin. Behind unity, division. And behind every show of

291

respect, a curse. So the best way was the middle way. Neither honour nor destruction. The middle way – the road to balance, to survival.

And this organisation had to be able to create the foundations for even further advance. It was not an end in itself, but a means to an end. It was not the ultimate destination, just a starting point. Everywhere I went I had to refuse the offer of titles. I had to order people not to squat or kneel before me. We were aiming for a new society, where everyone was equal as human beings.

'Why does Sudara still use the title of Raden Mas?'

'Only to ensure that I retain my rights to *forum privilegiatum*, so they can't haul me up before some Native court where I can't defend myself.'

And the term 'sudara', began to replace all the other forms of address that had hitherto existed. One Moslem was the brother, sudara, of all others.

Princess never accompanied me on any of my journeys. Neither Marko nor Sandiman would allow it. And even at home there were always seven fighters from Banten on guard. They all wanted to ensure our safety, husband and wife.

On every tour there was always somebody – once three in one tour – who proposed that I marry their prettiest daughter. The reason – so that I might leave my seed amongst their family. And so I had to become a teacher who taught that it was not blood or ancestry that determined whether a person would be successful or not. Rather it was a question of the education he received from those around him and a question of his own determination. Success was not a gift from the gods, but a result of of hard work and study.

This wrong view about blood and ancestry had such strong roots in the literature of Java. The Mahabarata and Bharatayuddha provided nothing to grab hold of for those who wanted to enter the modern era. These great epics had become obstacles to the people's advancement. These century-old teachings had lost touch with real life. They did not teach how rice was planted, or houses built, or how it was that people must sell what they produce. They only taught about fighting, and how good it was to become a lover of the gods, and thus further and further away from being human.

A pathetic people, Herbert de la Croix had said. For me too it was pathetic. This people waited for the Gong, the Messiah, the Mahdi, the Just King. And he whom they awaited never came. That power that could change everything and all the prevalent thinking never arrived. Every time somebody emerged claiming the mantle of the Just King, from whatever village, wearing whatever kind of cloak and *fez*, he was always welcomed and hailed as saviour. Then the people would return to passivity, though never tired of waiting for the new Messiah. And Minke is no saviour, neither is it his work. At the most, I am a drum that introduces some disharmony into the melody.

Wherever I went, I came across such superstitious thinking, thinking that had lost touch with even the most basic of realities.

'Sudara, this is what I think: It is best that this branch of the SDI doesn't accept any more members, because we have already reached the figure of – '

'Why can't you go beyond that figure?'

'The number nine is a perfect number, Sudara. If we go beyond it by one, there we arrive at the emptiness of zero, only having to start over again from one.'

Or: 'There is no way we can hold our branch conference during this coming month, Sudara. We can't find any auspicious days, not on the Javanese calendar either. In fact, the month is riddled with unlucky and inauspicious days.'

'Has Sudara ever heard of the Roman Empire?' I replied that time.

'No, I have only heard of Rum from the dramas.'

'Rum is the city of Constantinople; Istanbul it is called now. It used to be called Eastern Rome. Now the Roman Empire dominated the world for almost eight hundred years. And they never bothered about looking for auspicious days or any such thing.' Perhaps I was wrong about this but that was what I told them. And so I had also to tell them a little about the Roman Empire, and about Julius Caesar, whose greatness was such that even the rulers of today still used his name as their title, such as Kaiser and Czar.

In another branch I came across this kind of Javanism: 'There is no way the Knijpers will ever come around our branch, Sudara. We have quite a few members whose powers make them invulnerable. They will tear apart anything like the accursed Knijpers.'

And so patiently and with great caution I had to explain that in the modern era those with invulnerability were no longer the objects of special admiration. We were aiming for a democratic society where nobody stood above another. There were no special people, who stood closer or were the special beloved of the gods or of God.

'See, Sudara, if those with invulnerability were so special, we would not have continually been defeated by the colonial armies. It's not that I don't believe in invulnerability. I do. But in the modern era, the position of such people is no more than that of a magician. As invulnerable as anyone might be, he is still bound by the earth, nature and his fellow human beings. And it is the organisation of people together that now looks after people's interests and unites them in defence of those interests.'

Such explanations were not really in tune with many people's sensitivities. They didn't depict a world of supermen in which they could immerse themselves. But this Javanism was potentially dangerous for any future democratic society. Every tendency for people to be elevated to the status of gods was a danger to this endeavour. Explanations had to be presented sensitively and gently because the new ideas went to the very heart of Javanism, those beliefs that had become so embedded in people's conscious-ness over centuries of colonisation.

293

Excuse me for using the term Javanism. Perhaps it offends some people. But what can I do? I couldn't find any other term. Of course not every Javanese is a Javanist. And not all Javanists are even Javanese. It seems that many Indos are Javanists as well.

Every aspect of life had come under the influence of Javanism. Words, for example, had been made into mantras. They were considered to have their origins with powers above humankind, and not with social and economic life. They were not seen to come from an agreement in society to make sacred some object or situation, a symbol or concept. These words were looked upon as some kind of supernatural acronyms, freed from semantics, cut off from their etymology, severed even from the word's own meaning. This people of mine had become isolated from the development of science and modern knowledge, deliberately isolated by their European conquerors. They were the residents of colonialism's special nature reserve.

So it was one day that a young leader from one of the sub-branches once challenged me: 'Just think, Sudara, just think. There is no way we can defend ourselves from these latest insults. They are saying that the word *sarekat* comes from the two Javanese words *sare* and *jepat*, meaning "sleep" and "erect". So they say now that the Sarekat is an organisation whose only activity is swapping wives and beds. They say it is an organisation of the devil. How can we answer this?'

So my journeys through Java not only comprised accepting half the honour bestowed upon me. It also meant entering the jungle that was Javanism. And the torch I took to show the way? Small and weak. No one knew better than I that my knowledge and wisdom was hardly sufficient for this task. Sometimes I asked myself whether there was anyone else who would undertake such a strange task as this? So far there was no one else but me. And there was always the possibility that I might lose my way in this jungle. My torch might go out. And doing this kind of work based on my little knowledge and wisdom alone made it all a very personal endeavour. There was a great danger that people may lose their faith and trust in me, if I were to offend this Javanism of theirs.

Syech Ahmad Badjened had been unable to give me any advice based on religious teachings. He didn't know anything about Javanism. He only knew about faith and superstition, *taqwa* and *musyrik*. He did tell me about a religious movement aimed at freeing religion from superstition, mysticism and other burdens of history, across the seas in some other country. But I never found out any more about it.

In this kind of work, I could openly grope about in the dark. There were no models to follow – I was pioneering the way and thus would be making many mistakes. Mistakes, yes, that was for certain.

Numbers, days, even the hour, the syllables of a person's name, the year, month, the points of the compass were all given a numerical value in

Javanism. Then they would be added together in some combination or another and the result used to foretell what would happen or to decide what shouldn't happen. No one had ever sat down and figured out if all these predictions had actually come true. And the predictions continued. All of this had the same origin – the refusal to face reality, the unwillingness to think for oneself. They were like Sastro Kassier, who when faced with what seemed like impossible difficulties, surrendered himself to the supernatural, thereby not having to fight back against his situation. Once you pawn your intelligence and power of thought, putting it in the grip of the supernatural, it, like false teeth, can suffer no decay.

How do you actually lead people who live in a world of ideas rusted over by Javanism? Especially when they themselves still admire this rust? There is no other way than to approach things as politely as possible, peeling off one layer this year, and one layer the next. For how many years would it have to go on? I didn't know.

The chairman of the branch in Pemalang was someone I had known when I was a child. He was two years older than me.

'*Dik*, ("little brother"), he called me, 'Why do we have to use Malay?'

'In branch meetings where everyone understands Javanese, there is no need to use Malay. But at congresses and at the national level or when you're communicating with the national level, you must use Malay.'

'Why should Javanese be subordinated to Malay?'

'You have to be practical, Mas. In these times whatever is impractical will be pushed aside. Javanese is not practical. All the levels it contains are just pretentious ways of allowing people to emphasise their status. Malay is simpler. The organisation doesn't need statements as to everyone's social status. In any case, all members are equal. No one is lesser or greater than another.'

'But Javanese has a richer literature. It has a greatness because of that which Malay does not have.'

'You are not mistaken. When the Javanese held sway over all the islands of Nusantara the language of diplomacy was also Javanese. But that time has passed. The times have changed and so have the demands of the times. During the time that the foreigners have controlled the islands, it has not been Javanese that has been the language of diplomacy, but Malay. Our organisation is not a Javanese organisation, but an Indies organisation.'

'But the Javanese members are in a majority.'

'The Javanese don't have to spend so much effort and time to learn Malay. It comes easily to them, if they don't know it already. On the other hand if we required the other peoples to learn Javanese, it would take them years and years to master it. We make the practical choice. And what harm is there if we Javanese let go of the greatness and richness of the past, a past that is no longer in accord with the needs of our age? For the unity of the Indies!'

'But the other peoples outside Java, they have no history or heritage of any worth.'

'Oh, no! Everyone has such history and heritage. In any case, our business is not the past but the present. The modern present. A time where people calculate what is useful and what is not, and discard what is not useful. It is a time when you go forward or you stagnate. And when everything is calculated precisely.' And I prayed to myself that he would not ask me what the word 'modern' actually meant.

A long debate ensued. He was too firmly committed to his Javaneseness. I failed. Well, what could I do? Anyway he obeyed the rules of the organisation. But what would happen later? We would split no doubt, and the organisation would be safe.

Dropping in on this friend of mine in Pemalang became a habit. Even though he too had had a European education, he could not or would not free himself of the burdens of history. Rather the past for him was a greatness and a thing of pride for his people.

And his, and mine, are a people who have been conquered now for centuries, a people who have lost land and sea as well as our own selves. All that is left is our history, which we still carry. And now I come along and want to steal that too.

I did not suceed in everything I did. And even where it did seem I was succeeding it was not always the case. The human heart has a million facets.

There was an initial incident, then a confrontation took place. And the story should properly be told like this.

'Look here, Mas,' Princess began on a quiet evening, 'there is a request for something to be written about Dewi Sartika.'

I remembered the letter from the girl in Jepara to Mei about Dewi Sartika: *I admire so much the firmness and resilience of that Sundanese girl. Dewi Sartika did not face so many problems, she could use the freedom to move socially that her environment allowed her. You said, my dear friend, that I too could be as free as that. Those are such beautiful words.*

That was a letter that Mei received before she and I went and visited the girl in Jepara. It was a long time ago now. But the problem she was addressing was still there: How did one find the way, the path, the right character that would reveal the gateway out of this wild jungle into the modern era?

Mei dived headlong into organisational work. The Jepara girl, despite all the doubts she had lived with, had written much of eternal value in her letters. Dewi Sartika had established her schools. And the Princess of Kasiruta? She was among the first group of Native women to edit a magazine in the Indies.

Some said that women began their life with the wedding bed. The

Governors-General of the Indies had the opinion that women could be silenced by bringing them to the wedding-bed. Princess, it seemed, was following an old saying – without actually doing it – marry, divorce, become a widow and live as one pleased.

'So what do you think?' I asked.

'No, Mas, what is your opinion?'

'Try to learn to decide for yourself.'

'I don't have enough experience yet.'

'Go and meet Dewi Sartika. You'll get a lot of material that way.'

No Native woman had ever conducted an interview. She didn't yet have the courage. Put together a list of questions first, I said. It didn't take her long to do that. But she still hesitated.

'What will people say? A strange woman arrives at the house of a good family and then begins to ask all sorts of personal questions.'

She was right. There were risks for our family. We had to find another way. We mobilised several of the SDI men to start collecting information indirectly about this much respected and admired figure. What we received couldn't be used. It was too extreme, exaggerated, no one would believe it all. It was just like with *wayang* – if it wasn't amazing and incredible, no one paid it any attention.

The thought that an article based on this material would not satisfy the readers made Princess regret that she wasn't able to do it herself. One regret led to another. But the other regret had a different origin – Princess was still not pregnant. I followed her feelings closely, especially when she sat alone, quiet but restless. She always rejected my suggestion that we go for a holiday to Sukabumi. She always had the same excuse – there was work to finish.

To help keep her spirits up, I took her to see Dewi Sartika.

Raden Tumenggung Sastrawinangun, her husband, was not at all a pretentious person, although he did try to be as Sundanese as he could. He didn't interfere very much at all in the interview.

Towards the end of the interview, Dewi Sartika told of how she wanted to establish a school to further develop the art of weaving in Cicalengka. The local weaving was already famous all over Priangan.

'Why don't you go ahead and start it, if you have the opportunity and the funds?' asked Princess..

'We are still struggling with the finances.'

'We will help you,' I said.

'Is that true, Meneer?'

'Of course it is,' responded Princess, 'even if we can't provide all the money, we can provide at least that which is needed most urgently.'

'Thank you very much. The young women need an education. They need to be able to educate their own children in the future as well. They don't need only to be able to read and write. They need also to be able to work.'

I saw a frown come over Princess's face when she heard those words, 'their own children'. Those words seemed to be targeted at her especially, and she still showed no signs of being pregnant.

We returned home, and Princess didn't move to start writing up the results of the interview. I had avoided so far speaking about the subject of children at all, but it was she who began.

'We will be helping her to educate other people's children. We ourselves have not yet been blessed with our own.'

'What is the difference? Children are the same wherever they are.'

She looked at me, trying to work out what my feelings were, then went on: 'How much I yearn to give birth to a boy child, like you – handsome, intelligent, and more than that, courageous. Courageous enough too to dare to make mistakes, to dare to be in error. I would hand him over to you every day, and you would never complain of not having enough time to cuddle him,' she promised, humouring her husband.

'That time will come too,' I spoke those words again for the umpteenth time.

Sometimes she felt she was being humiliated. I had to try every method to calm her down again.

Our marriage seemed to be a happy one to all observers. I too had convinced myself of that. I was happy in this marriage. My wife was devoted to me and that was what was important to a Native man from whatever class and whatever region.

The days went by, yet she had not written one word about Nyi Raden Dewi Sartika. Then came the confrontation. One afternoon we were sitting in the front yard when the Lendersma boy came into the front yard. He was dirty as usual but he had a certain intelligence about him.

'Look at that boy! He's trying to work out a way to get one of those *jeruk* without having to climb the tree.'

She refused to look, but instead let out a sigh of exasperation.

'What's the matter with you?' I asked.

She sat there like a statue. I watched her silently. Some inner conversation was taking place. Eventually she could not keep it in any more. She ended it with an explosion: 'If Mas wants a child so much then all I can do is state that I am willing to see Mas marry again. I accept it, Mas.'

'You will have a child.'

'It is not I who decides whether I shall have a child, or whether it will be sooner or later.'

'We haven't even been married two years yet. Why are you so sensitive about having a child?'

'And isn't it you who have demanded from me to have the child quickly?'

'I'm sorry. But we don't want to have an argument, do we?'

It was only then that she raised her face to look at me and whispered:

298

'You are the man, you must decide.'

'I have no intention of marrying again.'

'I will accept it if you marry again.'

'Why do we have to go on like this?'

'Every time you talk about a child, you mean to tease me. I can't stand it.'

'Then we won't talk about it any more.'

'Sometimes you don't speak with your mouth but your eyes.'

'You're tired. You've been working too hard. You should rest. You won't even agree to a holiday in Sukabumi.'

I had suggested several times that she be examined, that perhaps there was something wrong with us. But she always refused, because it was something that was in God's hands.

Then one day, before going into the office, I took myself to a German doctor to be examined. My heart was pounding with the doubts I had about my own ability to leave behind any seeds that might indeed grow. When he came out of his examination room, all my doubts were confirmed. It was I who was infertile. And it could be forever. Perhaps the doctor was wrong. So I followed in the footsteps of Frischboten and sought out Pengki near the Buitenzorg markets. This time his teacher, writing once again on a little piece of paper, added the uncomforting words: 'I am sorry, Tuan, but this time *sinse* is unable to help you.'

The doctor from the bamboo house, with his lips blue from smoking opium, didn't take me straight into his examination room. First of all he interviewed me in his broken and hard-to-understand Malay. He examined my eyes. Without excusing himself first, he began to examine my hair. My hair! And then plucked a hair from my leg. This part of the examination went on for a long time, while he continued to ask me all sorts of questions about my past. Finally he did take me into his examination room.

The floor was bare and damp earth. The bamboo walls had holes in them. He ordered me to take off all my clothes and left me lying on a bench, without a mattress, or mat, and with a pillow that was by no means pleasant to look at, let alone to smell. He came back with a young Chinese man.

They started talking excitedly with each other. I couldn't understand a word.

The young one started massaging the iliopsoas group of muscles. Suddenly: 'Do you get backache?'

'Never.'

He examined the front section of my thigh, right up to near the testicles, and then the scrotum, plucking some hairs and examining their root. He told me to turn over then examined my backbone. The examination took quite some time. It was only after all this that he told me that I could get dressed again.

They didn't talk to each other again.

They brought me back to the waiting room. The *sinse* wrote the little note for Pengki.

'Yes, well,' said Pengki, letting out a sigh. 'The only thing to do is to pray to Him that Created Life, Tuan.'

I would not say anything about this at home. The matter of a child stopped here. At the very least I would not be bringing forth any creature that I could call my child during these next several years.

Now it was I who was often disturbed. What was I working so hard for if there was to be no child to savour the fruits of my work? What did it mean, this 'single people' or 'multi-people' nation, if none of my blood was mingling in it?

It was an emptiness for which there was no answer. Limp, empty. A litre of my perspiration every day would not fill this emptiness. A *kati* of protein and another of minerals and sugar would not produce enough energy to bear this burden. Often as I sat in the stillness of the night I could see in my mind's eye huge fields of wilting flowers, without new seedlings coming forth. For over a week I did not go up to Bandung.

Hendrik and Mir and their baby came to visit and to see if I was sick. They didn't stay but went back to Bandung on the last train.

'It's better not to get pregnant too early, anyway,' said Mir to Princess before they left for the station..

Just a few minutes after they left, someone came into the front yard. He was big, an Indo, and he had four others with him. His face was covered in hair, as if he had fertilised his face every day with manure. He didn't introduce himself. But as soon as he sat down I recognised him – Robert Suurhof.

'So, what do you want this time?' I got in first.

His eyes popped out.

'Tell him,' said one of his friends.

'Yes, I've received your letters. I recognised your handwriting, your "r". But letters like that don't deserve any attention.'

'You began it,' he suddenly accused me.

'We began everything together in Wonokromo. When do you want to finish it?'

It was at that time that Princess came out, carrying some papers.

'One of your gangs started it in Pameoungpeuk.'

'We have no gangs. We are not some group of thugs. Our organisation has been legalised by the Government. If you haven't forgotten how to read yet, you can check for yourself in the *State Gazette*.'

'It doesn't matter. You've been attacking the Indos.'

'Very well. Tell me what your complaints are. I will take them all up with the Assistant Resident. With the Governor-General, if needs be.'

'You've got a big head. Everything in the Indies is decided by the Indos – good and evil, black and white, what will survive and what will be destroyed, everything.'

'Princess, did you hear what he said?' I said to my wife, who was standing at the door watching our 'guests'. She understood the blinks of my eye. She put the papers down on the table and went back inside.

Following in the footsteps of all those who managed big firms, I had taken advantage of my right to own a gun and acquired a colt revolver. There was an agreement between Princess and me that whoever needed to use it would do so. And Princess understood. In a few moments she returned to the veranda with the revolver in her hand, pulled over a chair, and sat down to watch our guests.

'These gentlemen say they have some business to finish, Princess,' I said, taking the lead.

'What is it they wish to end?' asked my wife.

'Ask them.'

'What business is it that you gentlemen wish to finish?' asked Princess of Robert Suurhof.

Now they all turned to Princess. Their fury had been swallowed up by the shock of her intervention. I stood up and moved away from them.

'Don't play around with that thing!' Robert Suurhof warned her.

'What is it that you gentlemen wish to end?' Princess repeated her question.

'We can also use those things,' Robert Suurhof warned her.

'What is it that you want to end?' repeated Princess for the third time. 'Do not come into my house without my permission. Finish your visit now or I will shoot without mercy. I will count to three. One . . .'

The five of them looked at each other.

'Two . . . '

They stood up.

'Three!' and Princess began shooting.

The explosions shattered the silence. The five of them ran off. Not one was hit. Princess fired some more shots outside the house. They were running as fast as their feet could carry them.

They disappeared from sight. We stood there, still in shock ourselves. Several soldiers from the palace soon arrived, asking what had happened. They did a quick examination of all the rooms. The gun was taken. They left, but gave us a receipt for the gun.

It was several minutes before the shock wore off. We stood there looking at each other like two children lost in the forest.

'You were courageous to shoot, Princess.'

'It is better that they should die than my husband.'

'Where are our guards, the men from Banten?'

'Some went off to get their replacements. The others I sent with the Frischbotens to the station.'

'We will lose the gun.'

'We haven't lost anything,' she said.

I rubbed her back, and she sat down again. Embracing her around the neck from behind, I whispered to her: 'When did you learn to shoot?'

She didn't answer straight away. Meanwhile I continued to reflect on my admiration for her. Natives generally were afraid of firearms, even to touch them. And then she told me how back home in Kasiruta all the members of her family, everyone ten years old and above, were instructed by her father to practice shooting, every Sunday afternoon in the forest. No, it wasn't difficult to get a gun. As long as you had a certificate of good behaviour from the police and you had the money, you could easily buy a gun, or even more than one.

It was a simple story. And that is why van Heutsz exiled her father. It seems that her father, my father-in-law, once had plans.

That afternoon we left Buitenzorg and travelled down to Sukabumi to see her father. My respect for him was now greater than ever. And he seemed surprised at my attitude.

'Princess needs to rest, Bapak, she's been working too hard, she's exhausted. While she's at home, there is no way I can get her away from her work. We will stay here for a couple of weeks.'

But I couldn't stay there for the full two weeks. The palace guards called me for an interrogation, even though no such thing was ever required of Robert Suurhof. They were investigating, they said, the discharge of a gun in the proximity of the palace. As the interrogation wore on and they concentrated on the reasons for my owning a gun, it became clear that they were looking for evidence that I was planning a rebellion or some other kind of attack against the Governor-General.

'Impossible. The former Governor-General van Heutsz often called me, and desired my friendship.'

'Precisely because of that,' answered the interrogator, who had no right to make such accusations. 'Now that His Excellency Governor-General Idenburg is here and has not called you, perhaps you feel slighted?'

'If that's all you can accuse me or suspect me of, then I could do the same to you too. What's the difference?'

'Everyone who lives within the proximity of the palace and owns a gun must report it to the palace security.'

'I have never read any such regulations. May I see them?'

'In any case you have fired a gun in the proximity of the palace. We will confiscate the gun.'

'Very well. I will be reporting this to the appropriate authorities. I have a licence for my gun.' I showed him the papers and also the bullets that I had stored away. 'And I have also reported to the police the fact that I have used two of the bullets that I am registered as owning.'

The interrogation came to an end. My revolver was later returned to me by the police.

It was becoming clearer and clearer – if we did not have the means to defend ourselves, all Natives, and not just myself, would become the playthings of the Robert Suurhofs. Well, that was just the way it was. Yet this incident brought those who were close to me, and perhaps many others that I did not know of, even closer. As we became a closer-knit group we also began to understand that the Knijpers had dissolved itself. There was now a new group – TAI. We didn't know what the letters meant, except perhaps that the last two stood for 'Anti Inlander', that is, 'Anti Native'. There was also a possibility they were trying to make fun of the fact that I often signed my articles with the initials TAS.

All the tension caused by our childlessness disappeared. Justice must stand firm, even in a colonised country like ours. Who else would ensure this, if not the Natives themselves? Because justice is something that is a purely human affair, it is only human beings that can defend it. The laws of the Netherlands Indies did protect life and property. But they protected only those who knew the laws and knew how to use their knowledge. Those who did not know were, in fact, the targets and victims of these laws.

Onwards even further, our Islamic Traders Union, our Sarekat. Onwards too, you, Minke. Don't be diverted by minor personal sentiments. You have begun, now you must show you can finish.

15

Boedi Oetomo continued on undisturbed. It was backed by the supporters of the Ethical Policy. The BO schools were even offered subsidies, as long as they used the official curriculum. Idenburg himself made the offer. BO did not suffer any moves against it like those against the SDI.

1911 seemed to promise more turbulent developments. Thamrin Mohammed Thabrie received orders that went one step further than previously – he was to drop his membership of the organisation completely.

'As a Moslem I must, of course, remain faithful to the SDI,' he answered.

The Government took action. He was dismissed from his post, with a pension. This incident was reported by almost all of the Dutch language papers in Betawi.

'What can be done?' he commented. 'The Government is fearful that I might use its authority to help the organisation. It has the right and the power to take the action it has.'

He lost his job. And *Medan*, which did not have a 'Transfers, Promotions and Dismissals' column, did not report it. Thamrin was pensioned off with an extra little gift as well – he was still forbidden to be active in the organisation. They continued to make all kinds of threats against him.

The Boedi Oetomo had founded three schools. The SDI had not founded even one – at least not yet. It was sticking to its policy of helping to fund other non-government schools, including those of the BO.

The example of the BO schools excited a lot of interest in setting up non-government schools that used the Government curriculum. The more independent-spirited teachers, those who had been involved in some kind of argument or dispute with their headmasters, always Europeans, started to get together to found their own schools, or joined up with the BO effort. Meanwhile schools that did not use the Government curriculum lost any status they once had, especially if they didn't teach Dutch. Even the Jamiatul Khair and Tiong Hoa Hwee Koan schools did not seem to be taken seriously any more.

The desire for education built up like a great wave ready to break. Where did the momentum come from? The Ethical Policy. Then the Jepara girl's book was published – *De Zonnige Toekomst* – 'The Bright Tomorrow'. The editor was van Aberon, a supporter of the Ethical Policy. The Ethical style came into fashion. A number of the educated, upper-class Native women eagerly sought out the book and became its great devotees. This phenomenon became even more pronounced when parts of it were translated and published overseas, in England and France. The Ethical crowd claimed that here was an example of the best the Ethical Policy could produce. Their opponents accused van Aberon of simply being interested in getting into the palace, in becoming the next Governor-General.

This debate was the main subject of conversation at all gatherings, formal and informal, among the Europeans. So what do you expect from these writings anyway? asked some. All you do is laud her writings to the sky, because you yourselves can't write as beautifully. Others held the view that perhaps it wasn't the girl herself that wrote them. Perhaps it was van Aberon! There was no committee to check this. How many of her correspondents did van Aberon approach to get copies of her letters ? Five or seven? Is it true that she only ever wrote to five or seven people in her whole life?

That the van Aberons' collection comprised letters to so few of her friends did give the critics some basis for their skepticism. But they were also jealous of van Aberon. The letters to the van Aberons, husband and wife, were full of praise for them and exhibited the girl's dependence on them. And on Europe. And on Holland. With the publication of *De Zonnige Toekomst*, said the opponents, all the van Aberons were interested in was having themselves praised, in showing how they were loved by the educated Natives.

I read the book, all of it. I think that van Aberon did indeed act unilaterally in publishing it. There were other letters. In my wardrobe there were eight letters from the girl to Mei. And they weren't all so self-deprecatory as the ones he had published. She was a bit like that when writing about herself. But when she was writing about other things, she wasn't despondent at all, indeed she was often very fired-up. I think there must have been at least two letters to Nyi Raden Dewi Sartika. When Princess and I had interviewed her, she mentioned that she had received correspondence from Jepara, but that she had never replied. And from what I had heard, the person whom the girl wrote to most was her brother, who was in fact her teacher. And van Aberon had not published even one of those letters. Wardi was also able to tell me that his friends in the Netherlands, including those in the Indies Students Association, had written to him to say that many of her letters that had been read out at their meetings were not in that book.

I think I could understand a little of the feelings of those who did not approve of what van Aberon had done. There was not one letter that he had published that had a firm or strong tone to it. She was a restless soul, but she did have firm and strong ideas on many things. There was very little biographical information in the book either, something that would have been very interesting as well. There were too many tears and too much despondency and too many sighs in the collection that he published; it didn't truly represent her. And perhaps all those tears and those sighs were indeed of van Aberon's making?

But neither amongst those for or those against was there any desire to see a proper commission established to investigate all this.

A movement under the banner of the girl from Jepara sprang up among the European and Indo supporters of the Ethical Policy. It was centred in Semarang. They planned to carry out what the girl had always dreamed of – to offer education to young Javanese women. Jepara Committees were formed in nearly all the big towns. Within two months they had collected enough money to establish a new school. And they chose for its location – Rembang.

A commission was formed and sent to Rembang to find a good site. The Inspector of Schools for Central Java, Raden Kamil, the highest Native education official, opened it. There was also a monument to the Ethical movement, but there was no inscription. No 'Long live the Jepara girl! Long live the Governor-General!' That was the real message of all this – look how fine things aré today in the Indies! The dark ages of Multatuli are past. Come on plantation capital, much empty land awaits you! Send your unemployed here too. Look, everyone, even the educated Natives have found their proper place in the embrace of the Government. All is well. Please come out, you're very welcome! And hip, hip, hurrah for Idenburg!

Meanwhile, without people realising it, the Tiong Hoa Hwee Koan had been quietly working away setting up many new schools throughout Java. During the past eleven years, the organisation had produced many young people whose education was oriented not to the Indies, but to China and to the international scene in general. There were even a few THHK graduates who had made their own contributions to the movement in China.

The Jamiatul Khair hadn't progressed at all. Its key leader had twice come to me to complain that contributions from the Arab community were drying up. Soon, he said, his only source of funds would be from the SDI. He was very ashamed of this situation.

By 1911 the Chinese had won a more or less total victory over the Arabs and the Natives, both in commerce and in general advancement. The Indos, who preferred to be soldiers or other eaters of salaries, had been left behind half a century ago.

There began to be talk within the governing circles as to how the balance between the races might become upset with the emergence of the new-found strength of the Chinese. Within the SDI we monitored things closely to make sure that the organisation wasn't used unfairly against any of the other groups competing to advance. In several places there were already some unhealthy developments. Some of the self-defence groups that had been sponsored by the SDI were being incited to go into action against the Chinese. The Knijpers weren't around at all. Those doing the inciting were businessmen members of the SDI. They thought the destruction of the Chinese businesses would mean that more profits would fall into their laps.

Trouble was being incited in more and more places. From Priangan it spread to Central and then East Java. My call for the Natives to live in harmony together with the other governed peoples fell on deaf ears. I was unable to conquer the dangerous economic illusions people had. SDI branches all over the place began to set up youth groups, with all sorts of names, who studied the martial arts for attack as well as defence.

The atmosphere of enmity that was spreading everywhere soon brought into the open the secret associations of the Chinese that had been lying dormant all this time. Everywhere, but especially along the coast, they rose up. The strongest was the one that called itself the Kong Sing.

The competition between the races left the Indos far behind. The umpire behind the scenes remained the same – the Netherlands Indies authorities, through Idenburg, the mighty Governor-General. The Arabs seemed to withdraw from public life, and thereby ended up indirectly drawing closer to SDI. I was kept busy writing letters to the branches warning them not to let the SDI be used to hit out against people's personal enemies, either groups or individuals.

A new development took place. A truly major event, huge, earth-shattering, its impact spreading everywhere, something that had a great influence on developments in the Indies.

On 10 October 1911 rebellion broke out in China, in the town of Wu Chang, Hu Pei province, led by the Young Generation. Dr Sun Wen alias Sun Yat Sen, who had been involved, it was said, in the Filipino revolt against the Spanish, was overseas when the revolt in Wu Chang started. He was in Tokyo but was soon expelled at the request of the Chinese Emperor. After going to the United States where he taught at Denver University, Colorado, and then to England, he returned to China to lead the Wu Chang Revolution. The Revolution spread throughout almost all of China. The Man Ching Dynasty was overthrown and a republic was established.

In Betawi a new paper was started, the *Sin Po*. Its task was to help unite and give leadership to the Chinese nationalists in the Indies. Within three months it had almost caught up to *Medan. Medan*'s own circulation dropped about 5 per cent. The Chinese leaped ahead further and further. Their overtaking of the Natives in commerce was becoming a part of the reality of social life. There was no way of stopping them. It reflected their superiority in organisation, commercial knowledge, loyalty, skill and their unconditional confidence in their organisations.

One of the features of these new developments was the clear role the newspaper played in leading the community that was its readership. The organisation itself wasn't really visible to the public. Rather it was the paper that they saw, and if that ever disappeared from the face of the earth, then so would the leadership capacity of the organisation.

Medan must live and stay alive. There was no other paper capable of leading the Natives.

The editorial staff suggested that we use smaller type-face so that we could put more in the paper. I continued to reject the idea. The Chinese readership of *Sin Po* could afford to buy glasses; the Native readership could not. We had to find some other way. There was nothing we could do to improve the paper technically because we were using the best technology available. There were plenty of signs that *Sin Po* – which published articles in both Chinese and Malay – would continue to press us. Our Chinese subscribers one by one withdrew their subscriptions. Sometimes a whole town would go. *Medan* was in trouble.

Frischboten didn't feel he had the right to interfere in editorial affairs, but he was able to point out how *Sin Po* had taken over some of *Medan*'s techniques. We used a legal advisor from Europe. They employed a pensioned European police commissioner, who really knew how the law operated, and about how the Indies laws worked too. A similar thing happened in relation to distribution and reporting. And there was one thing that we could not fight. They were able to get news reports from outside. They could afford to pay for them. If *Sin Po* could keep going for another five years, perhaps all of the Indies Chinese would be nationalists, except the older generation who were incapable of change.

All this time, the colonial press never tired of publishing their reports of the activities of the Jepara Committees or of praising the glories of the Ethical Policy. *Medan* and *Sin Po* did not join in. It was my own view by then that this whole campaign was indeed an attempt by the supporters of the Ethical Policy to have van Aberon made Governor-General in 1914, or, at least, to build support for the Liberal Party. Those opposed to the campaign argued that the Governor-Generalship was not a social position but a political one. The Ethical policy supporters had the illusion that with a Governor-General who was a genuine Ethical Policy supporter, the welfare of the people would be improved.

Princess and I, accompanied by some of Sandiman's men, went to Blora to visit family.

The Bupati of Blora, a grandfather, was so proud that I had a Princess as a wife.

Princess and I met with the two old people, husband and wife, in their back parlour. The conversation was opened without any unnecessary formalities.

'Gus, Tuan Assistant Resident sent us a message a little while ago, just a few hours after you arrived. Perhaps you can guess what it was, so don't be surprised – the Sarekat is banned from any activity in this district.'

'I'm not surprised, and I understand completely, *Nenenda*.'

'Very good, If you wanted to start something you would have to stay in a *losmen*, and their are no good *losmens* here. If you stay with any other official, he will receive the same warning.'

'I understand, Nenenda.'

'In other words, while you stay here you must not contact the local Sarekat branch.'

The old woman, Raden Ayu, listened silently, hardly blinking an eyelid. Princess was straining to hear what was going on.

There was no one else allowed to attend this discussion.

'Even so I myself want to know as much as possible about the Sarekat.'

'But that would be Sarekat propaganda.' I turned him down. 'It's better that I don't speak about it.'

'No. It would be just a grandson talking to his grandfather.'

'But it would be a Sarekat activity, because I would, of course, be highly recommending and praising it.'

'Yes, yes, it would be Sarekat activity,' the Bupati repeated. 'In that case, tell me about something else, whereby the Sarekat is mentioned in passing, is not praised, and also is not the main topic of discussion.'

He burst out laughing, really enjoying his suggested ploy. I was carried away with laughter as well. And that was the first time I had laughed befored a *bupati*. It was a complete surprise to me to see him giggling uncontrollably. Then the old woman joined in as well. It was only Princess who sat there open-mouthed, not knowing what was going on. So, as I had done before for Mei, I now did for Princess – I became an interpreter.

Now Raden Ayu couldn't restrain her giggling as she watched me interpret, unable to restrain her amusement at my having a wife who understood no Javanese. Not knowing Javanese was the same as being totally uncivilised.

Seeing everyone else laugh, Princess joined in, though feeling that she was the only one not knowing what was going on.

The old Bupati suddenly stopped laughing when he saw a granddaughter-in-law dare laugh in front of him, without covering her mouth, without bowing her head, and without lowering her voice. A stern frown was soon on his forehead as he looked at Princess.

It was like some comic farce that was not funny enough to make anyone laugh.

Princess stopped laughing while I explained everything to her. After hearing my translation and knowing how things stood, she burst into even more raucous laughter, not caring who else was there. So did I. Finally so did the Bupati.

The laughter died down when some refreshments were brought in. The Bupati took the opportunity to take charge of proceedings: 'You may begin,' he said.

So I told him about all that had happened since the founding of the Tiong Hoa Hwee Koan, about the competition between peoples of the Indies, and how all but the Europeans had been left behind by the Chinese.

'And what will the Sarekat do about all this?'

'Oh, a thousand pardons, but in this district, your humble servant here will not speak about such things,' I said firmly to show respect to his position and to the instructions he had been put under.

He then asked what were the reasons for all the fuss over the Jepara Committees, even here in Blora. And I explained to him about the campaign to try to put van Aberon in the Governor-Generalship.

'But who is this girl from Jepara? Wasn't she the late wife of the Bupati in the neighboring District, Rembang?'

'You are not mistaken, Nenenda.'

'Why isn't it her own husband that is setting up the school for his late wife, who indeed died in his arms?'

'Most Natives, even her own husband, do not understand what it was that she dreamed after, Nenenda. It is mostly the Europeans and other foreigners who understand. The Natives are still groping about.'

'And how is it that a woman can be more respected by the Europeans than a man?'

And now he listened to my words, concentrating like an obedient child before his teacher, forgetting all about his curiosity concerning the Sarekat. As a *bupati* he had about fifty thousand people under him. The Sarekat now had about seventy thousand people, including the families, under it. And among the fifty thousand residents of Blora, not all of them would listen or obey him. The Samin people obviously would ignore everything that came from the Government.

I explained to him about the dreams of the girl from Jepara. The old woman also listened attentively. And my story ended with her instructions to her sisters that they educate their sons to respect womankind, and not be like most of the wealthy and powerful men of Java, who considered their wives to be no more than an ornamentation. While he needed such ornamentation his wife would be looked after and loved. If he no longer needed her, he could kick her out, not caring where she would end up.

'She must have been a goddess, Child,' said the Bupati, intervening, 'and she sent these thoughts all the way to Holland?'

'Not just to Holland, Nenenda, but after she died her writings were translated into French and English as well.'

'And where is England and France, Child?'

'England is to the west of Holland, and it has the biggest empire in the world, controlling one eighth of the world. France is to the south-west of Holland, and is itself much bigger than Holland.'

'Yes, I have heard about that school to honour the late wife of the Bupati of Rembang. Why didn't he do something like that himself earlier?'

'If other people had not moved to honour her, perhaps the Bupati himself would have forgotten that he had even taken her as a wife. That is why today he is the object of many insults. From the Europeans, and from the educated Natives also.'

'A *bupati* insulted! Such things never happened except in a time of war,' the Bupati commented.

'How would you feel if you were the object of such insults?' I asked.

'What is the point of a being a *bupati* if you just become the object of insults? It would be better to resign and go into meditation in the mountains.'

'Nenenda.'

'What?'

'Why don't you, as way of showing honour to women, also establish a school for girls? Without any help from the Europeans, but by yourself? That would be something, Nenenda.'

'You've got all sorts of strange ideas,' he answered.

'Not all sorts, just one, and not so strange. If Nenenda carries out this idea, for sure you will be more honoured and respected than the Bupati of Rembang.'

'I have never treated your grandmother in the way the Bupati of Rembang treated his late wife.'

'Then, if not to honour womankind, Nenenda, do it at my request.'

'You can found one yourself. The Sarekat has enough money.'

'I will not speak about the Sarekat here in this building, Nenenda. And if you did set up a girls' school here, with the aims that were espoused by the girl from Jepara, your superiors would truly respect you, even though you set it up at my request.'

'Yes, all sorts of strange ideas. I want to see if you can establish such a school yourself.'

'I can do that any time, easily, the thing now is you, my grandfather.'

'Are you challenging me?'

'Perhaps you could interpret it that way.'

'And where would your Nenenda obtain the money to establish such a school as that?' asked his wife.

'Money is no problem if the will is there.' And then in Malay to Princess, 'Isn't that so, Princess?'

'Isn't what so? I haven't understood a word.'

So I translated it all for her again.

'So what is your opinion then, Princess?' the Bupati asked in Malay.

'The money can always be found, Nenenda, if the will is there.'

'Ah, you're just saying that to back up your husband.'

'My heart will be full of joy and gratitude if Nenenda agrees to this idea.'

'Is that so? And what is the reason that you should be so grateful?'

'Whosoever obtains a modern education, like this your servant, soon understands that women are not at all respected by men. And when I see a woman suffer disrespect or humiliation, it is as if I myself suffer that humiliation too.'

'But your husband has never humiliated you?'

'Never, Nenenda. He has always honoured me, and with great sincerity.'

I quickly followed this up with the story of how Princess had chased off the Knijpers that day and how she had fired off the revolver at them.

'You fired at them with a revolver?' he asked, amazed and full of admiration at the same time. 'You?'

'They ran off and have never returned, Nenenda,' answered Princess.

'My granddaughter-in-law shot at some thugs with a revolver,' he shook his head. 'You?'

'Just to chase them away, Nenenda.'

'You saved my grandson, Princess. Your grandmother would shake just at seeing the revolver,' and he looked at his wife, who did not understand Malay. 'From whence comes your courage?'

And Princess didn't answer. She just smiled and looked at me, hoping that I would help her answer.

'Ah, enough of this. It's not important. The important thing now is what about this school for girls that Nenenda is going to set up. If you are not convinced that you should do it as a mark of respect for women, or because I asked you to, perhaps you will do it for the first Native woman to edit a magazine and who saved your grandson.'

His wife slapped me on the thigh, and that meant I had to translate for her.

Princess listened and was embarrassed. Then lifting up her face, she spoke in Malay: 'Not because of or for me, Nenenda. If this your servant may tell a story . . .'

'Yes, go ahead, Princess.'

'I have read the book *De Zonnige Toekomst*. The most interesting part was when she told how the Bupati of Rembang proposed to her. He told her that when his wife was dying, she instructed him that he must wed that flower of Java, the girl from Jepara. My husband has told me that when a *bupati* says 'his wife', he means his official wife. They married, and the girl from Jepara was taken off to Rembang. There she was met by a six-month-old baby and several *selir*, his 'unofficial wives'. I cried when I read that, Nenenda. How evil it was to trick a woman who was as educated as she was. No, it wasn't that she was tricked. There was something that made her powerless to refuse. I do not want to see other women trapped like that. So that is why I would be so grateful to see

Nenenda establish such a school for girls.'

The Bupati laughed slowly: 'I hoped to hear something about the Sarekat. Now this is something else again that we are talking about. This husband of yours, Princess, he got up to all sorts of things when he was a child. Now, when he is grown up and much older, he is still the same,' he turned to his wife and translated into Javanese what he had just said.

'Yes, what is wrong with the idea if we indeed we are capable of doing it?' she answered. 'It would be good if many girls knew these things, then they will never be tricked like that.'

We sat there silently listening to this conversation between the two old people. I deliberately didn't tell them that the girl from Jepara knew that her suitor was deceiving her, and she also knew that behind the Bupati were his superiors and the Government. She knew too that she had to accept this humiliation as the consequence of her own vacillation. She entered that hell because her love and devotion to her father was greater than her commitment to her own ideals.

'I've never deceived you, my wife, have I?' asked the Bupati, as if he himself had been the object of the criticisms.

No one responded. And the discussion did not reach any decision.

The next morning I received a message from the local Sarekat branch that they wanted me to attend a meeting. To ensure that I didn't violate the instructions my grandfather had received, I told them that I could meet them at Cepu station at nine o'clock the next morning.

The next day at Cepu station I was met, not just by one person, but by twenty-one, including the whole of Cepu sub-branch. We had no choice but to stay overnight in Cepu. We held our meeting in the Cepu soccer field, the first time it had been used for a public meeting. There was nothing important discussed. They just wanted to meet someone from the Central Leadership, and to appy for Cepu sub-branch to be made a full branch. The discussion was held in Malay and Javanese.

Princess stayed in a *losmen*, guarded by Sandiman's men.

At this meeting I told them that while they had no doubt studied about the boycott method, they must not use it without permission from the Central Leadership. I also told them that they must not do anything against the Samin movement. If they were not in a position to help the Saminites, then they should just remain silent. They mustn't join the *priyayi* in insulting them.

But there was something more important that I discovered during this journey. It was late evening by the time I returned to the *losmen*. I found Princess asleep, curled up around the pillow. Underneath the pillow I saw some papers with writing on them. Slowly I pulled them out and tried to read them by the wall light. She had written, in Dutch, a commentary on *De Zonnige Toekomst*.

But it was not just a commentary on the book itself. She also attacked the Bupati of Rembang for deceiving the girl from Jepara when he proposed to her. At the bottom, she had signed Princess Dede Maria Futimma de Sousa. But then she had crossed out that name. I put the papers back under her pillow.

As I lay there next to her I began to wonder whether my wife had been writing for some of the Dutch publications. She had never mentioned it. Perhaps her experience in editing the magazine had given her the confidence to submit some articles without telling me. As I neared unconsciousness I came to the tentative conclusion that she was writing for Dutch magazines. The girl from Jepara's book may have also encouraged. her.

Now I couldn't sleep. Why had she never told me? Had she written anything else major that was not for publication? I got up again and groped around looking for other papers. I even opened up the suitcase. But I could find nothing.

Let's hope that she had not revealed anything about the inner workings of the Sarekat, deliberately or otherwise. Her secretiveness was suspicious. What were her motives? It wasn't just to practice her Dutch! Perhaps she was afraid I would stop her? No, that was also impossible.

I must watch this development closely.

The second day back I started work again at the office. I read Princess's article in one of the Dutch papers, although her name wasn't there. A few days later a great storm engulfed the Bupati of Rembang.

I pretended not to know. But then I understood, Princess had been disappointed all this while that *Medan* had never published anything about the girl from Jepara. And I continued to pretend I didn't know. She herself didn't say a word, as if nothing was happening. But the attacks on the husband of our late friend became stronger and stronger.

I once tried to start a conversation about the article that had started all the furore. But she didn't say anything, pretending she didn't know anything about it. Later, I tried a second time. This time she replied: 'Yes, I would like to read that article.'

'Don't tell me you haven't read it yet?'

'No, not yet.'

I showed her the article. And then both of us started up a little play of our own. I went on: 'The author is obviously a woman. And not just any woman. I can tell from the anger she displays towards the husband of that girl, that perhaps she herself is also upset with her own husband, if she has one, that is. In any case, she is obviously very intelligent. And such intelligence just adds to the beauty of any woman. And if she is a woman who is already beautiful, then all this will make her a star that will shine out among all women.'

She didn't read the article, but listened to what I said.

'How can you tell all that, Mas?'

'Well, what do you think?'

'In my opinion, the author is obviously an old Indo who has been disappointed by his marriage. He lives in a dream that the girl from Jepara is his wife and he loves her and cares for her in accordance with her self-respect, education and dignity.'

She was imagining me as an old Indo, I thought.

'But I'm not old yet,' I disclaimed.

'I didn't mean you, Mas.'

'But you haven't read the article yet.'

She groped about, realising that I knew that she had already read the article. Not just read it, but that she had written it herself.

'I contacted the editor of the paper. He happens to be a good acquaintance. I asked him who was the author. He wouldn't tell me. I went down into the print shop. One of the setters showed me a copy of the original that hadn't been destroyed yet. But unfortunately there was no name there. So when did you read the article?'

'From this clipping.'

'You've only read two lines and you're giving your opinion.'

'Yes, I am a fast reader. Mas didn't observe very closely this time. I've actually read all of it, not just two lines.'

'Buy you haven't even unfolded it yet.'

Again she groped about.

'Princess, why won't you admit that you have read the article?'

'I can tease my husband occasionally, can't I?'

'Of course.'

'Yes, I have actually read the article.'

'But I have never brought this newspaper home,' I said, smiling. 'And we don't subscribe. So where did you get a copy?'

'From the wrapping of the fried peanuts.'

And that was as far as I could take things. We had bought some fried peanuts the day before and they had been wrapped in newspaper. I had failed to get her to confess. And I had no right to try to force her. That was her right, the right of privacy of a modern person. She didn't want to be known as the author. And I respected her attitude and her privacy.

And the waves of attacks of the Bupati did not abate. One day three people brought in another article, which they had signed, attacking the Bupati. They were all middle-ranking officials from Rembang and they wanted *Medan* to publish it. They had listed the time and place where the Bupati had carried out the things they accused him of. And what was the point of *Medan* helping fan these attacks? Who would benefit if the target of all these attacks was removed? One of the newly announced candidates for Bupati who had not yet got a district and who were all favourites of the Government?

And in Rembang, he who suffered this storm of insult and criticism without having any means of defending himself, fell sick. Ah, the Liberals' game of lauding the girl from Jepara! The girl from Jepara raised up van Aberon, so that van Aberon might then stride upon the stage as Governor-General.

The Knijpers had disappeared from the face of the earth. TAI now emerged, though cautiously and somewhat afraid. A feeling of hostility developed amongst us towards the Indos. Douwager perhaps understood my feelings because he never came around any more. Wardi now spent more time with him and did not come any more to the offices either. *Sin Po* kept stealing *Medan's* readers. If this kept on *Medan* might have to close up.

The editorial staff decided to join the fray and suggested we publish reports from Rembang, though not as sharp or as detailed as the others. I did not agree with them. We had to find another way to keep up *Medan's* circulation.

The key to solving this problem came to me indirectly from my father-in-law. During one of our visits to see him came this question: 'Where is your friend, Child, the one who came with you here the very first time?'

'You mean the one who drove the automobile?'

'Yes, he said he was on his way to Jeddah.'

'Ah, Hans Haji Moeloek, Bapak.'

'Yes, yes, Haji Moeloek. How is he?'

This little bit of a conversation reminded me of this Indo author, who wrote so simply and interestingly. I telegrammed Marko to come straight away to Buitenzorg.

I returned to Buitenzorg from Sukabumi, together with my father-in-law. Two hours later Marko arrived in a taxi. I gave him part of the manuscript of *The Tale of Siti Aini.*

'Set it all, Marko. Publish it as a serial. Don't lose or damage any page. There are no other copies. Guard this manuscript as your life.'

'Very well, Tuan.'

'You understand what I'm saying?'

'I will guard this manuscript, Tuan.'

'Good. Go back to Bandung now. Begin things tonight.'

And so it was that I showed the good side of this Indo, just when his people were threatening us. His writings redeemed all the evil doings of the Indos. Such a story has never been published before, even in Dutch.

My predictions weren't wrong. After just a week of its appearing in *Medan*, everyone was going crazy over the serial. Our subscriptions didn't go up, but they stopped declining. Meanwhile our sales in the kiosks, especially in the sugar towns, shot up. After three months and the story still hadn't ended, we started to receive letters asking who was this Haji Moeloek, because his writings did not exhibit any *haji*-ness or religiosity, and they told about the life of Eurasians in the sugar plantations. What a pity that he himself did not want to be known by anybody.

One of the colonial papers said that it guessed that Haji Moeloek was the pen-name of an Indo, given the background in which his story was set. The paper praised *Medan* to the heavens for winning the confidence of such an Indo writer, who was by no means a lesser writer than Francis. Francis was, at that time, considered the great teacher of the Indos.

These words kept the TAI movement under control for the time being. *Medan* could breathe easily for a while. Subscriptions began to increase again.

'These Indos are always off balance,' Hendrik Frischboten commented.

'You're an Indo too, Hendrik,' I reminded him.

'Yes, but not a part of them as a social group, a group whose fortunes are affected by the ups and downs of the Indies economy. Whenever things are going bad for the big European companies – and therefore the Government – they became vicious. When things are profitable, they became tame again. Minke, have you studied the latest statements of the Sugar Syndicate?'

Here was a new issue to be faced. The Sugar Syndicate planned to reduce the rent they paid to peasants for their land from 130 cents per *bahu* to 90 cents per *bahu* for eighteen months.

This was not just a matter for the newspaper.

I summoned all the leaders of the SDI to discuss the matter. I explained to them, based on all the material I had gathered together, what a disaster this would be for the farmers in the sugar areas. I began my story by telling them about one of the first victims of sugar – Nyai Ontosoroh. Then I mentioned other names such as Troenodongso, Piah, Sastro Kassier, and Plikemboh, and now there was this new problem which would hit everybody. From one hundred and thirty cents to ninety cents at a time when the sugar price was riding high on the upsurge of the world trade in sugar!

No doubt new regulations would be announced that fitted in with the Sugar Syndicate's plans, just as Ter Haar had once explained. The sugar plantations would expand, and the land available for growing rice would decrease. Meanwhile the sugar mills and plantations would not be able to provide jobs for those pushed out of rice farming. The TAI would also no doubt be used to ensure that these plans of the Sugar Syndicate would be implemented successfully.

This would mean a new struggle and I had to convince the SDI leadership of this. But they didn't understand that the interests of the farmers and their interests were the same. They considered that the losses that were going to be suffered by the peasants would not affect them, the independent class, the free people, the merchants.

'As the farmers' incomes decline, so will the merchants' trade,' I said during the meeting.

They did not want to understand. While the craftsmen still worked, and the factories and workshops still employed their workers, and the number of *priyayi* didn't decrease, the merchants' incomes would not suffer.

'We share no interests with the peasants,' another contradicted me.

'But these farmers are our brothers, our sudara, our fellow countrymen. The big European, Arab and Chinese companies want to squeeze all the money and land out of them that they can. If we let this happen, then it will be the same as giving our approval to it, we will be approving this evil. Is this allowed by Islam? Won't we, as Moslems, be ashamed of allowing this to happen?'

'But the Europeans, Chinese and Arabs are very powerful! How can we stop them?'

'Does it mean that just because they are powerful everything they do is right and cannot be opposed?'

That meeting resulted in something I had never expected – the SDI split into two. My group called the others hypocrites. And they called us the *ngawur* group who didn't know what we were talking about. They continued to use the name Sarekat Dagang Islamiyah. We gave in on this and called ourselves the Sarekat Dagang Islam.

According to Hendrik Frischboten a split like this was a normal part of the life of an organisation. No organisation could avoid it forever, no matter in what country.

'It is a crystallisation that takes place naturally but is also scientific,' he said confidently, 'there is no need to be discouraged.'

I convinced myself not to be discouraged. This split meant now that the SD Islam had to fight the decision of the Sugar Syndicate and side with the farmers. The split in fact gave us all a great boost in spirits. At some considerable cost we printed up leaflets and statements to be distributed to all the branches around the Indies that were willing to listen to us as their leaders.

Sandiman, Marko and all their people were mobilised to travel right round Java visiting all the branches. We did not allow our material to be sent through the post. I soon started to hear of their travels as they moved around by whatever means possible – bicycle, horse, train, buffalo cart, even by foot.

If the Syndicate continued with their plans the SD Islam would launch an immediate and total boycott.

A letter from Jeddah, from Haji Moeloek, whispered gently to me: *Tuan, I am truly concerned about what Tuan is planning. The Syndicate is the power behind the Government. I hope that you do not continue with your plans. I know many of the sugar czars. I don't side with them, don't think that, but I doubt that you are strong enough to take them on.*

318

And indeed I have never been so happy as when I saw The Tale of Siti Aini *published in your paper. But these new moves you are taking, I hope you are just joking. And if you are serious, Tuan, please make sure that you safeguard my manuscript, as not all of it has been published yet.*

And if you do carry out your plans, Tuan, all I can do from here is pray for you. I can do no more than that. Yes, you are on the side of right, but victory demands that other conditions also be met.'

I did not reply to his letter. But across the oceans and waves of the Indian Ocean I whispered to him: You will see, Tuan. Here in the Indies the weak now have a weapon. Its name is boycott. You will witness how we wield this weapon. Just wait for it to go into action, Tuan Haji, and you will hear the earth shake here in these islands of the south. The whole world will feel the tremors. Tens of thousands of SDI members will bring an end to the Sugar Syndicate. The world will be short of sugar.

The storm surrounding the Bupati of Rembang no longer had any meaning. In any case, that was only the case of one man and his family. Tens of thousands of farmers and their families were more important. The bell would be rung to call for a boycott the moment the Syndicate implemented its plan. And that bell would sound the death knell of the Syndicate. Idenburg's plans for increasing the country's revenues would fly out the window and away on the tropical clouds.

And from Paris came another refreshing whisper:

You are a good child, my son. You are avenging me against Sugar.

How beautiful would that day be . . . No, I and all of us no longer hesitated. The girl from Jepara gave us an example of what happened when you gave in to vacillation – you became its victim. If you have to become a victim, at least do so after conquering your own hesitation.

16

Mother arrived at the newspaper office in a very agitated state. 'What is going on inside you now, Child, my son?'

I took her to the Frischbotens' house.

'Your father is very worried about you and about your safety. Tell me everything honestly, Child, before I return to your father!'

'What has made Mother so worried and anxious like this, as if you were being chased by a whirlwind?'

'You know better than I. It is you who should explain things to me.'

'What did Father say?'

'He said, Child, that your group . . . here, there, everywhere, is very active. He said that it was all happening on your orders. People are flocking to hear the SDI leaders so they know what your orders are. Child, my son. What is it that you want to do?'

Frischboten was at his office. Mir left us alone. Mother had forgotten that she was in a European's house. She paid no attention to the furnishings. She was oblivious to the atmosphere there. All she cared about was her child.

'Didn't Mother already give her blessings to my endeavours as a *dalang*? Mother knows too that I am a *brahman* and *sudra* together. I need not kneel to anybody nor do I need others to do obeisance to me. And neither am I a *kedasih* bird that sings alone.'

'But those other people can endanger you, Child?'

'They do not endanger me, Mother, it is I who bring danger to myself and to them too. They face the danger of their own accord. Not because of me, but because . . . ' and I told her the situation that faced the farmers.

'No one has ever cared about the farmers before. It is only you who concern yourself so. No one has ever done it before. And people should listen to their superiors, because that is the purpose of having superiors, and that is the purpose of the farmers in the eyes of their superiors.'

'And who decided this, Mother?'

'They who are the most powerful amongst all men, that which is more powerful than all men. Have you ever seen a farmer in any *wayang* story? Never. Because they are just not there. There are only the kings, the knights, the priests. The closer a person works to the land, the less honour there is

320

to him, the less he is thought about by anybody.'

'But Mother has heard my story of the French Revolution.'

'A beautiful legend, Gus, my child.'

'In China the Empress has been overthrown, Mother. They do not need kings any more.'

'In China? Those Chinese? What is it to us if something happens in China? The Chinese know nothing of Java. They don't know how to behave.'

'Ah, Mother, do not look down on other peoples. This Java of ours is only a tiny spot on the oceans, Mother. Every people has their own greatness.'

'Of course I believe you, Child. But your error is that you have distanced yourself from the knights, and from knightliness. That is the big error you have made.'

'I am not able to insult and humiliate those who are close to the land, Mother.'

'You yourself are far removed from the land.'

'Do you remember, Mother? You used to tell me of the knight Bisma? He died in the battlefield. You told me how he would always come alive again, every time his corpse touched the earth? He lived again, did battle again, died again, and then came alive again as soon as he touched the earth.'

'And what about Bisma, Child?'

'He lives eternally, Mother, as long as he stays in touch with the earth. And the earth is the farmers, Mother, the farmers, yes, Mother, those very same farmers.'

'This has nothing to do with Bisma. Listen, I am here with a message from your father.'

I sat and listened to her while my eyes roamed round the room, which was simply furnished with things from Europe. On a big sideboard I could see Chinese ceramics and copper and *prastika* ornaments as well. Mir's baby cried from his crib outside in the sun. But none of this was noticed by my mother.

'I want you to think now not of what I have already heard from you, nor of me, your mother. I want you to think now of the worries your father has.'

I wanted to take her home to Buitenzorg but she refused because she wanted to return home quickly with my reply.

'I will write him a letter.'

'Good, Child. But even so, I want you to tell me yourself what you will say to him. So I can see your face as you tell me.'

'Who is it that Mother is worried about? This your son or Father?'

'Both of you. Both of you can suffer because of all this, Child.'

'Has Father received orders from his superiors?'

'How would I know? You know about those things better than I.'

I didn't want to say anything.

'You never think about me, Gus, my child. You don't even want to speak to me.'

I stood up and went across to take in a breath of fresh air. And my mother felt she was being ignored.

'Child, sit here, don't leave me here by myself like this.' I went across and sat down beside her. 'Now tell me what it is that you want to do.'

'Just because Father has received orders from his superiors, does not mean there is anything I can say to him.'

'Nor to your mother?'

'Only that your son, Mother, will still do what he intends to do. That is all.'

'Very well. Then write that letter.'

'There is no need now. What I have said is enough.'

Now mother was silent. She watched me closely, and there was disappointment written all over her face. Eventually she took hold of my hand. She asked: 'I understand, Child. You have dreamed all this time of becoming yourself. Are you prepared to see your father fall from his position?'

'That has nothing to do with me, Mother. If Father is dismissed it is not because of me. No.'

'Then why?'

'Because he has superiors that have the power to dismiss him.'

'You are firm in your decision?'

'As Mother can see for herself.'

'You do not hesitate?'

'No, Mother.'

'You will not regret it later?'

'No, Mother.'

'Is it true that you are a *kedasih* who does not sing alone?'

'That is I.'

'You are not wrong again, Gus, my child.'

'No, Mother.'

'Let there be no shaking of your legs. No trembling in your voice.'

'I stand resolute, Mother.'

'Let you not blink when your father falls from his position.'

'I will not blink.'

'Tomorrow I will go back, Child. Your mother will still pray for your safety.'

And I don't know how many times I had done this before, but again I kneeled in obeisance before her and kissed her knee.

'Gus, my son.'

'Mother.'

'You still remember that your mother has never forbidden you anything?'

'That has always been my talisman, Mother.'

'You have knelt down enough before your mother. You need do that no longer, not ever again. Rise up.'

'Why am I not allowed to kneel before you any more, Mother?'

'You have become yourself. Now it is your children who must kneel before you,' she spoke slowly, heavily, her voice tense with all of humankind's concern for its children.

As I stood and lifted up my face, I saw Mir coming up the steps into the house. But she didn't come in and I saw her go into the kitchen carrying a serving tray.

We both sat there silently. Mother's last words truly cut within me: Now it is your children who must kneel before you. They will never kneel before me, Mother, and I wanted to tell her the truth. I wanted to, but I never did. A picture of Hendrik and Mir when they were at their loneliest appeared before me. And then I heard the words of the German doctor in Bandung: You have no seed, Sir, they are too weak. Then there was the scene in the *sinse's* place in the bamboo house in front of the Buitenzorg markets . . . No, Mother, no child will ever kneel before me. And if there were children, I would never make them do such a thing, I would not allow it, because they would already be themselves, because they would be my friends in goodness, and my enemies in evil.

The next day Mother returned home, escorted by Marko.

The evening before she left, when some of us were discussing what my mother had reported, both Marko and Sandiman succeeded in convincing me that the reports about people flocking to the SDI branches could not be believed. What was closer to the truth was that the Government and the Syndicate had somehow discovered the Sarekat's plans.

1911. Inside the SDI and in my own heart there was much tumult and excitement. Outside, the Government was no less busy.

Medan's circulation continued to rise because of *The Tale of Siti Aini*. Marko's and Sandiman's assessment of the news that my mother had brought was proved wrong. Wherever there were sugar mills and plantations people flocked in huge numbers to the SDI, all registering as members. And they weren't just traders. Now there were farmers, Government *priyayi*, work-men, sailors, apothecaries and hospital laboratory workers. Then came the railway workers. The Sarekat had blossomed and its membership had trebled.

The TAI wasn't to be seen anywhere. But something new had risen from its corpse.

It was Buitenzorg and twilight was at its zenith.

Princess and I were sitting in the garden. Quite a way from us sat a man on a bench facing the main road – it was one of the fighters from Banten.

A hired carriage stopped before the front gate and a gentleman alighted. He wore glasses, a white buttoned-up shirt, black shoes and no hat. He was a big man. He carried a cane. He walked confidently up to us, bowed in respect, and asked in Dutch: 'Good afternoon. May I speak to you for a few moments?'

I invited him to sit down while glancing across at our bodyguard, who was sitting in the corner of the garden, his legs swinging below the bench. He was watching us closely.

'Let me introduce myself, Sir, my name is Pangemanann, with a double "n" at the end.'

'Pleased to meet you, Sir,' I said.

Princess stood, bowed to the guest and withdrew inside and did not come out again.

'I have wanted to meet you for a long time now,' he said very politely.

I examined this Pangemanann for a moment. He was obviously a Menadonese. He was perhaps fifty years old. I thought he was being unnecessarily polite, as a Menadonese to a Native Javanese. He had the same official status as a European. Thus I found his behaviour quite intriguing. And even more intriguing were the two 'n's at the end of his name, and that he felt the need to mention them.

'I am one of your admirers, Sir,' he spoke again, 'as many are. I read *Medan* not only so I can follow your writings, Sir, but also because you've started publishing *The Tale of Siti Aini*. Nothing can compete with *Medan* now. I, of course, will not be like everyone else and ask who Haji Moeloek is.'

He spoke fluently, quickly, and there was not the slightest hint of Malay influence on his Dutch. And I had to be patient and wait to find out what it was that he really wanted. He had placed his cane between his legs. His face, which was totally clean-shaven, seemed tanned. Perhaps he spent a lot of time outdoors. Perhaps he was a plantation employee.

'When do you think Haji Moeloek's story will finish?'

'Perhaps another six or eight months.'

'That's quite a thick book for something in Malay.'

'It seems that you are very interested in these matters.'

'I am among those who admire very much the ability to put down thoughts and feelings in writing, Sir. If he had written his story in Government Malay, like in Francis's *Nyai Dasima*, I don't think it would have been so alive.'

'So you do not approve of Government Malay?'

'It's not that. No one speaks in Government Malay, not even the Government. That's why I think you, Sir, are absolutely correct in continuing to use living Malay in *Medan*.'

'Thank you, Meneer Pangemanann with two "n"'s.'

'Actually, Sir, I am here for a specific reason. Perhaps it is not important for you, but it is for me.'

Aha, now I will learn what he's here for. I listened, but with heightened vigilance. Who knows, perhaps he was a member of the Indo gang.

'In my spare time I too like to write stories, Meneer, in Malay, but in school Malay, Government Malay.'

So he is a Government man, I thought, and: 'Aha!' I cried, 'and where have they been published?'

'Nowhere, Meneer. I've always held back, all these years. I have never felt satisfied with what I've written. There is just one novel left that I have kept.'

'Why have you held back? Why haven't you been satisfied?'

'It's not just that. I was ashamed to publish them because of Francis, Meneer. I knew him all his life, that king of storytelling! The Will of God! He has gone on before me. Now there is a new king of storytelling. From studying its style and vocabulary, as well as its subject matter, it is clear that the *Tale* was not written by you.'

'Of course not.'

'It's like this, Meneer. When the *Tale* is finished, is it possible that you could publish my story? Although it is not as great as Haji Moeloek's.'

'It's difficult to give such a promise.'

'Of course. I can understand that. You haven't studied my manuscript yet. You have to read it and consider it properly before you make a decision.'

'Did you bring the manuscript?'

'I will bring it to you in Bandung later.'

'What is it about, if I may ask?'

'It is about Pitung, the bandit, Meneer.'

'You mean it's a *lenong* story?'

'It's an attempt to improve *lenong*.'

'Improve it? How can you do that when the *lenong* actors themselves can't read or write? Yes, Francis tried to improve on the *lenong* story of *Nyai Dasima*. And he didn't succeed either.'

'Of course, while the *lenong* actors themselves cannot read, any attempt to improve the *lenong* repertoire will not succeed. Nevertheless the two of us have tried to do it.'

'It sounds very interesting. And meeting another writer is also always interesting. Even more so reading his work. I am looking forward to seeing it.'

He looked very pleased. Then suddenly he changed the subject: 'Meneer, it is very worrying hearing all these reports about the Knijpers. Very worrying. They say they have reappeared again as the TAI. Now there is a new group of these trouble-makers, Meneer, calling themselves De Zweep, the Whip. They say it's the same people as before, but a smaller and tighter group this time. Just a couple of score of people. And with more specific targets this time too.'

'Very interesting,' I commented.

'No, not interesting at all.'

'Who do you think they will target?'

'How would I know, Meneer? People they don't like, I suppose.'

'And no doubt it will be like before. None of them will be arrested by the police, or if they are they will be released even before they get to the police station.'

'Could be, too. Ah, it's already dark. I must go. Please excuse me. I will visit you in a few days' time in Bandung.' He stood up, held out his hand and said 'Good evening', then strode calmly out of our grounds.

That night I studied all the reports we had from the sugar regions, both reports from the branches and letters from readers. I rushed off an article about how justice was implemented there. This will be the first shot fired at the Syndicate.

The article itself didn't discuss the most important issues. It just reported to those people who knew nothing at all about life in the sugar areas what happened to children who took cane from the mills, how they were maltreated by the plantation officials. They would be detained until their parents came and paid a fine of one hundred cents. Their parents' wage, if they worked in the sugar plantations, would be seventy cents at the very most. But it wasn't the fine itself so much that signalled the injustice but the fact that the children took the cane out of hunger and need for sugar, took cane grown on the land of their own ancestors, sometimes even from their own parents' land, land they had been forced to rent to the mill.

I hadn't quite finished writing when Princess called me in for dinner. She asked then: 'Who was that, Mas?'

'Pangemanann with two "n"s, I answered.

'I didn't like him from the moment I saw him. Even the spelling of his name is strange, with two "n"s. What did he want? Was he making threats?'

'I think that was what he was here for. Now they're called the Zweep.'

'If they bother us again, I will shoot them again.'

'Is that necessary yet?'

'Rather than them get in first.'

She was talking out of anger and frustration.

Three days later, my article touching upon the power of Sugar was published. And on that day too, just a few hours after publication, Pangemanann was sitting at my desk. He had his manuscript *Si Pitung* with him. I observed him closely. I could see him furtively glance down at an envelope that was lying on my table. Its corners were marked with red stripes.

It was possible he recognised the letter. With a somewhat piercing look from his eyes, he handed over his manuscript, saying politely: 'I hope you like this and will decide to publish it.'

'Do you have a copy at home?'

'Unfortunately, no, Meneer. But I know it will be safe in your hands.' He stole another glance at the envelope on the desk, then returned to watching me.

I returned his gaze with a patient smile. The letter was a threat from the Zweep that they would move against me if I did not withdraw the article about the cane fines and the maltreatment of the children who were hungry and did not have enough sugar. *Medan* was supposed to explain that the article wasn't serious and the things described in it never happened. At the bottom were the words the Zweep, and there was a signature. The name seemed European.

I thought that Pangemanann was going to discuss the letter, but it didn't happen. Then he suddenly turned the conversation: 'It seems you are really determined.'

'There is nothing to be afraid of, is there, Meneer? What is it that we should be afraid of?'

'He-he-he, no. I mean it seems that you are very determined and committed in carrying out your work. Committed people must be respected. That is why I respect you.'

'And where do you see this determination in me, Meneer?'

'In your attitude.'

'It appears that you seem to see some danger ahead of me. Or perhaps it is you yourself, Meneer, that is the danger to me?' I joked.

He let out a rather indecent laugh. He wasn't carrying his cane this time. He wore clean white clothes but now his shoes were brown. As before he wore no hat, and his rather golden hair – there was no grey at all – shone with hair oil.

'I like the way you talk, Meneer. Bold. Sharp. No mincing words or suchlike.'

'You are a true man of letters,' I said, praising him, 'taking so much notice of every word spoken and how they are spoken.'

'Yes, it is a hobby of mine. Could I have a receipt for my manuscript? I must go, I have other appointments.'

I made him out a receipt. He took it and excused himself, leaving behind the words: 'May you have success, Meneer.'

I didn't escort him to the door. And I began to examine the day's mail. At that moment I heard a voice thundering before me: 'Are you withdrawing the article or not?'

I jumped up. Before me there stood three Indos, each one hiding his hands behind his back. At the front was someone I had known since the last century – Robert Suurhof.

Before I could answer, I heard a cracking sound. My vision went black, I saw stars everywhere. My face and body felt the lash of whips again and again. My mouth was hit. I tasted a salty taste. Blood.

I don't know how many times I felt those lashes. I felt my body fall, after staggering for a moment, crashing into the arms of the chair, then . . . nothing. All I could hear was the voice inside me shouting: 'No! No! I will not withdraw it!'

As I regained consciousness I heard voices about me. I couldn't tell who they belonged to. Perhaps Suurhof and his friends. I tried harder to tell. It was Hendrik's voice that I heard first: 'How are his eyes, Doctor? They're not damaged, are they?'

'They'll need care for quite a while.'

I tried to speak. But my lips refused my orders to move. My hand seemed to move by itself, groping for my lips. I had no lips. All I could feel were wet bandages. And now I could smell medicines.

'Minke!' I recognised Mir's cry.

I moved my hand, and I felt it grasped and caressed by a smooth palm. I felt the slipperiness of a metal ring. There wasn't a sliver of light that penetrated my vision. My eyes were also covered with bandages.

'Tuan,' I heard Marko's voice. 'Everything happened so quickly. I was in the print shop. Sandiman heard the noise first. He came up to the office. The attack was already under way. He grabbed a typesetter's hammer and threw it at them. He got one in the shoulder. They fled. Sandiman went after them. But they had horses waiting and escaped on them.'

I gave a weak nod accepting his request for forgiveness. I moved my hand again and my fingers indicated they wanted pencil and paper. As soon as someone put them in my hand, I wrote these words: 'Continue with all our work. Study all the reports from the sugar regions. If they seem to be more or less accurate, then publish them. Watch security. Take me to Buitenzorg.'

'And this incident, Minke, are you going to remain silent about it?' asked Hendrik. 'I don't think it is right that we keep quiet about it. We should begin now.'

'Yes, we will now begin publicising this terror,' I wrote. 'But keep a good watch on security. And you too, Hendrik, Mir, be careful.'

'Thank you, Minke.'

Mir and Sandiman took me by taxi to Buitenzorg. Mir sat with me in the back. Sandiman rode in front with the driver.

'Is the driver an Indo?' I wrote on a piece of paper.

'Yes,' whispered Mir in the bandage that covered my ear.

'Be careful, Mir,' I wrote again.

'Don't worry,' she whispered, then kissed the part of my face that was not bandaged. 'Sandiman is armed.'

She spoke no more, but just caressed my hand.

As we journeyed along I thought of my mother, and Mama and Princess, three extraordinary women whom I had met during my life. Then I saw Ang San Mei, pale, skinny and narrow-eyed. It was as if she came to me at that moment, knowing the helpless state I was in, as helpless and powerless as a worm. And I thought I heard her whisper: As long as you realise, Minke, this is just the beginning. And I nodded that I understood. Then I saw Khouw Ah Soe waving to me and then suddenly he vanished. But SDI had already announced itself to the world. They had written that the Indies bourgeoisie is beginning to rise. And now its *dalang* lay bruised and beaten in the care of a European woman.

Suddenly my heart started thumping. The idea that the Syndicate would get a laugh out of all this made me furious. And I couldn't picture them in my mind, they were abstract and anonymous.

'Your pulse has got faster, Minke, what are you thinking about?'

I shook my head.

I felt the taxi come to a stop. We must be in the grounds of the house in Buitenzorg.

Mir led me out of the car, and up the steps.

'Princess! Princess!' Mir cried out.

It wasn't long before I heard running footsteps and cries: 'Mas, what has happened? Why are you like this?'

I felt her hand take mine and she led me into the room.

'He can't speak yet, Princess. And he can't use his eyes yet either. It was the Zweep.'

'The Zweep,' Princess whispered into the bandage over my ear. 'I should have shot that Pangemanann.'

'Don't be a hot-head, Princess.'

'I know that one day I will have to shoot them.'

'Don't think about such things, Princess, for God's sake you'll just make him worried and anxious,' said Mir.

They led me onto my bed.

I could hear Sandiman giving orders to the men from Banten. Nobody was allowed on the grounds, except with the permission of Princess. Anyone who did come in had to be taught a lesson so that they understood next time.

That afternoon Hendrik arrived, with the nanny who looked after the baby. He came straight to me and reported that everything had been done as ordered. He also passed on a message to Sandiman to go back to the office in Bandung as soon as he could.

Reports of the attack, my wife told me, were published in some of the Betawi and Bandung papers, mentioning the names of the attackers. The SDI was moving into action and demanding revenge. I wrote a message to the Central Leadership that there should be no action taken against the Zweep. They were just the instruments of greater forces. We must not be side-tracked from our challenge to Sugar. Victory in the struggle against Sugar was the most important thing.

Hendrik Frischboten had also been at work. The attackers had been detained and would be put on trial as soon as I was well.

One afternoon Douwager came to visit me to say he was sorry to hear what had happened. My mouth had been unbandaged by then, though my lips still felt swollen.

'Where is Wardi?'

'He hasn't been in Bandung for a while,' he answered.

'He's been travelling around propagandising for that new party, perhaps.'

He didn't confirm or deny. 'If he knew what had happened, he would have come straight away.'

'It doesn't matter. The propaganda work is important too.'

And it was then that it also became clear to me, even though my eyes were still covered – he and Wardi were not joining in the fight against the Syndicate. Not with deeds, and not in their hearts either. Indies Nationalism was more important to them.

And I was not discouraged because of it.

The trial proceeded quickly and without complications. The motive for the attack was that Robert Suurhof did not like the article in *Medan*. Why didn't he like it? No reason. He just didn't like it.

I tried to open up the trial to broader issues, but the court wouldn't let things go outside the actual attack and firmly rejected moving even an inch off track.

Robert Suurhof and his friends were found guilty of premeditated assault and were sentenced to four months each. And with that, the matter was considered ended.

But for me the matter had not ended at all.

While they were shut away in gaol, we published even more reports about the sugar districts. In some areas people went into action and began setting the cane-fields alight. This movement began in Sidoarjo, where Mama was born, the place where my story began. One of the laboratory workers who was a member of the SDI taught people how to set the cane alight. When the dry season had reached its peak, it was enough for one person to slip in amongst the cane at night and pour phosphorus over the leaves that lay on the ground after the cane had been pruned. Then next day, as the temperature rose, the phosphorus would ignite by itself. The fallen leaves would burn. If the guards looking after the cane were at all slack, the fire would spread very fast. Even if they acted quickly, they would still lose a quarter of a hectare that would be burnt to the ground. And there would be another hectare of cane that could no longer be sent to the mill. To put the fire out, all of the coolies would have to be mobilised. The cost of putting out even a small fire would at least equal that of putting down a rebellion.

At first, the sugar barons didn't understand exactly what was happening. After there had been twenty fires in just one month in Central and East Java, they organised a conference. The results – security of the plantations would be strengthened. The fire epidemic stopped, but not because of the increased security. The wet season had arrived.

Reports from the sugar areas became more and more popular in the press, especially the Malay press. There were no signs of any activity from the Indo gang, perhaps because their ringleaders were still shut away in gaol.

Then came one more trial, the heaviest of all.

One afternoon a man came to see me. He was already beginning to show his age. His clothes were dirty and faded. He wore a black Malay *fez*, so that you could hardly see his hair. He was an Acehnese named Teukoe Djamiloen. This name indicated that he had been a traditional leader in Aceh.

'There is nothing else for me to do than come and see you, Tuan,' he said in a rather strangely-pronounced Malay. 'After living some time now in these uncertain straits, and after asking here and there, it seems it is only Tuan who can perhaps help me. So here I have come. Who knows? Perhaps it is God Himself who has led me here.'

I observed his lean dry skin. He moved lithely, and had the appearance of someone from Southern India. He was perhaps forty-five years old. He wore a week's growth of moustache, beard and whiskers along his neck under his chin.

'What is it you want?' I asked, impatient with his ornate and overpolite manner of speaking.

'At first I humoured myself that it did not matter being here in Priangan because our leader Tjoet Nya Dhin too was exiled here. But as time passed I have found less and less consolation in this thought. The feeling that I had been treated unjustly, Tuan, began to gnaw at my soul more and more, day and night.'

'What was it that happened?'

'Yes, Tuan, just before the Aceh War ended, the Army captured me in a *blang*.'

'A blang?'

' A field, Tuan. They caught me after we had been surrounded. Then they beat us. Several of my comrades were killed. They took the rest, all badly wounded. It was about the same time that Tjoet Nya Dhin was caught in the jungle and exiled here to Priangan. I and some of my friends were put in gaol – for five years. After they let me out, I lived in Kotaraja back in Aceh for four years. I got married again and had a child. Then one day I was summoned to the office of Tuan Kontrolir of Kotaraja. All he asked was: Is this Teukoe Djamiloen? Then and there I was taken to the harbour and put on a ship. I had nothing with me. I was brought here to Priangan in Java, and then just let go like that.'

I took him to see Frischboten and I told him to repeat his story.

'Barbarians!' hissed Hendrik, who himself was unable to control his fury. His eyes burned.

'Then how did you live after that?'

'I have trodden all roads, Tuan, all roads – and they all led to gaol.'

'You've been in court?'

'Several times.'

'The matter of your being exiled here from Aceh without any Court Order has never been raised?'

'Never.'

'Can you prove what you have told us?' I asked.

'I am an Acehnese, Tuan, and a teukoe, who for more than fifteen years fought in the battlefield. Is it right that I should now lie?'

'We're sorry, don't be angry.'

'What is the point of lying and cheating if I can still use my muscles and my mind? Yes, I have stolen, fought and robbed. But lie, Tuan, and cheat, that is not in my character. I am a true Acehnese.'

'Fine,' said Hendrik. He took some paper and started to question the Acehnese in more detail.

Two hours passed. The questions were finished. Teukoe Djamiloen was asked to come back the next morning to continue the interview.

'Have you ever met Tjoet Nya Dhin?' I asked.

'I have never been able to find her. How could I look for her when my situation is like this?'

'This is enough now. You can go.'

He didn't seem to want to go.

'Where will you go?' I asked.

'If you would allow me, I could guard your door at the office?'

He had no place to stay.

Hendrik looked at me, nodding. He believed all that Teukoe Djamiloen had told him. And that meant that the Teukoe's request was agreed to, and so he joined Marko's men.

As soon as he had left, I asked Hendrik; 'Could a Kontrolir exile someone without any recourse to the law like that?'

'It's happened before, hasn't it, Minke. Not just in the Indies, but in all the colonies. This is not the only case.'

'And the person has no way of defending himself?'

'He could, if there was someone who could handle his case.'

'So it is because he has no money that he can't defend himself?'

'No, it's more than that. Look, Minke, according to the law, the only person who can act arbitrarily like that, who has a legal right to do that, is the Governor-General. You know yourself about the Extraordinary Rights, rights which only the Governor-General has. But there are those local officials, who, because they're crazy with power, or because they don't understand the limits of their authority, or because they've been bribed by the local Native rulers, come to think that these rights extend down to them, and they use them. They use them without ever requesting permission from the only one who has such rights under the law – the Governor-General. It's always been like that.'

'We can take legal action, can't we?'

'Yes. The Kontrolir of Kotaraja will lose, but nothing will happen to him. He will not undergo any punishment.'

'Even if found guilty?'

'Even if found guilty. Because he has the right to request his superiors to give him the protection of his office. And they always agree.'

'In that case we should just publish the story then.'

'That is the best thing to do.'

And so it was that the case of Teukoe Djamiloen was launched in *Medan*. I was immediately summoned by the authorities. A preliminary investigation took place, but they were not concerned about whether the report was true or not, rather with why I had decided to publish it. The examination wasn't even completed, and I was further summoned to meet the Assistant Resident.

'How could you believe, Meneer, that such a thing could actually happen?'

'The man is with me now, Mr Assistant Resident. I can bring him here if you wish. Perhaps that is the best thing to do.'

'What is the point of bringing a madman here?'

'Madmen are not sent into exile, Meneer.'

'Are you prepared to bring witnesses that he is not crazy?'

'Why not, Mr Assistant Resident?'

'Be careful, Meneer. Your report has already come to the notice of those above. It is better that you withdraw the story before things go too far.'

'*Medan* intends to report further on this case.'

'It's better that you don't, Meneer. The world is still going to go on. There is still much time ahead, and this life is so enjoyable.'

He escorted me to the door.

And we continued our campaign on Teukoe Djamiloen's behalf.

Everybody's spirits at *Medan* were high because of all the victories we had won. The Syndicate was clearly not going ahead with its plan to lower its rent payments to the peasants. We had so far got away with only a mild warning from the Assistant Resident. The Zweep were still shut away in gaol. SDI was bounding ahead – it membership had trebled.

For me the whole world had opened up. All obstacles moved out of my way, running away in embarrassment and shame. All the *Medan* publications, newspapers and magazines, circulating more and more widely, were entering the minds and hearts of their readers, and were leaving behind seeds that would surely one day grow.

Haji Moeloek's serial was almost finished. I had begun to prepare another story, called *Nyai Permana*. It was also a story of the sufferings of a farmer and the unworthy behaviour of the Native officals. A few years ago, the Government had carried out a land redistribution. But the Native officials had grabbed the land for themselves, and had often sold it for their own profit as well. I wrote the story myself. I based it on real events but mixed in things reflecting the dreams of the girl from Jepara, especially about the rights that must be possessed by women – the right of a woman to divorce her husband, for example. Such a right should not only lie with the husband who can then get rid of his wife whenever he likes.

I was so involved with writing this story that all the many other major problems had to wait their turn for my attention.

But then came our greatest trial, as I have mentioned earlier.

As soon as I had stepped off the train in Bandung, Sandiman was there, along with Teukoe Djamiloen. Both of them seemed exhausted. Sandiman was carrying a big package. I could tell from his eyes that he was very worried.

'This is all I could get, Tuan,' said Sandiman, opening proceedings.

'What is it?'

'The manuscripts and papers from your office.'

'Why have you brought it here?'

'We have all been evicted from the printery and the editorial office.'

The Zweep have moved into action again. I thought. 'There wasn't any fighting, was there?'

'How could we fight, Tuan. They all carried rifles. The police!'

'The police have evicted us?' I asked unbelievingly. 'What for? What reason did they give?'

'They just threw us all out. They didn't say what it was about. The office has been locked and sealed. These papers were all I could save.'

We left for No 1 Naripan Street. The office was sealed. Marko was sitting on the step, his head in his knees.

'You all go home, Keep these papers safe,' I gave orders.

I jumped on a *dokar* and headed off to the Assistant Resident's office. He had no other visitors, but I still wasn't invited in from the waiting room. My legs and arms all wanted to do something. My patience was wearing thin. The Assistant Resident came out and pretended not to see me waiting. He went in again, having looked at me, still pretending not to know anything. That was enough. So the sealing up of the offices was on his orders. His direct orders!

Without waiting to be summoned, I knocked on his door. He nodded, smiled sweetly, and invited me to sit down. Then he stood. I sat down and he pretended he was busy and had to go outside again. As if I didn't know how busy an Assistant Resident really was!

Now I sat waiting at his desk. There were no papers on it anywhere. There were no books of law statutes or dictionaries. Nothing. In a sideboard there were a whole lot of porcelain ornaments and a collection of pipes. When I saw them, I realised that the room was permeated with the smell of tobacco tar.

Was he punishing me for knocking on his door and ignoring protocol? To hell with it, my business with him is also important. If *Medan* doesn't publish, it will confuse the whole of the Sarekat and the campaigns against abuse of power will stop, because only *Medan* is capable of carrying out those tasks, at its own risk.

Five minutes went by. He still hadn't come back. Damn! Why are you avoiding me? Don't worry, I have no power over you, do I? Or are you afraid, Meneer Assistant Resident?

A servant came in and placed a glass of water on the desk. He pushed the glass away from me. Then he left, disappearing behind the door. It was another five minutes before the Assistant Resident of Priangan appeared again. There were no signs of perspiration on his neck or face. Perhaps the business he had to attend to involved nothing more than moving his pipe from hand to mouth and back again. His pipe was back in his mouth now, and he mumbled: 'Forgive me, Meneer.'

Before sitting down, he took out his pipe, picked up the glass of water and drank it all down. It was he who was nervous. He needed something to calm himself.

He sat down. He still didn't speak. Slowly he knocked out the tobacco ash from the bowl of his pipe into an ashtray, and refilled his pipe. Then he lit it with matches two or three times, drawing in slowly and then exhaling even more slowly. Only then: 'There is no doubt something important.'

'More than just important,' I answered. 'Why has *Medan* been sealed up, Mr Assistant Resident?'

'Why haven't you made this enquiry through a letter?'

'This is better. Moreover the action that has been taken was also done without anything in writing. It's better that we do this face to face.'

'And when did this sealing up of *Medan* take place?' There was a glint in his eyes as he spoke, like a clown who had no more audience.

'I suspect precisely at the time that you ordered it.'

'Oh, yes. Was that what those there said?'

'That is what I say. Meneer.'

'Oh, is that right? So you want . . . ?'

'I want to know the grounds upon which you have sealed up *Medan*.'

'Oh, is that all? You just want to know the grounds?'

'If I find them acceptable, yes, that is all.'

'Do you remember the report you published about Teukoe Djamiloen?'

'So your intention is to turn me into a Teukoe Djamiloen here in Priangan too?'

'No,' he answered uneasily, 'I mean that isn't it true that I warned you about that report. I was clear, wasn't I?'

'Very clear. And it turns out that there were no inaccuracies at all in that report. No one ever refuted it.'

'Not yet.'

'Very well, not yet, but *Medan* has already been sealed up.'

He was silent a moment. He picked up the glass, but he couldn't drink because it was already empty. He drew on his pipe, but it had gone out. He lit a match and started up the pipe again, drawing and exhaling quickly.

'So can you explain to me what valid reasons you have for closing *Medan*?' I asked.

'I warned you.'

'That is not grounds. Neither are the ten anonymous letters I have received giving me such warnings.'

'Are you equating the warning of an Assistant Resident with anonymous letters?'

'We both know that you are the only person making such a comparison.'

'Very well. What are your views since you have received that warning?'

'My opinion? The Government, of course, will investigate the Kontrolir of Kotaraja.'

'So your purpose is to set the Government and the Kontrolir against each other?'

'That is your question, not my answer. In any case I have come to see you, not to be examined when there is no summons, but to receive an explanation, Meneer, as to why *Medan* has been sealed up.'

'Are you sure that *Medan* has been in fact sealed up?'

'Why, hasn't it?'

'Did you yourself see?'

'There was no need for me to see for myself.'

'In that case, you had better check again. You don't want to be mistaken.'

'It seems clear that you do not want to give any reason. That's OK, too. It seems I will have to go to higher authorities.'

'And where will you go?'

'I think that is my business. At least three levels above you.'

'That's a bit silly. Don't you think so?'

'No.'

'Don't be so quick to anger, Meneer. You see I received an order to freeze all businesses under your control in my district.'

336

'Now we're getting somewhere. You are only carrying out somebody else's orders. Who asked you to do this?'

'I'm not allowed to say. But may I ask how is your account with the Handels Bank?'

He was looking for excuses. Our account was in quite a healthy state. But this person needed to be taught a lesson. I answered: 'Perhaps the bank owes us too much?'

He laughed, enjoying the joke. Nodded. Tapped his pipe on the table.

'So, that's the answer?'

'Yes, that's about it. You check with the bank.'

'But the Handels Bank has no right to sequester property without discussing things first with me. We are its clients and they are our clients. The accounts aren't always in balance, but that's normal.'

'Go and see the bank first, Meneer.'

He wasn't going to discuss it any more. I went straight to the homes of *Medan's* workers. The houses we provided for them had also been sealed up. Their inhabitants, with their belongings, were outside, huddled in groups under the trees. They all stood up when I arrived. But I was unable to give them any firm promises. I suggested that they find somewhere to stay for the time being with friends or relatives.

The Assistant Resident's obvious intention was to try to destroy *Medan's* public and commercial standing. As soon as I left, he would have telephoned the Handels Bank, giving them instructions as to what they must do when I arrived. If that's what he is really trying to do, he will soon be looking in a mirror and seeing his own stupidity.

Before I set off to the bank, I remembered Hendrik Frischboten. I turned back to the workers and told them all to go to stay at the Frischbotens'. All of them!

As soon as I entered the bank, several employees stopped working just to watch me. Then someone came out to greet me and took me straight to the Director, Meneer Termaaten. He invited me to sit down, and then: 'Meneer Minke, our bank serves its clients. The bank takes a neutral position in any dispute between its clients and anyone else, including the authorities. Except, of course, if there is some law that says otherwise. And even then we will also consider whether the law is acceptable or not. If we cannot accept it, then the law must concede or we will close up and move to another country.'

'Thank you, Meneer.'

'We also do not wish to know what has happened between *Medan* and the Assistant Resident.'

He stopped talking and waved his hand at a clerk.

The clerk brought over a big book. He opened the book and placed it on the table.

'As you can see here, Meneer, *Medan* has a surplus of almost ten thousand guilders. Only the bank and you know this, Meneer, no one else. Outsiders have no right to know, except with your permission.'

After visiting the bank I went straight to a *warung* to eat. As soon as I sat down in the corner, someone else sat down beside me.

He ahemmed once.

My thoughts were still occupied by the beauty of the power game that the Assistant Resident had tried to play. He clearly had no legal authority over the bank. Very beautiful.

The person next to me ahemmed again.

When I turned to look at him, it was none other than Pangemanann with the two 'n's. I was quite startled, and quickly put on my guard.

There could be no doubt that somewhere nearby were the Zweep. I regretted not ordering Sandiman or Marko to accompany me. There was nothing I could do now. I would have to face this situation by myself. 'Oh, Meneer Pangemanann.'

'Good afternoon, Meneer. I saw you from afar, so I hurried along and caught up with you. Unfortunately I have already eaten, so I cannot join you. But you don't mind chatting a bit while you're waiting for your meal to be prepared, do you?'

'Please, please.'

'So what did you think about *Si Pitung*?'

'Yes, your style is very much like Francis'.'

'He was my teacher,' he explained. 'So Meneer will publish it?'

'Certainly,' I said. 'But not yet. After Haji Moeloek's serial finishes, there's another story that I want to publish first.'

He put on a disappointed look when he heard that. Crocodile!

'No doubt a more interesting story,' he said, fishing.

'Ah, that is up to the tastes and needs of the reader,' I replied, while trying to work out what kind of finale this chit-chat was leading up to.

'Meneer, your report about Teukoe Djamiloen was truly interesting. If it wasn't for your report no one in the Indies would have known that there were European officials who took actions that were completely outside the law. I know truly that such behaviour is contrary to the Europeans conscience.'

'Contrary? Why?'

'I lived in Europe for a long time, Meneer, long enough for me to become European. I know that Europe could not survive without the law. Since they are babies, Europeans are educated to follow rules. There are indeed many theories about the law, but one thing at least is clear – it is the law that has made Europe great. Then it seems that as soon as they leave their own land, many Europeans forget the education they received at home and the law that has brought them up.' He was silent a moment. Then he pretended to be startled. 'Oh, what are we doing talking about the law just before eating?

Ah, I see your dinner is ready. Heh! One white coffee for me, please.'

He watched me as I was served with my food. 'Hearty eating, Tuan, please, please.'

I ate slowly. My appetite had disappeared because of this person. And I didn't want to eat much because of the fight that I might very well have to face before this was over. All the while I was eating I tried to see outside without making him suspicious.

He sipped on his coffee without paying me any attention.

'With a simple *warung* like this people can still live decently, serving everyone who comes – everyone who has money in their pockets. Why do people go to so much trouble to seek a livelihood? But is one's livelihood the only important thing? Huh!' he sort of hissed to himself. 'There are other more important things, especially for those people with ideals, of course. But there are not many of them. Not many! There are almost none in fact. But they do exist.'

He looked at me again. 'Why don't you finish your meal, Meneer. No appetite?'

'I can't eat much, Meneer.'

'Or perhaps you have lost your appetite because of the law?'

'No.' I stood and moved across to the bench opposite, where I could see out onto the main street.

Pangemanann seemed to turn around spontaneously to look behind out onto the main street, 'It seems you like to watch the traffic, Meneer.'

'Yes, things that are alive and moving always interest me.'

'You won't be bored, will you, if we talk more about the law.'

'It seems that you are an expert in the law, heh?'

'I know a little bit about it, yes, but that's all.'

'How many years did you live in Europe?'

'Almost nine years, Meneer, in France.'

'A beautiful country, a country of myths and legends. It's understandable then that you like the law. And perhaps that's also why you use two "n"s.'

'You are very clever, Meneer. With just one "n", the French would pronounce the last syllable of my name "nang", so I changed it to double "n", so they woud pronounce it properly, "naan".' He laughed, laughing to himself.

'And perhaps Meneer does not simply like the law, but also carries it out, heh?' I asked.

He laughed again. He neither confirmed nor denied. Suddenly: 'Tell me, what is your personal opinion about what the Kontrolir of Kotaraja did?'

'As to the legality of it, I am sure Meneer would know better. But to me it seems rather odd. It is the Dutch who make the law, and it is the Dutch themselves who trample on it. A bit of a costly joke, don't you think?'

'Yes, I think that is exactly what it is,' he shook his head. 'And your opinion of the Extraordinary Rights of the Governor-General?'

'So that's what you want to know? Those rights place him outside the law, or more precisely, above the law, like the ancient kings of Java, isn't that so? Yes. So that means there has been no advance in the Indies since those times, yes?'

'But below the Governor-General there is law. Under the kings of Java, there was nothing, absolutely nothing, like . . . yes, like what, I wonder?'

'If you say there was nothing at all, I think that's a bit of an exaggeration.'

'I don't think so, Meneer. There was no positive law, nothing written down, nothing definite and solid that people could grab hold of. Any ruler or official could do whatever he liked.'

'Yes, like the Kontrolir of Kotaraja.'

His next words suddenly evaporated out of my consciousness. Across the road I saw a woman carrying an umbrella. I could see the bottom half of her body. She was wearing a silk blouse, a *batik kain* and velvet slippers. She had no escort. A very strange scene. The umbrella was a plain black one. I thought to myself that her gait and stride would have been better matched by a beautiful light floral umbrella. She carried a rather large leather handbag. She walked slowly. I saw her stop just as a bicycle caught up to her. And there could be no doubt that it was Sandiman on the bicycle. But he didn't stop or alight, even though the woman stopped. He pedalled on, and disappeared. The woman continued walking with that gentle, swaying gait.

I knew that bag with the roses pictured on it. I watched more closely and tried to imagine what the figure behind the umbrella would be like. But why didn't Sandiman stop, get off and pay his respects? Wasn't that Princess? My wife?

I no longer heard Pangemanann's chatter. If that was my wife what was she doing in Bandung without an escort? And now she had disappeared from my view.

I stood, called over the *warung*-keeper and excused myself from my unhoped-for friend. He also stood. Just as I was about to put the money in the *warung*-keeper's hand, we heard two revolver shots. Then there was silence. The money left in my hand dropped by itself into that of the *warung*-keeper.

'Shots,' hissed Pangemanann.

Ignoring me, he dropped some money on the table and disappeared outside, I couldn't see where.

Then I left myself, walking quickly in the direction of the shots. The woman whom I suspected was my wife was nowhere to be seen. At the edge of the road there were three men collapsed on the road. Two of them were bathed in their own blood. The other showed no signs of a wound. Pangemanann was already there. He was bending over examining those covered in blood. By the time I got there one had just died, shot directly in the heart. One of the others was moving and trying to sit up. As soon as I saw him, I knew who it was – Robert Suurhof.

I covered my face, as I knew I was now amongst the Zweep. There may have been more than just these three.

The one who didn't seem to be wounded was thrusting his legs about.

Pangemanann called out for people to help. A few people then came across, and he told them to find something for stretchers. He told others to fetch the police. Then he examined the one who didn't seem to be wounded. He opened up his shirt. It was only then we would see that there was a knife buried in his waist. Buried right up to its hilt. There was only a small ring of blood visible.

I walked away quickly. My eyes roved about wildly looking for that black umbrella. Or a bicycle with Sandiman on it. Neither was there. A few score metres away from the site of the killings there was a man squatting, with his *sarong* pulled up covering the top half of his body, except his face. No one who had just heard shooting nearby would be still hanging around like that. He was turned away from me so I could see his face from the side. I knew that profile – Marko! He turned away to avoid my gaze, then stood up, wrapped his *sarong* around him and moved to sit down at a stall selling snacks.

Good. I know where you are. But where are the black umbrella and Sandiman?

I walked and walked. I was bathed in perspiration. I couldn't keep going like this. I went into a taxi depot. The office was in the back corner, on the right behind the garage, which had places for nineteen automobiles.

I already knew Meneer Meyerhoff, the owner.

'Need a car, Meneer?'

'Yes, Meneer.'

'You can use whichever one you like. You can keep it for a week, as long as there is a driver available.'

'I see you've rented out five already.'

'A quiet day today.'

'Some were hired to go to Betawi perhaps?'

'Yes, Meneer, three. One very early this morning. Another one three hours or so ago. And one more just now.'

'Oh, perhaps Meneer Helferdink has already gone then?'

'Yes, Meneer Helferdink, and a Native too, hired the car for five hours, he did.'

The taxi was brought out onto the road and I excused myself.

The driver was a middle-aged Indo. I told him to drive all round town. And the black umbrella was still nowhere to be seen. I stopped at the Assistant Resident's place for a minute but his gate was locked. Then we went to the

Frischbotens'. But they had left. It wasn't clear where they had gone. Then I stopped at one of the bigger shops. I hurriedly alighted and went in to buy myself a hunting knife. I slipped it into my belt.

'Buitenzorg,' I ordered the driver. 'What's your name?'

'Botkin, Meneer.'

'Russian descent, perhaps?'

'You're not mistaken, Meneer.'

I offered him a cigarette. He took one without looking, nodded, mumbled, and put it in his mouth. I lit a match. Smoke soon billowed forth from his nose and mouth.

You can try something with me if you like, Botkin. And I sat there watching him vigilantly. This taxi must travel straight on, without stopping, until it gets to my home. If it stopped in the middle of the journey, nah, that meant danger.

That journey, which wasn't all that long, was a very tense journey. And Botkin did indeed take me straight to my house. I told him to stop in front of the main gate. After I gave him a tip he departed for I don't know where.

I examined the ground round the front gate. There were no tyre tracks or other signs of a car stopping there. There were no tracks either in the front grounds. As I climbed onto the veranda I heard a lot of shouting. I looked up. There were many people in the front parlour – Hendrik and Mir Frischboten, a Native man and a woman, perhaps his wife, that I didn't recognise. And children.

My wife came out, greeting me with a reprimand: 'There are many guests waiting, Mas. They've just arrived!' She smiled so sweetly, as if everything was as usual. She brushed off the imaginary dust from my shirt – just as she always did.

I looked deeply into her eyes, and she avoided mine. That was not normal. I quickly put on a happy face and went in to greet my guests. But who were the Native man and his wife and children?

'Have you forgotten me?' he asked. 'Panji Darman.'

He embraced me and we embraced each other.

'This is my wife. Look, already four children.'

His wife was an Indo woman. She had become too fat after giving birth to four children. Perhaps she had been slim and pretty before.

Fortunately Panji Darman was able to bring himself under control and he sat down again. His wife took my hand, and nodded as we shook hands, smiling.

I excused myself for a moment to change clothes.

As soon as I was in the bedroom I opened the wardrobe. I examined the shoes and slippers at the bottom. There was one pair of Princess's slippers that were covered in dust. Yes, the velvet slippers! The black leather bag, with the picture of the rose, was indeed the one I had seen earlier. I smelt inside and there was a strange smell there – gunpowder! Perhaps it was just my imagination. And where was that black umbrella? It wasn't hung in the corner wardrobe where it usually was. I closed the door. And I found the umbrella on top of the wardrobe.

I examined the object. There were three holes in it.

I opened the key box. And with one of the keys, I unlocked the dresser. The revolver was there. But not in its right place. And there was only one bullet left!

I sat down on the bed. My wife, Princess of Kasiruta, was a . . . No, I had no right to make accusations.

Princess entered and came across to me. 'We've got many guests. Are you ill, Mas?'

I looked her in the eyes. Again she avoided my gaze.

'Where have you been, Princess?'

'To the markets.'

'You don't usually go to the markets.'

'No. But I just felt like it this time. Why? You seem to be very suspicious today?'

And indeed I was becoming more and more suspicious because of how calm she was.

She took me by the arm and brought me to the door. As soon as I sat down I realised that I had neither changed clothes nor locked the door of the dresser where the revolver was kept. I wanted to go back to the room, but Princess hadn't come out yet.

'What time did you all leave Bandung?' I asked the Frischbotens.

'We didn't look at the time. As soon as all the *Medan* workers started flocking to the house, we set off for here. There was nowhere left for us at home!'

'About four hours ago,' added Mir.

My wife came out and then announced to everybody that their rooms were ready. They all went in to change clothes and have a rest.

I too went back into my room. I repeated my examination. Now the umbrella was back in its proper place. The slippers were no longer covered in dust. And now the number of bullets with the revolver was the correct number, not more or less. Did I count them wrongly before?

Perhaps Princess was already suspicious of me. She rushed back in the room. I saw her glance for a moment at the wardrobe and then at the dresser.

'I am very tired, Princess,' I said.

'How would you like some *jeruk* juice? I'll make some.'

And so I sat on the edge of the bed. She stood just a little way from me.

'I'd prefer it if you massaged my neck. It feels so stiff and it aches.'

She came closer.

'Put your legs up here, so I can massage from behind.'

I did what she wanted and she began to massage me.

'Did you come home by yourself just now or with Sandiman?'

'Sandiman? Is Sandiman in Buitenzorg?'

'Oh, yes, he's in Bandung. Why I am so forgetful today?'

'Yes, you're too tired, Mas. Your throat is all hot. Go to sleep, I'll explain to the guests.'

I lay back on the bed. Before she left, I grabbed her arm. And I saw there was a cut, about twenty centimetres long, on the back on one of her arms.

'What did you do to your arm?'

She smiled at me sweetly as if she was trying to seduce me.

'A nail at the markets.'

'And in what part of the markets is there a nail that is allowed to wound my wife? And you haven't tended to it yet. You seem to be in such a rush with everything this afternoon.'

'Heh, you're becoming so suspicious these days.'

She embraced me and held herself up against me. And I whispered into her ear: 'Where did you get the three bullets?'

'There are no three bullets. There is no cut on my arm. And no one has been in a rush this afternoon.'

I pulled her body down harder onto mine until I could hear her gasp for breath. 'So what is there then?'

'All there is for me is my husband, my leader. And I am not prepared to let anyone leave any wound upon him, let alone to his mouth and eyes, and his face.'

'So it was you who killed them?'

'It doesn't matter,' she was gasping more now. 'All that matters is my husband. Let me go.'

'No, not before you answer.'

'Do you want me to shout it out aloud – that all that matters is my husband? Oh, you, Mas, you have married a woman of Kasiruta, but you do not understand how they feel about their husbands.'

I lifted her up onto the bed. 'And how do they feel?'

'They will kill an evil husband. And they will also kill those who do evil to their husbands whom they love.'

'So you killed them.'

'I don't know anything. All I know is my husband. Don't ask me again.'

She pulled herself free from my embrace, hopped down off the bed and left the room.

I didn't have another chance to get near Princess for the rest of that day.

In the evening everyone gathered together in the front parlour. The reunion with Panji Darman was not as merry as it might have been because of the Frischbotens' presence. I could tell from his eyes that there were many things that Panji Darman wanted to talk about.

Frischboten also seemed to have things he wanted to discuss, but he held back because of the presence of Panji Darman and his family.

That evening we talked late into the night, but no one was able to discuss any of the personal or important things that they actually wanted to discuss.

It was only in the quiet after everyone had retired that I had Princess to myself again. Lying beside each other, out of everybody's hearing, with the wind blowing loudly outside, all doubt disappeared.

'Now, tell me all about it,' I proposed the program.

'I have told you everything,' she answered in a yawning voice, pretending to be sleepy. 'May I go to sleep now?'

'Not yet. I have only realised now that you are so stubborn.'

She laughed, happy. 'And my husband doesn't love me any less for it, does he, Mas?'

She didn't want to know how disturbed her husband was to sleep next to a murderer.

'You shot people who were not ready to defend themselves.'

'I only have one husband. My husband's work involves taking care of many things. My main work is to look after my husband. They were preparing to attack when I shot. They were just about to attack. It is their business to know how to defend themselves. I do not want to lose my husband, my one and only husband.'

My wife, it turned out, was someone who knew how to fight. Her father had begun training her when she was a child in Kasiruta to face the armies of van Heutsz. It was clear as day why my friend the former Governor-General had refused her permission to return home to her island. And I understood too why she had wanted to take back an understanding of the boycott as a souvenir for her people.

For one or two seconds then memories of my two late wives shone before me – the *Flower of the Century's End* and Ang San Mei. The two of them were people of impressive qualities. And the further I moved away from them in time, the stronger their qualities shone. It was only after she died that I found out that Mei was colour-blind. And this my present wife was a person of great quality. I should get to know and understand her better. I must not be too late as I was with Mei, I must love her more than those I loved who went before. But the other thought, that she was a killer, who one day would not shrink from killing another victim, whoever it might be, turned me away from my desire to get closer to her.

This battle within my mind had to be brought to a quick end. I had to honour and respect her opinions and the way she viewed things.

I held her and stroked her hair, whispering: 'Do you love your husband so much?'

'It is said that an egg is perfect in its totality,' she whispered back onto my throat, 'so the people of Kasiruta say. In such perfect totality is to be found the essence of living.'

I don't know whether that all came from her people or whether she made it up herself.

'And life means two bullets,' I said, ending this discussion.

'What about the closing up of *Medan*?'

And with that question, all this effort at love and romance dissolved. A truly terrible image appeared before me – Princess stalking through some trees aiming the revolver straight at the heart of the Assistant Resident of Priangan.

'I'll look after that myself tomorrow, Princess.'

'I think that's the best thing. You're worrying that I might decide to look after it myself.'

She was not at all disturbed by what she had done, as calm as ever as if nothing had happened. Perhaps this was not the first time she had killed someone. The hairs on the back of my neck stood on end. Had I all this time had a killer as a wife? And I never knew?

'I have a headache, Princess.'

She got out of bed and went to get water and aspirin. I took them and gulped them down, buried myself under the blankets and pretended to sleep. I had failed! There was a distance that now separated me from her, because of her love for me, because it was so deep, so unconditional.

Panji Darman returned to Surabaya without being able to revive the old intimacy.

Princess and I, together with the Frischboten family, went back up to Bandung. I went back again to the Assistant Resident's office, only to be told that he was not receiving any visitors that week. I then went to the Resident's office. There everyone pretended not to know who I was. And they also pretended never to have heard of a paper called *Medan* that was published in Bandung.

None of the papers published any news about the shooting of members of the Zweep. And, of course, Princess and I also pretended we knew nothing about what had happened. Pretended! Just like the Assistant Resident and the people at the Residency Secretariat. It was all a stage play! Them and us.

Very well. We will continue this little game, Meneer!

As soon as he appeared at the office, I took the opportunity to go with Sandiman to Lembang. During the journey a whispered conversation took place.

'Princess has told me everything. Sandiman. How could you have let her become involved in such a dangerous enterprise?'

He didn't answer. He just kept looking calmly out to the front. And that made me furious.

'If it was just you and your men I could understand. What would have happened if the police discovered who was involved?'

He was still silent.

'Why won't you answer me?'

'What must I answer, Tuan? I don't know what you mean.'

First Princess and now Sandiman – everyone was pretending, playing their part in a drama. My headache came back. All round me I found an impenetrable wall of silence. They all wanted to keep the truth from me.

'Where were you when the shootings took place?'

'What shootings, Tuan?'

'Where were you on the day that they sealed up *Medan*?'

'I met Tuan at the station. Then I helped the workers move to the house of Tuan Frischboten, until evening.'

'And Marko?'

'He was with me all the time. It was to me that Tuan Frischboten handed the keys after he went. I didn't know then where to. Apparently to Buitenzorg. So I don't really understand Tuan's questions. I did hear about some shooting incident. But I have no idea what it was all about.'

A stupid answer from a journalist!

'This is the first time I've met a journalist who didn't want to know about such things,' I grumbled at him.

The taxi took us back to Bandung and then it returned again to Lembang. I still had not found out anything more. Very well, I had failed for the moment.

Later I tried with Marko. The same result.

Why should I give myself such a headache thinking about this? If they consider this affair a personal matter, and nothing to do with me, then fine, I don't need to know. I know anyway that they did it all out of love for me, to save my life.

And so it was that ever since then I carried the revolver with me. I no longer left it lying in the dresser. Because I knew that from that moment on it might be me that had to shoot . . .

17

Robert Suurhof did not die. The bullet pierced the sternum and nestled underneath the collar-bone. The doctors were able to get the bullet out. His two friends died. One died on the spot, shot in the heart. The other died two days later from the knife that was buried in his waist. The knife was made of brass gilded with copper. Apparently it was designed to wound without causing bleeding. It was probably Sandiman who threw the knife and Princess who did the shooting. I guessed that Marko was assigned to keep watch, no doubt along with numerous others of his men.

It was certain all this would mean the police would be paying more attention to me. Many eyes would be on me now.

Sandiman came to warn me that he had found out that Pangemanann was a police commissioner from Police Headquarters in Batavia. Well at least he knew where I was when the shooting took place – with him. And if what Sandiman said was true then it meant that there was a relationship between the Knijpers, TAI and the Zweep on the one hand and the police on the other. So the Government not only had a force that – so it claimed – acted to carry out the law but also a force that acted outside the law.

For the time being anyway, I had to accept this as the truth. I had to be on my guard. I was now in a situation of constant danger. Relations with the official authorities had to be conducted through talk and smiles. Confrontations with the other authorities outside the law had to be met with action and violence.

And in that way the play could go on, whether that's what we wanted or not. The schools never taught anyone that such were the ways of the world. It seems that so it has been since I was born, and so it will be until this earth of mankind explodes. Perhaps these indeed are the rules of life, and this is the way things have to be handled.

The closure of *Medan* for ten days effectively lost us 25 per cent of our circulation. My serial, *Nyai Permana,* did not succeed in attracting back our readers.

But the Sarekat continued to expand. Its total membership was now over fifty thousand, and reports began to appear in the international press again about the giant organisation that had emerged in South-East Asia.

While all this was going on the Sarekat branch in Solo kept asking that the Central Leadership visit them. Central Leadership! Who sat in the Central Leadership now? Everyone had become afraid following the recent events. One by one they had resigned. In the end the Central Leadership comprised only me and a new unelected Secretary – Princess.

There was nothing we could do about this situation yet. The problem would be solved as things developed.

So when I did go to Solo I had to take Princess with me, but under very tight escort.

We entered the front grounds of Haji Samadi's house in the suburban hamlet of Lawean. It was surrounded by a cement wall. There was a group of people sitting round not doing anything.

Haji Samadi himself was busy inside. We were invited to sit.

A clerk sat at a nearby table noting down the names of all the people waiting. They were all applying to become members of the Sarekat.

Haji Samadi was quite startled to find out that a big entourage had arrived from Buitenzorg and that the unexpected guest who stood before him was myself. He began to speak, but his Malay was difficult to follow, so I replied in Javanese to make things easier for him, and he too switched to using Javanese.

'Raden Mas, why didn't you send news that you were coming? What a pity. We have made no proper preparations. Ah, no matter. Praise be to God that you and your wife have arrived safely.'

Princess was shown the way out the back, as is common Native custom. She went, smiling so sweetly, head bowed, eyes to the floor, just like a woman of the Javanese nobility – but not at all happy at doing it. In any case, we all continued to play our parts in this drama.

After I reprimanded him for addressing me with my title, he switched to using the Malay *tuan*.

'Tuan,' he began, 'You can see yourself, Tuan, all these people are flocking in to become members. God has shown them the way that they can unite together with their brothers in Islam.'

We went across to the clerk who was noting down the membership details. He listed name, address, age, occupation, sex and took a membership fee of one *benggol* from every person. Dues of one *benggol*! That was only one hundredth of the Boedi Oetomo membership dues. The membership dues according to the Sarekat Constitution were one *tali*, equal to ten *benggol*. Haji Samadi had unilaterally reduced the dues .

When we sat down again, he explained: 'Forgive me for not seeking permission before I reduced the dues,' he said patiently. 'Sudara (now he used *sudara*) will no doubt reprimand me.'

I didn't respond. Anyone who has to deal with traders or businessmen knows that their mind is always set on the problem of getting as many customers as possible in whatever way they can. I thought that this was no doubt the case with the Branch President as well. He had completely violated the Constitution. One *tali* was indeed burdensome. A *ringgit* was even more burdensome. But it was set that way to be a test of whether or not the new members were prepared to give up a day's meals to pay their dues. The heart of the issue was that it was a test of people's seriousness.

My guess was this man here, the Branch President sitting before me, wanted, openly, and legally, to use the Sarekat to tie the community closer to his businesses.

'If the Sarekat will not approve of this, then I will, of course, make the difference up out of my own money,' he added, seeing that I wasn't answering. 'It seems Sudara is not yet prepared to answer.'

'Of course Sudara will be able to make up what is missing,' I said, 'but it is still a violation.'

'They cannot afford to pay one *tali*. Does that then mean they do not have the right to become members? It is not just that people be separated from their sudara only because they are poor?' he answered.

'Look, Sudara Haji, if each branch started changing those sections of the rules which they didn't like, then, eventually there would be no rules, and as a result, no organisation either.'

'But the rules may not seem such a burden in other areas and for other branches,' he answered, 'but they are very much a burden for us here in Solo. And in those areas that are even poorer, it will be felt as an even greater burden.'

I knew, however, that one *tali* was not too expensive for Solo. It was a prosperous town and cash was in wide use. The businesses were all still in the hands of Natives. The handicrafts were alive, well and prospering. Agriculture was in a good state as well.

'We must learn to implement those decisions that we all voluntarily agreed to.'

Merchants and entrepreneurs are all very good talkers. Haji Samadi was no exception. With lots of smiles, laughs, elegant hand movements, twinkling eyes, and without once touching his *destar*, he continued his defence: 'In all of Java it is Solo that has been able to keep commerce in Native hands. To make sure that this situation remains the same and in fact develops and improves, we feel that all methods that are right and proper should be used to develop the relationships between producers, merchants and the consumers. We are not prepared to let it happen that even one person puts more trust in a non-Native merchant than a Native merchant. Every individual person who loses trust in us will undermine others' confidence in us.'

And so on: 'And it is our view too that our merchants should not do business with foreigners when buying their raw materials. We have set up a special body in the Solo branch to ensure that we no longer buy from the Chinese merchants here, but approach the big European trading houses in Surabaya. We are also working out a way to import these things ourselves – the dyes from Germany and wax from BPM, the cotton from England, and the copper for the *canting* from Japan. Then we may also be able to control the prices. The most important thing though is to create confidence in our efforts and to eliminate speculation.'

And so as he went on I came to understand even better that this Branch President was totally preoccupied with commercial matters. And, in fact, it wasn't even commerce in general, but only the *batik* business.

'Yes, we did deliberately lower the dues. But for the small traders it is still twenty-five cents, and for the medium size and big merchants it is from five to fifty guilders. I still believe that a cent weighs differently in different people's hands. Not everyone obtains a cent equally quickly or with the same effort.'

His eloquence was quite impressive.

'Sudara, as a member of the Central Leadership, you are quite welcome to examine our accounts at any time. Every cent can be accounted for.'

Without waiting for my agreement, he clapped his hands.

A man wearing a traditional striped Javanese tunic and a *kain* that was so long that it polished the floor as he walked came up to Haji Samadi. Still speaking in Javanese, my host took the account books from the man.

With even greater eloquence he explained all the figures, lined up as they were like rows of soldiers. The wealth of the branch as set out in the books was twenty-seven thousand guilders.

And I was totally amazed that this man could read so quickly without glasses. I pointed to a section he was explaining and asked: 'What is this entry, Sudara?'

'This one?' He was silent for several moments. He didn't read it. He pulled over the clerk and told him to explain.

The clerk read out the section, and the Branch President nodded in agreement.

'This is our Branch Secretary Sudara, Raden Ngabehi Sosrokoornio.'

We shook hands.

'And where is all this money now?'

'It's all been invested in commercial dealings.'

'God Almighty!' I swore. 'So what do the members get, if they are just looked upon as a source of capital? Is this true?'

'To start with, all members can buy from shops that belong to the Sarekat at special lower prices.'

'God forgive us!'

'What's the matter, Sudara?'

It was now revealed that the Solo branch saw the Sarekat as a business with the members as voluntary shareholders, volunteering to own shares without having any proven ownership of the shares.

'But that is a business arrangement, not the kind of organisation that is set out in the Constitution and Aims and Objectives.'

'Look, Sudara, this is what most people want. You yourself have seen the people flocking to join the branch. Every day. Are we in the Solo branch in error? We are convinced also that things will continue to improve. And if the Central Leadership does not approve of what we have done, where will we send all these people? The people of Solo have trade in their blood. They know what they need.'

'So you have been hoping that we would come here and make this all official?'

'Not so much that. We just wanted you to see the situation as it really is and then have the opportunity to study and consider it. We estimate that by the end of this year, 1912, we will have twenty-five thousand members in our branch. That is not something that should be considered lightly. And it is something that is sure to happen.'

The Solo branch wanted to confront me with a fait accompli, with what their leadership had carried out without ever telling the Central Leadership. And whatever else may be the case, it was true that these were major developments and should be studied seriously. Twenty-five thousand members – in Solo alone. All those people wanted leadership, not just cheaper prices and not just to be with other Moslems. Perhaps they wanted more than leadership, though.

This was a serious matter and we couldn't conclude a discussion on it in just one or two hours. I asked that the discussion be postponed so that we could discuss it with the whole branch leadership.

Then I called over one of the people who was there to join up. It happened that he was a farmer. You could tell from his tattered pants and his farmer's bamboo hat. His legs were filthy from working in mud every day and never having known soap. He approached bowing all the time and then crawled along on the floor.

I looked at my host and he didn't seem to be bothered by this scene. Rather he waved to the man that he approach closer. I wanted to tell him to sit in a chair. But these were not my chairs and this was not my house. I would have to find another time to discuss this matter, while making sure I did not offend anyone.

'What is your name?'

'Krio, Ndoro.'

'Don't crawl like that, Krio. Stand up.'

His eyes showed nervousness. He wiggled his fingers nervously. But he still remained glued to the floor.

'Forgive me, Ndoro, but it is better like this.'

'You are applying to join the Sarekat?'

'Yes, Ndoro.'

'Stand up,' I ordered.

Hearing me speak in such a sharp voice, he stood. He kept his hands clasped before him.

'What kind of work do you do?'

'A farmer, Ndoro, sometimes a coolie,' he answered, while wiggling his thumb.

'Don't call me Ndoro, use Sudara.' He didn't respond. 'Why do you want to join the Sarekat?'

'All my neighbours have joined, they often go to Sarekat meetings . . . '

'What do they talk about?'

'I am not allowed to attend, so I don't know. That is why I am asking to join.'

I waved my hand and he left.

His answer was enough. The people needed somewhere they could gather together as a group and become a part of a bigger union. The question of cheaper prices was not important to them. And it was true that they did need the protection of being in a bigger grouping. They needed leadership.

Haji Samadi requested very vigorously that we stay at his house, and we granted his request.

That night the meeting with the Solo branch leadership took place. There were ten people gathered. I was introduced to them one by one. There was one young man with a *haji's* cap on his head who sat a few metres away from the table. His body seemed bloated even though he was quite a tall man. Because he was so big, he seemed short. His two hands always rested on his lap. He didn't wear a *batik kain* like the others but a plain *sarong*.

As gently as I could I explained that it was not the Sarekat's function to collect money from those who wanted to be organised, who wanted to learn about organising, to form capital for the use of any other particular group. I told them that what the branch had done in using the money to buy the materials for *batik*-making was a useful thing, but it was not the real aim of the Sarekat. The real aims were still those set out in the Consti-tution – comradeship, to develop confidence in our own efforts, to build unity through joint endeavours, to face troubles and problems with a united approach, and to build a joint fund for the members' mutual benefit. So the appearance of a small group that decides what is in the common interest is not correct unless approved of by all members.

They were not ready to hear about nationalism at that stage, so I proceeded to discuss other things first. They were still preoccupied with their businesses and hadn't yet glimpsed the outside world. It would be necessary to spend time educating them on other things before we began discussing nationalism.

There was one thing that they had studied well, however, and that was the ins and outs of the boycott. But that weapon was not yet needed in Solo. The social and economic life of the town was still in Native hands.

It was only when the clock indicated nine o'clock that I started to introduce them to the foundation stones of Indies nationalism, but without using those terms. What I told them was based on the reality that our ancestors had left us, not just on the daydreams of one or two people, as was the case with Douwager. I explained how it would be the Native middle class that determined what happened in the Indies, how Islam was the foundation of a brotherhood between everyone, and how independent endeavour and commerce was the basis of our communal life. And I told them also that the unity that would give birth to Indies nationalism would stretch beyond Java to wherever there were people who spoke Malay, who were Moslems and who engaged in independent endeavour.

Sosrokoornio took down all that I said as soon as I said it.

The young man in the *haji's* cap and *sarong* picked up his chair and brought it closer so that he could hear better.

'Yes, here, closer,' I said.

Close up he looked even more swollen, huge, his body swollen with muscles. His fingers were huge like bananas.

'What is your name, Sudara?' I asked.

'Haji Misbach.'

We greeted each other. I introduced him to the people in my entourage. With those huge, strong fingers of his, if we had shaken hands European style my hand would have been crushed. There are obvious advantages in the Islamic style of greeting, where your hands just briefly touch, and then you pull them back to touch your heart.

I explained to them that in Siam there are thirty thousand people who speak Malay, and in Malaya everyone except the Chinese speaks Malay. There were more in Singapore and in the Philippines. In the Indies we could say that everyone understood Malay.

'So, my brothers, our nation is not just that of the Javanese, but includes many other peoples as well, bound together by the things that I have explained to you. It is much greater than that which people have described as the Indisch nation or the Indies nation. As for its name, I do not have one yet. Perhaps we will need a new name for it. And the Javanese are only a part of this great nation.'

I understood that they weren't all that interested in this kind of story – a story that did not promise some new monetary gain! I had to add some fire to this story for them.

'Here in Solo business and commerce is already quite advanced. You are all receiving a good living due to the blessings of God Almighty. This would be even more the case if our nation were to become much bigger, covering the peoples outside the Indies as well, and if all the business and commerce was in the hands of Natives. Try to imagine how great will be the prosperity from God that you, my brothers, will be able to harvest. And all this can come to pass if the Sarekat can grow and expand in all the corners of the Indies, and even outside it. If the Sarekat does not strive to achieve this then it will all just remain dreams and nothing else. The Sarekat will try to form an army of propagandists who will be sent off to all the regions.'

And so they began to pay more attention. One interrupted to ask that I put my ideas on this question of nationalism in writing so they could study it more closely and develop the ideas more easily.

I promised I would do that.

'Today our biggest factories cover an area equivalent to fifteen houses. When we extablish our new nation then our factories will expand in accordance with how big our nation is. Perhaps they will become as big as whole towns, like in Europe and America.'

Then discussion ensued – and in this there was something very strange – about just how to unite all the component peoples, exactly how could we go about doing it. But not a single person even mentioned the fact that the Indies was under the political control of the Dutch.

'And just think, if everything is in the hands of the Natives like it is here in Solo, then there will be no more the Knijpers, TAI or the Zweep, because we will be deciding everything. And also what the Government is allowed to do will be up to us.'

I saw their eyes shine with idealism, as if they wanted to convince me that they had grasped the essence of what I was saying. The Government would bow to us, without resorting to arms as they had in Bali, as they had against Diponegoro, Imam Bonjol, Troenodjojo, Troenodongso and Surapati. It was enough for us to be united, it was enough for the Islamic Traders Union, the Sarekat, to be strong and resolute.

To close the meeting I recommended that they put right their leadership methods. They mustn't allow the membership to end up losing faith in them. The membership needed clear leadership.

The clock struck twelve times and the meeting adjourned.

As soon as I returned home from Solo I began making plans for the expansion of the Sarekat to all Malay-speaking areas, in and outside the Indies. In the article I wrote I also included the Malay-speaking peoples of Ceylon and South Africa. For the time being I called them all the Greater Malay Nation.

As soon as it was printed it was distributed to all Sarekat branches and down to the sub-branches too.

The decision that the Sarekat would use *Medan* as its beacon meant that our circulation jumped up again. But we still couldn't catch up to *Sin Po*, which was the beacon for the young Chinese nationalists in the region.

Requests for legal assistance no longer only came direct to Frischboten. The Sarekat branches now also received cases. Hendrik had to employ several assistants.

And the Central Leadership, namely myself, had also prepared its plans for the coming year, 1913. Because there were no longer any disputes over the question of religious versus modern education, it was now time for the SDI to start its own schools. They would provide a general, modern education, with religious instruction provided in the afternoon. I drew up the curriculum myself. I took the ELS curriculum as my base, except that I cut out Dutch history and replaced it with Indies history. Dutch language lessons were cut by two hours a week, which were to be used for instruction in Malay.

A two-month course for propagandists was held in Buitenzorg. There were delegates there from all the branches in Java. I, Sandiman and sometimes also Frischboten spoke to them – Frischboten about the law. The two months passed and they returned home, taking with them resources they did not possess before.

These sixty propagandists immediately began work. They also took back ideas on how to improve their organisation. The result was even further increases in membership. And not just in Solo. Everywhere! Outside Java too. So I dared come to the conclusion that all these developments proved that we had chosen the right basis upon which to build the organisation. We were indeed providing what the people needed in the way of organisation. It was now clear that a great movement, encompassing tens of thousands of the peoples of the Indies, as well as the Malay-speaking peoples outside the Indies, was possible. All that was needed was for just one propagandist to take on the task of visiting the new areas.

I never dreamed that it would be as great and wonderful as this, Child. You are greater than I ever guessed. You have made my life here far from the Indies so beautiful, wrote Mama from Paris.

Om, wrote Maysoroh, *I have seen two reports now in the French papers about the movement that you are leading. It is indeed true that you are needed by your people. I often think about how you have achieved so much, just as you had always hoped. It stirs deep feelings within me. The Indies will be bright now, Om. May you also be bright and clear under His blessings.*

I have now appeared in Paris society as a singer, not a famous singer, Om, but singing in certain small circles.

I always think of you, my good and kind Om. Papa is often ill these days. Jeannette, my little sister, is growing into a sweet and pleasing child. Mama is as healthy and as devoted to her work as always.

Not yet, Om, I am not yet married. I have no desire for that for the time being.

Rono Mellema never wrote.

My son, wrote my father, for the first time since I left Surabaya. *For all these years I have thought to myself of how must I act towards you. The answer that you sent back with your mother truly startled and shocked me. For a long time I could not sleep or eat because I was thinking about it. It is not easy to understand your thinking and your actions, your ideals and your works. But now I have made a decision. I am on your side, Son, fully and with all sincerity. You are my teacher. Secretly now I have been protecting the Sarekat in my region.*

My Son, may God grant his blessings for eternity.

Meneer, wrote Hans Haji Moeloek from Jeddah, *I have received news from the Netherlands that the Syndicate has been forced to drop its plans for reducing the land rents it would pay. This news I have for you is from very reliable sources. Congratulations, Meneer. No Native has ever before been able to defy the will of the Europeans. You have proved that it is possible. But, Meneer, don't ignore my warning, a warning from a friend – they will not take this lying down. I don't mean in regard to the land rent issue itself, but as regards you yourself, Meneer. Be careful, and be even more than just careful.*

He was right. The bigger the victory, the less vigilant one became. And lack of vigilance was the path to one's demise. I must be cautious in enjoying the fruits of these victories.

The last portion of *Nyai Permana* was published. The letters that came in, all from men, almost all asked: If women were given the right to divorce their husbands, what then would become of the position of men? Was not such an idea leading people astray? Did it not violate the laws of religion?

These were all very important matters. But for the time being I put them aside.

The land question that I had also discussed in my story did not, however, elicit any reaction at all.

No matter.

There were so many organisational needs pressing in on us that the question of re-establishing a competent, honest, and most important of all, a courageous Central Leadership became urgent. I myself had decided that I should become the Central Leadership's main propagandist. I planned to travel from region to region, both within the Indies and outside.

I summoned the presidents of the Solo and Jogjakarta branches, and all those branches where Native commerce was expanding or at least holding its own, to Buitenzorg. We held a small conference that discussed the questions of the Central Leadership and of our long-range propaganda activities. Of course, it is not of interest to note here all the ins and outs of the discussions. What needs to be noted down are the decisions. The conference agreed to the proposal that I begin propaganda work, with the condition that I be accompanied by my wife. Secondly, on my own recommendation, the General Chairman of the Sarekat, namely myself, should transfer the mandate of Central Leadership to Haji Samadi in Solo.

The handover took place that night after I had edited and improved the text of the mandate that had been agreed to by the little gathering. From the moment the mandate was signed, the Central Leadership was transferred from Buitenzorg to Solo.

The conference, having also discussed the countries that I would visit, which included Singapore, Malaya, Siam and the Philippines, finally adjourned. All the delegates from the branches returned to their respective regions.

Sandiman and Marko, with Frischboten's help, would continue to publish *Medan*.

But I would not be completely honest if I did not explain here the personal reasons I had for taking on the propaganda tasks that would take me outside Java and even outside the Indies. The shooting of the Zweep had been worrying me for some time. If it were true that the assassinations were carried out by those close to me, then it was likely that there would be some kind of revenge – open and through the law, or outside the law, perhaps open, perhaps not. If it were done through the law, then the whole affair could also be used to destroy the Sarekat.

Once I was travelling outside Java and the Indies, and with full authority over the Sarekat now with Haji Samadi, the integrity of the organisation would be protected if I or any of those close to me were charged.

I did not dare discuss any of this with Frischboten. He should not know anything of this, even if I guessed he might know anyway. Even those involved were not prepared to open up to me about it. I had no real evidence. As busy as I was with all kinds of activities and ideas, I could not overcome my anxiety about this.

'Princess,' I called her one afternoon after telling Sandiman, Marko and their friends that they would have to run *Medan* themselves from now on. 'We are going on a long journey.'

'You mean together with me?'

'Of course. You are my wife, aren't you?'

'But will I be allowed to leave Java?'

I was stopped in my tracks. I had never thought about that.

'Ah, you forgot about that, didn't you, Mas?'

'We needn't mention that you are a Princess, the daughter of a king. We will just list you as my wife. We will try that if you agree.'

'Do you need my agreement?' she asked. 'I will always do everything that you want, Mas.'

'You are not a doll, Princess,' I said. 'You are my wife, whom I respect fully, as I do myself. I need your agreement.'

'Of course I agree, Mas. Take me wherever you like and for however long you like.'

'No, that's not the kind of answer I want, even though I am grateful for such a selfless statement. I need your answer as an individual in your own right.'

'I agree,' she answered seriously.

I looked at her face. There was no joking smile. Her lips were relaxed and her eyes calm. She did not look me in the eyes. She sat straight in her chair. Her unblinking gaze was fixed on the door.

For the umpteenth time I found myself convinced again that this obedient woman had been trained since childhood to be a fighter. Had her father, the king, not been exiled and separated from his people, perhaps she would already have strode the battlefield and have been defeated or killed.

'Can you ride a horse, Princess?'

She smiled. She was obviously remembering past times back home in Kasiruta. 'We all had to learn to ride horses, across the fields, and through the scrub and forests . . .'

'Who made you do this?'

'My teacher of course. Can you ride a horse, Mas?'

'No doubt not as well as you. I have ridden one.'

She laughed happily, held my hand, and suddenly kissed it. I pulled it away and corrected her: 'It is I who should kiss your hand.'

'I am not a European woman, Mas. I am your wife. I have no desire to be praised by men, not even by my husband. But you are the husband of a Moluccan woman.'

'And what does that mean for a woman of Molucca?'

'Her husband is her star, her moon, her sun. Without him, nothing will exist, including herself.'

'They have all sorts of strange ideas, these women from Kasiruta,' I interrupted. 'So you give your agreement in your own right and not just as my wife?'

'I agree.'

'Then let's start making preparations.'

And she began to prepare things for our departure.

One of the first things that we had to do was get all our travel papers and documents. While we were doing this, Sandiman and his friends had taken over the complete running of *Medan*. Hendrik Frischboten still acted as legal advisor.

Then suddenly something happened. I found out about it one day when I visited Meneer Meyerhoff's place.

'I'm sorry, Meneer, I can't provide you with a car today. All the taxis have been hired. You will have to take the train.'

'Twenty-five taxis all hired at once! Never has such a thing happened before. May I ask who was it that hired them?'

Meyerhoff just laughed.

When I arrived back at Buitenzorg, there was more news. All the best taxis in Betawi had also been hired out. All the taxis from Bandung and Betawi that were in good condition were being checked over in a workshop in Betawi. The best mechanics in all Betawi and Bandung had been mobilised. Then things became clearer. Eighty taxis had been hired by the State Secretariat. His Excellency the Governor-General was going on an outing.

I cabled the news to Bandung and asked them to try to find out where he was going. It wasn't clear. No one knew what were his destinations. What we did know was that the taxis had been hired for a week.

Such major preparations were very suspicious when there were no major events coming up. But no one would say what all the preparations were about.

The next morning I found Sandiman and Marko hotly debating a report that Marko had prepared. The Governor-General's entourage, comprising eighty taxis and ten private automobiles, had departed and were heading east, steadily eastward.

By the afternoon the news began to spread. Governor-General Idenburg was heading for Rembang, accompanied by several hundred high officials and their guards.

By the evening things were even clearer – they were going to Rembang to attend a funeral.

The Governor-General himself, with a huge entourage, going to attend a funeral! Who had died in Rembang?

That night I stayed in Bandung so I could obtain a more complete picture of what was going on, and this is what emerged – the Bupati of Rembang had died. The Bupati of Rembang, the husband of the girl from Jepara, may her soul rest in peace!

The very next morning, the press, especially the journalists who supported the Ethical Policy, were all abuzz. They were amazed that the Governor-General should go to so much trouble to travel so far to attend the funeral of a Native official who had been the object of so much public criticism. But they also realised that Idenburg was making a political statement: it was an illusion on the part of the supporters of the Ethical Policy to think that van Aberon could become Governor-General!

With the news that the Governor-General was attending the funeral, all the *bupatis* of Java made sudden preparations and headed off in that direction. Several journalists hired second or third-class taxis and sped off to Rembang

360

too. I could imagine what it would be like in that little town that had probably never even seen a single automobile, when perhaps more than one hundred turned up. Everyone would throng to the main square to attend the funeral, and also to get a look at the automobiles. And they could fly along without horses! They could all spew out smoke and dust! They could all growl and roar. And they were all equipped with shiny copper carbide lamps.

And in the *Medan* office, people were no less busy. In the discussions it was none other than Marko who insisted: 'We cannot let them get away with this without us saying something.'

'The Governor-General is trying to rehabilitate the name of the Bupati of Rembang,' followed on Sandiman, 'and we cannot let it pass without comment, but we don't need to go overboard.'

I just listened to them debate.

'We were among those who attacked him, the Bupati, even if not directly. Not he himself personally, but his behaviour. We shouldn't be cowed just because the Governor-General is attending his funeral.'

'Yes, but we shouldn't be too extreme!'

'The Governor-General is using money taken from the people – their tax money – to defend the Bupati of Rembang. Just think how much it cost for eighty taxis. And the other costs would probably amount to ten times the cost of the taxis. And even if he was paying for it out of his own pocket we should still be objecting.'

The Governor-General's attendance at the funeral was surely a political act. Only a few people, so simple that they can be easily deceived, really thought that the Governor-General was honouring the man who had died. He wanted to demoralise the Liberals who had got carried away with their illusions. He wanted things to be as they had been before with none of this activity and movement. He was also sending a message to the Sarekat that the Government of the Netherlands Indies honoured and defended its officials and that the Sarekat therefore should not get too disrespectful towards them. Be careful! He was warning us.

On that day I had to say goodbye, as our departure was now only three days away. I handed over the publication of the newspaper and all the magazines to my two friends. They would now be totally in charge of editorial and all other policy. How to deal with this initiative of the Governor-General was also up to them now.

Back in Buitenzorg there was a letter from Princess. She asked forgiveness a thousand times over that she had gone to Sukabumi to stay with her father for the next two days. She asked that I follow her there later.

I will be down in two days, Princess. In the meantime I will use these two days to say goodbye to others of my friends, especially Thamrin Mohammed Thabrie. I would say goodbye to him while making a visit to Betawi.

I saw that the suitcases were packed and ready, all locked. We were indeed planning a long journey. If possible, we would travel on to Europe.

It was late evening and I was very tired by the time I had finished saying my farewells to all my friends in Buitenzorg. I went to bed and slept, overwhelmed by a feeling of being at ease and safe.

At nine the next morning a young boy arrived with a copy of *Medan*. Lazily I unfolded it. Eventually my eyes hit on a headline and suddenly my whole nervous system went into shock. I jumped up. My eyes popped out and a scream uncontrollably came from my mouth, like a monkey shot with an arrow: 'The fools!'

The Banten guards outside all came running. My hands, which held the paper, were shaking.

'Master!' the chief guard reported.

I waved them away and they moved off.

My legs moved and I stalked back and forth like a bear in a cage. I tried to calm myself. I couldn't. My hands quivered with tension. As I strode back and forth, I read the paper again. I wasn't wrong.

'Idiots! Donkeys!'

Those children had launched a crude attack on Governor-General Idenburg himself. It was now in print and being circulated. There was no way to stop it now. What did they want to achieve with such a crude attack as that?

'Idiots!' I roared in pain, as if it was my body that had been struck by an arrow.

I ran to the back and bathed. I went into the room and put on my clothes from yesterday. Everything else was locked away in the suitcases or wardrobe. The key box was also locked. The master key had been taken by Princess. God knows what I looked like. I put on my *destar* not bothering to check how it looked. And my other shoe . . . ah, shoe where are you hiding? Why are you too trying to annoy me like this? It looks as if the neighbour's dog has hidden it, or taken off with it.

'Piaaaah!'

Our maid came running in, her hair still in a mess.

'My shoes! Where are my shoes?'

She crawled about looking under everything but couldn't find them. She ran out the front and out the back. Nowhere to be found.

Exhausted from the tension of it all, I finally flopped into a lounge chair. The noise outside wouldn't have caught my attention if it hadn't continued to get worse and worse. Why did they launch such a crude attack on the Governor-General over his attendance at the funeral – they didn't even mention his title or position, they referred to him sarcastically as *kyai-ne*, 'his holiness'? As I angrily asked myself this question once more, I glanced out the front window.

362

It was as if I was nailed to the lounge chair.

A detachment of police had rounded up all the guards, the men from Banten. I could hear shouted threats.

'Where are the others?' in Malay, 'Come on, don't lie. There are fifteen altogether, aren't there? Watch out.'

The fighters were huddled under a tree guarded by three police with carbines.

I saw a police official, escorted by six of his men, head towards the house. Outside the fence there were scores more lined up, arm's length apart.

So, they are going to arrest me.

I could hear their footsteps more clearly now. The police officer climbed the veranda steps and entered the room without waiting for my permission.

I remained seated.

A man in civilian clothes stopped in front of me and paid his respects. Then: 'In the name of Her Majesty, and of justice, I place you under arrest, Meneer.'

He took out a piece of paper and gave it to me.

The paper was from the Office of the Court, an order for me to be detained in lieu of non-payment of debts. For non-payment of debts!!! The debts of my people perhaps, held under my name. This is worse than what they did to Teukoe Djamiloen.

After reading it, I looked up at the officer.

'Do you understand?' the officer asked.

I saw his eyes, his nose, his cheeks. Yes, it was none other than Pangemanann with two 'n's.

I nodded.

'Don't be angry, Meneer. You have a pistol, do you not?'

'Not a pistol. A revolver.'

'Yes, revolver,' without looking at his subordinates, he ordered one to search me.

I still did not rise from my chair. And they did not find the weapon on me.

'Where do you keep the revolver, Meneer?'

'In the bedroom. Under the pillow.'

'Fetch it,' he ordered one of his men in Malay.

'Do you still remember me?' he asked in Dutch.

'Pangemanann,' I answered, standing up.

He saluted me, held out his hand and greeted me: 'I carry out an unpleasant task against a human being I much admire and respect,' he said, 'a person who has begun to change the face of the Indies.'

My spit fell and splattered on the floor.

'That is right, Meneer. It is right for you to humiliate me. And it is also right that I still respect and admire you.' He turned to his men. 'Get outside all of you,' he ordered in Malay. 'I am taking you away from here today, and you will not return.'

'I cannot go today, I am waiting for my wife.'

'Your wife? Yes. The Princess will not be accompanying you. She is not allowed to leave Java.'

'So I will be taken off Java?'

'Not yet, not now. Get whatever things you need. Do it now.'

The policeman who had gone into my room came out with the revolver and handed it to his superior.

Pangemanann examined the papers with it and counted the bullets.

'None of the bullets have been used,' he spoke aloud to himself. 'Good. There will be no additional complications. Why have you not asked the reason for your arrest, Meneer?'

I shook my head.

'You have been detained for not paying your debts.'

'Debts?'

'You have received reminder letters several times now and you have never replied.'

'Reminder letters?'

He showed me the letters demanding payment and pointed out that they had been signed as received by one of my clerks – Dolf Boopmjes, that child whom I had taken off the streets. But even if there had been no such letters, I would never have been able to pay the debts that now fell upon me.

Pangemanann dropped his gaze. He whispered: 'The debts of your people, Meneer, which you will have to pay yourself.' He ahemmed. 'I am not saying that just to humour you, Meneer. Nobody could have done more than you have done.'

His voice made me bow my head. Without realising it, my hand had reached into my pocket and taken out a handkerchief. I wiped my face. He looked the other way.

'Yes, power has its own kind of face and heart. It can peel off its morals according to need. Please forgive me, Meneer. I understand that you will not be able to forgive me. But I have asked for forgiveness all the same.'

'Where are you taking me?'

'Oh, don't forget, Meneer, I respectfully request that you return to me my manuscript of *Si Pitung*. You have not had a chance to publish it yet.'

I opened the bureau where I kept all my papers. I pulled out his manuscript from amongst the others. I gave it a brush in case there was dust on the packet. I put it on the table and inspected it page by page.

'Please return the receipt I gave you,' I said.

He took out a piece of paper from his top pocket and gave it to me.

'Check the pages again,' I requested, and I studied and then tore up the receipt. 'There is not a single mark on them.'

I left the two of them standing there. I sat down at my desk and wrote a letter to my wife. I stole a glance at them and saw that Pangemanann had sat down in the lounge chair without even asking first.

Princess, the moment of our separation has arrived at last. You are still my wife, so it is your duty to listen to what I say. All that I have built has been destroyed. You will find out for yourself about those who have pierced me from the front and stabbed me from behind. Your life, which has just started, need no longer be devoted to your husband. My future now is very uncertain. Thank you for all your love and all your sacrifices. Thank you for the happiness I have enjoyed as your husband. I will take the memories of that happiness to wherever it is that I go now. Consider this letter as a valid and legal divorce. Marry a man who will not demand of you so much sacrifice. You are still very, very young, beautiful, charming, educated, patient and courageous. You are not yet twenty years old.

You are still my wife. Do this which I tell you. Take this letter to a penghulu as proof of talaq. Goodbye my darling, drink of life to the very dregs of the cup. Make sure you achieve all of your youthful dreams, be they ones that reach up to the heavens. Seize from life all that is rightfully yours. Give my greetings to Mir and Hendrik. My respects to your father, the Raja. All from the bottom of my heart. And to Sandiman, Marko, Djamiloen, Wardi, Douwager, Tjipto, all the branches and sub-branches and members of the Sarekat.

Pangemanann has said that I will never return to this house and that I will be leaving Java. So do not be sentimental over this separation. Things will go hard for me now. I have always been hard with the world. You too must be hard with the world, so that your sleep will not be disturbed by bad dreams.

Tomorrow, when you enter this house, know that your husband will be in some place and time unkown. All that I own is now yours. With this letter, I also attach an authority for you to withdraw the little savings we have in the bank. I hope the bank has not frozen the account. Princess, go now into the world and face life without tears, and do not think of your husband, because, as soon as you read this letter, your husband will then only be an ex-husband. May peace be with you, Princess. Goodbye.'

'Piaah!' I called.

The maid appeared in the distance. Her whole body shook with fear.

'Over here. Come closer!' She shook even more, even though she moved no closer. 'Listen, I am going off, I don't know where, perhaps far away, very far away. You stay in this house until your mistress returns.'

'I will do as you say, Master.'

'Tell the men from Banten to return to their homes. Tell them thank-you from me. And I thank you too, Piah. Bring me the suitcase in the storeroom.'

'The old dinted and dented suitcase that's used for the rice, Tuan?'

'Used for the rice?' I put aside my surprise. 'Fetch it.'

She almost ran as she left the room. When she came back, she was shaking less. In her hand she was carrying an old suitcase, brown, with even more dints and dents in it now, and with the rust around it even merrier.

'Stand there, Piah, I will still need you.'

'Yes, Tuan.'

I shifted my papers from the bureau into the suitcase.

'Fetch me a towel, toothbrush and toothpaste, Piah.'

She ran out the back again. She returned, no longer shaking, carrying all that I had asked for as well as some unironed underclothes and Princess's towel.

'Why have you brought me mistress's towel?'

'Take it, Tuan, so that you can take with you at least one thing of my mistress's,' her voice suddenly broke, she was sobbing. Without saying any more, she put the towel in my suitcase.

'Don't cry, Piah, don't leave here before the mistress returns. Don't let in any guests.'

'I will not leave, Tuan.'

'Even so, Piah, I want you to swear before me and these others that you will not leave.'

Suddenly she squatted at my feet. In a very gentle voice, but pregnant with protest: 'How can you demand an oath from me, my master? An oath for my master, for my leader? Is it not enough that I am a member of the Sarekat?'

'Piah!' I could not hold back my tears. Piah, my servant, a member of the Sarekat! The second woman member out of fifty thousand men. I stood and raised her up: 'Why do you, a member of the Sarekat, kneel before your leader?'

'I feel that you are going far away, Tuan, and will not return.'

'Very well, Piah, I will not demand an oath from you. Stand up. Tomorrow give this letter to your mistress.'

'Yes, Master.'

'If you love your mistress, then stay with her always.'

'Do not forget or neglect my mistress's towel, Master. It is Tuan's duty to always look after it and to remember the wife of my leader, who is also my leader.'

'I will always remember, Piah.'

I glanced at Pangemanann and he was wiping his eyes. When he noticed me looking at him, he brought himself under control, and asked: 'Are you ready?'

'Piah, I cannot go without leaving you something. All the keys are with your mistress. All I have is . . . ' I searched around in my pockets. There was only some coins, about three guilders or so. I grabbed them all and held them out for her. 'For you, Piah, take them.'

She took them and then put them back in my pocket.

'You will need them on your journey.'

'No.'

'You will need them.'

'Then give them to the men from Banten.'

'No, it is us who should be helping you, Tuan. Leave me behind some words, Tuan, good words that I might remember all my life.'

'Very well, Piah. Become a propagandist for the Sarekat. Call upon all women to join. Become their leader.'

'I will remember, Tuan, and I will do what you ask.'

'I must go now, Piah.'

'You will always be in our hearts, Tuan.'

As I walked down the front steps of the house, I couldn't help but turn and look back at her – Piah, a pearl whom I had never got to know all this time. Princess had taught her.

And I didn't notice that I wore no shoes.

Buru, 1975

Glossary

A

Assistant Resident	for each regency there was a Dutch Assistant Resident in whose hands power over local affairs ultimately resided

B

bahu	a measure of area, equivalent to 7096.5 square metres
Bandung	Bandung was, and still is, the major town in West Java outside Batavia (now Jakarta)
Bandung Bondowoso	a figure in folk mythology who built one of the Prambanan temples in one night
bapak	literally 'father', used to indicate respect
Bathara Narada	a figure in *wayang*, a messenger for the gods
batik	a Javanese process for decorating cloth by using wax to prevent some areas from absorbing dye; material made by this process
benggol	a 2-1/2 cent coin
belikat	sternum
bendi	vehicle similar to a surrey
bendoro	a term of address equivalent to 'master' or 'lord'
Betawi	the Malay name for Batavia, the capital of the Dutch East Indies, now Jakarta
Bharatayuddha	a famous Hindu epic, depicting a great war between two families of nobles

biawak	iguana
brahman	the priestly Hindu caste; the highest caste
bupati	the title of the Native Javanese official appointed by the Dutch to assist the Dutch Assistant Resident to administer a region; most *bupatis* could lay some claim to noble blood

C

canting	a small tool used in 'writing' *batik* on cloth with hot wax
capjiki	a kind of lottery game
cokek, dogar, gambang kromong	forms of folk drama and dance
Culture System	the system of forced cultivation of certain crops enforced by the colonial authorities; under this system, Javanese peasants had to grow export crops such as coffee and sell them to the Dutch authorities at extremely low prices

D

dalang	the puppet master who recites the stories and manipulates the puppets at *wayang* performances
delman	a kind of horse carriage
denmas	short for the title *'raden mas'*
destar	an East Javanese form of head-dress; a kind of head-band
dokar	a two-wheeled horse cart
dukun	traditional Javanese magician and/or healer
duren	a highly aromatic and popular tropical fruit
Dutch East Indies Company (VOC); the Company	*Vereenigde Oost Indische Compagnie*, United (Dutch) East India Company

E

ELS	Dutch-language primary school
engkik	term of respect for a woman by a younger person; 'aunt'; used by Chinese Javanese
engkoh (abbreviation *koh*)	Chinese for 'uncle'
Roorda van Eysinga	a writer (1852–1887), expelled from the Indies in 1864 because his writings were regarded as harmful to the colonial government

F

forum privilegiatum	the right to appear before the 'White Court'
Francis, G.	Eurasian author of the early Malay-language novel *Nyai Dasima*.

G

gamelan	traditional Javanese percusssion orchestra
garuda	the mythical magical bird upon whom the gods rode
gus	a term of affection used among the families of the Javanese aristocratic elite by parents towards their male children; short for *gusti*
gusti kanjeng	a term of address used for higher aristocracy, meaning 'exalted lord'

H

haji	title of a Javanese Moslem who has gone on the pilgrimage to Mecca
HBS	the prestigious Dutch-language senior high school
Dr Snouck Hurgronje	a Dutch scholar who was an influential adviser on Native Affairs to the colonial government

370

I

ibu	literally 'mother'; used as a term of address for respected women
ikat	binding, belt, etc

J

Java Doctor	someone trained in the Dutch-run medical school, STOVIA
jeruk	a sweet citrus fruit, something like a cross between a lemon and a mandarin

K

kabupaten	the formal local term for the administrative area that an Assistant Resident (through the *bupati*) administers
kain	traditional dress worn by Javanese women; a kind of *sarong* wrapped tightly around the waist and legs
kampung	a village within a city environment
kecap	Indonesian soy sauce, sweetened with thick palm sugar syrup
kenanga	a kind of flower
keris	traditional curved-bladed Javanese dagger
kliwon	one of the days of the Javanese five-day week
kontrolir (Controller)	the junior Dutch administrative officer in charge of a sub-district, one level below that of an Assistant Resident; being close to the grass roots, they often wielded much power on a day-to-day basis
kopiah	a traditional Javanese-style Moslem fez
kromo	High Javanese spoken to and between the upper classes
kroncong	a form of music and song adapted from Portuguese folk music
ksatria	knight; nobleman; the caste below *brahman*

371

kyai	an Islamic teacher or leader

L

'landschap'	a territory ruled by a king or under the sway of customary law
lasting	a kind of plain material
lenong	a form of urban folk drama popular in Betawi and performed in the colloquial Malay of the Betawi people
Liberal Movement	the Liberal Movement was a political movement based amongst the Dutch bourgeoisie in Holland and the Indies; it called for the government to implement policies to improve education and irrigation in the Indies and to promote transmigration (then called 'emigration') out of Java
londo godong	literally 'Dutch page'; a Javanese who has been given the same legal status as a Dutchman
losmen	inn

M

magrib	the name of the prayers that are carried out after the sun has set but before it is dark; the Moslem creed sets down five obligatory times for prayer
Mahabarata	epic story in which the Pandawa and the Korawa wage war for possession of the realm of Ngastino
makmum	in Islamic practice, when more than one person is carrying out ritual prayer, the group selects the oldest or most know-ledgeable man to lead the prayers; the others, known as the *makmum*, stand behind him and follow as he guides them through the prayer ritual
mantri	village official below the *wedana*

mas	Javanese term of address literally meaning 'older brother'; used by a young woman towards a man, it indicates an especially close, respectful affection; it can also be used between men, indicating respectful friendship; by a sister to her older brother; and also by a wife to her husband; a title of the lesser nobility
Max Havelaar	novel by Eduard Douwes Dekker (Multatuli)
meneer	Dutch for 'sir' or 'mr'
mevrouw	Dutch for 'madam' or 'miss'
Multatuli	pseudonym of Eduard Douwes Dekker, an outspoken humanist critic of Dutch colonialism and author of the anti-colonial novel *Max Havelaar*
musyrik	fearing other than God, elevating others to the level of God, giving God partners, idolatry

N

ndoro	a term of address used by a lower-class person when speaking to someone in the feudal class or of similar status
nenenda	grandfather, a term of great respect used when speaking to an elderly person, ususally of one's grandparents' generation or older
nyai	the Native concubines of Dutch men in the Indies
Nyai Dasima	the heroine of G. Francis' popular Malay-language novel
nyo	abbreviated form of *sinyo*, used to refer to young Dutch boys, or Dutchified Eurasian or Native boys

O

om	uncle

oma	familiar term for 'mother' used as honorific

P

Pasopati	magical weapon used by Arjuna in the *Bharatayuddha*
patih	the chief executive assistant or minister to a *bupati*
pendopo	a large roofed verandah or reception area at the front of a Javanese dignitary's residence
penembrana	a traditional welcome for VIPs, usually comprising special Javanese music and singing
penghulu	local chief; (religious) head man
pici	small black velvet cap, originally a sign of Islam
Prambanan	a great Hindu temple complex located near the town of Jogjakarta
priyayi	members of the Javanese aristocracy who became the salaried administrators of the Dutch

R

raden ayu	title for aristocratic Javanese woman, especially the first wife of a *bupati*
raden mas	'*raden*' and '*mas*' are titles held by the mass of the middle-ranking members of the Javanese aristocracy; *raden mas* is the superior title
raja	king
ringgit	2-1/2 *rupiah* or 2-1/2 *perak*
rodi	the right of the government, through the local native administrators, to require villagers to provide free labour for government or other projects as directed

rotikalung	a type of wooden knuckleduster used in martial arts
rujakpolo	weapon used to completely destroy your enemy
rupiah	basic unit of currency (100 cents)

S

selangka	collar-bone
selir	the 'unofficial wives' of Javanese aristocrats
sembah	homage, tribute, respect, reverence
silat	a Malay form of self-defence
sinkeh	term used to refer to a Chinese immigrant
sinse	a traditional Chinese healer
sinyo	form of address for young Dutch and Eurasian men or Europeanised Native young man, from the Portuguese '*senor*'
songkok	black Moslem fez
STOVIA	*School Tot Opleiding van Inlandsche Artsen* (School for the Education of Native Doctors); the STOVIA was the only institute of higher learning established by the Dutch colonial authorities during the early twentieth century
sudara	brother
sudra	the lowest Hindu caste; the mass of ordinary people
Sugar Syndicate	the sugar planters' association
Sultan Agung	one of the most powerful of the early Moslem rulers of Java
surjan	traditional Javanese top-coat or shirt, worn with a *batik sarong*

T

talaq	the Moslem divorce procedure whereby a

	husband can divorce a wife through uni-lateral decree
tali	a 25-cent coin
tape	fermented rice mixture
taqwa	worship of only one god; fear or awe of God
teukoe	an Acehnese title for a traditional leader, sometimes translated as 'prince'
Tjoet Nya Dhin	a heroine of the Aceh War, the woman who led the Acehnese guerillas in the last phase of the war against the Dutch; she was captured and exiled to West Java in 1910 and died a year later
tricolour	the Dutch flag
tuan	Malay word meaning 'master' or 'sir'

W

warung	small shop, booth or stall
wayang	shadow puppets
wedana	the head of a municipality, one of the lower administrative positions
Marie van Zeggelen	Marie van Zeggelen went on to write a number of books sympathetic to the Natives' struggle for freedom; these included *A Biography of Kartini* (1908), a book on the struggle of the Buginese, *De Onderworpenen (The Vanquished)*, *Gouden Keris (Golden Keris)* and *Oude Glorie (The Golden Age)*, about Aceh during its hey-day in the 16th and 17th centuries – this book was not published until 1935

PENGUIN – THE BEST AUSTRALIAN READING

ALSO BY PRAMOEDYA ANANTA TOER

This Earth of Mankind and **Child of All Nations** now published together as **Awakenings**

Minke, a Javanese student and aspiring writer, optimistic in his faith in European teaching, is drawn into the mysterious mansion of the Mellema family. Here he finds a new love – the exquisite but fragile Annelies, and a new teacher – the charismatic concubine Nyai Ontosoroh.

Through these extraordinary women he begins to confront his divided world – the ideas and values of the Europeans who have given him literacy, and the political struggle of his own people against their Dutch rulers.

Pramoedya Ananta Toer's epic novels are banned in his own country, Indonesia, but his writing reaches far beyond politics, to achieve a vivid historical picture of the richly varied culture of the Dutch East Indies, and a deep understanding of a people's painful emergence from colonial domination.

PENGUIN – THE BEST AUSTRALIAN READING

BOOKS BY BLANCHE D'ALPUGET IN PENGUIN

Monkeys in the Dark

Young Australian journalist Alexandra Wheatfield takes a job in Djakarta at a time of chaotic change: President Sukarno is about to be overthrown, and he has warned the people that without him they are like 'monkeys in the dark'.

Alexandra is moved by the raw colour and sullen violence of life in the city, and it mirrors her affair with Maruli Hutabarat, poet and party activist. But she is faced with the conflicting demands of two societies – her own and that of her lover – and she is finally betrayed by both.

'Blanche d'Alpuget's novel reveals more about the cultural, social, political and sexual tensions of Australians working – or filling in diplomatic time – in Indonesia than a thousand guarded press releases.'

Financial Review

Turtle Beach

Judith Wilkes, an ambitious journalist, goes to Malaysia to report on an international refugee crisis. Ten years before, Malaysia had provided Judith with her first major career success . . . but also with personal disaster.

Through her encounters with Minou, exotic, young French-Vietnamese wife of a high-ranking diplomat, the ambitious Ralph Hamilton and, ultimately with enigmatic Kanan who tries to liberate her, Judith is thrown into dramatic personal and professional conflicts.

The train of events has a Graham Greene sense of inevitability as the characters move between cultures and the tensions heighten.

It is on the East Malaysian coast, when turtles gather to breed, that the dilemma reaches its tragic, brutal climax.

'The sort of novel one encounters at very rare intervals: broad in scope, ambitious, yet written with a crisp breezy intelligence . . . '

Newsweek

BOOKS BY MARION HALLIGAN IN PENGUIN

Spidercup

Does a wife exist only when her husband is contemplating her? . . . A wife is called into being only by a husband; therefore does she cease to exist when he stops observing her, stops regarding her?

Elinor leaves her husband suddenly and goes to France, to the village of Sévérac-le-Château. There she ponders the lives of other women. In the seventeenth century a wife is murdered for faithlessness; in the early twentieth century a woman embroiders sheets for a trousseau never needed; in the 1980s a successful pediatrician may or may not know what her husband is up to.

Elinor's process of transformation – from a wife to a self – is written with subtlety and humour. The journey she undertakes is more than a journey of the flesh.

The Hanged Man in the Garden

' . . . the Hanged Man dangles gallantly by one foot and turning upside down observes the world. Its powers cannot harm him, he sees it clearly and afresh, all new. He is an individual. And he has a halo round his head.'

The Hanged Man represents a turn-around of perception that often occurs when an individual confronts pain. A baby dies, a husband is unfaithful, a woman spends a week in a cupboard, people strive to come to terms with grief and loss – variously they choose humour, despair, irony and hope. It is the unexpectedness of this illogical reversal that makes the experience precious. And, how ever hard life may be, the sensuous beauty of its surfaces is a source of pleasure.

One of Australia's foremost short-story writers, Marion Halligan explores, through the interweaving lives of a group of individuals, the complexities of pain.

PENGUIN – THE BEST AUSTRALIAN READING

BOOKS BY MARGARET BARBALET IN PENGUIN

Blood in the Rain

Jessie's life is, in many ways, ordinary – a young girl growing up and reaching for maturity in the Australia of the Great War and the Depression, as she moves from country town to country town and eventually to Adelaide. But Margaret Barbalet's evocative novel follows Jessie's odyssey to self-acceptance with a perception and compassion that reveals a person who is quite extraordinary.

Steel Beach

'The view from the house distracted me from my work. Held between the beach and the escarpment, I would look up from my papers and my eye would take in the sweep of the coastline – the same coastline that Lawrence and Frieda had explored half a century before. Now I was the explorer, mapping out the life they had led there.'

'I met a surfer on the beach yesterday who was the image of Lawrence. As soon as I saw him, I knew he was important. *He* was my first clue.'

BOOKS BY PETER CORRIS IN PENGUIN

'Box Office' Browning

Richard Browning is a crack-shot, six-foot, all-Australian ex-private-school horseman. He is determined to con his way into the new world of film-making, but his way to Hollywood is thwarted by World War I, a series of unfortunate affairs and a disastrous marriage. In his developing career as box office poison, Browning makes far more enemies than movies.

'Box Office' Browning is Browning's recollection of his early days from an ungraceful old age. The truth may be filtered through booze, drugs and a lot of years, but the escapades with the famous and the infamous are a delight.

'Beverly Hills' Browning

Richard Browning has a marvellous talent for mucking up even lucky breaks. In fact, he's only really good at one thing; that is, getting away.

Sure, the would-be Aussie movie star makes it to the U.S. of A., but San Francisco proves to be a long way from the starlets, palm trees and swimming pools of Hollywood, at least by the route only he could choose, through Mexico. And then, when he gets to Beverly Hills, he finds bootleggers in the swimming pools, anarchists on the movie sets and starlets just too hot to handle. Not to mention making an enemy of the 'king' of Hollywood, Douglas Fairbanks – the 'city of dreams' becomes nightmare land.